BEAUTIFUL *Hate*

LORRAIN ALLEN

Published by Lorrain Allen

ISBN: 978-1-7342309-8-7

This book is a work of fiction. All names, characters, places, and incidents either are a product of the author's imagination or are used fictitiously. Any resemblance to events, locales, or persons, living or dead, is coincidental.

The author acknowledges all song titles, song lyrics, film titles, film characters, trademarked statuses, and brands mentioned in this book are the property of, and belong to, their respective owners. The publication/use of these trademarks are not authorized/ associated with, or sponsored by the trademark owners.

Lorrain Allen is in no way affiliated with any of the brands, songs, musicians, or artists mentioned in this book.

Editors: Abby Gale & Owl Eyes Proofs & Edits, LLC.
Proofreader: Chrisandra's Corrections
Interior formatter: Champagne Book Design
Cover designer: Black Widow Designs

AUTHOR'S NOTE

If you've read my previous books, then you already know my antiheroes aren't here to be redeemed. For the uninitiated, proceed with caution. Sam, aka Sandman, takes what he wants without remorse or apology. Groveling? Not in his vocabulary. Expect murder, mayhem, betrayal, and some of the most jaw-dropping noncon scenes you've ever read. Dare to enter the world of the Gods… but don't expect to leave unscathed. Scan QR code to view content warning.

DEDICATION

To all my hater fans, thank you so much for your continued support.

PLAYLIST

"Bring Me To Life" – Evanescence
"Play With Fire" – Sam Tinnesz featuring Yacht Money
"Prisoner" – Raphael Lake, Aaron Levy, and Daniel Murphy
"5 Seconds of Summer" – Youngblood
"Watch Me Burn" – Michele Morrone
"Mirrors" – Justin Timberlake
"Down with the Sickness" – Disturbed
"Paint It, Black" – Ciara
"Dangerous Woman" – Ariana Grande
"Without Me" – Halsey
"Just Give Me A Reason" – Pink featuring Nate Ruess
"I Don't Wanna Live Forever" – Zayn and Taylor Swift
"Sweet Dreams" – Marilyn Manson
"Believer" – Imagine Dragons
"Apologize featuring OneRepublic" – Timbaland
"Infinity" – Jaymes Young
"Under The Influence" – Chris Brown
"Sweet Nothing" – Calvin Harris featuring Florence Welch
"Elastic Heart" – Sia

BEAUTIFUL
Hate

PART ONE

Fates Collide

STOP!!! Are you sure you want to read this book? It's EXTREMELY dark, almost pitch black, and is not for the faint of heart. Sandman is NOT a hero and does not magically become a good guy by the end of the book. He makes no apologies for his behavior. If you're still here, then consider this your final warning.

CHAPTER 1

SAM

Twelve years old

RAP MUSIC PENETRATES MY FOGGY BRAIN, THE WORDS BOUNCING around the box they shoved me into. I groan, my joints stiff and screaming from being folded into myself like trash in a compactor. My mind drifts between consciousness and oblivion, making it impossible to tell one moment from the next. Minutes, hours, days—I have no clue how much time has passed.

I crack my gritty eyes open to darkness. Panic sets in, clawing at my chest until every breath burns.

You're okay. You're okay. You're okay.

I chant in my head over and over again, trying to steady my ragged breathing. Then I hear laughter. *Hers.*

Brandi. My tormentor. The daughter of my mother's latest boyfriend. At sixteen, she's sadistic and rotten to the core, with a smile that promises pain. I was mesmerized by her beauty, but soon enough, I found out she was venom wrapped in sweetness.

After just two weeks of dating, my mother invited them to move into our cramped, one-bedroom trailer. No warning. I came home one day, and they were already here. Brandi got the couch, and I was demoted to a blanket on the stained carpet. That was nearly three months ago. She swears Merle's "the one." But he's the *fifth* "one" this year.

I'll give their relationship another month. Katherine "Kitty" Hendricks isn't satisfied unless there's a man in her life. I've never been a priority for her. Just dead weight she complains about every chance she gets.

More often than not, it's just Brandi and me. Mom and Merle disappear for days, sometimes weeks, at a time. No calls. No texts. No money left for groceries. Not a single thought given for the children they left behind.

That's when things go from bad to worse. Brandi and her friends go on days-long benders—hardcore drugs, endless liquor, and reckless hookups everywhere you look.

I survive it all. *Barely.*

This time, I'm not so sure. Brandi found out about my claustrophobia and ordered her friends to stuff me in the trunk at the foot of my mother's bed. I don't think I can last much longer.

I've hated tight spaces ever since I was four years old.

My mother's boyfriend at the time would lock me in an old freezer in his garage. When he was really pissed, he'd turn it on.

At least in the freezer, I was safe from his beatings. He'd use anything within arm's reach on my tiny body. Belt, hammer, frying pan, baseball bat, hanger—it didn't matter. I should be dead, even wished for the final blow that would end my life.

Where was God then? Where is he now?

I flex my aching fingers, the skin scraped raw from trying to escape my tight prison.

"Let me out," I croak, my voice barely more than a whisper.

I grimace and swallow hard, hoping to soothe my parched throat. It's been a while since I had anything to drink. I muster all my strength and bang my shoulder against the padded top.

"Please let me out!" I scream as loud as I can. "I can't breathe!"

The music drops to a low pulse.

"Oh, he's awake again," Tanner jeers. Brandi's stupid boyfriend. He's the person I hate most in the world after her.

"Brandi, please! Let me out! I can't breathe in here!"

"Come on, you've had your fun," a girl says. "Let him out. He could seriously die."

Brandi scoffs. "Oh please, he's just being dramatic."

"Fuck that, man," a hard voice snaps. "I ain't gonna be an accessory to no murder."

"Yeah, me neither. I'm on my second strike. If I catch another charge, they're going to throw the book at me."

Some voices sound familiar, others I don't recognize, but at least there are people here who care if I live or die—whatever their reasons might be.

"Okay, fine," she gripes. "I'll check on him, but I'm not letting him out."

This is it. My chance to make a break for it. The second the lid cracks open, I lunge forward, fueled by adrenaline and desperation. I slam into Brandi, sending her careening into the dresser with a pained gasp.

"You little piece of shit," she screeches. "I'm going to kill you."

I tear through the living room. Heart thundering. Lungs searing. Every face and piece of mismatched furniture a blur in my hurry to get away. I zero in on the screen door and bolt toward it—the promise of freedom just steps away.

"Get him, baby!"

I'm almost at the door when something barrels into me from behind. I hit the floor hard, the sound echoing in my ears.

"You're dead meat, bro," Tanner sneers, flipping me over and straddling my chest. His weight bears down on me, crushing the breath from my body. My mind screams at me to get up, to run—but I'm stuck.

"Get off me!" I flail beneath him, every muscle straining to escape.

"Hold him down," he orders the onlookers. One person grabs my wrists and pins them high above my head, while two others press my legs to the floor.

I thrash against my human shackles, fighting like an animal caught in a trap, but it's no use. They're bigger. Stronger. Meaner.

"Let me go!" I yell, my voice cracking.

"Give me that," Brandi barks, snatching a cigarette from one of her friends and stabbing it into my neck. It sears through my skin like a hot blade. A scream rips from my throat. It hurts so bad I can't even think.

"Shut him up," she hisses.

Tanner's fist slams into my cheek, and a sharp pain slices across my face, freezing me on the spot. He doesn't stop—his punches come fast and brutal, one after another, crunching bone and cartilage. My head snaps sideways. Blood fills my mouth. My vision splits in two. Everything is pain and fists. Hot tears spill from my eyes as their cruel laughter rings in my ears.

I need to act fast before he kills me. I go limp, pretending to be unconscious, but the punches keep coming. I force myself to lie perfectly still, barely breathing. When you've been abused your whole life, pain becomes second nature—you learn how to disappear without leaving.

My plan works. The hands holding me slip away.

"Dude, chill. He's out cold."

It's now or never. I arch forward, smashing my forehead into his mouth.

"My tooth!" Tanner squeals, diving after it as it tumbles across the carpet.

I don't think. I just move—leaping to my feet and sprinting toward the door.

"Grab him!" Brandi shouts. "Don't let him get away!"

I dodge the hands reaching for me and burst outside, falling down the stairs in my desperation to escape. I'm back up in a heartbeat. Getting caught means another beating and being thrown back into the trunk. I race into the humid night, my bare feet slapping hard against the warm pavement. I can hear them behind me, closing in like a pack of wolves.

"I'm going to beat the snot out of you!" Tanner bellows.

I pump my legs faster, not daring to glance back.

Move it, Sam. Don't let them catch you.

Lightning cracks across the dark sky, and a single raindrop lands on my nose. I close my eyes, savoring the coolness on my scorching skin. Then the sky breaks open, dumping cold rain all over me.

"You can't run forever!" Brandi yells after me. "You'll be back and I'll be waiting!"

They turn back, but I don't stop running. *I can't.* A soothing voice whispers in my head, telling me everything will be okay, promising things a boy like me could only dream about.

Soon my surroundings become unrecognizable. Big houses. Perfect lawns. Clean streets.

I don't belong here.

My legs give out, and my face meets the drenched concrete with a hard whack. I roll onto my back, wanting to disappear. Not die. Just… be gone.

I'm a shadow in a world that doesn't see me—unloved, unnoticed, alone.

I clamber to unsteady feet and wrap my arms around my belly.

What am I going to do? I can't go home. Not with Brandi and her friends there waiting for me.

I spin in a circle, searching—for what, I don't know. That's when I see it. A tree house between the hulking branches in the backyard of the biggest house on the street. Clutching my throbbing side, I limp across the lawn and haul myself over the wooden fence.

CHAPTER 2

Zilphia

Ten years old

"Oh, Momma, don't start," my mother snaps, rolling her eyes.

"All I want is for my daughters to get along." Grandma's voice cracks, and tears shimmer in her eyes. "Is that too much to ask for? Growing up, you two were inseparable."

I love when my grandma comes to visit. She bakes cookies with me, reads bedtime stories, and teaches me to knit with her warm hands wrapped around mine.

Momma never does any of that.

I just wish her and Momma would stop fighting. Grandma used to visit for a whole month, but now she only stays for two weeks.

I pick at my food, losing my appetite. Momma and Aunt Sheila have hated each other since before I was born. Grandma says it's because Momma stole Daddy from her way back in high school. I don't know if that's true, but it's the story they all whisper when they think I'm not listening.

"Well, it's not me that's holding on to the past," Momma huffs and slams her fork onto her plate. "Sheila needs to get over it. It's been fourteen years for heaven's sake, and it's not my fault she can't keep a man."

Grandma inhales a sharp breath. "That's unnecessary, Loretta."

"See, you're always on her side," Momma snaps, her espresso-brown eyes narrowing to tiny slits.

Daddy clears his throat, looking uncomfortable. "This conversation is not for young ears."

My older brother, Nolan, doesn't seem to be fazed by the confrontation unfolding. He's too busy stuffing his mouth with pot roast.

"I'm not on anyone's side." Grandma sighs tiredly. "Please call your sister and have a heart-to-heart."

"No, I will not," Momma responds with finality. "She's older and therefore should extend the olive branch."

"For shame, Loretta." Grandma shakes her head in disappointment.

"I will not be guilt-tripped into apologizing. Sheila's just jealous of me." Momma fluffs her shiny, silken curls and proudly squares her shoulders. "Look at me. Married to a doctor, living in a five-bedroom house with granite countertops and a big pool in the backyard. Meanwhile, Sheila's still in the hood with a baby daddy doing forty to life."

Heavy rain, accompanied by thunder, causes the lights in the dining room to flicker.

"May I be excused?" I ask, desperate to escape the suffocating tension at the table.

"Sure, sweet—"

"You may not." Momma cocks an eyebrow at Daddy, daring him to challenge her. He averts his gaze and drinks a sip of his water. "I spent hours preparing this lovely meal, and you're not going anywhere until your plate is empty. And stop slouching and get your elbows off the table. I am not raising a wild animal."

Nolan snickers, but Momma's glare instantly silences him. I shouldn't have said anything.

Momma's judgmental eyes land on me again. "Your hair was a complete mess this morning. How many times have I told you not to go to bed without your bonnet on? No man is ever going to marry you if you insist on behaving like a little savage. Perfection twenty-four-seven is absolutely mandatory."

I shrink in on myself. Momma wears makeup, pretty dresses, and high heels all the time. Her hair is always done up nice too. Men stare at her wherever she goes.

"I'm sorry, Momma," I say in a low voice, hanging my head low. "I promise I'll be a better daughter."

"I told you to stop slouching!" she admonishes. "Sometimes I'm convinced the wrong baby was given to me at the hospital."

Her words land like a slap. I don't say anything. I just keep staring at my plate and do what I'm told.

"Slow down, Winston." I giggle, watching my hamster devour a strawberry. "You're going to get a tummy ache."

Daddy gave Winston to me for my tenth birthday. I asked for a puppy, but Momma said no and refused to budge on her decision. Daddy talked her into getting me a smaller pet. And then came Winston. He's the best birthday present ever. I even took him to school for show-and-tell once. The entire class loved him.

"Okay, all gone." I scoop him up from my lap and climb out of bed. "It's time to go to sleep."

I slip him inside his cage.

"Nighty night, Winston." I scratch his head before securing the latch. "I'll give you more strawberries in the morning."

Movement near the swimming pool catches my eye, and I peer out the window. Through the downpour, I spot a boy scurrying up the stairs to the tree house Daddy had built for Nolan and me.

"What's he doing?"

I can't see his face clearly. Maybe he's one of Nolan's friends. They come over a lot, but never this late.

I leave my bedroom and tiptoe downstairs, curious to discover who the boy is. I grab an umbrella, a flashlight, and my bright yellow rain boots from the closet by the front door, then hurry to the kitchen. A creaking noise stops me in my tracks. I hold my breath until all is silent before disabling the alarm and sneaking onto the deck. I quickly make my way to the tree house and cautiously push open the wooden door. It's pitch black inside. I close the umbrella and prop it against the wall.

"Hello?" I call out, clicking on the flashlight.

I find the boy huddled beside the bookshelf, his knees pulled tight to his chest. He's got no shoes. His jeans are dirty and have holes all over. His hair is a big, tangled mess. There's blood under his nose, and his lip is split. Then I look into the prettiest blue eyes I've ever seen—both dark purple and swollen, one almost closed shut.

"W-who a-are y-you?" I stutter, tightening my grip on the flashlight.

"My name is Samuel," he answers, his voice tiny. "But everybody calls me Sam."

"You're not supposed to be in here."

"I just… needed somewhere to hide."

I warily approach him and sink to my knees in front of him. "From the person who hurt you?"

He nods. "Can I stay here for a while? I won't be any trouble."

His voice is barely there. Like if he speaks too loudly, I'll hit him. "Okay, but you have to leave before morning. My momma will be real mad if she catches you here."

He blows out a deep breath and slumps forward. "Thank you."

I look at him for a moment longer. Sam definitely looks like he needs a friend. I can be that. For tonight at least. I point at the television. "You want to watch a movie?"

He shrugs, and that's all the encouragement I need.

I bounce to my feet and select *The Avengers* before plopping down on the futon. Sam stays in the corner like he's afraid to move.

"Come on." I wave him over. "There's plenty of space, silly."

Sam bites down on his bottom lip, but after a few seconds, he moves to the futon, though on the opposite end. I blink back tears. His shirt is ripped down the middle, revealing scary bruises—big ones, little ones, all different colors. He's the skinniest person I've ever seen. Every rib sticks out. And he's so pale, I can see his veins. Maybe his momma is mean like mine. I want to talk to him, but I don't know what to say, so I just keep quiet. Not long into the movie, his stomach rumbles.

"Are you hungry?"

He nods, bowing his head like he's ashamed. "I haven't eaten all day."

"I'll make you something," I chirp, standing. "Be right back."

I dash across the slippery grass and quietly enter the house. After whipping up turkey sandwiches, I gather some other things for Sam, then sneak back to the tree house. He smiles timidly at me. Nervous flutters fill my belly. He's a cute boy, even though he's dirty and skinny.

"I have loads of goodies for you." I sit beside him and hand him a large tote bag. "There are extra sandwiches for later, plus snacks, drinks, clothes, shoes, a first aid kit, and a towel so you can dry off."

He stares at me like I'm the best person in the whole world. "Thank you for being nice to me," he says, sadness creeping into his voice. "No one else ever is."

I want to know everything about him. Why hasn't he eaten today? Where are his parents? Where does he live? And most importantly, who hurt him, and should the police be called? Asking these questions could scare him away, and I'm not ready for him to go yet.

The first sandwich is gone in seconds, then Sam digs out another one. Once he swallows the last bite, he looks at me and a real smile appears on his face. "What's your name?"

"Zilphia."

"That's a pretty name."

"Thank you," I mumble, the unexpected compliment starting a fire in my cheeks. "You-you have pretty eyes."

He lowers his eyes and rummages through the bag, a flush creeping up his pale face. "Whose clothes are these?"

"My brother's. I snagged them from the dryer, so they're clean, but probably a bit too big for you."

"Wow!" he exclaims, whipping out the expensive sneakers. "These are the new Thunderbolts."

"Can you fit them?"

"Maybe, they're a half size smaller than my shoe size, but they'll work." He looks happy and carefree at that moment, but then his smile suddenly melts into a thin line. "But I can't take them."

"Why?" I frown, confused.

"Brandi will just sell them to buy crank. She's the daughter of my mother's boyfriend."

"Oh." What is crank? It's obviously something bad. Concern for his safety twists my belly into knots, but I don't ask any more questions.

We watch the rest of the movie in silence while I clean and bandage his wounds. I feel his eyes on me, but every time I glance at him, he looks away. All too soon, the credits start to roll, but I want my new friend to stay a little longer.

I offer him the remote. "You choose the next movie."

About an hour into the movie, my eyes get too heavy to keep open. I doze off and on until the sky begins to brighten. Next to me, Sam is fast asleep, the blanket tucked around his shoulders.

I gently nudge him on the arm. "Sam, it's almost morning."

He stretches and lets out a big yawn before his sad eyes land on me. "Well, I guess I better get going."

I don't want him to leave, and I can tell he doesn't want to go either. I'm scared for him. *What if we never see each other again?* My tummy aches at the thought.

"You can come here whenever you need a safe place to hide," I tell him.

His eyes fly to mine. "Really?"

"Of course. Do you have a cell phone?"

"No." He looks down at his clutched hands.

I take his hand and lead him to the window. "My bedroom's the one with the pink curtains. If you ever need me, just throw a rock."

"Okay. Thank you for helping me."

I hesitate. "Do you want to come back tonight?" If he's here with me, I won't have to worry about him being hungry or hurt.

He nods.

I smile and pull him into a tight hug. He doesn't move at first. But then his thin arms slowly wrap around me, like he's afraid he'll break me—or himself.

PART TWO
Birth of a Monster

CHAPTER 3

Five years later

Zilphia

I SIGH, PRESSING CLOSER TO THE WARM BODY BESIDE ME. SAM SHIFTS in his sleep, his hand brushing mine, and for a second, I pretend we don't have to get up. The sharp chatter of birds shatters my peace, and my eyes fly open. Beyond the tree house window, streaks of color stain the sky, signaling the approaching sunrise. *What time is it?*

My gaze shifts to the clock hanging on the wall. *Holy crap! What the heck happened to my alarm?* I reach down and snag my cell phone off the floor. *The freaking battery's dead.* Dang it! I fell asleep last night and forgot to charge my phone.

"Sam, get up," I whisper urgently, roughly shaking his shoulder.

"Ten more minutes," he grumbles, his eyes still closed.

"Uh-uh. Up. Now," I order, scrambling off the futon.

"Stop being mean," he whines, pulling the blanket up to his chin.

"Come on, Sam," I grab a pillow and whack him on the head, but he doesn't budge. "It's ten to six. You know my momma will be waking up soon."

And if she happens to stop by my bedroom and I'm not there… I shiver. She'll beat me senseless and ground me until I'm married.

"Maybe…" I hesitate. "Maybe you shouldn't come over so much."

"Whoa." Sam bolts to his feet, shaggy blond hair flopping across his tan forehead. "Where is this coming from?"

"It's becoming too risky sneaking out here all the time. My momma's going to pitch a fit if she catches me."

Recently, Momma's gotten stricter about my comings and goings. And that's not the worst part. I've caught her staring at me with a calculating gleam in her eyes more than once. I can't shake the feeling that something bad is going to happen.

"Don't worry." He curls his hands around my slender shoulders and gives me his signature lopsided smile. "I'll be your human alarm clock from now on."

I scoff. "Sam, you sleep like the dead."

"Dang, have some faith in me," he gripes, giving my earlobe a playful tug.

I sigh contentedly and lean into his hand. Most nights, I fall asleep curled against his chest, lulled by that same gentle touch.

"All right, I'll give you a chance to prove yourself." I hold up one finger. "Don't let me down."

"You know I got your back, girl." He gathers me in a tight embrace and drops a soft kiss on my temple.

I pull back and meet his twinkling blue gaze. "I'm happy we're friends."

He's always been more than that, though. He's my secret. My shelter. My other half when everything else is going to shit.

He's the one bright spot in my controlled existence. When Momma pushes me to the brink, he stops me from tumbling over the edge. What would I do without his constant presence in my life?

I hope I never have to find out.

A faint frown flickers across his expressive face, but disappears just as fast.

"What's the matter?" I ask, furrowing my eyebrows.

"Nothing." He shrugs nonchalantly.

"You sure?"

"I'm cool, Zilphia," he clips out.

"Okay. I'm looking forward to kicking your butt in Monopoly again tonight," I tease to lighten the mood.

"Hey," he scowls in mock anger. "You won because you cheated."

"I did not." I chuckle, punching him in the arm. "You're just a sore loser."

"Yeah, yeah, whatever," he says, shooing me toward the door. "Go on, get outta here."

"I'm going, I'm going." I slide my feet into my comfy pink bunny slippers. "See you later."

I dash to the mirror and snatch my bonnet off. It won't take too long to style my hair. I plug my flat iron into the outlet and switch it on, then liberally apply heat protectant onto my thick strands.

"Hey, shit for brains." Nolan strolls into my bedroom and stretches out across my bed. "Momma said get your ass downstairs pronto."

"Get out," I snap, picking up my hairspray and launching it at his fat head.

He easily dodges it. "Nope."

"I mean it," I bite out between clenched teeth, scouring my dresser for the next haircare product to use as a makeshift missile.

"Don't kill the messenger." He leans to the side and lets a big one rip. "Damn, that stench is going to linger in here for days."

"Ugh, you disgusting pig!" I charge at him, my fist raised. "I'm going to murder you!"

Before I can deliver the blow, he bolts out of the door, cackling like a hyena. Living with him is a nightmare! And since we're going to the same school this year, he's my ride in the mornings. *Grrr!* Being in a confined space with him is a true test of my patience, and that's putting it mildly. He blasts the radio, farts, picks his nose… basically doing everything he can to annoy me during the entire twenty-minute drive.

Thank the heavens above, he's graduating next year and heading off to college—hopefully somewhere thousands of miles away. I'm literally counting the days. I pluck my honeysuckle body spray from the dresser and liberally spray the sweet scent around my room.

Great, now it smells like flowers and rotten eggs.

Nolan is popular and well-liked by his peers. I don't understand it. Girls even compete for his attention. It's sickening to watch. What the heck do they see in him? It can't be his stellar personality. Okay, yeah, playing sports has toned his body, but he's short and resembles a naked mole rat. He's seriously butt ugly. And I'm not just saying that because he's the worst brother on this planet. It's a fact.

Nolan doesn't take after our parents, who are very attractive people. Maybe he's adopted. That'd explain a lot.

I quickly run the flat iron through my silky mane, then slick down my baby hairs with edge control. A few coats of watermelon-flavored lip gloss, and I'm ready. I study my reflection, turning from side to side, checking that everything is perfect.

"Zilphia Theresa Kensley, your behind better be at the kitchen table in two minutes!" Momma yells upstairs.

Crappity crap crap. It spells disaster whenever she uses my full name. I'm in for the 'you're a bad daughter' lecture interspersed with head shakes of disappointment. *Yippee*.

"Coming, Momma," I call out, grabbing my inhaler, my purse, and my backpack. I yank my door shut and race downstairs.

"Good morning." I bustle into the kitchen and slide into a chair.

The table is laden with bacon, eggs, potatoes, grits, and pancakes.

"Morning, baby girl." Daddy beams, placing his coffee mug on the table. "Did you have a good night's sleep?"

"Yep."

Momma stops filling the dishwasher and immediately starts airing my shortcomings. "You are so irresponsible, Zilphia. Why can't you be more like your brother?"

Daddy shoots me a pitying look but doesn't utter a word in my defense. We're in the same boat. Momma is always jumping down his throat for one reason or another, mostly about finances. She spends more than he earns. I wonder if he regrets choosing her instead of Sheila.

"I told her to hurry up, Momma, but she was taking her sweet ole time." Nolan smiles smugly.

Oh, how I want to smack it off his fugly face.

"Do you need a bedtime at fifteen?"

"No, Momma," I answer respectfully. "I forgot to charge my phone last night."

"You're too old to be this stupid and irresponsible," she snaps, glaring at me with disdain.

"I'm sorry," I mumble, clasping my sweaty hands together beneath the table. "It won't happen again."

She lets out an annoyed huff and turns back to her task. I release a relieved breath and begin stocking my plate. I'm careful to serve myself small portions so as not to incur her wrath.

Momma prepares a feast every morning, dressed as if she's heading to a red-carpet event.

Today, a ruffled apron is cinched tight around a yellow sundress. Designer, of course—same as the white stilettoes adorning her dainty feet.

Her red lipstick hasn't smudged. Not a single hair out of place in her perfect bun.

Who cooks dressed like that?

She doesn't have anywhere to be. Not this early. Unless "somewhere" means lunch at the country club or a shopping spree with the same women who kiss each other's cheeks and roll their eyes the second backs are turned.

"Have you made a decision about me visiting Grandma for Thanksgiving?" I ask her.

My grandmother fell and broke her hip two years ago. She had surgery to repair the damage. I haven't seen her since—traveling is just too exhausting for her now.

"I have and the answer is no."

"Please," I beg, clenching the fork in my hand. "I miss Grandma so much."

And I want to get to know my aunt and cousins too.

Deja and I are the same age, and Terrence just turned three.

"Well, I don't want Sheila and your cousins' ghetto behavior rubbing off on you. If Momma had her own place, I'd let you go."

"But—"

She slams the dishwasher shut. "This topic is closed. Do I make myself clear?"

"Yes, ma'am," I answer, sinking into my chair.

I blink back tears, my heart splintering into tiny pieces. It's not fair. The feud between Momma and Sheila has nothing to do with me. Why should I suffer because they don't get along?

"Argh!"

My head snaps up at Momma's outraged cry to find her bristling near the open refrigerator, holding a medium-size storage container.

Oh no. I'm in big trouble now.

“Why is there only one chicken breast left? I cooked extra to use for stir fry tonight.”

“I didn’t eat them,” Nolan announces, saturating his pancakes in syrup.

“Wesley?” she growls at Daddy, planting a newly manicured hand on her hip.

“It wasn’t me either,” he responds.

Suddenly, three pairs of eyes land on me, and I fidget in my seat.

“I got hungry in the middle of the night,” I explain lamely. It was either that or “Oh, I took a plate of food to my secret friend last night.”

“No wonder you’re getting fat,” Nolan retorts.

Momma rushes forward and yanks me out of the chair. “Bathroom. Now.”

I know what this means.

Weight check.

My mother trails behind me, shoving me toward the digital scale when we reach the bathroom. “Move it!”

I step on the smooth metal surface, shaking in absolute terror.

121 lb.

“You’ve gained six pounds!” she screeches and slaps me hard across the face. “Why are you trying to embarrass me?”

“I’m not, Momma, I swear,” I say, tears staining my cheeks.

“You don’t deserve to be a majorette!” She slaps me again. “You’re disgusting and bring shame to the uniform!”

I didn’t even want to try out for the team. Momma was a majorette and forced me to follow in her footsteps.

“No fried foods, starches, or sugar until I say otherwise.”

With the taste of blood in my mouth, I choke back a sob and whisper, “Yes, ma’am.”

CHAPTER 4

SAM

"I'M HAPPY WE'RE FRIENDS."

I kick a rock and watch it flit across the deteriorating concrete. My emotions are in an uproar. Friendship isn't enough for me. Zilphia earned a special place in my heart on that rainy night five years ago. Since then, my love for her has grown to immeasurable heights.

We belong together. Fuck the status quo, and fuck what anyone has to say. They can all kiss my ass. None of them could ever comprehend the unbreakable bond between us. I'd crawl through broken glass for her. Doesn't she realize that? I'm willing to spill blood, every last drop of it, for her… always anything for my Zilphia.

I'm nothing without her.

My eyes touch on my threadbare blue jeans and scuffed sneakers. I can't buy her fancy things, but she's never been a materialistic girl. And money can't buy what we share. It's priceless.

I'm going to take a risk and lay it all on the table. Explain my true feelings to her. She fears her mother, but that vile woman won't be able to control her forever. I'll protect her.

I know she feels something for me. The way we hold hands, comfort one another, cuddle, laugh, and joke goes far beyond friendship. Zilphia thinks she can pretend there's nothing between us, but I won't let her.

I wipe my sweaty forehead and follow the street that leads toward home. It's already a scorcher outside. Southern Texas weather ain't for the weak.

As I near the trailer, shouting spills out to meet me.

It's too early for this bullshit.

The front door flies open. "Can't a man have peace in his own house?"

"Come back here!"

"I've had enough of your constant nagging!" Emmett shouts, bounding toward his truck.

"Where were you last night?" my mother asks, trailing his footsteps with only a towel covering her slim figure.

"Working!" Emmett calls out. "I had to work a double."

"Why weren't you answering your phone then, huh?"

They put on a show for the neighbors nearly every damn day. An audience is already gathering to watch my mother and her boyfriend make spectacles of themselves yet again. Frankly, I've seen this rerun way too many times. On the plus side, at least this is the longest relationship my mother ever had. A year and two and a half months to be exact. I guess that's cause for celebration.

"Because I left it in my locker, you crazy bitch."

"You must think I'm an idiot!" she rages, beating on his back. "You were out fooling around with Birdie again!"

Emmett whirls around and seizes her wrists. "You need a psych evaluation."

"I'm tired of you cheating on me!" she wails. "I have gonorrhea because of you!"

"Oh shit! Kitty's got the clap, y'all," someone chortles, and the crowd roars with laughter.

"Stop telling our business to these fucking gossipmongers," Emmett growls, shoving her to the ground.

"Let them talk," my mother sobs hysterically. "I don't care."

"I'm staying at my sister's until you calm down."

"No! You're lying." She wraps her arms around his leg, dislodging the towel. "You're going to go see Birdie."

He kicks her off and dives into his truck, tires shrieking as he tears down the asphalt. She runs after him bare-ass naked. Catcalls echo through the neighborhood.

"That's right, girl, go get your man!"

"Another day in paradise," I deadpan and stroll into the trailer.

CHAPTER 5

Zilphia

"YO, SIS, HOW'S THE FACE FEELING?" NOLAN SMIRKS WITHOUT taking his eyes off the road.

"Shut up or the next time you go to sleep I'll disembowel you," I fume, balling my hands into fists.

"Damn," he laughs. "You get slapped into next week and now you wanna commit a felony?"

"I mean it, Nolan." I twist in my seat, ready to do some bodily damage if he keeps pushing me.

When the jokes didn't start the moment we got into the car, I foolishly thought Nolan took pity on me and breathed a sigh of relief. Silly me. Should've known it was too good to be true. He will never be a protective big brother. Our mother's relentless coddling turned him into a selfish, spoiled brat with an ego to match.

Momma hates me, though. Why else would she treat me the way she does? I try my hardest to meet her expectations, but she always finds me lacking.

Nolan slows his Mercedes-Benz to a stop at a four-way intersection. "Shit,

I bet the whole county heard it. Momma laid the double whammy on your ass. Sure you don't have a concussion?"

"I hate you!" I scream. I'm about to land a punch when he strikes me first.

A sharp jab to the gut.

I double over, gasping for air, blinding pain rippling through my intestines.

"Jesus," he grumbles. "Overreact much?"

I throw the door open and retch, but nothing comes out. Nolan unbuckles my seatbelt and shoves me headfirst to the pavement. Frustrated drivers blare their horns and speed around us, pissed at being delayed.

"Walk it off," he sneers and tosses my belongings after me before peeling down the street.

I pluck my compact mirror from my purse and examine the damage. No bleeding, but my forehead is scraped up pretty bad. I'll put on a little more makeup at school.

I stand tall. Straighten my spine. Pretend I'm not screaming inside.

It's just another day, Zilphia… Don't think. Don't cry. Don't let him win.

Holding my head up high, I begin the ten-minute trek to school. Walking is preferable to riding with Nolan anyway.

My thoughts drift to Sam. It'll be especially tricky sneaking food to him now. After this morning, Momma will for sure keep track of groceries. Without me, he wouldn't eat dinner most days.

I can't let that happen, not ever.

My calves burn as I hike up the steep hill leading to the hulking taupe-colored brick building. "FeFe, over here, boo!" Claudette shouts in her nails-on-a-chalkboard voice.

Ugh! I loathe that stupid nickname!

God, she is beyond irritating. I've asked her not to call me that a trillion times, but does she listen? *NOPE!*

I count to five Mississippis and slide my lips upward in a fake smile.

We've been "friends" since kindergarten—because our mothers said so. They're meaner than rattlesnakes and have PhDs in starting drama. Every day it's the same ridiculous competition over who can flaunt the most overpriced outfit, shoes, and jewelry. It's aggravating.

I don't trust them as far as I can throw them. But Momma says these are the right girls. The right crowd.

"Hey," I wave at the three girls clustered near the marble sculpture of Bart the Bear, Pinkerton High's mascot.

"Ew, what happened to your forehead?" Savannah asks, backing away like I have the plague.

"I fell." I shrug. "It's nothing serious."

"You are such a klutz," Phyllis chastises me. "Do you have two left feet or what?"

"Well, I didn't fall on purpose, Phyllis."

"Oh, honey, what are you going to do about the homecoming dance?" Savannah tsks. "You can't waltz into the gym hanging on Redmond's arm looking like something the cat dragged in."

"Still don't get why he asked you in the first place," Phyllis quips, throwing shade.

Savannah snorts, and Claudette snickers behind her long coffin-shaped acrylic nails. Truth be told, I have no clue why he asked me either. Sure, Redmond and Nolan are best friends, but he never paid attention to me until a few weeks ago. What's changed? Unlike my brother, Redmond's tall, ripped, and freaking hot. He could've gone to the dance with any girl he wanted, but chose me.

"Don't fret." Claudette squeezes my hand, offering false comfort. "Foundation will cover that nasty little bruise right up."

"I have an important announcement," Savannah states cheekily, changing the subject.

"Do tell." Phyllis waggles her eyebrows. "Is it something juicy?"

Savannah flips her lemonade braids over her shoulder. "Super juicy."

Claudette sucks her teeth impatiently. "Well, what is it?"

"I'm going to have sex with Briceson on homecoming night."

"What?" I exclaim, wide-eyed. "But that's tomorrow and you're only fifteen."

And she just started dating him. They can't love each other this soon. Sex is a huge step and shouldn't be taken lightly. I, for one, want my first time to be special.

"But you're only fifteen," Savannah mimics in a whiny tone. "Gosh, you're such a baby. It's not a big deal. My cousin lost her virginity at thirteen. Anyway, it's my duty to keep my man satisfied."

"Yeah, hello, we're not in middle school anymore, FeFe," Claudette retorts. "Do you think Redmond is going to stick around if you're not giving it up? He'll drop you like a bad habit, girl. Remember, whatever you refused to do, another bitch won't."

"And being a virgin at fifteen is so 1960s," Savannah proclaims, giving me the stink face. "You really need to get with the times."

"Creeper alert," Phyllis mutters suddenly, wrinkling her nose.

Savannah follows her gaze. "Who?"

"The dingy white boy sitting on the stairs."

I glance over and my breath stalls in my throat.

Sam.

Sitting on the edge of the brick steps like he belongs nowhere. Hoodie half-zipped. Knees drawn up. But it's his eyes—those glacial-blue eyes—that pin me to the spot.

He's staring at me. *Just* me.

What the hell is he doing?

We made a rule. No looks. No words. No acknowledgment.

And he's burning a hole through me in front of the worst gossips in the entire school.

My skin prickles. My throat dries. My brain screams, *"Look away, look away"*—but it's too late.

"He's staring at you, Zilphia," Savannah remarks.

"Like he wants to eat you alive," Claudette adds.

"Wait a minute," Phyllis says, her eyes darting between Sam and me. "Do you two know each other?"

"Are you serious?" I snort, loud and dismissive. "He's not even my type."

"Come on, girl," Phyllis croons. "You can tell us. We're your friends."

Friends don't study your face like it's evidence.

"I have never even spoken a single word to him," I lie, praying my acting skills are sufficient.

Claudette bumps her shoulder against mine. "Maybe he has a crush on you."

"Gah, he looks stank, and has he never heard of a comb?" Savannah retorts.

"He doesn't stink," I snap before I can stop myself.

Silence.

Shit.

Phyllis blinks slowly. "And how exactly would you know that?"

I laugh, tight and too fast. "I walked past him in the hall. Once." I need to end this conversation before I give myself away. "I'm heading to the bathroom to clean up before class starts. See y'all later." I practically run to the entrance.

Sam is on their radar now, which means they'll be watching him and his reaction to me. This isn't good.

SAM

Zilphia's rich, dark-caramel skin is unparalleled. My famished gaze drinks her in, seeking sustenance only she can give me. I shouldn't gape, but I'm hopelessly riveted by her. She's my sunshine in my otherwise cold, dark world. Everything that is me belongs to her. I am her property. I'll forever be at her beck and call.

I slip my fingers into my pocket and caress the gold cuff bracelet there. It's a surprise gift for Zilphia. Our names are engraved across the surface in fancy script. I mowed lawns all summer long to save money for the expensive purchase, but she's well worth the days spent slaving in the blazing heat. I'm waiting for the perfect moment to give it to her.

"Take a picture, it'll last longer," Jiminy teases, plopping down next to me.

I jab my elbow into his ribs. "Zip it."

"Dude, quit being so obvious," he cautions, pushing his overgrown chestnut hair from his eyes. "That's all I'm saying. It's curtains if Nolan finds out you hold a torch for his sister."

I scoff. "That fucker doesn't scare me."

Nolan and his entourage used to make my life hell. Freshman year was pranks, verbal warfare, and locker-room beatdowns. Sophomore year, I hit back. Hard. But I never told Zilphia. She doesn't need that. Our tree house time is sacred. I won't stain it with his name.

Nowadays, our run-ins are few and far between.

"What's your end game, huh? Marriage, babies, and a desk job?" he questions sarcastically. "It ain't happening, Sam. Not with Zilphia. Her family isn't going to roll out the welcome mat for you."

"She'll choose me," I respond, though doubt digs its razor-sharp talons in my heart. "Eventually."

The silence that follows cuts deeper than laughter.

"Look," he finally says. "Zilphia isn't built for the path we walk. That girl's got a glass life. You throw one rock—"

"You don't understand," I fire back. "Zilphia and me, we share something special."

"Okay, I get it. Romeo and Juliet 2.0," he deadpans.

"Fuck you, Cricket." He's my best friend, but sometimes I want to throttle him.

"Dude, fairytales aren't real. Girls like Zilphia don't date, let alone marry, white trash." I wince, rearing my head back as if dealt a violent blow. "Hey, no offense, man. Hell, I'm white trash too."

I glance down, trying to rein in my emotions. "I love her."

"I know, but you will never exist for her outside that tree house. The sooner you realize that, the better."

"You done?" I snap, refusing to acknowledge the truth behind his words. "I shouldn't have told you shit. You throw the situation in my fucking face every chance you get."

"Hey." His voice softens. "I'm not trying to kill the dream, Sam. I just don't wanna be scraping your heart off the pavement later."

"Thanks, but I don't need a goddamn watchdog. I'm fully capable of taking care of myself."

"Hendricks," Nolan calls, marching toward me. Redmond strides at his side.

"Here we go," Jiminy mutters.

I grab the rusted metal handrail and push to my feet. "What do you want?"

Jiminy stands too, ready to throw punches if necessary.

"Damn, why so hostile?" he asks, his eyebrows dipping low in mock concern. "We just wanted to check on you. Make sure your mom's okay."

My jaw tightens, knowing exactly where this conversation is headed.

"Saw a video of her giving the whole neighborhood a show," Redmond chimes in, barely controlling his laughter. "Shame there wasn't popcorn."

The fuckers cackle like they just heard the funniest joke on Earth.

"I gotta hand it to her, though." Nolan leans toward me, his voice low and taunting. "For an old bitch, she looked pretty good."

"Back off," Jiminy growls.

"Or what, pussy?" Nolan sneers.

"I'll smash your shit in," I threaten, my fists clenched and itching to land a hit.

"Space and opportunity," he goads me, spreading his arms wide. "Space and opportunity."

"Hey!" the security guard yells. "Is there a problem?"

Nolan plasters a smile on his face. "Not at all. We're just having a friendly conversation."

"Save it for later. The bell's about to ring."

"You're lucky," Nolan mumbles, giving my cheek a quick slap before he and Redmond amble past us.

"Your future brother-in-law is a major asswipe." Jiminy slings his arm across my shoulders. "Family gatherings should be a blast."

"Shut up, Jiminy." I shrug him off and stalk into the building.

CHAPTER 6

SAM

I enter the tree house, surprised to find Zilphia curled up on the futon. She usually doesn't sneak out until around eleven or twelve.

"Hey," I say, smiling at her. "Eager to see me, huh?"

"Yeah." She pads across the wooden floor and wraps her arms around me. "Rough day."

I hold her tight against my chest, relishing the feel of her in my arms. "Wanna talk about it?"

She shakes her head. "No."

I pull back and frown, noticing the bruise on her forehead. "What happened?" I ask, softly brushing my thumb over the raw skin. My stomach knots with rage. I don't need to ask who the culprit is.

"Nothing." She sighs, blinking back tears. "Same ole, same ole."

"It's not nothing, Zilphia."

She shrugs and returns to the futon, pulling her legs to her chest. "What does it matter? I'm stuck here until I graduate."

I sit beside her. "Let's run away," I say, needing to get her away from her toxic family. "Tonight. We can—"

Zilphia presses her slender fingers to my lips. "Sam, please. Just drop it."

I nod because I can't stand seeing the sadness in her brown eyes. "Okay."

"Sam," she hesitates. "Today… at school. You can't look at me like that. People will talk."

"Don't give a fuck," I reply tightly, rolling my hands into fists. "Let them."

"Well, I do!" she exclaims, desperation in her voice. "You were watching me like… like…"

I cup her cotton-soft cheek. "I can't help it. You're beautiful."

"Don't." She stands and walks away, keeping her back to me. "If my mother finds out about our friendship, we'll never see each other again."

Zilphia's words are a cold dose of reality. I know she's right. Mrs. Kensley would transfer her daughter to another school just to keep her away from the likes of me.

I saunter over to Zilphia and grasp her shoulder, turning her around to face me. "I'm sorry. It won't happen again. I promise."

I'll do whatever it takes to keep Zilphia in my life.

"Thank you, Sam."

"Don't mention it." I glance back at the board games stacked on top of the bookshelf. "Chess?"

A faint smile tugs at her lips. "Yeah."

I grab the box and arrange the pieces on the table. "Get ready to lose."

She playfully swats my arm. "Hey, I've been getting better."

Three games in and she hasn't won yet. I have no problem rubbing it in either.

"Checkmate!" I crow in triumph. "Three wins in a row."

"Hey, not so fast, the game isn't over yet," Zilphia grumbles, flinging a rook at me.

I catch it. "Have some dignity, girl, and accept your defeat gracefully."

Her fiery gaze narrows on me. "You're a real butthole, Sam."

"Dang, is the name-calling necessary?" I ask, feigning hurt.

"If you shut your big fat mouth, I could concentrate," she snaps, hurling a bishop this time, striking me in the nose.

"Ouch," I whine, rubbing the spot where the piece landed.

"Not another word," she hisses, pointing a finger at me.

"Aight, you got it." I slash my index finger and thumb across my lips in a zipping motion.

"Good." Zilphia's perfectly shaped eyebrows dip over her vibrant, dark-maple gaze as she intently studies the brown-and-beige checkered board.

My lips flatten into a thin line to keep my amusement in check. I don't want another chess piece thrown at my face.

Minutes tick by, but Zilphia hasn't attempted a single move. There's no way she's going to win. She's done and knows it, but is too freaking stubborn to admit the inevitable.

I yawn dramatically, stretching my arms high above my head. "Sometime this century, please."

She growls in frustration and flips the chessboard, scattering the chess pieces across the worn floor.

"I can't believe you did that," I say, gawking at her in disbelief.

Zilphia's lips lift in a self-satisfied smirk. "Now no one wins."

"Oh, you're in for it now." I wiggle my fingers, and apprehension immediately replaces her glee. "Prepare to be tickled until you pee your pants."

"I'm sorry," she squeaks, scrambling backward on her bottom.

I move to my knees and inch after her. "It's too late for apologies."

"Sam, don't." Her eyes shift between my wiggling fingers and the door.

I arch a knowing eyebrow. "You wouldn't make it one step."

"I'll do your homework for a week," she offers, sweeping her tongue across her plump bottom lip.

I shake my head. "Nah, not good enough."

"Two weeks?" she asks, aiming to sweeten the pot.

"Nope," I reply, drawing out the P. "You should've just taken the L."

"Three weeks then? Please, Sam!" she pleads, holding a hand up to ward me off. "You know I can't take being tickled."

"Welp, you should've thought about that before acting like a brat." I shrug, closing in on her.

"I'll bake you a humongous strawberry shortcake with extra strawberries and whipped cream," she says, upping the ante. "Just how you like it."

"Mmm… humongous, huh?" I grip my chin contemplatively. "Now we're getting somewhere."

"And I'll do your homework for a whole month too," she adds, her posture visibly relaxing. "Think about—"

I lunge at her, shamelessly using her false sense of security to my advantage. Zilphia's high-pitched yelp resounds in the tree house as she tries to scuttle away.

"No, you don't." My long fingers dig into her midsection mercilessly.

"Sam, stop! I can't breathe!" Zilphia laughs uncontrollably while trying to pry my hands away from her belly. "I'm sorry, okay? I promise never to act like a brat again."

"Shh... you're going to wake up the entire neighborhood," I warn in a teasing tone.

"Then quit tickling me!" she shouts, crying tears of laughter. "My kidneys are going to burst!"

"Okay, but under one condition."

"Anything you want," Zilphia readily agrees between gasping breaths. "Just name it."

"Repeat after me."

"Okay."

"I, Zilphia Kensley, acknowledge Samuel Hendricks as master of all board games."

"I'll say it, but it's not—" I go for her belly again. "Okay, okay! Don't be so rash." She fakes a cough, then clears her throat with a dramatic flair. "I, Zilphia Kensley, acknowledge Samuel Hendricks as master of all board games."

"See, that wasn't so hard," I tease, gliding my thumb over her bottom lip.

She playfully nips at it, sending a violent jolt straight to my gut. Suddenly, our innocent banter ventures into forbidden territory, and I become acutely aware of my lean body pressed flush against her delicate curves. We're so close that my reflection shines clearly in her soulful brown depths.

"Sam," she gasps in a breathless whisper, feeling the shift too.

"Zilphia," I murmur and gingerly seal my mouth to hers.

Flames dance through my veins the moment our lips touch, unleashing an explosion of need through my body. Zilphia lies motionless beneath me. My heart skips a beat, afraid she'll pull away from me. But she doesn't—she burrows her slender fingers through my hair and kisses me back. I've dreamed of this moment for so long, but I never truly believed it would happen. I want to shout. Tell the world that Zilphia is mine.

Blood swooshes in my ears as my cock grows hard against her. I push my tongue deep into her mouth and nudge my hips between her thighs, pressing my length against her warm center. I want to devour every inch of her. Her moans encourage me to delve my hand beneath her camisole, but before I can reach her breasts, she tears her mouth away.

"Stop!" she cries, pushing at my shoulders.

I sit back on my haunches as she frantically scurries to the nearest corner.

"I'm sorry," I start, but that's a lie. I'd do it again. "No, you know what? I'm not sorry."

"You have to go."

"Why?" I growl, my nails biting into my palms. The pain keeps me in place; otherwise, I would've gone after her.

"Please, Sam," she begs.

I leave, though my heart and mind rebel against it.

CHAPTER 7

Zilphia

DANIKA'S FINGERS GLIDE THROUGH MY HAIR, MASSAGING TEA tree oil into my scalp in soft, practiced circles. She tousles my curls one last time before unsnapping the cape at my neck.

"You're good to go, baby doll," she announces.

I turn toward the mirror and run my fingers through the shiny, shoulder-length ringlets and smile. "Thanks, Danika. I love it."

Momma's making a big to-do about the homecoming dance. After school, she took me to get a manicure and pedicure, then dropped me off at the hair salon. She even bought me a gorgeous fuchsia satin dress and matching lace-up stiletto heels a few weeks ago, but I wasn't expecting the full-fledged prom treatment.

"You're welcome." She squeezes my shoulder. "Knock 'em dead tonight."

"I plan to." I grin and exit the salon, stepping into the humid evening.

I spot Momma's shimmery yellow-gold Audi across the street, and self-doubt's nagging voice booms in my mind, faltering my steps. She let me choose my hairstyle, which means either she's in a good mood… or something more sinister is awaiting me. I whisper a silent prayer, cross the street, and open the door.

"So what do you think?" I ask, sliding into the passenger seat.

"You look stunning," she says, a calculating smile tugging at her lips as her eyes scan me like merchandise.

"I'm glad you like it," I mutter, my internal alarm bells going off.

"I stopped by Lilac Fashion Boutique and got you a little something extra special for the homecoming dance tonight." She plucks a small pink paper bag off the back seat and places it onto my lap. "Take a look."

I excitedly rummage through the bag, expecting jewelry, but find a white lace bra and thong set. Confusion swiftly replaces my exuberance, angering Momma.

"Well?" she huffs.

"Um…" I'm at a loss for words.

There's an ulterior motive behind this purchase, and I'm terrified to learn what it is. Undoubtedly, the nefarious scheme will benefit my mother the most.

"It's beautiful," I answer to appease her.

"Redmond's going to lose his tongue when he sees you in it," she boasts, her lips stretching wide.

Crippling dread unfurls in my belly. My fingers tighten around the bag. "Why would he see me in it?"

She laughs, but the sound is hollow. "You're almost a woman, Zilphia. You know why."

I swallow, forcing down the coiling apprehension lodged in my throat. "Y-y-you want me to have sex with him?"

Her hand cracks across my face, sharp and fast. My head whips sideways, and I curl in on myself. "Don't be stupid," she hisses. "Never give yourself away for free. Tease him, but only enough to drive him crazy," she cajoles, lightly skimming her fingertips over my stinging skin. "Let him explore your body… fondle your breasts… touch between your legs. You can jerk him off and even suck his dick, but do not fuck him. Not yet anyway."

I sit frozen, bile burning the back of my throat.

"But I don't love him." A single tear leaves a wet trail on my cheek and drips onto my trembling hand.

"Love doesn't pay the bills. Your top priority should always be financial security. Redmond's family comes from old money. Play your cards right and you'll be set for life."

Momma's enthusiasm when I told her Redmond asked me to the dance, and the costly preparations make sense now. She plans to pimp me out, use me as her personal cash cow, and elevate her status in Texas's upper echelon.

"Do you love Daddy?" I ask, already knowing the answer, but needing to hear her say it.

Emotionless eyes cut me to the core. "No, I don't."

My heart crumbles at my feet, disintegrating into specks of dust. I can't deny the truth any longer. My mother is a monster.

"No curfew tonight," she announces, then seizes my chin in an ironclad grip. "Show Redmond a good time. Am I understood?"

"Yes," I croak, suffocating nausea bowling me over.

The underlying message is unmistakable. Willingly participate in her convoluted plot or suffer the consequences.

She kisses my forehead. "Good girl."

The engine reverberates through my paralyzed limbs, and soon we're joining rush hour traffic on the highway. Though the air conditioner is set to max, anxious sweat dots my skin.

What mother encourages her teenage daughter to seduce a boy?

My gaze clings to the small pink paper bag still on my lap. It weighs a few scant ounces, but mentally it's crushing me. I roll my hands into tight fists to keep from ripping the racy lingerie to shreds.

My morals can't be exchanged for monetary gain. I'd rather be dirt poor. Love is supposed to develop naturally. It shouldn't be forced. Marriage is a sacred union, and mine will not be based on lies. And, heck, I'm only fifteen. Tying the knot isn't on my radar. There are so many goals I want to accomplish before settling down.

Momma turns on the radio.

"Oh, I haven't heard this song in forever," she gushes, notching up the volume.

While she sings along to the lyrics, my heart and mind scream in silent agony.

I hadn't even planned on giving Redmond a good-night kiss, let alone allowing him access to my most private areas. Sam is the only boy I've ever been intimate with. Our kiss was explosive, but it's a line we shouldn't have crossed. There is nothing for us beyond friendship. We're destined to walk separate paths in life.

The sudden silence alerts me that we're home.

"Go shower. I'll be in soon to do your makeup."

"Okay," I reply tonelessly.

I follow her into the house and listlessly climb the stairs to prepare for my downfall. My inner turmoil intensifies with each wavering step. The second my bedroom door clicks shut, my legs buckle under the oppressive burden heaped onto my shoulders, and I crumple to the carpet in despair.

My airway contracts, limiting oxygen flow and constricting my chest painfully. I reach for my purse and frantically fish out my asthma medication, then quickly inhale two deep puffs. Once the wheezing recedes, I drag myself to the bathroom. I shower and slip into my silk robe in a foggy daze before perching on my bed. The thong is a size too small, making it impossible to sit comfortably. It's sure to leave an indent around my waist.

Momma scurries into my room, all smiles, large aluminum cosmetics case in hand.

"It's almost time!" she exclaims, depositing the case next to me and promptly beginning my beautification process.

"You are so lucky. I didn't have much growing up. Momma barely earned enough money to buy the bare essentials. All my clothes and shoes were hand-me-downs or from the thrift store. The uppity bitches at school bullied me every day. I wanted a better life and your father was an easy target. I seduced him and have no regrets."

A sour taste slithers along my taste buds at her selfish admission.

"But you betrayed your sister," I whisper.

She bends down until we're eye to eye. "And I'd do it again in a heartbeat. You're young, but one day you'll realize the world is a cold place. If you want something, you have to take it by any means necessary. Everyone is expendable, including family."

Nolan appears in the doorway. "I'm heading out."

"You look devilishly handsome," Momma raves, giving his designer outfit a once-over. "Have a great time."

"I will. See you in the morning," he says before strutting down the hallway.

Momma grabs the blush palette and sets to finishing her task. My curfew is lifted for tonight, but Nolan is always free to come and go as he pleases without question, even when he was my age.

"Flawless." Momma beams, spritzing setting spray over my face.

Ding-dong.

"That's him," she breathes, her eyes sparkling like a schoolgirl about to meet her celebrity crush. "Hurry up and get dressed, and remember what we talked about."

I nod, blinking away the tears threatening to spill free.

CHAPTER 8

SAM

"Coming here is a colossal mistake," Jiminy gripes, trailing behind me into the building.

I sigh, pinching the bridge of my nose. He bitched the entire walk here. I usually avoid school functions, but Zilphia's going to be here tonight. I need to speak to her before I lose my nerve.

We stroll down the hallway, bypassing a few kids tucked in corners doing only God knows what. I haven't seen an adult yet. They probably wouldn't care anyway. Most turn a blind eye to the shit that goes on around here. They do the bare minimum to keep their biweekly checks coming in.

"We're parading straight into the lion's den," he adds, continuing his gloom and doom narrative.

A giggling couple darts past us, undoubtedly seeking privacy to engage in some teenage debauchery.

"You insisted on coming, remember?" I remind him. "I told you to stay your ass home."

"Who else is going to have your back when things go south, hmm?" he asks, pursing his lips into a paper-thin line.

"You know, silence is a virtue," I deadpan.

"Excuse me for trying to talk some sense into you," he huffs, flinging his arms up in exasperation.

"Positive thoughts equal positive results," I tell him.

Jiminy scoffs. "You'll be singing a different tune when Nolan and his henchman beat the brakes off you."

"Well, at least you'll be right beside me, getting the brakes beat off you too," I joke, flicking his earlobe.

He smacks my hand away. "Oh, you think putting our lives in jeopardy is funny?"

"Relax, no one's dying tonight, except maybe you, if you don't chill the hell out."

"Can't wait to say I told you so," he grumbles under his breath.

I ignore him and squeeze through the crowd mingling near the gymnasium entrance. All dressed to impress. Me? Same threadbare jeans and scuffed sneakers that scream "nobody." I'd love a steady job, but there aren't many positions available in town, and public transportation is nil. If I had a car, finding work would be a breeze.

The instant we push through the double doors, my gaze scans over the gaudy yellow-and-purple-decorated gym, searching for Zilphia. It's jam-packed, making it difficult to locate her among the attendees.

"Ah fuck," Jiminy mutters.

"What?" I ask, prepared to spring into action if somebody's looking to start some shit.

He jerks his head to the left. "Over there."

The music and boisterous chatter fade away until the only sound inundating my eardrums is the blood thundering in my veins. Black spots dance in my vision. I blink once. Then again—hoping I'm wrong. But there she is.

Redmond's slimy hands mold over her bottom, pulling her flush against him like he owns her.

"Let's get outta here," Jiminy says.

"No," I grit out, storming toward the gyrating bodies.

"Don't be stupid, man. She's not worth us getting our asses kicked," Jiminy calls after me.

I latch onto Redmond's shoulder and spin him around.

"What the—" I swing. My fist crushes his nose, and he folds like a chair.

"Oh my God," Zilphia gasps, clamping a hand over her mouth.

Before the sheep realize one of their precious idols was dropped by a nobody, I'm already barreling out of the rear exit with Zilphia in tow.

"Are you insane?" she yells, her heels scraping the vinyl tile as I drag her behind me. "Let me go!"

After trying several doorknobs, I find an unlocked classroom and haul Zilphia inside. The candescent moon shines through the tall, rectangular casement windows lining the entire back wall, casting her in a fluorescent glow. She's breathtaking. The short clinging dress displays her cleavage and shapely legs.

And fuck…

Her shimmery white-polished toenails are the beautiful bow on the package. Zilphia's feet deserve the highest praise. The soft, slim soles are perfection. I've fantasized about gliding my tongue over the delicate arches more times than I can count.

Every inch of her is designed to wreck me.

"Do you realize what you've done?" she asks, nervously wringing her hands. "People will for sure talk now."

"I don't give a damn!" I roar, my nostrils flaring in anger. "How could you let him touch you like that? That fucking bastard doesn't deserve to be anywhere near you!"

"Redmond's my date, and we were just dancing."

"Your date!" I bellow. She stumbles back a few steps, her lips quivering. "You never said anything about a date!"

"I'm not obligated to tell you everything that goes on in my life!"

I close the distance between us. "You didn't tell me because you know it's fucking wrong!"

"You and I are just friends, Sam," she fires back. "I'm sorry if you got the wrong idea."

"Bullshit." I grip her arms. "We kissed."

"No." She jerks her head from side to side. "You kissed me."

I rub my forehead along hers. "And you kissed me back."

"It was a mistake," she whispers, her voice cracking the slightest bit. "Please don't make this harder than it has to be."

Mistake. That one word hurt more than anything I've ever endured. But it's still nothing compared to my fear of losing her.

"You're lying." My throat muscles clench and warm tears drench my cheeks. I'm a snowflake for crying, but she's my soulmate. I can't lose her.

"Please don't cry, Sam," Zilphia pleads, emotion spilling out with every word.

I gently cradle her oval face in my large hands. "I love you."

"Sam—"

I swallow her words, closing my lips around hers, pouring my desperation into her. Telling her without words that she is my North Star, brightening my path across the murky, treacherous sea of my life. I need her to understand the sincere depth of my feelings.

With a gasp, Zilphia twists her fingers into my shirt, responding to my urgency.

Thank God.

She said yes.

To me. To us.

My hands travel the length of her spine and skate under her dress. I finger the waistband of her tiny thong before gripping her velvet-smooth bottom and lifting her onto a desk.

"I love you, Zilphia," I rasp against her lips. "I love you so fucking much—"

The door slams open and light floods the room. "What the fuck are you doing with my sister?"

Zilphia scrambles off the desk, stark terror transforming her features. I face down Nolan, Redmond, and three other guys. Satisfaction puffs my chest at the sight of Redmond's swollen nose.

"Nolan, I—"

"Save your excuses," Nolan barks, jabbing an accusing finger in her direction. "You're nothing but a fucking whore."

"Call her another name and stars will be the next thing you see," I growl, taking a threatening step toward him.

"Enough yapping," Redmond snarls. "This hillbilly needs to be taught a lesson."

"Wait till Momma hears about this," Nolan crows, rolling up his sleeves. "She's going to beat your ass good, but first I'm going to crack your boyfriend's skull."

"I-I h-have no idea w-who this guy is," Zilphia stammers. "I-I s-swear."

"Liar," he accuses, his mouth twisting into an ugly sneer. "You were all over each other. From here on out, your life is going to be a fucking nightmare."

She shakes her head, panic flickering in her wide eyes. "He forced me in here… and just started kissing me. But I'm fine, really."

"Zilphia," I whisper, her words hitting like a bullet to the chest.

This isn't the girl I fell in love with.

Her betrayal is more crippling than the deadliest poison on Earth. We could've stood together in unity, but she chose to throw me to the wolves to save her own skin. Like mother, like daughter after all.

"Motherfucker!" Nolan shouts and rushes me, clocking me in the jaw.

I quickly recover and retaliate, landing a two-piece combo to his grill. The group converges on me and wrestles me to the floor. Five to one—the odds aren't in my favor. Fists and expensive shoes fly, pummeling my body. I nestle my knees to my stomach to protect my vital organs and curve my forearms over my head. Luckily, adrenaline numbs me against the brutal beating.

"Stop!" Zilphia cries, hurling herself between me and my attackers.

Too little, too late.

She sealed my fate the moment she falsely accused me of sexual assault. No point in pretending to care now.

Nolan pushes her, and she crashes into the whiteboard. "Stay out of this!"

"Cocksuckers!" Jiminy roars, coming to my rescue, but a blow to the face takes him down too.

Two on him. Three on me. As he predicted, getting our asses beat.

"Move!" Nolan orders.

The battering stops, and something hard is smashed against my temple. Then… complete darkness.

"Sam, wake up." Jiminy's worried voice penetrates my fuzzy brain. "Can you hear me?"

My eyes blink open to his bruised face hovering above me. I grimace, struggling to an upright position, though my body protests in agony. I scan the four corners of the classroom, searching for *her*.

"She's gone," Jiminy answers my unspoken question and offers me his hand. "You were out for about five minutes. That fucker Nolan decked you with a chair."

I slump my weight onto the nearest desk. "She said she didn't know me," I murmur.

"I know."

Zilphia tore my heart out and spat on it. She didn't just leave me. She left me bleeding—literally.

And somehow, I still love her.

But it's a twisted love now—the kind that wants to maim. I want to hurt her and worship her at the same time. She's my weakness… the one person who could break me. I thought she was my savior, but she was my tormentor in disguise all along… just a trick of the light.

"Your ear is bleeding," Jiminy observes. "You should go to the hospital to play it safe."

"Give me your lighter," I say, ignoring his advice.

He delves into his hoodie pocket and drops the small brass canister in my outstretched hand. I detest cigarettes, but tonight his bad habit works in my favor.

"Go home," I instruct him and hobble toward the door.

Jiminy barricades himself in the doorway. "What are you going to do?"

"It doesn't concern you. Go home," I reiterate between grinding teeth.

"Leave it be, Sam," Jiminy warns. "Zilphia made her choice. The pretend world you two created was bound to crumble eventually."

Jiminy pours salt into the festering wound, and the last fiber holding my control intact unravels. I capture his neck and slam him into the wall.

"Go the fuck home!"

I release my hold and burst into the hallway, taking off at a dead run. Identical to the rainy night almost five years ago, a voice beckons me, but it isn't destiny's lulling drawl. It's wrath's sinister monotone, goading me on, demanding I *burn it.*

Burn it.

Burn it.

Burn it.

My rumpled sneakers sail over the terrain at top speed, only sliding to a halt when the tree house fills my vision. Memories taunt me, cackling at the stupid boy for daring to hope. I should've stayed in my own world. Violent tremors rock me to the core as tears fall down my cheeks. My heart is in ruins.

I want to forget her. Press the rewind button and change the course that led me to her doorstep. I peer at the inky-black sky, damning the Fates for cruelly tempting me.

Single-minded determination propels me across the freshly cut grass. I hop the wooden gate and clear the stairs to the tree house in seconds, then my rampage commences.

The TV's first. Gone.

The bookshelf. Splintered.

Board games, memories, promises—all torn apart.

I stand in the middle of the wreckage, my rib cage heaving and mind in chaos. Still, above the clamor, the mantra persists, seeking my undivided attention.

Burn it.

Burn it.

Burn it.

I pick up Zilphia's heather-gray fleece blanket and draw in her titillating honeysuckle fragrance, getting drunk off her sweet essence one last time.

My Zilphia. No, not my Zilphia.

I let the blanket slip from my fingers. The girl I thought I knew was a mirage.

I pluck Zilphia's nail polish remover from the scattered debris, pour the clear liquid onto the futon, then set it on fire.

I stumble down the stairs and watch the flames spread, incinerating my once-coveted sanctuary.

Our story, our safe place… gone.

PART THREE
The Killer

CHAPTER 9

Three years later

SANDMAN

I PALM MY THROBBING DICK IN ONE CALLOUSED HAND AND HOLD A doobie in the other, higher than the Milky Way. My boy Ghoul hooked me up. He grows the best Hindi Kush this side of the United States. I place the rolled Bambú paper between my lips and pull the potent herb into my lungs.

My boneless body sinks farther into the mustard-colored armchair, dopamine levels kicking into overdrive. This shit will have the most seasoned stoners tweaking. I part my lips, releasing smoky ringlets into the hazy air. The strong pinewood aroma cloaks the room in a thick, calming blanket.

Between the weed and girl-on-girl action taking place on the bed, my cock is ready to do parlor tricks. Riley's lithe frame undulates on the mattress, her legs spread eagle while she kneads those lovely raspberry-colored nipples of hers. Cherry, her fellow twinkie and companion, goes to town on her bald pussy real messy like, soaking the mattress in cunt juice.

They're wet dreams in motion—blonde, sun-kissed, tight waists, big tits, and squeezable, round asses. Just my kind of art.

I avidly watch the steamy performance, chasing my high while briskly coasting my hand along my silken length, using the pearly pre-cum beading at my bulbous tip as lubricant.

The door flies open, striking the wall with a shuddering bang. "Get your ass home pronto," Draco growls, his fists clenched at his sides. "We have Church in thirty."

I take in his snarling countenance and hold out the jay in offering, knowing my gesture will only raise his hackles further. It's his second dramatic entrance in less than twenty minutes to relay Zeus's summons. He faithfully follows the dictates of his master.

Fucking lapdog.

"Wanna hit?" I ask, then nod toward the writhing bodies. "Or maybe you'd prefer a little dessert."

"Double penetration," Riley purrs, licking her lips. "Yummy."

"Me first," Cherry says, her voice low and teasing.

"Your presence is required now," Draco reiterates, anger rippling under his granite jaw.

"Well, as you can see, I'm preoccupied at the moment." I shrug and wave for the show to resume.

"Zeus shouldn't have brought you here," Draco seethes, resentment pinching his hard features. "You'll never be a true God."

"Pull the wedgie out of your ass and relax, *big bro*," I drawl, flashing him a crocodile smile.

Draco pounds into the room, blocking the carnal display from my view. Indignation stains his skin ruby red. I stay planted in the chair, unbothered by his mounting fury. He doesn't like being reminded of our shared DNA. I'm not exactly thrilled to be related to the fucker either.

Regrettably, one can't choose who their family members are. Three years ago, I learned my father wasn't dead like my mother led me to believe. I have a younger brother too—Lucien, aka Snake. He and I get along just fine.

The almighty Zeus is our father and the president of the Gods of Ruin, the most notorious motorcycle club in the Western Hemisphere. Draco is the veep. We have different mothers—all were twinkies at one point. Mine aspired to upgrade her status to old lady, but Zeus isn't the settling type. She ran off pregnant and pissed, without telling him about the life growing in her womb. Her vindictiveness caused a domino effect, resulting in the permanent scar on my heart.

"Do something," I dare him, stuffing my dick inside my boxer briefs.

Hostile energy vibrates off him in droves. Yeah, he's raring to cave my shit in, but surprisingly, he pivots on his heel. Too bad, I was looking forward to stomping his ass into the next century.

"Catch you later, *Julian,*" I mock, because the pettiness in me couldn't resist pushing his buttons a bit more.

He stops dead in his tracks.

Come on, give me a reason to rock your jaw loose.

I flex my fingers, itching to send him to the emergency room, but he storms into the hall and disappears.

Draco detests his government name. A bigger person would've left well enough alone, but mayhem is my mistress. The fickle bitch gets antsy if I don't lick her pussy every now and again. Guess that's why Zeus dubbed me a liability, says my thirst for trouble makes me impulsive, but my reckless behavior benefits the brotherhood. It's me who's tasked with disposing of our enemies. All the fuckers get a first-class ticket to Hell, courtesy of my Glock.

I wish disposing of my demons could be as easy.

Zilphia's beautiful image materializes in my mind, stirring up memories best left forgotten. Unfortunately, every part of her is etched into my psyche—from the arch of her feet to the shape of her mouth.

I didn't belong in her world. The universe fed me a pipe dream, and like a besotted fool, I greedily devoured it. My obsessive need for her surpassed common sense, but the fantasy unraveled on homecoming night. I lost my boyhood aspirations, my freedom, and the ability to hear in my left ear. A steep price to pay for unrequited love.

The doc put me on steroids, but that didn't help. Neither did hearing aids. Ultimately, I was diagnosed with profound hearing loss. Tinnitus was the worst part—the relentless ringing in my ear nearly drove me insane. After two years, the grating sound became sporadic and eventually disappeared altogether.

That was a very dark period in my life. Black hate filled the organ in my chest, and fantasies of torturing Zilphia filled my head. The hearing loss doesn't bother me much anymore. I've grown used to my impairment, though at times it's difficult to pinpoint where sound is coming from, especially in crowded places. It's a reminder never to fall victim to my feelings again.

In the aftermath, I was charged with second-degree arson. Fire spread to the house, and it burned down too. Luckily for me, no one was home at the time. The court-appointed attorney showed me more empathy than my own goddamn mother. That bitch didn't care if the judge threw the book at me.

My attorney discovered my old man was still alive and residing in Kent, Oregon. She contacted him, and he immediately came to my rescue. Subsequently, the felony charge was reduced to a misdemeanor. I got a year of probation, community service, and a hefty fine. Zeus paid the fine on my behalf, and the rest is history.

I shake my head, dispelling her enticing vision, and refocus my attention on the bed. It's best to let sleeping dogs lie. Rehashing the past serves no purpose.

I straighten to my six-foot-three frame and saunter to the bed, gray jeans hanging low on my hips. Riley's quivering thighs cradle Cherry's head, locking her in place.

I tangle my fingers in her golden strands and guide her lower. "Gotta eat her ass too or the meal isn't complete."

While she feasts, I glide my hand over her impeccably smooth bottom before smacking the supple skin until the jiggling flesh turns crimson red.

I admire my masterpiece, lightly tracing my fingertips over the visible handprints on her backside. "Lovely."

My cell phone rings in my back pocket, interrupting my vibe. It's probably Zeus, ready to tear me a new asshole. I let the call go to voicemail. I'll deal with him later.

I lean close to Cherry's ear. "Fuck her and make it hurt."

She pushes three slender digits into her companion's drenched pussy. Riley gasps, rotating her hips in tandem with the fingers plunging in and out of her tight body.

"We can't neglect this, now can we?" I rasp, pinching Riley's engorged clit.

Her back bows off the mattress, mouth opening in a soundless scream. I alternate between squeezing and kneading her sweet spot until she's writhing in pleasurable agony.

I hold the joint to her lips. "Want some?"

"Uh-huh," Riley hums and inhales a long drag. "Mmm, so good."

I take another hit before snuffing it out in the skull-shaped ashtray on the windowsill and stripping down to my socks.

"So heavy," Riley murmurs in awe, caressing my aching testicles. "These need to be emptied."

"I agree." I pluck a rubber from the glass bowl on the nightstand and roll the latex down my length. "Now open that pretty little mouth."

I ram my cock between those made-for-sin lips over and over again. Mascara streaks down her face as she gags around my erection. She tries to twist away, but I seize her long ponytail, keeping her right where she is.

"Tsk, tsk, tsk," I croon. "No running. Take my cock like a big girl."

The monster in me sings a dark lullaby at the panic brimming in her jade-green irises. I pound into her throat, almost shooting my load just from watching her struggle. Alas, I'm not done having fun yet.

I pull my dick from her mouth and climb onto the bed. Cherry pushes to her knees, bending that perfect ass in my direction.

"Good twinkie," I praise and slam deep inside her heated depths.

She lets out a sharp cry, her body going rigid at the sudden intrusion.

"Eat," I growl, shoving her face back into Riley's cunt.

I dig hard fingers into her tiny waist and jackhammer into her pussy, zero fucks given that her snug walls barely accommodate my cock.

I'm not the gentle type, but my partners are never left unsatisfied. For them, a chafed pussy is worth the mind-blowing orgasms. Cherry's impassioned moans reverberate through the room as her creamy passage chokes my length. I join her in release moments later, spilling my seed into the condom.

"My turn," Riley announces, snagging a magnum. "Need to rest, big boy? Or are you ready for round two?"

I smirk. Bitch doubting me, but she about to learn—I'm not new to this, I'm true to this.

CHAPTER 10

SANDMAN

I AMBLE INTO THE BAR, FRESHLY SHOWERED AND CONTENT AFTER curbing my sexual appetite. It's filled to capacity. "Livin' on a Prayer" comes on over the sound system, prompting more people to flaunt their dance skills. Others entertain themselves playing pool, foosball, or darts. There's even axe throwing.

Saturday nights are always crankin'.

A vintage jukebox sits in the corner, lending an old-time feel to the atmosphere. It's rarely shown any love, though.

There's a full-service kitchen too, and man, the grub is top-notch. The kind that causes heartburn and clogs the arteries, but the greasy deliciousness is worth going to an early grave. The garlic parmesan chicken wings with extra sauce… that's my poison. I can demolish a dozen in ten minutes flat. Add some loaded curly fries, and I'm in glutton heaven.

Zeus didn't just build a clubhouse—he built a legacy. After his rise to power, he brought in an architect like some hotshot Hollywood director, sketching out his empire in blueprints and concrete. The hulking structure has two main entrances: the bar and The Sanctuary.

We call it The Sanctuary for a reason—the first floor alone boasts a rec room, kitchen, dining area, gym, laundromat, and even a movie theater. There's also an office for Zeus. Twelve motel-style rooms span the second and third floors. Each club officer has their own private room. The others bunk out back in two barracks-style buildings.

Then there's the rooftop—complete with pools, jacuzzis, and grills. A space created for celebrations or escape, depending on the day. Below it all, the basement holds an auditorium. Two hundred patched brothers and counting gather there once a month, and every time, I still feel the weight of that number.

The bar is open to club affiliates—family, friends, anyone loyal to the Gods. They're welcome to eat, drink, and use one of the five bedrooms in the back—for a little adult fun or just to sleep it off. But that's where their access ends, unless Zeus says otherwise. Breaking this rule will result in a swift ass whooping.

People learn real quick why disrespecting the Gods is a bad idea. More often than not, we don't need to make an example out of anyone. Word gets around. Nobody crosses the brotherhood and lives. Still, despite what outsiders think, it's not all blood and mayhem. Some days are downright boring as fuck. We watch over the neighborhood, attend local events, and even cut checks to charity. Not exactly the Wild West fantasy people like to whisper about.

Earning a place in the brotherhood takes time, and for good reason. One rat could wreck everything. Recruitment's no joke—truth serum, lie detector tests, extensive background checks. Zeus doesn't cut corners when it comes to protecting the MC.

Civilians who show real interest get invited to hang around for a year. During that time, loyalty isn't requested; it's expected. Absolute obedience or you're out. Only a unanimous vote from the executive board earns you the right to prospect. Make it through two more years, and if you're still standing, you earn your patch.

The board answers to no one but Zeus. He handpicked each board member, and our voices are the only ones with any weight. The rest of the brothers hear the final word at meetings—simple as that.

The MC is doing better than ever. Zeus owns a trucking company, a gentleman's club (aka a prostitution ring), a crematorium, and a string of houses, apartment buildings, and gas stations. All solid earners, but nothing touches the real money—guns and heroin. The weapons come from shady dealers right here in the States. The H rolls in from Mexico.

Everyone gets a cut based on rank and time served. The businesses help clean the cash. The crematorium? That was bought with one purpose in mind—getting rid of bodies. No evidence, no investigation. Around here, the cops don't chase ghosts, especially not the kind with rap sheets.

On paper, the crematorium belongs to Kirk, Zeus's old marine buddy. Most people don't even know they served together. That's by design. Zeus nearly died taking a bullet for him, and Kirk's loyalty is ironclad. He plays the part, keeps his head down, and never asks questions.

"Sandman." The familiar timbre of Jiminy, aka Cricket, catches my attention above the din.

He hops off the stool at my approach, sporting a shit-eating grin on his lean face. We recently got our colors. I'm officially unofficially the club's hitman, and I have to admit, I fucking love coming to work every day. Killing motherfuckers is my passion.

Of course, Cricket wasn't going to let me leave Texas without him. According to him, his guidance was essential for my survival. Zeus, being financially well-off, didn't mind adding another mouth to feed to his household. Cricket's uncle has three small children at home to provide for and was happy to get rid of him.

"What the fuck are you smiling for?" I grumble.

His name should be Smiley since his teeth are showing half the damn time.

"They were some juicy gashes." He waggles his eyebrows. "Am I right?"

I lift my shoulder in a shrug. "They were okay."

"Just okay. Cheri has a—"

"Cherry," I correct him.

"What?"

"Her name is Cherry, not Cheri."

"Fuck her name, bro." He blows out an exaggerated breath. "Her name could be Fido for all I care. The point is that bitch has a super soaker and Ryan—"

"Riley," I correct him again, but he ignores me and keeps talking.

"—has the longest nipples I've ever seen. Fuck, is that a birth defect or something? Shit, I don't even give a damn. Them things are amazzzzing."

Cricket has fucked every club twinkie. He doesn't discriminate. All pussy is the same to him.

"Draco is pissed at you," he states, changing the subject. "He could've spit nails."

I snort. "When is he not pissed at me?"

Cricket chuckles. "True, true."

"Where is he?"

"He left about an hour ago," he responds.

"We should ride too."

Church is usually held at The Sanctuary, but there's an office for the scarce meeting at home too. Some heavy shit must've gone down. I got two more missed calls from Zeus while showering. We hustle through the crowd and step into the warm night. A few prospects man the electric fence, ensuring no foes slip onto the property.

"What do you think happened?" Cricket asks.

"No clue, but it must be serious." I straddle my Harley and slip my helmet on.

If any of our enemies stepped out of line, there's going to be hell to pay.

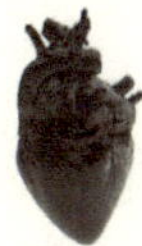

I'm barely inside the foyer before Mayhem and Harley plow into me, nearly knocking me to the porcelain tile.

"Hey, chill out," I gripe, but the spoiled Dobermans bark in protest, rearing up on their hind legs.

These two are always on me the second I walk through the front door. Sneaking past them would take ninja-level skill. I've had the sister and brother since they were pups, going on two years now. Both have black-and-rust coats with amber eyes. From a distance, it's easy to mistake one for the other.

I stoop to my haunches, and wet tongues greet me in welcome.

"Nasty." Cricket gags. "Dude, you're gonna smell like dog ass."

"Shut up. You're ruining a beautiful moment."

"Whatevs, butt-crack face. I'll be in the living room," he says and strolls down the long hall. Cricket is like a son to Zeus, but that doesn't mean he's allowed in Church.

"Got shit to handle right now, but I'll take you delinquents on a walk later."

They circle me in unrestrained excitement, catching on to their favorite word. I give both a pat on the head before making my way to Zeus's office. I stop at the console table next to the closed door and drop my mobile device in the ceramic bowl along with the others. I saunter into the room, and Draco promptly voices his grievances.

"We've been waiting over an hour!" he bellows, neck tendons stretching taut. "Your cavalier attitude ends today."

He occupies the chair to Zeus's left, and Jigsaw, the sergeant at arms, sits on his right. Butch, Snake, Tank, and Buffalo are also seated around the long rectangular table, which has the club's logo intricately etched in the center. The rest of the opulently furnished office boasts a matching cherrywood desk, a cozy sitting area, a stocked bookcase, a liquor cabinet, and an electric fireplace. I pad across the wool carpet and drop into the seat beside Snake.

"Well, I'm here now." I wink at him, fueling his rage.

"You degenerate piece—"

"Leave off it, Draco," Zeus cuts in.

"You're fucking kidding me, right?" he spits, his nostrils flaring wide. "You allow this wild animal to run amok with no consequences."

"We have more pressing matters to address," Zeus reminds him.

"Why do you allow this—"

"Enough!" Zeus booms, and Draco's lips snap together. The irritating fucker may be dumb, but he ain't stupid. He don't want no smoke for real.

Zeus's fearsome reputation, coupled with his brawny six-foot-five frame, makes motherfuckers think twice before crossing him. I have witnessed hardened criminals sob and piss themselves when facing his wrath. He will lay anybody out, even his sons.

We went toe-to-toe about two and a half years ago. And he taught me "respect" with a black eye, broken nose, and three cracked ribs. But a lot has changed since then. It won't be so easy to take me down if we square up again.

The sound of the gavel hitting wood draws my attention to the front of the table.

"I've called Church because we have a shit storm on our hands," Zeus states gravely, then nods at Buffalo. "Tell them what you told me."

"Caesar didn't double-cross the club." He pauses and swallows hard. "It was Brick. He's feeding intel to the Disciples."

Tank leaps to his feet, murder in his dark-brown gaze. "What the fuck you say?"

Fuck me. Caesar leads the Latin Maniacs—a fast-growing street gang with ties across several states. Zeus supplies the firepower they and other criminal groups need to protect their territories for a steep sum. It was a shaky alliance, but it worked until three weeks ago.

Five of our brothers went to deliver guns. None came back. Slaughtered. The weapons, gone. Caesar swore innocence, asserting his people arrived at the meeting location after the bloodbath. Efforts to locate the merch and uncover the truth led to a dead end. The brotherhood couldn't take Caesar at his word and let the slaying of five Gods go unpunished. Blood had to spill.

We hit back hard. His crew lost twice what we did, ending the business arrangement and igniting a war. Now Buffalo's saying Brick sold us out to the Disciples instead. If true, we're in deeper shit than we thought.

An alliance broken and a possible snake in our midst. Mistrust is bound to spread and chip away at the brotherhood's once-ironclad bond.

This isn't just bad. This is catastrophic.

"Let him finish," Jigsaw says, his stern tone brooking no argument. He's a no-nonsense type of motherfucker. I don't think I've ever seen him crack a smile.

His aquamarine gaze shifts to Buffalo, waiting for him to continue. The healed lacerations dominating Jigsaw's rugged features resemble a puzzle, hence his road name. In addition to ensuring club laws and rules are upheld, he used to handle Zeus's kill orders until I inherited his unofficial secondary position. Jigsaw was far more ruthless in the role. He prolonged the agony until his victims begged for a bullet.

The tragic story behind his horrific disfigurement is a mystery. That hasn't stopped the speculations, though. Zeus is probably the only person who actually knows the truth. A confidence he'd never betray. They've had each other's backs since basic training.

"I overheard Brick on his cell talking all whisper-like," Buffalo recounts to the group. "I could tell he was real pissed—"

"Get to the fucking point, Buffalo," Zeus growls.

"I heard Brick say, 'That wasn't the deal, Spider. You promised me a quarter mil for the guns.'"

"Hearsay," Draco protests, skepticism evident in his voice. "Do you have any proof to corroborate your story?"

It's hard to believe Buffalo would fabricate a claim like this, especially against his own cousin and roommate. They were patched in together. What would he even gain from lying? Nothing, as far as I know. The decision to come forward must've been a difficult one, knowing the revelation would result in Brick's death sentence.

And it's no secret Spider has a personal vendetta aimed squarely at Zeus. His ragtag MC, the Lawless Disciples, ruled the heroin and gun trade around here until Zeus rolled into Kent and gutted his empire in under a year. Blood painted the streets.

In the end, Spider folded. Been lying low ever since, licking his wounds. But maybe now he figured it's time to slink out of the shadows and make a power play. Bad move. He doesn't stand a snowball's chance in hell.

"No," he admits. "I could try to get his cell phone, but he has the face recognition and passcode lock on."

"Bring it to me," Snake offers, interlacing his fingers on the table. "I can unlock it, no sweat." At seventeen, Snake is already a tech genius. No title, but he's on the board. Being the president's son gets you perks.

"What if he notices it's missing?" Butch questions. "He could get spooked and be gone with the wind."

As the club treasurer, Butch cleans the cash and keeps our finances in order. At sixty-two, he's also the oldest member of the brotherhood, but he's still a force to be reckoned with.

"Where is he now?" I ask Buffalo.

"Still at home," he replies, leaning back and propping his elbows on the armrests. "Said he wasn't going out till later."

"You four, head over there now. Check his call log, text messages, voicemails, emails… leave no stone unturned. Nip this situation in the bud tonight," Zeus orders, then looks at me. "There's only one place for a rat."

I dip my head, acknowledging the unspoken order. "Say less."

Zeus slams the gavel down and we disperse. The night is about to get bloody, and bloody is what I do best.

I swing the driver's side door shut and join the others on the sidewalk. We took the SUV instead of riding our bikes—better to catch Brick off guard. The night is still. No nosy neighbors. *No witnesses.*

In grim silence, we start toward the deteriorating single-family home. It's a wonder this place hasn't been condemned. I'm betting a strong wind would blow the peeling wooden structure clear across the county line. The lawn, if you can even call it that, is predominantly dirt and overgrown weeds. A weathered garden duck is the sole adornment.

Buffalo slowly opens the rusted chain-link fence surrounding the property, and we follow behind him with quiet footsteps. It's dark inside the house, save for the dim light visible through the curtains hanging over the window to the left.

My hands buzz. Heart hammering. *I love this part.* Killing hits like a high. Twisted? No doubt, but damn if it doesn't get my dick granite hard.

We scuttle up the rickety porch steps and stealthily enter the house, turning into the scarcely furnished living room. There, we find our target conked out on the tan leather sofa, snoring loudly and mouth agape. A commercial for a popular fast-food restaurant plays on the muted flat-screen television.

I perch on the coffee table, pulling a Glock from my shoulder holster. Another Glock is strapped to my ankle, and a knife rests at my hip. My holy trinity.

Cricket grabs the half-empty beer bottle next to me and dumps the amber liquid over Brick's face. "Wakey, wakey, motherfucker."

He sputters, lurching to a sitting position. "What the fuck?"

"Sorry for disturbing your beauty rest," Snake retorts sarcastically.

Brick's wide gaze darts between us, anger quickly morphing to trepidation. "What's going on, boys?"

"Give me your phone," Snake states, motioning for him to hand it over.

"Why?" He chuckles nervously, his beady eyes glued to my firearm. "Did you lose yours?"

I latch onto the fucker's scrawny neck and yank him to the edge of the sofa. "Where is it?"

"On the charger," he croaks, grappling for air. "In the kitchen."

"See, that wasn't so hard," I quip and shove him away from me.

Cricket retrieves the device and tosses it to him. "Unlock it."

"What's this about?" he asks, sweat forming on his blotchy forehead.

I slide my finger over the trigger. "Unlock it. Now."

He scurries to obey, prompted by the unspoken threat. Snake plucks the mobile from his trembling grasp and begins searching for the smoking gun. Brick looks to Buffalo for help, but his cousin planted himself in a corner and noticeably avoids eye contact.

"Who are all the unknown callers?" Snake asks, his thumb flying over the screen.

"Telemarketers," he answers, his Adam's apple bobbing.

"Or maybe you have something to hide," I accuse.

"Is this a joke?" he scoffs, feigning nonchalance, but he isn't fooling anyone. He's scared shitless.

"His call log and text messages are clean, but—"

"See, nothing to hide," Brick gloats triumphantly.

"I wasn't done talking, pencil dick. As I was sayin', his call history and deleted texts are easily retrievable." Snake aims a taunting smile at him. "You gotta love technology."

And abracadabra, Brick's exuberance disappears in a flash.

"Did you think it'd be that easy, you rat fuck?" Cricket crows, bouncing around like a goddamn lunatic. "Snake is a tech genius, motherfucker."

"Here's the thing, Brick," I announce, pausing to study my fingernails for several beats. "We know you sold us out to the Disciples."

"I didn't—"

"Listen, tell the truth and I'll convince Zeus to spare your life." I aim the gun at his protruding midsection, which is weirdly disproportionate to his thin frame. The sleazy scumbag is skinnier than a two-dollar crack whore. "Lie and kiss your ass goodbye."

"Okay, okay," he concedes, threading a hand through his mousy-brown hair. "I set it up, but Buffalo was in on everything."

"You lying motherfucker!" Buffalo shouts, charging forward. He punches his cousin in the mouth before Snake manages to haul him back.

Brick spits blood onto the worn carpet. "Why am I not surprised you skipped the part about your involvement, little cousin?"

"Don't believe this piece of shit," Buffalo sneers, jabbing a finger at him. His voice is too loud. Too panicked.

"I brought him on for twenty grand, but later he switched up and demanded more money. I refused and he got pissed," Brick explains, pinning his narrow gaze on Buffalo. "Thought I'd be killed right away, no questions asked, huh? Too bad for you."

Buffalo pales, guilt written all over his face. "H-he's l-lying—"

I raise the gun and fire once, silencing him forever. His lifeless body crumples to the floor, blood oozing from the gaping hole in his skull.

"Thanks a lot," Snake grumbles, wiping blood and brain matter off his face with the hem of his shirt. "Some got in my eye too."

"My bad," I say to him before giving my full attention to the disloyal fucker cowering on the sofa. "Any last words?"

"Wait a minute," he shrieks. "You said you would talk to Zeus."

"Oh, about that," I drawl, scratching an imaginary itch on my neck. "I lied."

Crocodile tears gleam in his eyes. "Honest to God, no one was supposed to get hurt."

"But they did." Two bullets enter his chest, and his eyelids stretch in terror.

Twin red spots bloom on his white tank, saturating the cotton in seconds.

I blow him a kiss. "See you in Hell."

Undoubtedly, Lucifer is eagerly awaiting my arrival.

His breathing grows shallow, then his journey on Earth comes to an abrupt end.

"Get the burner from the car and call the cleaner." I issue the directive to Cricket. "Tell him to get here ASAP."

"On it," he says and leaves the house.

"You shouldn't have killed Buffalo without the okay from Zeus first," Snake remarks, shaking his head at me. "He's going to bust a vein."

"Fuck his bureaucratic bullshit." I dismiss my brother's warning and stand, dropping my sidearm back in its holster. "Help me find something to wrap the bodies in."

Zeus will have to wait to chew me out. Right now, we need to get these bodies to the crematorium, then regroup. We're bound to find more dirt in these fuckers' cell phones.

CHAPTER 11

Zilphia

"WAITER!" MOMMA YELLS IN A HAUGHTY TONE, HER DELICATE features bunching into a contemptuous sneer. "More wine now!"

I duck my head, my cheeks flaming. Honestly, I should be used to her embarrassing antics by now. The woman is notorious for making a public nuisance of herself.

"One moment, ma'am." Selene, our unfortunate waitress, places two sizzling entrées on the table across from us.

The elderly couple glares at my mother, and I don't fault them one bit. Their disdain is warranted; her behavior is disgustingly atrocious. She missed the memo to treat others the way you want to be treated or, more likely, just ignored it. As far as she's concerned, people below a certain tax bracket don't deserve her consideration or respect.

"What the hell are you two staring at?" she slurs, directing her scorn at the pair. "Mind your own goddamn business."

They quickly avert their gazes, choosing wisely to avoid a confrontation with the crazy inebriated person. I silently thank them. The last thing we need is airport security on our case.

I clear my throat. "Momma, don't you think you've had enough wine?"

She already drank three glasses; any more alcohol, and I'll have to carry her on my back.

"Don't question me," she admonishes, her dark-brown irises shooting laser beams at me. "I'm the adult and you're the child. It's best you remember that."

"Sorry," I mumble, my gaze fixed on my untouched lunch. "I didn't mean to upset—"

"Another word and I'll slap the black off you," she threatens, shaking a dainty finger in my face.

My body flinches before I can stop it. I bite my tongue, following the elderly couple's lead. Though humanly impossible, I'm positive my mother will indeed attempt to slap the black off me.

"Eat!" she orders, pouring more vinaigrette onto her tossed salad. "We don't have all damn day. Boarding starts in thirty minutes."

I cut into my salmon and force myself to swallow down a small piece. The flaky fish settles heavily in my stomach. It's delicious, but I'm too anxious to enjoy the smoky flavor. The last five months have been emotionally draining to say the least. Either someone is playing a cruel prank on me, or I'm unknowingly the lead character in a Lifetime movie.

The nightmare began on a typical Friday. I came home late from Redmond's, and my father's car wasn't in the driveway. Call it a sixth-sense moment, but I knew something was wrong. He never stayed out that late. A thousand scenarios ran through my mind.

Momma brushed off my concerns and waited until morning to file a missing person's report. The following week, we learned the gut-wrenching truth. Daddy was being investigated for health insurance fraud. He knew it was only a matter of time before his crimes were brought to light. Rather than face prosecution, he emptied his bank account and fled. We haven't seen or heard from him since.

That's just the tip of the proverbial iceberg. Unbeknownst to us, Daddy was practically bankrupt and took out a second mortgage. He also has multiple malpractice lawsuits pending against him.

Momma isn't blameless, though she does play the victim so well. Her selfishness and obsession with expensive things escalated my father's financial ruin. She never took an interest in the bills and due dates. That responsibility was left to Daddy. It's a miracle she didn't send him over the edge sooner.

"Sorry for the delay, ma'am." Selene appears at my mother's side and fills her glass. "It's always busy around this time."

"Spare me your excuses and don't expect a tip either," she sneers.

Selene gives a jerky nod. "Again, please accept my apol—"

"Move along," Momma snaps, shooing her away.

I peek up from under my eyelashes and covertly study the woman who gave birth to me. Was she born a narcissist? Or did something happen in her life that caused her to become this unfeeling monster? It's a question I've asked myself often, but I'm too chicken shit to seek an answer. Here we are, practically destitute, but her spending habits haven't changed.

Glossy hair styled in a trendy pixie cut, radiant espresso-brown skin, impeccable gel manicure and pedicure, and dressed head to toe in the latest fall fashion—one would think she was cruising on easy street. She grudgingly sold some of her jewelry and other valuables to keep up appearances, including a pair of diamond earrings Daddy had gifted me on my sixteenth birthday.

When the house went into foreclosure, the furniture, sterling silver cutlery—basically anything that could prolong her lavish lifestyle—was sold too. But the money is dwindling fast. We shouldn't be in this restaurant, eating this overpriced food, about to board a first-class flight to Oregon. There were cheaper ways to travel, considering our dire circumstances.

And then there's Nolan. He took the fall from grace harder than any of us. He literally ugly cried, snotty nose and everything. An ugly person ugly crying is an alarmingly grotesque sight. I thought we were going to have to call an ambulance when he fell out on the floor, his limbs spread wide. His dreams of being the campus playboy? Gone with Daddy's bank account.

Heck, after January, he might be dropping out anyway; tuition is only covered until then. He'll have to learn to fend for himself. We all do, but unlike my brother and my mother, I'm willing to do whatever it takes to achieve my goals and pave my own way. I'll find a job and save every cent I can for college. Then there's financial aid, loans, grants, and scholarships.

Redmond dumped me the second Daddy's name hit the news. I didn't shed a tear.

The relationship was never mine—it was Momma's. Her blueprint. Her social-climbing scheme.

We only ever made it to second base, per my mother's stringent seduction guidelines. *Thank goodness for that at least.* He cheated the entire time we were together. Not that I gave a flying crap. It kept him from pawing at me every chance he got. I shiver, recalling the many times he tried to force himself on me. Momma excused his behavior, asserting, *"Boys will be boys."* It was a relief when he graduated from high school and went off to college.

"I have to pee." Momma stands, swaying on her feet. "Tell that idiot to bring the check."

"Okay," I mumble and watch her stagger to the restroom.

Dear God, please, please, please let my short stay in Oregon be drama-free.

I have a gut feeling my prayers will go unanswered. We'll be staying with Sheila, though she didn't extend the invitation out of the kindness of her heart. It was for Grandma's sake. Her health has been deteriorating for some time now, and the added stress of worrying about us hasn't helped matters. My once lively grandmother spends most days in bed. Maybe her daughters' temporary truce will help improve her condition. One can only hope.

Sheila and her husband, Keith, relocated to Oregon about a year ago. They met while living in Delaware and have been married going on two years now—give or take a few months. Of course, we weren't invited to witness their special day. Keith works in banking and transferred to the West Coast office after getting a promotion. Sheila finally has everything she's ever wanted. I'm thrilled for her, but Momma is green with jealousy.

"Excuse me," I call out to Selene as she walks past the table. "We're ready for the check."

"Sure thing," she replies. "Need any boxes?"

"No, we're good. Thanks." Momma only has a few bites left, and my roiling stomach can't handle any more food.

"You're welcome," she says, collecting the dishes from the table. "Be back in a sec."

"Wait." I glance toward the restroom door before rummaging through my purse and plucking a twenty out of my wallet. "Here you go."

"Thank you." Selene beams, stuffing the bill into her apron.

"Hey, you earned it." *And it's the least I could do after my mother's behavior.*

That's the last of my cash. I have sixty-four dollars left in my checking account, but that won't last long. Finding a job sooner rather than later is paramount. Hopefully someone is willing to hire an eighteen-year-old with no work experience or references. *Fingers crossed.*

“Momma, please calm down,” I plead, clasping my sweaty palms together in an ironclad grip. “Maybe something came up. Unexpected things happen all the time.”

The drama floodgates crashed open the second our plane landed. Sheila and her husband were supposed to be our ride from the airport, but she texted Momma telling her they couldn’t make it. Thus, the ranting and raging began. My anxiety is skyrocketing.

I inhale deep, measured breaths to ease the tightness in my chest. This is so not the time to have a freaking asthma attack. I need to placate my mother before we get to my aunt’s house and all hell breaks loose.

Frank’s—our Uber driver—saucer-eyed gaze collides with mine in the rearview mirror. He’s probably thinking the mentally unstable lady forgot to take her daily crazy-people meds. I wish there were a reasonable explanation for her tirade, but entitlement is her only ailment, and there’s no treatment available for that.

I sigh, massaging my throbbing temples. Fantastic, the first stirrings of a headache. Soon the dull ache will develop into a full-blown migraine.

“I can’t wait to give that bitch and her dog-face husband a piece of my mind,” she rages on.

“Sheila is pregnant, remember? Maybe she isn’t feeling well and Keith is taking care of her,” I say, attempting to soothe her hurt pride. “Isn’t morning sickness rough during the first trimester?”

“Stop making excuses for her!” Momma shrills, her lips curling into a sneer. “She’s a vindictive whore and wants to lord it over me. Oh, but I’ll have the last laugh. Mark my words.”

Apprehension cramps my abdomen at her bitter declaration.

What havoc does my mother plan on causing?

The minivan comes to a sudden stop, and I frantically glance around, zooming in on the house number to my left.

Crap in a fucking handbasket. We’re here.

Momma is out of the minivan and jetting down the walkway in the blink of an eye.

“Momma!” I shout, running after her.

"Hey, a little assistance with the luggage, please," Frank calls out to me. "These old bones can't do too much heavy lifting nowadays."

"Oh, I'm so sorry." I hurry back and help the flustered driver unload our overstuffed suitcases onto the sidewalk.

Seven in total—two belonging to me and five belonging to my mother. The baggage fees were outrageously high.

I hear angry shouts coming from inside the three-story home. The pounding in my head increases. This isn't the reunion I imagined.

Frank deposits the last suitcase at my feet. "Good luck," he says, shooting me a sympathetic look before fleeing to his vehicle.

"Luck won't cut it," I grumble to myself. "This family needs divine intervention."

I steel my resolve and forge ahead, joining the chaos. I go no further than the staircase, unsure what to do. Momma and Sheila are nose to nose, screaming the house down, while Keith unsuccessfully attempts to defuse the situation.

My poor grandmother sits huddled on the sofa, crying hysterically. Terrence, my little cousin, lingers at the kitchen entrance, watching the explosive argument. He doesn't seem distressed by the verbal melee but rather curious. How did a six-year-old kid reach this level of unbothered? I need to learn his secret.

"Let's all sit down and have a sensible conversation," Keith suggests, squeezing his distraught wife's shoulder.

"No!" she exclaims. "I want her gone now!"

"Fine by me," Momma responds haughtily. "Zilphia, let's go."

"We don't have anywhere else to go," I remind her.

Unless sleeping on the street is preferable.

"Stop it!" my grandmother wails, her frail body shaking violently. The emotional entreaty effectively silences my aunt and mother. "Sisters shouldn't be fighting like this. You're supposed to love each other."

I rush to her side and wrap my arms around her slender torso. The once buxom woman has wasted away.

"Don't cry, Grandma," I murmur, consoling her. "It's going to be okay."

I haven't hugged my grandmother in eight long years. On the rare occasions we video chatted, her deteriorating appearance escaped my notice. Maybe that's why she preferred talking on the phone versus video chatting. She knew I'd eventually notice and worry. Her coffee-brown skin resembles worn leather, and deep wrinkles line her haggard features. Even her hair has lost its healthy glow. The tresses are now dull and brittle. I'm afraid my time with her is running out.

"I need to lie down," she croaks, her body going limp. "I'm so tired."

Keith rushes to her aid in a few long strides and lifts her slight form in his arms. "I'll take you to your room."

"No more fighting," my grandmother pleads with her daughters, her voice barely more than a whisper. "Please. My heart can't take it."

My aunt and mother have the decency to look ashamed. Serves them right, but they'll be back at each other's throats by the end of the week. They hate each other too much to put the well-being of their ailing mother—or anyone else, for that matter—first.

I follow Keith up the winding staircase to the second level. He enters the second door to the left and gently places my grandmother on the queen-size bed positioned against the wall. Her bedroom is small but nicely set up—beautiful alabaster-white furnishings, a huge flat-screen television, and a plush recliner. I'm glad to see that she's living comfortably. Sheila is doing right by her, unlike my mother.

"Thank you."

"You're welcome." He pulls the comforter to her chin and plants a kiss on her forehead. "Get some rest."

I already like my aunt's husband. The adoration and patience he shows my grandmother are commendable.

"Zilphia," Keith says, turning bright, friendly eyes on me. "It's nice to finally meet you."

I accept his outstretched hand. "Likewise, though I wish it were under different circumstances."

"Me too, but I believe everything happens for a reason. The good, the bad, and the ugly." He gestures toward the open window. "I assume the suitcases on the sidewalk belong to you and your mother?"

"Yeah."

"I'll bring them inside."

"Thanks." I perch on the bed, suddenly feeling twice my age. "I'm sorry for my mother's behavior," I add, accustomed to apologizing on her behalf.

"Don't worry about it. It's been a rough day for everyone." He gives me a reassuring smile before leaving the room, closing the door behind him.

Keith is short in stature, average physique, not the typical man women would drool over, but handsome nonetheless. The silver-gray sprinkled throughout his low fade and beard lends him a distinguished air, though in my opinion, his skin is his greatest feature. The beautiful hue is so dark it resembles purple.

I slip out of my sneakers and denim jacket, then snuggle up next to my grandmother, who's already fast asleep.

"It's going to be okay," I repeat my promise to her, though the words ring hollow in my ears. "You'll see."

Please let everything be okay.

CHAPTER 12

Zilphia

I POUND MY FIST AGAINST THE FLAT PILLOW, HUFFING IRRITABLY. IT'S freaking impossible to find a comfortable position on this air mattress, but beggars can't be choosers. It was this or the floor.

My mother and grandma are bunking together. I get the musty basement, caged between the boxes and plastic bins. I don't have the convenience of a bathroom either. Traipsing upstairs in the middle of the night to relieve myself is going to be a major pain. I suggested bedding down on the sofa in the living room, but Sheila wouldn't have it, stating she won't have her living room resembling a pigsty. Definitely not an ideal living situation, but on the plus side, the washer and dryer are close at hand.

I roll onto my side and check the time on my cell phone. It doesn't have service. Momma canceled the plan months ago, but it's still useful for apps. Of course, she and the prodigal son have working cell phones. *"I can't afford service for you too, Zilphia."* Whatever.

Great, eighteen minutes before the alarm goes off.

No point in trying to go back to sleep now. The poor sleeping conditions aren't the sole reason for my restlessness. Despite less-than-favorable circumstances, I'm excited to start a new school and develop a close bond with my cousin, Deja. We're the same age, and I know we'll get along great. I'm betting we have a lot in common too.

She missed all the drama yesterday and still hadn't gotten home by the time I turned in for the night. I'm looking forward to hanging out with her today. I can't wait to talk about boys, watch movies together—all the normal stuff teenage girls do. Maybe we'll even become roomies.

I won't miss my old school or my so-called friends one bit. From the outside, my life seemed like a modern-day fairytale. Girls envied me, would've killed to take my place given the chance. I had everything they coveted—popularity, money, and a smoking-hot boyfriend.

What I truly craved was the freedom to make my own decisions, though. I was nothing more than an unwilling pawn in my mother's quest for power and wealth. That woman would sell my soul to the devil himself to acquire both. Now it's my turn to shine. Real friends. Real choices. A fresh start without Momma's shadow clawing at my every move.

School started a month ago, but my cousin will help me settle in and bring me into her fold.

A depressing thought suddenly intrudes on my excitement, causing a sharp pang to bloom between my breastbones. *What if Deja hates me?*

Sheila does, and she showed me just how much during dinner yesterday evening. While Keith and Terrence were kind and welcoming, she was cold and indifferent. Resentment practically spilled from her pores.

My aunt wasn't keen on sharing either, serving me minuscule portions. She barely spoke two sentences to me and cast withering glances my way throughout the entire meal, making me feel unworthy to sit in her presence. I received the same hostile look from my own mother on too many occasions to count.

Momma was still livid about the airport and didn't come down to dinner, which was for the best if you ask me. Undoubtedly, the sisters would've ended up in another shouting match. Grandma stayed in bed, too exhausted to join us. I'm praying her offspring put their differences aside and start playing nice for her sake. Easier said than done, unfortunately.

Deja and I don't have to inherit their war. Maybe we can even plan a family intervention and force them to settle their feud once and for all. My trepidation eases a little.

I perk up, hearing footsteps on the basement stairs, and shift onto an elbow to see who it is. Bright light spills into the compact space, stinging my eyes.

Deja.

She's almost a replica of her mother; seriously, they could be twins—tall, curvy figure, pecan-brown skin tone, a shade lighter than her mother's.

I bound to my feet and offer her a timid smile. "Hi."

"Shut up and listen, bitch," she snarls, folding her long arms across her ample breasts. "One: Don't talk to me. Two: Don't touch my shit. Three: Stay the fuck out of my way. Four: Keep your dirty whore hands off my boyfriend. Break those rules and I break your face."

With that warning, she spins on her heel and sashays back upstairs.

I'm at a loss for words. Sheila got in her head, painting me as the villain in some fanciful story. What lies has she told her? I doubt anything I say will change Deja's mind about me. Not with my aunt in her ear stoking the flames.

"Oh, and one more thing." My cousin stops in the doorway and peers over her shoulder, her contemptuous gaze slowly perusing my skinny frame. She smirks, finding me lacking. "Don't expect me to chauffeur you to and from school. Find your own way."

I lean closer to the bathroom mirror and study my puffy, bloodshot eyes. *Perfect. Everyone will think I have conjunctivitis.* A search through the medicine cabinet yields no eyedrops to clear the redness. This day just keeps getting better. I broke down in the shower and couldn't stop crying. It's so unfair.

Deja crushed all my hopes about a better life. I'm always getting the shitty end of the stick. Should've known things would be the same here.

I have no idea what to expect at school now that my cousin has shunned me. Being the new kid is never easy. I sigh, running my fine-tooth comb through my heat-straightened mane for probably the twentieth time, though every single strand is neatly in place. I'm just not ready to go downstairs and face the double dragons.

"This is stupid." I toss my comb into my purse and zip it closed. "I live here now. We all just have to learn to get along. Simple as that."

I grab my purse off the sink and draw the long strap across my torso before exiting the bathroom. I pause at my grandmother's bedroom and press my ear to the door, hearing light snoring. She and Momma are still fast asleep. I'll catch up with them after school.

A wonderful aroma hits my nostrils as I make my way downstairs. *Breakfast.* My pace quickens, following the smell to the expansive kitchen. There, my aunt and cousins sit at a small round table in the corner, sharing the morning meal. Time to put on a brave face.

"Good morning," I chirp and slide into the empty chair next to my little cousin.

"Good morning, Zilphia," Terrence returns my greeting, but the double dragons do not.

"Ew." Deja snickers behind her hand. "That outfit is so juvenile."

Self-doubt rears its ugly head. It took me nearly an hour to decide on what to wear. What exactly does she find juvenile about my attire? I glance down at myself. Floral print top, high-waisted yellow shorts, and chunky white sandals. Looks good to me.

I furtively examine my cousin's skimpy ensemble. Low-cut blouse barely holding her huge boobs. A microscopic skirt leaves little to the imagination. It's giving "desperate for attention." Does Bentworth High School not have a dress code? I mean, come on. Her shirt was not made for huge boobs. One wrong move and free nipple show for anyone nearby. I'm loving her wedges, though.

My scrutiny moves upward, taking in her impeccable makeup, fake, extra-long eyelashes, exaggerated baby hairs, and wavy, butt-length wig. Future Instagram model in the making here.

"Sorry," Sheila states insincerely, interrupting my assessment. "There isn't any food left for you."

Why am I not surprised?

"That's okay," I mumble. "I'll just have some apple juice."

Deja seizes the jug of apple juice and empties the last bit into her glass. "Oops, all gone."

Bitch.

"I'll share with you," Terrence announces, pushing his plate and cup toward me. "My teacher said leaders share."

He beams, and I feel myself melting a little inside. His kind gesture earns him disapproving glares from the double dragons, though.

"Thanks for the offer, but I'm not hungry," I lie. *I'm freaking starving.*

Yesterday's meager dinner wasn't enough to fill a toddler. I'll eat breakfast at school, though. No biggie.

"You're welcome," he replies, showing his toothy smile.

"Eat," Deja snaps at her brother. "We're leaving in two minutes."

"Okay," he grumbles and scarfs down the rest of his food. "I'm finished!"

"See you later, Ma," Deja says and prances out of the kitchen.

Rein it in, Miss Diva. You're not walking the runway.

Terrence gives his mother a peck on the cheek before darting after his sister.

"Have a good day," she calls out, then shifts her spiteful gaze to me. "Shouldn't you be going too?"

"Yeah, umm… Is Keith home?"

"Why?" she asks, her eyes narrowing on me. "What do you want him for?"

Oh God, does she think I'm crushing on Keith?

"Just to see if he can give me a ride to school. That's all," I quickly answer before her wild imagination gets me into trouble.

Keith is old enough to be my father for crying out loud!

"He left for work," she says sharply. "My husband's not your personal driver. Walk or take the bus."

Sheila flips her flowing lace-front install over her shoulder and begins clearing the table.

I need to make my aunt see that I'm not the enemy.

"I know what Momma did. It was wrong on so many levels," I state, shifting in my seat to follow her movements. "I'm so sorry—"

"I'm not," Sheila cackles, keeping her back to me. "Loretta did me a favor. Your father turned out to be a lowlife criminal. Now leave."

I stand. "I'm not my parents and shouldn't be judged based on their actions."

She stiffens but continues wiping down the counter.

I'm done.

Trying to repair the damage in this family is a lost cause.

I march into the hallway and stop dead in my tracks. What the heck? I left my backpack propped against the basement door, and now it's gone. I'm confused for a second, then understanding dawns on me.

Deja.

She took my goddamn backpack. *Ugh!* I storm out of the front door, single-minded determination goading me on. I slip my cell phone out of my back pocket and search for the school's address in Maps. Thank goodness service isn't needed to use it.

Okay. Thirty-minute walk, but I can get there in twenty.

I tilt my face toward the cloudless sky, relishing the sun's beautiful rays. Soon the climate will shift, bringing colorful leaves followed by freezing snow. The cold and I do not get along. I'm built for Texas heat, not Oregon winters. I'll need a sturdy coat, warm clothes, suitable footwear, and funds to buy it all. Too bad money doesn't grow on trees.

I raise my hand to my forehead, using the appendage as a makeshift visor to shield my eyes. The vibrant azure sky is utterly stunning. The same color as *his eyes. Sam's eyes.*

His name whispers through my mind, stirring restless emotions within me. I have so many questions.

Where is he? How is he doing? Is he happy?

Guilt has plagued me since that tragic night three years ago. That night everything changed. That night I betrayed my best friend and became the villain in my own story. I became my mother.

Selfish. Despicable. Conniving.

I will never forget the unadulterated pain reflected in his poignant gaze. It gutted me… flayed me to the marrow. I felt his hurt as if it were my own.

A solitary tear leaves a wet path on my smooth cheek.

God, I miss him so much. His lopsided smile. His corny jokes. His hugs. His… everything. But his warm, lulling voice most of all. Sam was my listening ear, my shoulder to cry on, and my loyal confidant—my savior on my lowest days.

I know we'll always be connected on an intrinsic level. Nothing will ever change that. Not time, distance, or the scheming woman who gave birth to me.

Shame stopped me from seeking him out. What would I say to him? Does he hate me?

I'm afraid to learn the answer.

Coward.

The self-recrimination booms in my mind.

My eyelids slam shut, recalling the last time I saw him. Bleeding. Broken. Still. So still. More tears start to fall.

And then the fire. I couldn't believe it. My Sam… responsible for burning my home to the ground. He didn't say one word to defend himself. Everyone thought he was just some psycho stalker obsessed with me.

Why didn't he talk? Did he keep quiet to protect me?

Another person in his predicament would've told it all. I wouldn't have blamed him if he had.

A blaring horn and skidding tires disband my morose brooding. The motorists, a man and a woman, lunge from their respective vehicles. Arms flap frantically as they yell obscenities, each accusing the other of almost causing the fender bender.

I continue on my way, veering around the next corner. Across the street, to my left, I spot the side view of an imposing brick building. The beige structure is the tallest in the general vicinity. A parking lot is directly below, with a long flight of stairs leading to what I assume is the main entrance. There aren't many people milling about, since the bell for homeroom rings in roughly fifteen minutes. I quicken my strides, not wanting to be late on my first day.

I enter the double glass-and-chrome doors, breathless and a bit sweaty. I burrow my fingers into my hair, and, sure enough, the roots are beginning to frizz.

I release a frustrated sigh and roll my eyes skyward. "Give me a freaking break."

This is one epic bad streak. My hair will be a puffy mess in a few hours.

"Chop, chop, young lady," a man clutching a walkie-talkie in his hand rushes me. "The bell for homeroom rings in ten minutes."

"I'm new here," I say in response. "Can you tell me where the main office is?"

He aims the walkie-talkie straight ahead. "Down this hall, on the right. You can't miss it."

"Thanks. My name is Zilp—"

"Hurry along now." He dismisses me and dashes down the hall. "Hey! You kids better get moving. Detention for anyone caught in the hallway without a pass after the bell rings."

What a total douche.

I continue on my way and enter the door with "MAIN OFFICE" in bold, black print across the front.

"Good morning." I fold my arms across the reception desk and read the gold nameplate at my elbow. "Ms. Leacock."

"Hello, dear." She beams, peering at me over the rim of her glasses. "What can I do for you?"

"I need my locker number and a printout of my class schedule, please," I answer her. "It's my first day."

Not that I have anything to put in said locker. *Fucking Deja.*

"First and last name?"

"Zilphia Kensley."

"Spell it for me, dear." Her deft fingers fly over the keyboard, typing out each letter. "Your locker number is 183." A few right clicks on the mouse, then she pushes away from the desk. "I'll be right back."

She walks over to the printer, grabs two papers from the tray, and hands both to me. "Here you are, dear. Your class schedule and instructions on how to set your lock."

"Okay. Thank you."

"You're quite welcome. Have a great first day."

My stomach rumbles, reminding me to seek nourishment ASAP. "Can you point me to the cafeteria?"

Please don't let it be too late for breakfast. Hunger headaches are a super bitch.

"It's closed until first lunch block, which starts at eleven ten," she responds, regarding me sympathetically. "If you want to catch breakfast in the mornings, get here by eight twenty at the latest. The building opens at eight if you want to come earlier."

I glance at my schedule and inwardly groan. Fuck my whole entire existence. My lunch block isn't until twelve twenty. It's the third and last lunch block of the day. That's a million hours away. Not really, but three and a half hours is a long damn time when you're hungry.

Ugh! I'm going to keel over and die from starvation before then. Maybe the cafeteria workers will have pity on me and toss me a stale muffin or something. No, I better get to homeroom. I don't want to risk the Hallway Scrooge giving me detention.

"You need a school ID to get breakfast and lunch. It's used the same way as a debit card. Stop by the library sometime this morning to have one made. It'll take about five minutes." Ms. Leacock plucks a colorful flyer from a plastic holder and slides it across the wooden surface for my perusal. "Create an account on this website. Enter the six-digit number on the back of the card and follow the prompts. You'll need to add a payment method if you don't qualify for free meals."

I knew all this beforehand, but the last twenty-four hours and hunger pangs have my brain in warp mode. The process here is similar to the one at my last school. I more than meet the criteria to receive free meals, but Momma refuses to apply for the program, and she didn't offer me a single red cent.

"Okay." I add the flyer to my other papers. "I appreciate all your help."

"It's what I'm here for, dear."

I step into the hall and study my schedule.

"All right. Let's see what we have here," I mumble to myself. "Homeroom is on the second floor with Mr. Larkin."

My eyes dart to the analog clock hanging above the office door. *Two minutes.* I spot the stairwell ahead and take off running. My precariously high wedges pound against the ivory-and-turquoise vinyl flooring as I race to my destination.

I launch myself into the classroom a split second before the bell rings. A few stragglers rush in behind me. I drag my feet to a vacant desk and limply drop into the chair, unsuccessfully trying to control my erratic breathing.

Having an asthma attack right now would be so sucky. It's been a year since my last attack, but I always keep my inhaler in my purse just in case. I straighten my posture and begin the breathing exercises my primary care physician taught me. Several long, deep breaths later, I'm back in tip-top shape, but my stomach isn't. It's snarling at me.

The girl sitting next to me giggles. "That's some growl."

Mirth-filled eyes regard me through thick lenses. She has vitiligo or some other skin condition, though my initial assumption is likely correct. Pale patches of skin dominate her face, neck, and hands. An oversized long-sleeved shirt and loose-fitting jeans cover the rest of her. She's not dressed for the weather. I wonder if her choice in clothing has anything to do with her skin condition.

"Sorry about that. My stomach usually has manners."

"No sweat." She giggles again, displaying lime-green braces. "I have a granola bar if you want it. It's vegan, though."

"Yes please." Saliva pools into my mouth. "I'm dying over here."

She rummages through her backpack purse and pulls out a mixed-berry granola bar. I want to shout for joy, but I doubt the teacher would appreciate my antics.

"Oh my God," I say instead, ripping the wrapper open. "You deserve the Presidential Citizens Medal. Seriously, I was seconds away from croaking over."

"You're absolutely right," she readily agrees, nodding her head once. "I'll write the president a letter, detailing my outstanding contributions toward eliminating teenage hunger."

We both laugh.

"Name's Zilphia, by the way."

"Neat name," she responds. "Leah, short for Sesalee."

"Neat name," I repeat her compliment to me.

I admire my guardian angel's gorgeous fuchsia-tipped micro locs while scarfing down my continental breakfast. The tiny locks hang over her seat. She must have started them when she was very young.

"Want another one?" she asks.

I cock an eyebrow at her. "Is the sky blue? Bring on the granola."

She brandishes a peanut butter granola bar this time.

"You truly are a lifesaver." I eagerly accept the sweet honey oat treat. "My stomach owes you a debt."

"No debt," Leah replies. "Helping a fellow peer is reward enough."

I smile. Maybe the day won't be a total bust after all.

"I noticed you're empty-handed," she mentions. "No school supplies?"

"Oh… umm." Leah's cool, but I'm not comfortable airing my family's drama to a stranger. "I couldn't find my backpack this morning. Everything's been hectic since the move."

"I have a tote bag and extra supplies in my locker. You're welcome to anything you need."

"Do you have a best friend? If not, I would like to apply for the position."

She grins. "You're in luck. I have several best friend positions available, actually."

"I can provide references too," I say cheekily.

Yep, the day is turning a new leaf. I met a genuinely nice person, and my belly is no longer grumbling.

"Zilphia, I presume?" Mr. Larkin asks.

"You presume correctly."

"Welcome to Bentworth High. This is for you." He hands me a laptop and two sheets of paper. "The first document is the laptop agreement. Sign and date the bottom. Your username and temporary password are on the second document."

I scrawl my signature and date on the appropriate lines, then hand the agreement back to him.

“Perfect. You’re all set.”

Mr. Larkin ambles back to his desk and sits on the smooth surface, placing the paper beside him.

“All right, everyone.” He thumps bony knuckles against the wood to quiet my chattering peers. “Settle down. It’s time for roll call, then we’re going to discuss everyone’s favorite topic.” Mr. Larkin pauses for dramatic effect. “Arriving to classes on time.”

A collective chorus of groans and disgruntled boos resounds throughout the classroom.

“Hey, spare me the attitudes,” Mr. Larkin admonishes. “You guys knew this was coming.”

He continues with the morning routine, despite his petulant audience.

CHAPTER 13

Zilphia

I SLOUCH IN MY CHAIR, MY LEGS SPRAWLED HAPHAZARDLY. MOMMA would have my head if she saw me right now.

"A lady must conduct herself with grace and decorum at all times."

But fuck that. Grace and decorum can go straight to hell.

I'm exhausted and a bit irritable. Sleep deprivation and traipsing around a new building are taking their toll on me. These damn shoes aren't helping either. I'm usually a pro at walking in uncomfortable shoes all day, but the straps on these particular wedges are too damn tight. My ankles are killing me. I bought these shoes a while back and decided to break them in today. Huge mistake. I'll definitely need to put some ice on my poor ankles later.

So far, all my teachers seem cool. The kids are okay too, but not as friendly as Leah. I haven't seen her since homeroom. I should've compared our schedules to see if we had any classes together.

Haven't seen my bitch of a cousin either, which is for the best. I'm the new girl, and getting into a spat won't look good on my part. Cussing her out at home—calling that place *home* feels so yuck—is a no-go too. Don't want to stir the drama pot there; it's already close to boiling over, and anyway, my grandmother's peace means more to me than getting even.

Most likely, I'll never see my pink and purple backpack again. It's probably on the way to a landfill at this very moment.

My belly grumbles; the granola bars didn't curb my hunger for long. I can survive the next forty-five minutes, though. This is the last class before lunch. I'm crossing my fingers that there are some good options on the menu today. Like baked ziti, grilled cheese, or chicken enchiladas. Anything with cheese will do. It's my absolute favorite thing to eat.

I went to the library after second period, so payment is good to go. Sadly, I won't be able to afford breakfast and lunch after next week. Keeping my belly full will set me back seven bucks a day. Doesn't cost an arm and a leg, but when you're broke it might as well.

Momma flat-out refused to consider any government assistance. Another reason why finding a job is priority numero uno.

What's her plan? Does she even have one? Sheila's shaky hospitality won't last forever. If it wasn't for my grandmother, we'd already be out on the street.

Leah walks into the classroom, and my mood instantly brightens.

"Leah," I whisper-shout, relieved to see her friendly face.

"Hey." She beams, sliding into the desk behind me. "How's your first day going?"

I twist in my seat, giving her my full attention. "Better than I thought it would. Even had a few cuties flirt with me."

"Nice."

"Yeah, thinking about starting a harem," I joke.

She bursts out laughing, shaking her head at me. "You're hilarious."

"Zilphia Kensley?"

"Yes," I answer, turning back around in my seat.

"I'm Mr. Beaver." He places an American Government textbook on my desk. "You're only a month behind, so you should catch up in no time."

"Thanks." I face Leah again as he walks away. "Did you have lunch already?"

"No, my lunch block is next."

"Mine too. Do you want to sit together?"

"Sure."

After roll call, Mr. Beaver instructs the class to review chapter three and complete the challenge questions at the end.

"Zilphia, you can start on chapter one," he tells me.

"Okay." I open my textbook and set to work.

The next forty-five minutes go by at a snail's pace. I love my country, but damn if this chapter isn't long and boring. I'm close to pulling my hair out when the bell finally rings. The shrill sound is music to my ears. I almost trip over my feet sprinting to the door. Leah is right on my heels. Guess she's ready for a break too.

"Wednesdays are always the slowest," Leah complains, arranging her beautiful micro locs over a slender shoulder. "I call it the mid-week slump."

I chuckle. "Fitting name."

We merge with our peers in the stairwell and head to the first floor. My locker is the first stop. I quickly toss the tote bag inside, then we walk down the hall to hers.

She slides her notebook and textbook on the metal shelf before grabbing the cheetah-print lunch bag hanging on the hook. "I pack breakfast and lunch almost every day, since the salad bar is the only vegan option our wonderful school offers. Blatant discrimination if you ask me."

"What'd you bring?"

"Vegan chicken salad and grilled pineapples," she answers, swinging her locker door shut.

"Excuse my ignorance, but how the hell can chicken be vegan?" I ask, thoroughly perplexed. "It's meat."

I'm not even going to get started on the grilled pineapples. Who decided grilling pineapples was a good idea? It's bad enough someone thought to put it on pizza for crying out loud.

"Tofu, chickpeas, or another plant-based substitution are used instead of chicken."

"Oh." We slip into the fast-moving crowd, weaving our way toward the cafeteria. "What do you put in yours?"

"Chickpeas, cranberries, almonds, celery, and vegan mayo."

I crinkle my nose. "Sounds very vomit-worthy."

"Hey," she growls, her mouth twisting in feigned anger. "Don't knock it until you try it."

"Noooo thanks." I vehemently shake my head in the negative. "The vegan granola bars were pretty good, but I draw the line at vegan meat. I'm a carnivore through and through."

"I can sway you to the vegan lifestyle," Leah remarks, arching an eyebrow in challenge.

"Ha," I bark. "It ain't happening."

The instant we step into the bustling cafeteria, delicious aromas bombard my nose. I'm ready to eat my weight in food or until the bell rings, whichever comes first. I survey my surroundings.

No wonder there are three lunch blocks. The room's crammed tight. Long, rectangular bench-style tables fill the compact space, with circular stools on either side. There's barely enough elbow room for a couple hundred students.

"Do you want to eat outside?" Leah nods toward the round metal picnic tables beyond the bay windows to the right.

"Sure."

"I'll find us a table while you get some food."

I give her a thumbs up and we temporarily part ways. The lunch line is lengthy, but it's moving fairly quickly. My greedy gaze scours the mouthwatering selections behind the plexiglass. The crispy chicken tenders, mozzarella sticks, and curly fries are calling my name. I shift on my feet, impatiently awaiting my turn. *Come on.*

"Next," an older woman calls out, waving me forward.

Hallelujah!

"Hi," I chirp and point out my selections.

I pay for my goodies, then make my way toward the outdoor dining area.

"Well, if it isn't Ms. Junior Slutbag." I come to an abrupt standstill, recognizing my cousin's scathing tone.

Her snide remark is met with jeering laughter. *Great, an audience.* I clutch my laden tray in a death grip. Deja sits regal-like at the overcrowded table to my left.

I raise my chin, displaying a boldness the pounding organ in my chest belies. "I'm not a slut."

"No?" Deja lifts a perfectly shaped eyebrow. "Ladies, keep an eye on this one. She's a slut like her mother and will fuck your boyfriend right under your nose."

"Liar," I hiss.

"Don't worry about them, babes." A cute boy with a high-top fade and mischievous brown irises winks at me. "You can be my slut anytime." He grabs his crotch and gives a hard squeeze. "How about now?"

More laughter. I squeeze the tray harder as sweat rapidly accumulates under my armpits.

"Me too, sweet cheeks." Another boy grins, showcasing slightly crooked teeth. "Interested in a threesome? Me and Xander will take real good care of your fine ass."

"This is my man," a girl sneers, possessively snaking an arm around the biceps of the boy beside her. "Touch him and you die, bitch."

I'm still a virgin, but I refuse to tell them that. Fuck them. There's no use in trying to defend myself anyway. They've already decided who I am.

"She's broke and homeless too." Deja resumes the attack on my character, tsking under her breath in disapproval. "And her father's a criminal."

Tears burn my eyes and threaten to spill over, but I blink them back.

"Aww, she's about to cry," Deja croons. "Poor thing."

"Where's my backpack?" I ask, resolving not to acknowledge my near breakdown.

The budding actress taps a finger against her cheek in bewilderment. "Whatever do you mean?"

"Don't play stupid, Deja." My voice wavers a tiny bit. "You know exactly what I'm talking about. I left my backpack by the basement door, and you took it. Tell me where it is right now!"

"Oh, that raggedy piece of shit," she states, her full lips curling into an evil smirk. "I thought it was trash, so I threw it out. My bad."

Don't react. Don't react. Don't react.

What am I going to do? I don't have the money to buy school supplies, let alone a new backpack. I can't depend on Leah's generosity every day. Admittedly, the loss is inconsequential compared to the hailstorm my life has recently become. It was stupid to think things would be different here. Hope is a dangerous thing for good reason.

I square my shoulders and stride forward, head held high. A second later, I'm sprawled on my face, and any hope of a dignified exit goes right out the damn window.

Deja, the spiteful bitch that she is, tripped me. *Ugh!* She's been getting the jump on me since this morning. Jeers and cackling fill my ears. I lie there, stunned, watching my bottled water skid across the floor. Most of my lunch and dipping sauces scatter behind the rolling plastic. So much for eating good. I hop to my feet and grab my tray, but fall again chasing after my bottled water. Ketchup packets are the culprit this time.

Stick a fork in me, I'm so fucking done.

I'm never going to live this down. The rest of the school year is going to be a freaking nightmare. I should've ignored her and kept it moving.

Why me, God?

I scramble upright again, tray in hand, then bolt outside as fast as my wobbly legs can take me. Fuck the bottled water. I'll die thirsty. I sink onto the metal bench opposite Leah, my eyes downcast, too mortified to look at her.

"Are you okay?" she asks softly.

There's genuine concern in her voice. I'll be forever grateful to her for not laughing at my expense.

I force a small smile. "You saw that, huh?"

"Yeah," she answers, abandoning her meal to focus on me. "Do you know her?"

I open my mouth to respond but hesitate. How much do I tell her? Disclosing my family drama could scare her away. Truth be told, I wouldn't blame her one bit if it did. Anyone with common sense would think twice before involving themselves in a messy situation.

Moreover, being my friend could make her a social pariah. It's better if she learns everything from me. She's bound to find out on her own anyway. I'm pretty sure Deja is making it her personal mission to alert the entire student population about my "slutbag" ways.

"She's my cousin," I admit. "Kinda hard to believe, right?"

Leah's lips form a perfect O. "Definitely wasn't expecting a blood relation."

"I don't know where to begin," I say jokingly, though my stomach is doing somersaults. "Deja… um… my mother—"

"Hey, you don't have to tell me anything you're not comfortable sharing." She reaches across the table and grasps my hand. "For what it's worth, Deja and her friends pick on me too. But only when my bestie isn't around. This is her lunch block, but per usual, she's off doing only God knows what. Just know that I'll be all ears whenever you're ready to talk."

"Thank you," I whisper. "Are we cool then? I completely understand if you want to think over hanging out with me."

"Of course we're cool," Leah assures me. "You can't get rid of me that easily. Anyway, it's still my goal to persuade you to the vegan lifestyle."

"You're barking up the wrong tree," I say, popping the lid off my marinara sauce. "I love cheese way too much to ever go vegan. *Real* cheese." I dunk a mozzarella stick in the sauce before taking a bite. "So, who's your bestie?"

"Her name is Meela. You'll meet her crazy ass soon."

Crazy? I hope this Meela is as welcoming as Leah.

I push the pending introduction to the back of my mind and gobble down the fried gooey goodness.

"Damn, that hit the spot." I grin, rubbing my belly. "All hail to the mighty cows for their delicious gift to the human race."

"Oh God." Leah chuckles, rolling her eyes skyward at my antics. "Dramatic must be your middle name."

"It is," I state sweetly.

Leah chuckles again and refocuses her attention on her lunch, biting into a pineapple.

Silence settles between us, and my thoughts shift to all the goals I need to accomplish before graduation. "By the way, where are you doing your community service hours? Think you can help me get on there?"

I need to get the ball rolling on completing my forty hours pronto. The sooner the better. Then I can focus on more important things, like finding a job and picking up as many shifts as possible. Graduation, figuratively speaking, is right around the corner.

"Sibley General Hospital, but not for community service hours," she states, slathering *chicken salad* onto a cracker. "I completed mine freshman year but still volunteer there."

"Damn, you're ready to walk across the stage while my procrastinating ass has zero hours."

She chuckles. "Well, not quite. I'm just a lowly junior."

"Really?" My eyebrows shoot to my forehead. "Thought you were a senior for sure."

"Nope, but I do have most of my credits already. I'm the resident brainiac." Leah shrugs nonchalantly. "Highest GPA in the whole school. Next year I'll have a half-day schedule and take college courses in the afternoons."

I whistle. "Must be nice."

"It's okay," she draws out. "Being the perfect student comes with a hefty price. I'm not allowed to make the slightest mistake, ever. Getting a grade lower than an A is unacceptable. I love my dad to death, but sometimes the amount of pressure he puts on me is just too much. I know he wants what's best for me, but sometimes I want to run away. Start over somewhere and just be a normal, carefree teenager."

I nod in understanding. "You're my kindred spirit."

My predicament is similar to hers. The only difference is that Leah's father wants what's best for her, and my mother wants what's best for *herself*.

Both aspirations are equally damaging to a kid. Enough gloom and doom for one day. On to the important stuff.

"What do you do at the hospital?"

"Patient care," Leah replies. "Delivering meals, toiletries, blankets, anything patients need."

"I can handle that," I assure her. "Easy peasy."

"Apply on the hospital's website under the community service tab," she instructs me. "There's a waitlist, but I'll put in a good word for you."

"Thank you. I'll get that done this evening."

"I work in the gift shop too. That's a paid position."

I could kill two birds with one stone. "Any openings?"

"Not right now, but I'll be sure to keep an eye out for you."

"Dang." I suck my teeth in disappointment. "Thanks for helping a sister out."

"Girl, don't even mention it. I volunteer Saturday and Sunday mornings, then start my shift right—"

A body drops heavily next to Leah, straddling the metal bench. "What the fuck is this shit?"

She goes ramrod-straight, her pupils dilating with unadulterated fear.

Who is this boy? Though referring to him as a boy isn't an accurate description by far. The newcomer resembles a full-grown man with his towering height, herculean build, and chiseled features. Obsidian eyes and a thick raven mane offset his olive skin perfectly. Dark prince comes to mind. With several piercings adorning his face and a cross dangling from his left earlobe that screams irony, he exudes danger.

An elaborate snake tattoo coils along his neck, disappearing underneath a fitted black hoodie. I study the sinister clown dominating the front, taking in its misshapen face, evil grin, and razor-sharp teeth. His broad shoulders are encased in a leather vest. *SNAKE* and *BLOOD GOD* are stitched above the right breast pocket, with *ORIGINAL CHAPTER* and *KENT* positioned identically on the left. Each word is embroidered in black on a white background.

The dark prince helps himself to Leah's lunch, scooping chicken salad onto a cracker and popping it into his mouth. He retches and spits the chewed remnants back into the plastic container, effectively ruining her meal, then leans his big body into hers.

"Disgusting," he whispers in her ear. "Just like you."

Leah's hands form tight fists on the table. Fat tears drip from her eyes, painting wet paths on her two-toned skin. I can't just sit here and do nothing while he trash-talks her. Granted, I don't know what caused the bad blood between them, but that's a moot point. I can't watch him make her cry.

"Leave her alone," I demand in a paper-thin voice.

His charcoal gaze bores into me, sending an arctic blast rippling down my spine. I collapse in on myself, bravado dissipating instantly. This guy is fucking scary as hell.

"I'll give you a pass for today only, since you're new here," he remarks in a deep, raspy timbre. "But you better learn damn quick that *no one* fucks with a God."

Imparting his words of wisdom, he gets up and ambles away. I spot a skull logo on the back of his vest, etched in the center. The letters *MC* sit to the right of the symbol. *GODS OF RUIN* span the top, with *OREGON* stretching across the bottom.

"You should've kept your mouth shut," Leah rebukes, her fingers roughly swiping at her wet cheeks.

"I-I'm s-sorry," I stammer. "I was only trying to help."

"Help?" Leah retorts. "You just made things worse. Snake has bullied me since middle school, and your attempt at *helping* won't change a damn thing. He's going to corner me later and finish what he started. He always does. I get through it by saying *nothing*… by doing *nothing*."

"What about telling an adult?" I ask lamely.

"You're fucking clueless," she ridicules, breathing out through clenched teeth. "I talk and the bullying gets ten times worse. The Gods run Oregon. Hell, they run half the states on the West Coast. No one would dare cross them. No one with functioning brain cells anyway."

My throat seizes, my muscles working nervously. "Who are the Gods?"

"A motorcycle gang you don't want as an enemy." Leah stands and gathers her stuff. "Look, I'm an outcast. I have one friend in this whole forsaken school. My life is hard enough. I don't need anyone in it that's going to make it harder."

"Leah, wait," I call at her back. "I didn't know. I'm sorry."

She keeps walking, ignoring me. My appetite disappears. I'm right back to where I started this morning—dejected and friendless.

The bell pierces my melancholy. I wrap my food in napkins to eat later and drag my feet to my locker.

Ten minutes later, I'm sitting in the auditorium, waiting for drama class to start. I fidget in the uncomfortable wooden seat, racking my brain about what to do next. Maybe Leah just needs some time to cool off. I'll try to talk to her after school and hope for the best.

Deja sashays by with a girl I recognize from the cafeteria, souring my mood further. She notices me and whispers in her friend's ear. They snicker at my expense, no doubt, and sit several rows ahead of me. I thrust my middle finger at their backs. *Bitches.*

"Hello, my darlings!" A bald man announces, waltzing into the auditorium.

This must be Mr. Rousseau, the drama teacher and a favorite among the students, judging by their enthusiastic responses. A colorful striped blouse and heather-gray slacks mold to his slim, athletic frame. His royal-purple high heels clink hard against the floor as he climbs onto the stage with an energetic bounce. Very chic and fashionable. He strides to the center of the platform. The overhead lights paint a bright spot on his hairless crown.

"Today, we'll conclude auditions for *Beauty and the Beast*," he continues in a thick French accent. "Stacy, Tina, you both would like to audition for the role of Belle, yes?"

They both express the desire to display their acting skills.

"And you are, my darling?" he asks me.

"Zilphia Kensley," I respond. "New kid on the block."

"It's nice to have you here." He bows slightly. "Would you like to audition for a leading role or a supporting role?"

I cringe, neither option appealing to me. "I prefer not to audition."

"Sure, my darling, but you must participate to receive a grade," he states. "We'll find a position for you on the stage crew."

The tension in my shoulder eases. "I can handle that."

"All right, let's begin," Mr. Rousseau announces. "Stacy, come to the stage, my darling. Henry, you as well. You'll read the lines for Beast. Act 5, Scene 1."

Deja turns around and sears me with her contemptuous gaze. "Like your nasty skank ass could've bested me anyway. I auditioned for Belle yesterday, and Mr. Rousseau will for sure give that part to me, guaranteed."

"Girl, yes, you have it locked down," her friend agrees, boosting my cousin's already fat head. "You're better than all these basic bitches in here."

"Period," she gloats.

That's it. I've had enough of her bullshit.

I raise my hand. "Mr. Rousseau, I changed my mind," I say, returning my cousin's hateful glare. "I want to audition for Belle."

"Wonderful, wonderful!" he exclaims, clapping his hands excitedly. "You'll audition after Tina."

I smirk at Deja. "May the best girl win."

She scowls at me, but no comeback is forthcoming.

I hope I haven't bitten off more than I can chew. I've performed on stage before, but that was thirteen years ago. My beauty pageant days are long gone. I remember absolutely loathing every second of it. I didn't aspire to become Miss USA. That was Momma's dream, and she just dragged me along for the ride, reliving her youth through me. She made the experience not fun.

I never won first place, and each loss resulted in a verbal tongue-lashing. In some cases, verbal abuse is far worse than physical abuse. Eventually she said I wasn't worth the trouble anymore, and my beauty pageant contestant days came to a sudden end. That was one of the happiest moments of my existence.

All too soon, it's my turn to audition. Mr. Rousseau hands me the script, and I mount the stage stairs, heart hammering in my eardrums. It feels like cotton balls are lodged in my throat. Oh God, what have I gotten myself into? Me and my big, gigantic mouth.

Chill. You got this.

I watched *Beauty and the Beast* a gazillion times. It was one of my favorite movies as a kid. Yep, this will be a cakewalk. I take center stage, and my confidence crumbles to dust. *Well hell.* I stand there, trembling in my wedges, words failing me. I part my lips, but only a croak emerges.

Deja snickers behind her hand.

That does the trick.

My vocal cords and limbs move into action, following Mr. Rousseau's every directive. I read the lines effortlessly, then dance, frolic, and sing—giving it my all. Broadway has nothing on me. I belt out the final note, breathless and with a smile on my face. I fucking killed it.

"Amazing!" Mr. Rousseau praises, applauding my performance.

Take that, Deja.

CHAPTER 14

Zilphia

I RACE DOWN THE HALL, NERVOUSNESS EATING AT ME. THE LAST CLASS just ended. Mr. Rousseau said he was going to post the cast list by the auditorium entrance. A crowd is already gathered at the bulletin board; some kids shout gleefully, while others stomp away in disappointment. I twist and dodge my way to the front and quickly scan the list. I pull in a deep breath, then let out a victorious cry.

I got the role!

In your face, Deja! This makes up for my diarrhea day. I break through the noisy mob and see my cousin approaching. She zooms in on my triumphant expression and her steps falter.

"Oh, don't waste your time, honey," I say, planting a hand on my hip. "I got the role of Belle. Who's the basic bitch now?"

"You're going to wish you never came to Kent." She pivots on her heel, sneering over her shoulder. "You just wait and see."

Uneasiness skates goose bumps across my skin. I'm going to have to watch my back every second until graduation. That's going to be a daunting task, especially since we reside in the same household.

"Hi, Zilphia." A cheery voice draws my attention. "I'm Jace. We have Mr. Rousseau together."

"Oh, hey," I respond, instantly recognizing him. "I remember seeing you."

"I'm your love interest." He grins.

"Huh?"

Is he seriously trying to flirt with me? That's random, but he's a heartthrob, though. Especially with those dazzling amber eyes and shaggy reddish-brown hair.

"I'm playing Beast," he states, absolving my confusion.

"Right, duh." I pop myself on the forehead. "Congratulations."

"Thanks, you too," he says, swinging his clunky backpack onto his shoulder. "Are you free to run lines on Sunday? We should get some extra practice time in whenever we can. The next six weeks are going to go by fast."

"Yeah, sure." I want to do my best and practice makes perfect. "Your place?"

Definitely can't have him entering the Double Dragon's Lair. They'll purposely embarrass me for sure.

"Eight good for you? I'm babysitting my little cousins until sevenish."

"Yep." I slip my cell phone from my purse. "What's your number?"

My fingers fly over the screen, keying in the information. "I'm going to text you now."

Since I use a third-party app, I can only get calls and texts when my phone is connected to Wi-Fi. But it's better than nothing.

"Cool," he responds. "I can pick you up if you want."

"That'd be great." I smile, grateful for the offer. "Thanks."

"Sure. Just shoot me your addy."

I send him the address, then tuck my mobile back into my purse. "I have to get going. See you tomorrow."

"Okay, pretty girl."

Well damn, he is flirting. I'll have to unpack that later. Right now, I'm on a mission to mend fences with Leah. I haul ass to her locker and find her rummaging inside the metal compartment.

I stop beside her. "Hear me out, okay? I'm—"

"We're good." She closes her locker and faces me. "I overreacted. Snake does that to me."

"Hey, Spot." A boy whistles at Leah, slapping his palms against his denim-clad thighs. "Come here, girl. I have a treat for you."

The asshole hovering behind him roars with laughter. "Man, you are so wrong."

"Hey, limp dick!"

I whirl around, the enraged shout startling me. I observe a girl barreling toward us at breakneck speed. She's wearing pink and black from head to toe, literally. Pink hair bounces with every determined footstep she takes. The fringe bangs and chin-length haircut frame a pretty face. A pink corset-style top, black patent leather skirt, and fishnet stockings hug her voluptuous curves—chunky pink boots complete the bold look.

My goodness! This girl even has pink eyebrows and contacts. Talk about fashion statement and color coordination. Colorful tattoos decorate her creamy olive skin. The anti-eyebrow, bridge, dimple, medusa, and three piercings along her left nostril accentuate her daring look. She comes to a hard stop directly in front of Leah's bully.

"You see this, bitch?" She jabs a long nail in Leah's direction. "This is my bitch. You fuck with her, you fuck with me." She grasps the boy's cheeks with one hand, squeezing until his lips pucker. "Capeesh, motherfucker?"

The scumbag swine drops to his knees, stars in his eyes. "Will you marry me?"

His heartfelt proposal earns him a chunky pink boot to the gut. "Not on your life, limp dick."

He yelps, fastening his arms around his midsection. His buddy helps him stand and carts him down the hall.

Leah rolls her eyes. "Extreme as always."

"Can't let these assholes pick on my bestie." The girl, whom I presume is Meela, flings an arm across Leah's shoulders.

"Missed you at lunch," Leah remarks. "Off somewhere getting high, no doubt."

"Maybe, maybe not," she replies cheekily.

"You need stronger body spray," Leah deadpans. "I can smell the devil's lettuce on your clothes."

"Okay, I may have smoked half a joint," she says with a grin, then directs her sassiness at me. "Who are you?"

"Zilphia," I answer her.

"Jameela, but everyone calls me Meela." She openly examines me for a few seconds. "My girl been showing you the ropes?"

"Yeah, she's great."

"Come on," Leah interjects, quickly spinning on her heel. "You know how Olive gets if I'm late."

We push through the heavy foot traffic toward the exit.

"Who's Olive?"

"My little sister. She's fourteen and a real pain in my ass," she gripes. "If I'm even two minutes late, she whines to our father, and then the responsibility speech commences. That spoiled brat always makes me out to be the bad guy, and my gullible father falls for it every single time."

"Do you drive?" Meela asks me.

"I have a driver's license but no car."

"How do you get home? Regular bus or cheese bus?" she questions further. "Or does someone pick you up?"

"None of the above," I respond. "I walk."

"Where do you live?" This question comes from Leah.

"Rochdale Boulevard. Right off Somerset."

We pad outside and descend the steep concrete stairs. The weather has gotten a lot milder since lunch.

"I would offer you a ride, but that's in the opposite direction of Olive's school," she explains.

"I'll be okay," I assure her. "It's about a twenty- to thirty-minute walk. Besides, you've done enough for me already today."

"I can show you a shortcut," Meela offers. "You'll be home in fifteen minutes flat. It's through the woods, though."

I could kiss her, because shit, my feet are on fire. I need to get these death traps off stat. RIP wedges. You will not be worn again.

"The woods don't bother me. Lead the way."

"See y'all tomorrow," Leah says with a quick wave and hurries toward the parking lot.

We call out our farewells and set off in the opposite direction.

"You walk too?" I ask.

"Hell no." Meela points to a small building two blocks ahead. "My sister owns that convenience store on the corner and the laundromat next to it. I usually drive to school every day, but she took my car keys because she's a big, fat, drooping labia."

I burst out laughing. She has a way with words, that's for sure.

"She makes me wait with her until closing time," she complains. "It's the worst torture imaginable."

"That sucks." I dutifully take her side.

"Okay, yeah, I snuck out of the house in the middle of the night." Her arms fling into the air. "Big fucking whoop! I come home and find her sitting in the dark, like she's fucking Hannibal Lecter or something. I swear she's thirty-four going on one hundred. Anyway, my car privileges will be restored this weekend. Thank the heavens above because having her chauffeur me around for the last week and a half has been a complete nightmare. That chick seriously needs some D.I.C.K in her life."

"Your sister sounds very strict," I remark. *Like my mother.*

"You have no idea." A prolonged sigh parts her lips. "So what grade are you in?"

"It's my last year."

"Ugh! You're so lucky," Meela whines. "I can't wait to graduate and tell my sister to stick her stupid, asinine rules where the sun don't shine. Aren't older sisters supposed to be fun? I think mine may be broken. Do you have any siblings?"

I scoff. "An older brother, and trust me, they aren't any better."

Her nose wrinkles. "Gross. I'm happy I don't have one of those. I heard they're smelly."

"You heard right."

My gaze roams over the neighborhood. I was rushing this morning and didn't pay attention to my surroundings. There isn't much in the general vicinity—just a gated apartment complex across the street, a park adjacent to it, and a storage place a little farther up.

"You can't ride the cheese bus since you live within two miles of the school, but you can get a transit pass from the office. It's free and you can use it for the whole school year."

"Really?"

"Yep, but honestly, it's better to walk if you ask me. With the constant stops, it'll take you almost an hour to get to school. That means earlier mornings and less sleep for you. It's good to use for rainy and snowy days, though. And you can use it on the weekends too, which is a plus."

"Thanks for the tip," I say, eternally grateful.

"No prob," Meela says, stopping at the entrance to the convenience store. "Cross the street here. You'll see the footpath leading into the woods in about a block."

"I want to come inside and take a look around."

"Cool." She opens the door, and the bell hanging above the entrance chimes. "After you."

I step into the air-conditioned building, my gaze immediately coasting over the food, snack, and drink options available.

I only added enough money to my student account to buy lunch for today, wanting to figure out a way to stretch my dwindling funds. Talk about right on time. I'll buy bread, lunch meat, cheese, and a few other goodies to tide me over.

"Hey," Meela greets a woman standing behind the counter. "New girl, this is my sister. Sister, new girl."

"Does new girl have a name?" she asks, smiling politely.

"Zilphia." I return her smile. "Does sister have a name?"

"Tulip."

There's no resemblance between them. Meela is thick and pint-sized, probably standing a little over five feet, with light-golden skin. Tulip, on the other hand, is tall and lithe with a pretty dark-brown complexion. Silken black curls are pulled into a bushy ponytail at her nape, exposing graceful features.

It must be a riot at their house. Meela is wild and vivacious, while Tulip seems calm and demure. I wonder if they clash often.

The shopkeeper bell chimes, and in walks the finest red-headed man I've ever seen. He's tall and ripped, with a perfectly creamy complexion. My fan-girling fizzles the instant my eyes land on his familiar leather vest. The same one Snake wore, except this man has a vice president patch. Uneasiness prickles my skin. Is this guy going to cause trouble?

He nods at us in greeting before going to the counter. Tulip blinks up at him, nibbling on her bottom lip.

"And the melodrama begins," Meela grumbles, rolling her eyes.

"What do you mean?" I ask, my fear increasing tenfold.

"That's Draco," she whispers. "He has the hots for Tulip, but she won't give him the time of day."

"He's wearing the same vest as the guy who was giving Leah a hard time at school."

"That's Snake," she says, already knowing who I mean. "They're brothers. And it's called a cut, not a vest."

Great, there are two of those assholes. And I've never heard anyone call a vest a cut.

"Oh." My gaze slides back to the front of the store, surreptitiously studying the pair. "They'd make an odd couple."

Oil and vinegar would mix better than these two. Not to mention he looks way younger than her—I'd say mid-twenties. Either way, she definitely doesn't seem like the type to flock to bad boys.

"Nah, they'd be good together," Meela states confidently. "Tulip's head is shoved too far up her ass to see that. Anyway, see anything you want?"

"Yeah." I grab a basket, and we start down the first aisle.

"What are you doing here?" Tulip asks, her tone tight with irritation.

Meela pins me with an "I told you so" look.

"I came to take a look at your freezer," he answers gruffly. "Smokey said it was making thumping noises yesterday."

"I don't need your help," she snaps. "Stop sending your goons to spy on me."

"You better start showing me some fucking respect," he growls, slamming his fist on the counter.

I jump, heart in my throat. "Should we call the cops?"

"Get out," Tulip orders, her voice shaking as she backs away from him. "A lowlife doesn't deserve respect."

"No, their little melodrama will be over in a couple of minutes."

I start loading my basket, sneaking glances at them every few seconds. Their argument continues in hushed tones. Suddenly, he catapults over the counter and crowds her against the wall, his muscular arms caging her in. I squeak, squeezing the metal handle of the basket in a death grip.

"Calm down, girl," Meela says. "He'd never hurt her."

"Are you sure?" I ask, literally shaking in my wedges.

"Yes."

My shopping is done a few minutes later, and we make our way to the counter. Thank goodness the scary carrot top is gone. Tulip ducks her head at our approach, but not before I notice her trembling lips and glossy eyes.

"I'll be back in a minute," she mumbles despondently before disappearing through a side door.

Meela stomps behind the counter. "I wish they would fuck already."

"Why doesn't she like him?" *Besides the fact that he's a big, scary outlaw biker.*

"Because our father was a God, and one day he got killed," she replies, quickly scanning my meager provisions. "We weren't told the specifics, but it had something to do with the club."

"I'm so sorry." My parents aren't perfect, but I can't imagine losing one of them.

Meela shrugs. "It was a long time ago. I'm just glad we had Zeus to look out for us."

"Is he a relative?"

"No. He's in charge of the Gods," she says, gesturing around the store. "Tulip wouldn't have any of this if it wasn't for him. He gave us seventy-five grand apiece. I can't touch mine until I'm eighteen, though."

That was very noble for a criminal. "Where's your mom?"

"She moved to boring-as-fuck Maine with her boyfriend about two and a half years ago. I only visit when she guilt-trips me."

I laugh. "Yeah, Maine doesn't seem like it'd be your speed." I grab three Blow Pops out of the plastic bin on the counter and slide them over to her. "These too." I pause, then finally ask the question I've been holding back. "What's the deal with Snake and Leah?"

"It's complicated," Meela replies, leaving it at that. "Your total is twenty-eight dollars and seventy-seven cents."

I don't press for more details. Maybe in time, Leah will tell me herself. I pay and collect my bags, then go on my way.

It's been an eventful day and that's putting it mildly. I'm actually looking forward to the damn basement.

CHAPTER 15

SANDMAN

"WHERE THE FUCK ARE THEY?" DRACO GROWLS, KICKING THE steel wall.

We lie in wait behind the warehouse, tension hanging heavy in the air. It's one of two locations used to store weapons and product. The area is secluded and surrounded by an electric fence, but as a precaution, prospects stand guard around the clock.

Those assholes should've been here fifteen minutes ago. Snake found more incriminating shit on Brick's and Buffalo's cell phones. The fuckers planned to meet the Disciples here at nine. The plan was to sell them the merch at half price, then frame the Latin Maniacs for the theft. They're in attendance tonight, lingering at a distance, whispering among themselves. Tension between the brotherhood and the gang is at an all-time high.

Zeus invited them to participate in the pending massacre, aiming to soothe hostilities. Enemies at our front and enemies at our fucking back. I have a gut feeling that some slimy shit is about to go down. My instincts are never wrong.

Caesar's beady, hate-filled gaze continuously seeks me out, knowing I led the assassination of his men. If he even farts in my direction, it's a done deal. I'm wilding the fuck out.

Snake leans on the steel wall next to me. "What do you think the holdup is?"

"Don't know."

He and I rode the dearly departed's bikes here and parked out front. The others pulled up, packed into two SUVs that are now stashed in the trees beyond the property line. We wanted to be as inconspicuous as possible.

"Maybe somebody tipped them off," Jigsaw speculates, absentmindedly stroking his beard. "Keep frosty. We can't let those bastards catch us with our pants around our ankles."

True, we actually don't know how many rats are in our midst. Someone could've alerted the Disciples that we're on to them and led us right to the slaughter, but I'm ready. I never ran from a fight in my life, and I'm not about to start now. Kill or be killed. That's the code. The motorcycle world is full of posers—loudmouths with no bite. But me? I made peace with death a long time ago. This life doesn't hand out tomorrows.

Live by the sword, die by the sword. Those words are inked across my shoulder blades.

"We'll wait another ten minutes," Zeus orders, his nostrils flaring. "If they don't show, then we go to their clubhouse. A message will be sent tonight. Blood will have blood."

"We should leave now," Draco barks, pacing back and forth. "Go to Spider's crib and light it up. That'll send those motherfuckers a message."

"I second that," Milo, a club prospect, agrees.

His lips are glued to Draco's ball sac.

"I said we wait," Zeus's authoritative tone cuts through the night. "And going to his house ain't happening. Just because we have public officials on our payroll doesn't mean we can act wild west in the streets. Making noise in a residential neighborhood would bring too much heat down on us. Especially if an innocent got hurt, or worse, killed."

Did something crawl up Draco's ass and die? He's been sulky since this morning, which is nothing new, but his theatrics are on a hundred today. I chuckle softly to myself.

Draco's angry gaze zooms in on me. "Something funny, motherfucker?"

"Yeah." I nod my head in the affirmative. "Your bitch ass."

He strides toward me, his fists clenched at his sides. "We'll see who's the bitch."

"Come on," Snake gripes irritably. "Can you two skip the pissing contest for tonight?"

"Can't," I respond, straightening from my slouch against the wall. "Gotta piss like a racehorse."

"Let it go." Cricket grabs my arm. "We got bigger fish to fry."

"It's cool." I wink, pulling away from him. "This won't take long."

"Rein that shit in before I break a foot off in both y'all asses," Zeus threatens.

"Then how would you walk?" I deadpan.

Zeus's eyes narrow to slits. "Don't test me, boy."

Draco hocks a loogie on the ground at my feet, then spins on his heel. Some of the thick mucus landed on the toe of my right boot. That's a slight I refuse to ignore.

"I saw Tulip yesterday." Draco stops dead in his tracks, body winding tighter than a virgin asshole. "I don't usually fuck older broads, but she was looking real sweet. Might make an exception for her and feed that lonely pussy some young dick."

"Savage," Cricket mumbles.

"Fuck, did you have to go there?" Snake whines.

Draco whips around and charges forward, a feral sound erupting from his throat. Just as we're about to clash, Snake jumps between us, his arms spread wide to stop the fight. The punch meant for me lays him flat on his back. He staggers to his feet, rubbing along his jawline.

"Fuck, Draco, you almost broke my goddamn jaw!" he exclaims.

"Your dumb ass shouldn't have gotten in the fucking way."

"Motherfucker!" Snake bellows, swinging a right hook into Draco's chin.

They go head-to-head—ducking, dodging, and throwing punches. Draco lands a calculated blow to Snake's abdomen. He grunts, air swooshing from his lungs.

"You're way out of your league, pup," Draco taunts, his knuckles barreling toward Snake's face.

Snake ducks the jab and strikes back, smashing his forehead into Draco's.

"You little shits should've been swallowed," Zeus snaps, stomping over to them.

Jigsaw keeps pace at his side. They work together to pull them apart.

Cricket sighs, pinching the bridge of his nose. "See what you started?"

"Well, you know me," I drawl, shrugging a shoulder. "I'm the life of the party."

Distinctive rumbling rends the air, and everyone stills. Adrenaline flares to life in my veins.

"It's go time," Zeus announces, then looks at Draco. "You, Rooster, and Tank cover the front. Wait here until the fireworks start and dead anyone who tries to make a run for it. The rest of you get ready."

The rumbling grows louder, and we huddle at the back entrance, weapons at the ready. I slow my breathing, both hands clasping my Glock in a firm grip. The engines cut and heavy footsteps can be heard crunching the gravel as our hapless prey file into the dimly lit warehouse.

"On the count of three," Zeus whispers. "One, two, three."

I storm through the door first, my gun drawn and finger on the trigger. The others quickly follow suit, fanning out around the spacious interior.

Our rivals freeze. Bear, the sergeant at arms, draws his firearm. Too slow. I release a single shot, putting a bullet hole in his hand.

I lower my weapon, aiming between his thighs. "Move again, and your balls are next."

He winces in pain, holding his bloody appendage against his chest.

We outnumber their eight. They don't stand a chance.

"Where's Spider?" Zeus's question echoes through the building.

He and his VP are conspicuously missing.

"He ain't come tonight," Bear grinds out. "You'll never get to him."

"Please don't kill me," a prospect blubbers, tears raining down on his chubby cheeks. "I'm only doing what—"

I empty two shells into his chest. "Shut the fuck up."

Crying is for babies, children, and women.

Shock widens his eyes, and he crumples to the concrete floor, still as the grave.

"You son of a bitch," Bear snarls, baring his teeth. "He was just an eighteen-year-old kid."

"Now he's a dead eighteen-year-old kid." I smirk, turning my gun back on him. "Play stupid games, win stupid prizes."

The guy to Bear's left brandishes his piece with a roar and starts blasting. Everyone scatters, running for safety. I take shelter behind a steel column.

"It's a good day to die, motherfuckers!" I bellow, spraying bullets across the room.

Zeus returns gunfire, diving for a large wooden crate. Cricket flips a table. He and another brother drop behind it, using it as cover. I've lost sight of Snake and Jigsaw, but spot a few other brothers ensconced in various positions.

From the corner of my eye, I glimpse Caesar centering his gun at Zeus's head.

"Zeus!" I swing my arm around and fire at the gang leader, striking him in the eye and neck.

He still manages to discharge one shot but misses his target by mere centimeters. I knew we couldn't trust those fuckers. Caesar falls to his knees and then topples over. His second comes at me with a hail of gunfire, grazing my left shoulder. I duck and roll into a low crouch, dispensing several slugs into his gut.

"Bye-bye, bitch."

I sprint back to the steel column, pumping lead into Maniacs and Disciples along the way. We'll be lucky to see tomorrow. A bullet whizzes past my head.

Fuck, that was close.

I quickly reload and rejoin the fray.

"Hold your fucking fire!" someone shouts above the din. "We surrender!"

"Gods, ceasefire, but stay sharp!" Zeus's booming edict ends the shootout.

The silence hits hard, like someone yanked the sound from the air.

"Identify yourself," Zeus calls out.

"Bulldog."

"Throw your weapons out and come out with your hands up," he demands. "Same goes for you, Maniacs."

Guns slide out, then five men emerge—three Disciples and two Maniacs.

We cautiously surface from our hiding places. Snake drags a limping Milo at his side.

"Call the doc!" he cries out hysterically. "I'm dying over here, dude."

"You're fine," Snake snaps, lowering him to the concrete floor.

"Fine?" Milo wails, gesturing wildly at his leg. "Dude, look at my fucking leg! I'm bleeding like a stuck—"

Snake's foot connects with his face, knocking him out cold. "I said you're fucking fine."

The others enter the warehouse, weapons locked and loaded.

"Rooster, get the car." Zeus digs the key out of his pocket and tosses it to him. "Take Milo to The Sanctuary. Naomi will meet you there, then I want you back here."

"You got it, Prez."

Draco surveys the carnage. "Any casualties?"

"Yeah," Jigsaw responds somberly. "Claw's gone."

"Fuck!" Zeus thunders. "Six brothers dead within a month."

"On your knees, you pieces of shit," I bark as I stride toward our enemies.

I place my Glock against the first guy's forehead.

"No, please—"

"God's Wrath has no mercy." I pull the trigger.

I train the muzzle on the second guy. "You have five seconds to convince me not to put a bullet in your head."

"I have two children—"

Bang, Bang. Bang. Three slugs enter his dome.

"Changed my mind."

The next man drops with two in the chest. I set my sights on the fourth man. He doesn't cower or snivel like the others. Respect—but he still has to die.

"Not the last two," Zeus commands, making his way through the carnage and shell casings. He stops in front of the tough guy. "You're going to deliver a message. Understand?"

The man gives him a clipped nod.

"Tell Spider death is coming for him. Now get the fuck outta here."

He pushes to his feet and ambles out of the door, cool as a fucking feather.

Zeus turns to the last man. "Tell your crew we can let bygones be bygones or we can continue to spill blood."

"Yeah, man, I'll let them know." He scrambles to his feet and hauls ass.

Lucky bastards must have a guardian angel.

"How's your shoulder?" Zeus asks, nodding at the bleeding wound.

"It's just a flesh wound," I respond, sliding my gun into my holster. "I'll have the doc take a look at it later."

I'm wearing a bulletproof vest to protect my vital organs—all the brothers are—but a well-placed shot can still take me out.

"You did good," Zeus remarks, slapping me on the back.

I dip my chin, acknowledging the rare compliment.

"Found this on Bear's body," Tank says, holding up a bulging envelope.

"Payment for the merch," Jigsaw states, taking the envelope from him. "I'll give it to Butch."

"All right, people, move like you got a purpose," Zeus orders. "Dump the bikes and disappear the bodies." He looks at Draco. "In the morning, gather some prospects to put the warehouse to rights, but the cleaner needs to come tonight."

He nods and pulls his cell phone from his cut pocket.

It's going to be a long fucking night.

"Twelve stitches," Naomi announces, securing the bandage around my shoulder. "You're fortunate your injury isn't more serious."

"Thanks, Doc," I mumble, rotating my shoulder.

The pain is minimal. I'll be back in tip-top shape within the week.

"You're welcome," she replies with a bright smile. "Keep the stitches dry for the first twenty-four hours. After that, you'll need to wash, rebandage, and apply petroleum twice a day. I'll pull them out in ten days."

I nod, taking in her instructions.

"Antibiotics to prevent infection." A pill bottle is pressed into my palm. "Take one three times a day for a week."

"Got it." I push the bottle into my inner cut pocket.

Zeus slides into the chair to my right and passes me an ice-cold beer. "Finally got your badge of honor, boy," he praises, a grin on his face. "And you took it like a soldier."

"I hardly call getting shot a badge of honor," Naomi scoffs, ramming her supplies back inside her medical bag. "He could've been killed."

"Shut your mouth, woman." He winks at me, mirth in his gaze. "I'm talking to my son."

Naomi is an emergency room doctor and a recovering gambling addict. She got in way over her head. I don't know the particulars, but rumor has it that she's millions in debt.

Zeus offered her a side gig patching up our wounded. He loves getting under her skin. They have a lust-hate relationship, though the hate is on her part. Zeus just wants in her pants. I see why he has a hard-on for her. Curvy waistline, double D's, and a plump ass with ham hock thighs—she's thick, thick.

Naomi springs to her feet, her hands balled into tight fists at her side. "I'm not one of your lackeys."

"But you're on my payroll," he quips, his sensual gaze slowly roaming over her. "And insubordination has consequences."

"Then fire me."

"I'd rather fuck you."

Naomi's fair skin turns bright red, and Zeus smirks. The tension between them crackles—lust and fury wrapped in barbed wire.

"Fuck you, Zeus." She snatches her medical bag off the table and stomps toward the door.

"Naomi!" His booming voice cracks through the air like a whip, halting her instantly. "Don't mistake my kindness for weakness. My patience is wearing thin."

His implication is as clear as a cloudless blue sky. One way or another he'll have her by any means necessary. Naomi bolts out the door without a backward glance.

"Run away, little rabbit," he growls. "I'll trap you soon enough."

I swing the beer bottle to my lips and down the bitter contents in a few gulps.

"Want another one?" Zeus asks.

"Nah, I'm good." I rub my gritty eyes. "I'm going to head upstairs and crash."

I'm too damn tired to drive home.

"Stop exaggerating!" Snake shouts, elbowing Smokey in the stomach. "I didn't fall. I dove on the floor so I wouldn't get my ass shot off."

"You fell harder than that new chick in the cafeteria yesterday." Smokey laughs, blocking Snake's elbow from digging into his midsection again.

"What's her name? It's some weird shit." He snaps his fingers. "Oh yeah, Zilphia."

I leap to my feet, toppling my chair to the floor. Just hearing that name is like a kick to the gut. The chances of Zilphia being in Oregon are slim, but I need to put my mind at ease. "What's her last name?"

Zeus locks eyes with me, fully knowing the pain she caused me.

Smokey shrugs. "I don't know, man."

"What does she look like?" I bite out, vengeful thoughts twitching my cock.

"I didn't draw her picture." He chuckles and takes a long swig of his beer. "Shit, man, I don't even remember what I ate for breakfast this morning."

Cricket walks over to me and rests a hand on my shoulder. "Relax, you don't know if it's her."

"Don't know if she's who? Am I missing something?" Snake's eyes dart between Cricket and me.

I pounce on Smokey, hauling him off the barstool. "Answer the fucking question!"

"Um, she's Black. Pretty," he rushes out, his eyes wide with fear. "Slender, about five five."

It's her. Has to be.

The girl who turned my heart black. I want to cut her open and bathe in her blood. It's a sick fantasy for a sick motherfucker.

"Who is she to you?" Snake asks.

I release the shirt clutched in my hands and leave the bar on autopilot. Three phrases ring through my mind on repeat.

Make her hurt.

Make her bleed.

Make her suffer.

"Where are you going?" Cricket calls after me.

I straddle my bike and start the engine, my hands shaking with the need to hurt her.

Cricket grips the stainless-steel handlebars. "Leave with your head all fucked up and you're going to end up roadkill."

"Back off."

"Don't do anything stupid," he pleads, worry evident in his voice. "Even if it is her… so fucking what. Keep that bitch in your rearview."

"You know what she did."

"I know, and it's fucked up, but don't go jumping off the deep end."

"Cricket, back off or I'll crush every bone in your fucking hand."

He sighs but steps back. I twist the throttle and speed toward home. My surroundings are a blur, whizzing past unseen.

Make her hurt.

Make her bleed.

Make her suffer.

If it's her… Hell hath no fury like a woman scorned? *No.*

Hell hath no fury like a *man* scorned.

Sweet, sweet Zilphia, the most sadistic atrocities await you.

I'm going to make her hurt… I'm going to make her hurt so fucking good.

CHAPTER 16

Three and a half years ago

SAM

"SAM, ARE YOU THERE?" ZILPHIA'S HUSHED VOICE DRIFTS IN THROUGH the open window.

I shoot up from the futon and sprint across the wooden floor. She sits curled in the window seat, her legs tucked at her side—barefoot, her hair cascading in loose curls around her shoulders, bathed in silver moonlight.

"They're gone," she squeals excitedly. "Meet me at the patio."

Her parents went to some fundraiser thing, and Nolan's staying with friends for the weekend, so we're having a movie night.

"Okay," I respond, my heart thrashing in my chest. "See you in a sec."

I swallow hard and count to ten before leaving the tree house. The balmy summer night instantly envelops me. Down the stairs, past the swimming pool, and across the deck. I've never been inside her house. That thought alone makes my pulse race.

My breath swooshes from my lungs the second she comes into view. She's so beautiful it hurts to look at her. The door flings open, and she launches herself into my arms, molding her softness to my lanky body. I encircle her petite waist, aching to bury my face in her neck.

"Ew, Sam, you're so sweaty." She pulls back, wrinkling her nose at me.

"S-sorry," I stammer, my gaze fixed on the shiny floor behind her. "It's warm out tonight."

"Oh," she mumbles, then runs her fingers through my hair. "You're due for a cut."

I inwardly groan, fighting not to react.

"Thinking about letting it grow out," I rasp.

"I can see it." A chaste smile spreads across her lips. "The surfer-stoner look would definitely suit you."

We stare into each other's eyes and something passes between us. Foreign and forbidden.

Zilphia clears her throat and sweeps her arm in a wide arc. "Welcome to my humble abode. What do you think?"

I walk inside and glance around. Exactly how I envisioned. Pristine, sparkling everything. No doubt the entire house matches the opulence of the kitchen.

"Very nice," I mutter.

The doorbell chimes and my entire body tenses—my fight-or-flight response triggered.

"Relax," she says, laughing. "It's just the pizza. I ordered your favorite."

"Supreme?"

"With extra everything, baby." She does a little shimmy dance.

"Large?" I ask, my mouth already watering.

"A super, enormous extra-large." She waggles her eyebrows and skips out of the kitchen. "Can you grab a couple of canned sodas from the fridge? Oh, and the bag on the counter. I got us some snacks."

"Sure." I amble over to the shiny silver appliance and pull it open. "There's enough food in here to feed an army." I'm lucky if we have bread and mayo at home.

I snag four carbonated drinks and toss them into the bag before heading into the living room. Zilphia hovers by the front door, clutching the pizza box between her small hands. The savory smells of pepperoni and sausage invade my nostrils.

"Come on," she chirps, starting up the stairs.

"Where are we going?"

"To my bedroom, duh," she teases, throwing me a playful look over her slim shoulder. "Where'd you think we were going? Mars?"

Apprehension clenches my stomach, rooting me to the spot. I thought we were going to stay in the living room. My hormones go haywire, a hundred different scenarios swirling through my mind. Things a friend shouldn't think. Are we going to watch movies on her bed? We've snuggled on the futon in the tree house plenty of times, but this is different. It's her bed. Her private domain. This is a really bad idea.

"Are you sure about this?" I ask her.

Her eyebrows furrow. "Yes. Why?"

I shrug. "You're always so intense about us never going inside, even when your parents and brother aren't home."

"Guess I'm a little more comfortable. As long as we're careful, there's nothing to worry about." She smiles, cocking an eyebrow at me. "Anyway, you can always jump out the window if they come home early. Now move it. I'm hungry."

I follow her lead, admiring her pink flannel shorts. The soft material clings to her bottom. I reach out, lightly skimming a finger along the hem, careful not to brush her thigh. It's risky, but touching her is an addiction. She's simply perfection in every way possible, and I'm a filthy black spot in her otherwise unblemished world. Be that as it may, I'm not going anywhere.

We get to her bedroom, and my probing gaze scans the silver and purple color scheme. No posters on the walls. Just one canvas of a woman with an afro, painted in graffiti-style brushstrokes, hanging over her queen-sized bed. Trophies and framed photographs are displayed on shelves mounted to the wall. More pictures are taped to the intricate oval mirror above her dresser. She happily poses for the camera, sometimes alone, sometimes surrounded by friends who aren't me. The sight stings more than it should.

"Sit," Zilphia says, patting the spot next to her on the bed.

I place the snack bag on the nightstand, slip out of my sneakers, then climb beside her—more nervous than I've ever been in my entire life.

"What do you want to watch?" she asks, pressing the power button on the remote.

"Doesn't matter." I open the pizza box and help myself to a cheesy slice.

"Romantic comedy it is," she singsongs, browsing through Netflix.

"Have some mercy on me, Zilphia," I plead around a mouthful of pizza.

"Hey, you're the one who said it didn't matter," she reminds me.

"Well, I lied," I reply, reaching for a second slice. "Find an action movie."

She rolls her eyes playfully. "Fine."

"Wait, scroll back up," I instruct her. "Right there, three spaces to the left."

"What? Aliens?"

"Yeah, oldie but goodie."

"Okay," Zilphia agrees. "I haven't seen my acid for blood friends in a while."

We eat, joke, and talk about how badass Ripley, aka Sigourney Weaver, is.

A short time later, Zilphia's body is pressed against my side with her head nestled on my chest. I cradle her to me, resting my hand on the warm skin exposed at her hip. The feel of her breast on my rib cage taunts me, bringing unplatonic thoughts from earlier to the forefront of my brain. Her flowery scent wafts into my nose, tormenting me further. I nuzzle my face into her hair while tracing circles on to her velvet-smooth flesh. My cock grows hard between my legs.

"Sam, are you sniffing my hair?"

"Um… yeah. I'm sorry," I utter hoarsely, pulling the cover over us to hide my erection. "It smells good. What shampoo do you use?" I always wanted to ask, but didn't want to seem like a creep.

"Honeysuckle Dreams," she replies sleepily. "It's my favorite fragrance. I have the whole collection."

"It suits you," I mumble.

Zilphia tilts her head back, peering at me with those exquisite chocolate eyes. "Are you okay? Your heart is beating really fast."

"Yes," I grit out. "Just watch the movie."

She nibbles on her bottom lip, wanting to say more, but refocuses her attention on the television. After a while her breathing becomes slow and even.

"Zilphia, are you awake?"

No response.

"Zilphia?"

Still no response.

A perverse voice whispers in my ear, telling me to touch her… to taste her. She won't know.

I know it's wrong—every part of me knows it. But fuck… I can't help it.

Once… I'll give in to my primal urge just once.

I place a kiss on the side of her neck, my lips lingering. Then I taste her skin. One long, deliberate sweep of my tongue across her shoulder.

How far do I take this? Fuck it. I already crossed the invisible line into immoral damnation; might as well stay the course.

My hand slips beneath the waistband of her pajama bottoms and into her panties. She moans and snuggles deeper into my side, but doesn't wake. I resume my exploration, delving into her warm, wet slit.

My dick throbs painfully beneath my zipper, needing to feel the slick suction of her body. I pull my hand free and bring my glistening fingers to my nose, inhaling her unique aroma into my body. My head spins. Time seems to move in slow motion. It would be so easy to slip inside her. Fuck, what am I saying?

I carefully extricate myself from her soft curves and stagger into the bathroom, locking the door behind me. Against my better judgment, I lap her sweet juices from my fingertips. I grip the edge of the sink, my legs going weak as her taste floods my senses, shaking the foundation of my control. My mind screams at me to go back into the bedroom and gorge myself on her pussy.

I need to leave. It's too dangerous to stay here.

I freeze. There it is. Tucked in the shower caddy.

I pick up the bottle with a trembling hand and flip the cap open, breathing the golden liquid deep into my lungs.

The tantalizing honeysuckle fragrance burns a hole through my mind, fueling the darkness trying to swallow me whole.

I shove my pants down and jerk off to thoughts of her wet pussy wrapped around my cock. My orgasm hits me with an intensity that buckles my knees and leaves me gasping for air.

CHAPTER 17

Present

SANDMAN

By some miracle, I make it home in one piece. I slam my thumb against the biometric screen, and the gate creaks open. Restlessness coils in my gut. I skid to a stop in the driveway, ditch my bike, and shove through the front door.

"Stay!" I shout before my beloved Dobermans can pounce on me.

I take the stairs two at a time, heading straight for my room.

My determined strides carry me to my en suite bathroom. I pull open the cabinet, my gaze quickly landing on the bodywash on the top shelf. The golden liquid in the clear bottle beckons me. I reverently wrap my hand around the bottle and flick open the top, inhaling the flowery fragrance. An electric pulse rips through my brain, sharp and sudden. I latch onto the wooden cabinet for support.

I bound into my bedroom and stretch out across the bed. Two depraved images hit me simultaneously. One: pounding my cock into her dripping wet pussy until she's swollen and delirious with pain. Two: slicing my blade through her velvet-smooth skin.

I unfasten my jeans and release my engorged length, hissing as the sensitive head brushes against the worn denim. I squeeze several drops of the gold liquid onto my calloused palm before gripping the base of my cock and sliding my hand along the rigid planes. I close my eyes and let my dark imagination take control.

I'm kneeling between her spread legs, pounding into her sweet pussy while slashing her beautiful brown flesh with my favorite Bowie knife. Her blood-curdling screams pulsate through my dick, intensifying my need to make her hurt more.

"Please stop!" she sobs hysterically.

Zilphia's pleas for leniency spur me on, having the opposite effect she desired. My hand lashes out repeatedly, decorating her breasts, shoulders, and belly with long, deep cuts. Her warm, sticky blood splatters across my face and chest, snapping the last thread of my control.

I slice the honed edge across her throat, severing muscle and tendons. Zilphia's dark-brown gaze bulges in horror as she grasps the gaping wound. Thick, crimson liquid oozes between her trembling fingers. I watch in complete awe as she exhales her last breath, and the life fades from her eyes.

"Fuck yes!" I bellow as my milky load shoots across the room.

If Zilphia knew the storm that was coming for her, she'd run far away from Kent. She broke me, so it's only fair that I break her too.

CHAPTER 18

Zilphia

I CREEP THROUGH THE HOUSE LIKE A THIEF IN THE NIGHT TO PACK A quick lunch. School doesn't open for another hour, but I'd rather sit on concrete stairs than have another run-in with the double dragons.

Yesterday morning was an epic disaster. Dinner was more tolerable, though Momma and Sheila hurled the occasional barb at each other. I didn't want to be there, but someone had to babysit the unpredictable woman who gave birth to me. Keith and I were the unofficial referees, preventing their insults from escalating into a full-blown argument or worse, physical blows.

Deja was absent from the evening meal again, which was probably for the best. She and my aunt would've surely double-teamed my mother—and Loretta Kensley doesn't back down from a fight, *ever*. It doesn't matter if the odds aren't in her favor; if they'd gone after her, nothing could've stopped the inevitable. It would've been an all-out battle.

My grandmother was safely ensconced in her bedroom and didn't witness her daughters' uncivilized conduct. I devoured the orange chicken and rice despite the oppressive tension.

After dinner, I spent some quality time with my ailing grandma, watching television and telling her about getting the lead role in the school musical.

Momma mostly ignored us and bemoaned how unfair life is, dragging the mood down like a wet towel.

At least the night ended on a positive note. I applied for several jobs during advisory, and one listing in particular caught my attention—a housekeeping position at a gentleman's club. Twenty whopping bucks an hour. The rest were minimum wage gigs. Not ideal for my short-term goals, but as I've said before, beggars can't be choosers.

I'll accept any offer of employment made to me, but luck was finally on my side. The HR assistant from the club called me, and we chatted for a few minutes. I never worked a day in my life, but answered each question with poised confidence and snagged myself an interview for tomorrow evening.

I got two more responses. My heart is set on the cleaning gig, but putting all my eggs in one basket isn't smart. I replied to both emails. Just waiting to see what happens next. Earning an income and not relying on my father's wallet will be a huge stepping stone toward independence. Something I've craved for a very long time but was forbidden to do.

I stroll into the dark kitchen, clutching the gifted tote bag to my shoulder. I'm not giving my despicable cousin the chance to toss it out. Not to mention my purse and laptop are stowed inside. I'm not letting it out of my sight for even a millisecond. I stop dead in my tracks, confusion scrunching my eyebrows.

"Where the hell is my bread?"

I left it right there on the counter, next to the toaster oven. I'm sure of it, but now it's gone. I turn in a circle, my gaze quickly scanning over every surface. Maybe Sheila moved it. I search the cabinets and pantry. Nothing. A sinking feeling unfurls in my gut. I jerk open the refrigerator and angry tears fill my eyes. My lunch meat, cheese, mayonnaise, and sodas are gone too. Everything was tied in plastic bags.

Deja.

She threw it all out—I'm sure of it. I rip open the trash can, but my missing groceries aren't there either. My fists clench.

I drop my bag and bolt upstairs, rage setting my legs on fire. That stupid bitch went way too far this time. I tear into her bedroom and yank the blanket off her.

Deja wakes with a startled shriek. "What the fuck?"

"You threw out my stuff!" I accuse.

She leaps to her feet and shoves me. "Get the fuck out of my room!"

I push her back. "You owe me money."

"I'm not giving you shit, bitch," she jeers, her spittle landing on my lips.

Before I can stop myself, my hand flies up and connects with her face, sending her silk bonnet tumbling to the floor. Damn. I've never hit another person in my life. Well, except for Nolan, but he doesn't count.

For a split second, we're frozen in stunned silence. Then she starts swinging on me. I mean really swinging. Beating my ass six ways from Sunday.

Adrenaline kicks in, and I latch onto her lace-front wig, yanking with all my might.

Light floods the room, then hard hands dig into my arms and yank me back. "Get away from her!"

"She came in here and attacked me for no reason," Deja snivels, crocodile tears already rolling down her cheek. Sheila wraps an arm around her before turning her cold eyes on me.

Defending myself is useless, but I can't just sit here and let her lie on me.

"That's not true," I began, pointing at the vile creature in human form. "She—"

"Save it," my aunt sneers at me. "Don't you ever come into my daughter's bedroom again."

"My hair," Deja whines, digging her fingers into her scalp. "It's lifting now."

"No one will notice," Sheila assures her. "I'll have Mae fix it this weekend."

Deja glares at me. "I don't feel safe with her here."

"Put your filthy hands on my daughter again, and you and your *whore* mother will find yourselves on the street." I shudder at the pure loathing in her brown irises. "Do I make myself clear?"

I nod, my throat too thick with raw emotion to form a single syllable.

"Furthermore, I don't house freeloaders. Water costs. Electricity costs. Gas costs. Food costs. Toiletries cost." Sheila lifts a finger with each point made. "You and your *whore* mother need to get jobs ASAP or it's the streets for you both." An evil smile curves her lips. "And the streets are a cold place to be during the winter. Now get out."

I hurry to the second level on trembling legs and lock myself in the bathroom. I stare at my reflection. I'm none the worse for wear. No bruising. Yet. Glossy eyes, wild hair, and a scratch along my chin are the only telltale signs of the fistfight.

I finger-comb my thick mane, putting the strands back in place before heading to my grandmother's room. She and my mother are still bundled in bed. The fight didn't wake them; thank goodness for small favors. I kneel beside my mother and lightly shake her shoulder.

"Momma, wake up."

She grumbles and swats at me.

"Momma, we need to talk," I say in an urgent whisper, shaking her harder. "It's important."

Her eyes pop open, a frown contorting her features. "What is so important that it couldn't wait until later? It's the ass crack of dawn."

Dawn has come and gone, but that's a moot point.

I gnaw on my bottom lip, tasting my cotton-candy-flavored lip gloss. She's not going to like this one bit. "Momma, you have to look for a job."

She sits up, scandalized. "Have you lost your goddamn mind?"

I can't tell her what Sheila said; she'll blow a gasket.

"We can't stay here forever," I say instead.

"And we won't." She lies back down and pulls the blanket over her shoulder. "Now go to school."

"We need money to move out and support ourselves."

Unless she plans to rob a bank, we need to find jobs like yesterday.

"I have a meeting at a matchmaking service today," she states proudly, like she just landed a CEO position. "They only vet wealthy men. I'll be married in less than six months."

I blink. She can't be serious! "But you're already married."

"I'll get a divorce."

"Momma, marriage is not the solution," I say slowly. "There's no guarantee someone will propose to you."

Sheila will have kicked us out way before then.

She lets out an annoyed breath, rolling her eyes at me. "We're going to be fine. I know how to catch a man's attention."

"But—"

"Enough," she hisses and points at the door. "Go to school and don't wake me up this early again."

I'm fighting a losing battle. I blow out a long breath, then trudge down to the kitchen to grab my tote bag.

"Maybe living in a homeless shelter won't be so bad," I mutter, detouring to the basement.

Fortunately, I didn't leave all my purchases in the kitchen. I grab a pack of ramen noodles and drop it into my bag. I'll find a microwave at school. I hid everything else in a plastic bin. My suitcase is left defenseless, though. Deja could waltz down here anytime she pleases and wreak havoc. I can't have that. I gather my clothes and other belongings, meticulously stashing them too.

"There," I say, satisfied.

I check the time on my cell phone—roughly forty minutes until school starts. I leave the Double Dragon's Lair, taking the shortcut to school.

As I approach the building, a man sitting sideways on a motorcycle catches my attention. His head jerks in my direction. I can't make out his features. The sun silhouettes his face, creating a halo around his golden shoulder-length tresses. Is he watching me? Did Snake tell his club friends about our spat yesterday? A flicker of unease settles deep in my belly. I lower my gaze and keep walking, but as I near him, curiosity pushes me to steal a glance.

The world stutters to a stop.

My breath freezes in my lungs.

It's… *Him*.

"Sam?" I breathe, an exuberant smile stretching my cheeks.

I race over to him and fling my arms around his neck. I'm taken aback. Gone is the lanky boy. His body is all hard planes and sculptured muscles. I notice my embrace isn't being returned.

"Sam, it's me." I pull back and stare into his cornflower-blue gaze. "Zilphia. Remember?"

They're the same cerulean depths, but somehow different. *Icy*. The innocent gleam is gone. Something's wrong. Very, very wrong.

His cheekbones and jawline are granite angles. Whatever happened in those three years, it hardened him. The septum piercing is new. So are the silver hoops adorning his earlobes. A blackout tattoo covers his right forearm and another spans his neck—some kind of bird.

He's on his feet in the blink of an eye, his nose gliding along my neck as he breathes me in. I stand stock-still, shock holding me immobile. An animalistic growl rattles in his chest, vibrating through me. Suddenly, his teeth tear into my skin.

The ache jolts me into action. I rear back and try to scramble away, but he digs sharp fingernails into my wrist. An ace of spades tattoo graces the back of the hand that's preventing my escape to safety. The letters G, O, D are inked separately on his ring, middle, and index fingers.

"Let me go," I demand in a panicked voice.

Sam doesn't say a word, but the hardness in those icicle orbs speaks volumes. Sharp nails burrow deeper, piercing my flesh. A pained whimper parts my lips.

"I'll scream," I threaten, frantically pulling against his iron grip.

But would anyone come to my rescue? Leah warned me that these biker guys are untouchable. Kent's Robin Hood criminals, according to Meela. I'm inclined to believe them on both accounts.

Sam releases me, and I crash to the concrete. My elbow hits first, and the breath whooshes out of me in a rush of pain. I clamber to my feet, struggling to inflate the pinkish-gray organ in my chest cavity with precious oxygen.

Sam hasn't forgotten or forgiven my betrayal.

And who could blame him? I falsely accused him of sexual assault.

"Sam, I'm so, so sorry about that night," I say, my gaze briefly landing on the grim reaper painted in shiny white on the gas tank of his motorcycle. "I was afraid, but that's no excuse. I shouldn't have lied. Can we meet later and talk?"

"You're sorry?" His deep, raspy baritone envelops me, scattering goose bumps across my skin. A slow smile spreads across his face. "Not as sorry as you're gonna be."

Danger. Run.

The warning rises unbidden in my mind, sending a jolt of adrenaline through me. I spin on my ballet flats and tear up the stairs into the building. I head straight for the girls' bathroom, my heart shattering. I dart into the first stall and bawl my eyes out. *Sam hates me.*

"Are you okay?" Leah asks me, concern in her soft voice. "You seem distracted today."

"I'm fine," I lie, picking at my cuticles. "Just sluggish from the move."

Meela pops my hand. "Stop that."

"Sorry," I grumble, thoroughly chastised.

Leah and Meela are cool peeps, but I'm not ready to tell them about Sam or the circumstances that led me here. No one wants a backstabber for a friend.

"Oh, okay," Leah chirps, closing her locker. "Only one more day until the weekend, then you can have some downtime."

We start down the hallway, following the throng of bodies outside. I don't recall today's lessons. I couldn't focus on anything but *him*.

I have to speak to him again. Beg for his forgiveness. We were once inseparable, facing life's harsh realities together. It'll take a while, but I know we can rebuild our friendship.

"Downtime?" Meela retorts, rolling her eyes. "Jesus, what am I going to do with you? Have I taught you nothing? I can't wait for the weekend so I can have some downtime," she says in an overtly whiny tone, "said no teenager in the history of forever."

Leah's response is to shake her head and laugh. They've been best friends since the sixth grade. I gather she's grown accustomed to Meela's spicy attitude.

"Listen, babes, pay this little peach no mind. She's still learning. Hang with me on Saturday, girly. I'm getting a new tattoo, then we can do lunch and a movie."

Meela is dressed head to toe in lime green today. Complete with lime-green eyes and a matching wig. Does this girl color coordinate every day? Way too time-consuming for me.

"Can't go," I mumble, my gaze downcast in embarrassment. "I'm strapped for cash."

I haven't mentioned my job interview to anyone. Don't want to jinx it. Even if I get the cleaning gig, splurging is completely out of the question. I'll need to penny-pinch every single cent. Money will only be spent on the necessities; nothing more.

"I got you, babe," Meela says, winking at me.

"Oh no, I can't ask you to—"

"I insist," she replies, her tone brooking no argument. "And you didn't ask, I offered."

"I'm not comfortable—"

"Just let it go," Leah interjects. "Meela never takes no for an answer. Trust me on this, you're wasting your breath."

"Well, if you insist," I concede.

She gives a decisive nod. "I very much insist."

When we reach the bottom of the stairs, an arm slips over my shoulders. I grimace, seeing the annoying boy from my science class. I had the displeasure of meeting him yesterday.

I dig an elbow into his side and shove him away. "What do you want, Sully?"

"Don't be like that, doll face," he croons. "Just making sure we're still on for eight tonight."

Double ew, he's so slimy. He asked me out once already, and I said thanks, but no thanks. Why he thinks my answer would change in less than twenty-four hours is beyond me.

"It's Zilphia, and for the second time, my answer is no!"

"Playing hard to get, huh?" he waggles his eyebrows. "Me likey."

Barf.

"Newsflash, she's not playing hard to get," Meela deadpans, rolling her eyes. "Get a clue."

Sully slips his arm over my shoulders again. "Come on, babe. I'm a really nice guy once you get to know me."

"Back the fuck up!" I snap my head toward the angry voice and see Snake barreling in our direction. "That's Sandman's."

Leah and Meela exchange "what the fuck?" glances.

"I didn't know, Snake," Sully squeaks, quickly putting several inches between us. "Honest to God."

"Get the fuck outta here." Snake takes a menacing step forward. "If it happens again, it's God's Glory for you."

Sully bolts around the block, falling twice in his haste to get away. What the heck is happening here?

"What do you mean by *'that's Sandman's'*?" I ask, frowning at him. "I don't even know anyone by that name."

"You'll see." Snake snickers and saunters down the sidewalk.

I look to my new friends for clarification, but no responses are forthcoming. "Somebody wanna tell me who this guy is?"

Meela speechless? That doesn't bode well.

"Snake's brother," Leah answers, wringing her hands.

"Kent's resident hellraiser and someone you never, ever fuck with," Meela adds. "He has a bad temper, bad rep, hell, bad everything. How in the ever-loving fuck did you get on his radar?"

I mentally rummage through my memory bank, but that name doesn't ring a bell.

"I don't know," I whine. "I swear, I never heard of him before now."

"Well, he knows you, sweetie," she quips. "Slapped his name all over that ass."

"Obviously he has me confused with someone else."

"I have to go," Leah says, then peers at me. "Watch your back. Sandman isn't right in the head."

I give an imperceptible nod, picking at my cuticles again, which earns me another pop on the hand. It's a nervous habit I've had since forever.

We maneuver through the congested sidewalk, retracing yesterday's path to the convenience store.

"What does she mean by he's not right in the head?"

"Exactly what it sounds like. There's regular crazy, medium crazy, and 'get this guy a straitjacket' crazy. Sandman falls into the last category."

Perfect. Just what I freaking need.

"Supposedly, he handles the club's *dirty* work. Hence his name," Meela whispers. "Of course, that's just a rumor. Hasn't been proven."

"He kills people!" I exclaim.

"Keep your voice down," she admonishes me. "You trying to have the Gods on our backs?"

"I'm starting to freak out," I pant, breathing becoming labored.

"Calm down, like you said, maybe he got his wires crossed." Meela points her index finger at her temple and moves it in a circular motion. "Straitjacket crazy, remember?"

Meela chatters all the way to the store, but I completely tune her out. I can't stop thinking about Sandman. How dare he lay a claim on me? I don't belong to him—psychopath, hitman, biker or not.

After buying more groceries—nothing that needs to be refrigerated—I leave the store and veer into the woods a few minutes later. Maybe Snake can arrange a meeting between me and his brother. I'd rather not talk to that arrogant asshole, but I need to get to the bottom of this situation ASAP.

Suddenly, the air shifts, causing the fine hairs on the back of my neck to rise. Something is wrong; I feel it in the marrow of my bones. I spin in a circle, but only trees greet me. *There's nothing out here. It's your imagination playing tricks on you.*

I keep walking, though my apprehension intensifies with each step deeper into the dense woodland.

"Get a grip, girl," I mumble, but quicken my pace.

The uneasy feeling won't go away. I can't put my finger on it, but something is terribly wrong. My intuition is screaming at me to get out of these woods.

A slight breeze ruffles my hair before everything goes still. I glance over my shoulder, hearing heavy thudding behind me. Two huge Dobermans bound straight toward me, and my knees nearly buckle from fear as my heart rate picks up.

I take off without a second thought.

The rule of thumb is to stand your ground when a dog charges, but that's easier said than done—especially with two dogs snapping at your ass.

Stumbling, I lose my footing and almost topple to the soft dirt. My ballet-style shoes aren't made for running. Sticks and rocks dig into the thin soles, making it a struggle to remain upright. The slippery leaves aren't helping either.

Climbing a tree is next to impossible because the branches are too damn high. Stopping is too risky anyway. Those rabid beasts will be on me in an instant. My best bet is to make it to the street and yell for help.

The pounding grows louder, but I don't dare look back. That would only slow me down. My breathing soon becomes erratic, my chest tightening painfully. *Asthma attack.* Fuck, I haven't had one in a long time.

Gasping for air, I trip over a root and crash to the earth with a resounding smack. My tote bag flies from my hand, sending my groceries, purse, and laptop scattering across the ground.

That's it. I'm dead.

The Dobermans circle me, snarling and barking. I curl into a tight ball, waiting for sharp canines to rip me apart.

God, please let me live through this.

Just then, a loud whistle rends the air, and the beasts fall back, answering their master's call. My gaze collides with blazing blue irises.

"Sam," I gasp.

He prowls toward me, his animal companions flanking him. *Beautiful.* It's not a word typically used to encompass an attractive man, but it suits him.

By no means does my chosen adjective diminish his masculinity. Samuel Hendricks is alpha male incarnate. His flaxen mane was left unfettered this morning, but now the silken strands are piled into a topknot, granting me an unimpeded view of perfectly sculpted features.

"Go," he commands the four-legged duo, and they disappear into the thicket, paws thundering through the dirt.

I swallow over the lump in my throat. "Sam—"

Hard fingers twist into my hair, yanking me to my feet.

"My name is Sandman," he growls in my face.

My eyes lock onto the patch with his biker name. In my excitement to see him this morning, I completely missed it.

"Please," I wheeze and point at my purse. "Asthma. Medicine."

He cocks his head to the side, studying me like I'm an insect under a microscope. "Maybe I let you die," he taunts, placing a feather-soft kiss on my lips. "Abandon you, like you did me."

"Please—"

"Shh." A calloused hand snakes across my mouth. "You cost me the hearing in my left ear. Tinnitus. Ever heard of it?"

I shake my head, tears spilling down my cheeks.

"It's a constant ringing in the ears." He falls quiet, a faraway look in his gaze. "I drove myself crazy thinking about hurting you… about burying my cock deep inside your body," he rasps, unbuttoning my blouse. "And now here you are."

I try again, "Sam—"

"That's not my fucking name anymore!" he bellows, slamming me into a tree.

"Sorry," I sob, fire burning a hole in my lungs. "I'm sorry."

"Sam is dead." He brandishes a knife and presses the tip into my left ear, but not enough to draw blood. "You killed him."

My blood turns to ice in my veins. "Please, no, no, no." I try to turn my head away, but his steel fingers clamp onto my jaw, holding me prisoner.

"What will you give me in return?"

"A-anything y-you w-want." I heave out each word between short inhalations.

Sandman deftly slashes the blade through my cotton bra, and warm air hits my bare chest as the fabric falls away. I cry out but keep my arms motionless at my sides, though my knee-jerk reaction is to fight. But fighting is suicide. He's bigger and stronger than me, probably faster too. I have to be smart about this. Compliance is all I have left.

"Sweet, sweet Zilphia," he murmurs, his voice dark and full of hate.

I whimper, feeling the knife's honed edge pierce between my breasts and continue downward, creating a thin red line to my belly button.

"Hurting you makes my dick rock-hard," Sandman groans, grinding his heavy erection into me. "Has anyone had you? Or is that pussy untouched?"

"Un-untouched," I stammer.

"All mine," he declares, reverently licking the blade clean. "Fear… nothing tastes more decadent than fear."

Acid churns in my stomach and climbs up my throat, making it harder to breathe. I'm at the mercy of a monster. I thought being mauled to death would be a cruel fate, but he's far worse. His eyes are blue glaciers of hate. The lines on his handsome face, once soft and welcoming, are now rigid and drawn. The kind-hearted boy I once knew is well and truly gone. He drops the knife in the sheath at his hip.

"Are you going to kill me?" I whisper, my vision blurry with tears.

The monster smirks. "Not yet."

He dips his head, his mouth closing around one nipple while his rough hand punishes the other—pinching, twisting, yanking until I'm shaking from the pain. I squeeze my hands into fists, letting him have his way. Then, without warning, he savagely sinks his teeth into the rigid peak.

"Please stop," I beg, struggling to pull oxygen into my burning lungs.

The monster sinks to his knees and yanks my denim skirt up.

My eyes widen. "What are you doing? Please don't."

His fervent blue gaze holds me captive as he slowly drags my panties to my thighs. Then, using his thumbs, he spreads my pussy lips open.

"So pretty," he murmurs as his thumb circles my clit. "The things I'm going to do to you would make the devil blush."

An involuntary moan escapes my lips. *No*. I don't want this, not from him. I focus on the long cut marring my torso, the red stark against my brown skin, reminding myself that he is a monster and my body shouldn't react to him. But it's a battle I'm quickly losing.

Sandman nestles his face between my thighs, languidly stroking his tongue over my clit. He takes his time, sipping and slurping my swollen clit.

Left to right, up and down, his tongue thoroughly explores my pussy. A warm spark flares to life in the pit of my stomach, then grows to a raging firestorm. I erupt, mentally disintegrating into a million tiny particles, reforming, then bursting apart again. My saturated walls pulsate and spasm uncontrollably, violently clenching my lower abdomen. It's white hot… the sweetest, cruelest encompassing torture imaginable.

I grasp his shoulders, my head dropping back against the tree. My eyelids flutter closed, mind rebelling, praying for this nightmare to end… hating that my body yields to his pleasure.

His hands slip over my hips and around my ass, his fingers meeting at my rimmed entrance, lightly fondling the tight ring.

"Untouched here too?"

"Yes," I whisper.

"Then I'll take this first," he rumbles thickly. "Your pain will be so delicious, sweet Zilphia."

Blinding pain sears through me as his teeth dig into my clit. It hurts so bad, my entire body shudders, every nerve ending wailing in protest. I try to scream, but I can't; my chest is too tight.

"Ow, ow, ow," I sob hysterically, snot trickling into my mouth. "Please stop."

He releases my clit and unfolds to his imposing height, seizing my throat in a crushing hold.

"That's how it felt for me that night," Sandman snarls, pressing his forehead against my tear-soaked cheek. "I was in heaven, your lips on mine, your skin under my hands. Then you tore a hole through my fucking heart. How could you betray me? How?" he roars, shaking me to the marrow of my bones. "I loved you!"

"Sam." His hand tightens around my neck. "Sandman," I correct myself, fumbling for the right words. "I meant Sandman."

"I would've done anything for you!"

"Please forgive me," I gasp between broken coughs, swiping a hand across my runny nose.

"I'm going to be your hell on Earth." His disdain-filled gaze rakes over me before he turns away and retrieves my purse. "Want this?" he taunts, presenting my inhaler like a cruel prize.

"Yes," I croak past dry lips.

The monster beckons me forward. "Then come and get it."

I take a hesitant step.

"No," he clips out. "Crawl."

Rough terrain bites into my skin as I sink to my hands and knees. Bleeding, half naked, and barely breathing, I push forward on quivering limbs—only stopping when my head bumps against his leg.

"Kiss my boots," he commands.

Having no other choice, I plant my lips on one dust-covered boot, then the other. My tears drip onto the worn leather, creating miniature puddles.

"Now lick them."

Again, I obey my tormentor, lapping the front of each boot clean. He ambles to my side and places his foot against my rib cage, roughly nudging me over.

"You belong to me. Every breath you take… every heartbeat… is mine," Sandman proclaims, brutally grinding his foot into my chest. "Don't bother going to the police. We own them. Cross me and your entire family is dead, starting with your beloved grandmother. I'm going to mindfuck you into oblivion… until you have no willpower left… until you're nothing but an empty shell."

He drops my inhaler and purse next to my head, then strolls back the way he came, whistling for his canine friends.

I scramble for the small metal canister and quickly breathe the medicine into my lungs. I lie there on the ground long after the monster is gone, digesting everything that's happened. I can't run. Even if I tried, where would I go? I'm trapped and completely under his control.

CHAPTER 19

Zilphia

I SPOT THE CLUB FROM MY WINDOW SEAT AND PULL THE BELL CORD, alerting the bus driver to stop at the next designated area.

"Thank you," I say, traipsing down the metal steps. "Have a good evening."

"You too," he chirps in a friendly tone.

I wish that were possible, but I'm too on edge. I tossed and turned all night, thoughts lingering on my ex-best friend, fearing he would be lying in wait to ambush me on my way to school.

Thankfully, he wasn't, but that didn't ease my mind. I took the long route versus cutting through the woods to play it safe. It doesn't really matter, though. Sandman can get to me anywhere in Kent at any time. I know that with absolute certainty.

Every lesson went over my head, and my lunch was left untouched, despite skipping dinner yesterday evening and breakfast this morning. I can't bring myself to eat anything.

Snake posed a whole other problem. He kept a watchful eye on me throughout the day—in the hallway, the cafeteria—and I even saw him standing outside several of my classes. No doubt reporting back to Sandman. His knowing glances and sardonic smirks sent my anxiety into a tailspin.

Meela and Leah knew something was up but didn't prod for details. My trepidation grew and turned into a full-blown panic attack by the time last period rolled around. I had severe nausea and spent the entire class ensconced in the nurse's office.

My life flashed before my eyes the instant the last bell rang. I was afraid to leave the building. Fortunately, Sandman hasn't made an appearance thus far, but he can pounce at any given moment. He made it abundantly clear that my debt must be paid in tears, blood, and pain.

The worst part is not knowing when. Will he corner me today, tomorrow, next week? Constantly looking over my shoulder is exhausting. An eye for an eye, a tooth for a tooth, the Bible says. But what about forgiveness? How much of my blood will it take to satisfy his bloodlust? I hurt him. I don't deny that, but does the punishment fit the crime?

The long cut on my torso and the teeth indentions on my clit are testaments to how ruthless he can be. Both war wounds are still tender, but it could've been a whole lot worse. He applied just enough pressure to inflict pain but not cause permanent damage or require a trip to the emergency room.

What untold horrors await me?

An icy chill skates through my veins at the thought.

June... I just have to survive him until then. I'll be gone far away from here right after graduation. I'll find somewhere to live until I can move into my dorm.

What makes you think he's going to let you go?

I ignore the subconscious warning and peruse the black, windowless fortress.

Shadows is inscribed across a chrome, parallelogram-shaped backdrop high above the entrance. The pictures online don't do this architectural beauty justice.

I press the shiny silver button on the intercom.

A woman's voice crackles through. "Hello, how may I help you?"

"My name is Zilphia Kensley. I have a five o'clock interview with Mr. Hayes."

After a subtle click, I pull open the heavy metal door and step into an aesthetically pleasing lobby. Three lantern-style spheres hang from the chrome tile ceiling. The red light bulbs inside the ornate fixtures cast a scarlet hue throughout the room. Graphic photos line the black walls—bodies tangled, mouths parted, limbs knotted in pleasure and power.

I come to a dead stop, seeing two men wearing cuts standing guard. My heart kicks into overdrive.

Relax. Maybe the owner just hired them for security.

"Have a seat." The woman behind the glass partition gestures toward a posh seating area. "Someone will be with you momentarily."

"Thank you." I sink into a butter-soft velvet armchair and place my tote bag on the stainless-steel table. I'm not going to let their presence bother me. I need this job.

After school, I changed into interview-appropriate attire—a red blazer, rose-print blouse, black pencil skirt, and ballet flats. I just hope it's enough to make a good first impression.

Fifteen minutes later, the door next to the teller window swings open, and a beautiful woman with an even more beautiful afro steps through.

"Zilphia?"

"Yes." I stand, offering a friendly smile.

"Imani Grove, Hawk's assistant. Follow me, please."

The receptionist buzzes us through the door. I match her steps, entering the main section beside her. An X-shaped stage is the focal point, with a dance pole at the base of each leg and three in the middle. Barrel chairs are arranged around it for patrons who desire a closer view. Small circular platforms are interspersed between the tables. There are two bars: one to the left and another at the back. Employees scurry to and fro, going about their daily tasks. No customers yet—the club doesn't open for another hour.

We ride the elevator to the fourth floor, making small talk until we reach a set of black, ornate doors.

She lightly knocks on the gleaming wood surface, and we enter once we're given permission. "Zilphia Kensley, here to interview for the housekeeping position."

God, he's wearing a cut too. How many of these biker guys work here?

Mr. Hayes nods at his assistant, then approaches me, a broad smile defining his deep dimples. This man is a freaking giant—at least seven feet tall. If that doesn't draw attention, his beautiful ebony-brown skin will.

"Nice to meet you, Zilphia."

"Likewise," I respond, accepting his outstretched hand. "I really appreciate this opportunity, Mr. Hayes."

"Please, call me Hawk," he says, motioning for me to sit.

Hawk settles into his chair and opens a drawer, pulling my résumé from a manila folder.

"You were a camp counselor," he remarks, scrutinizing the tiny black text.

"Yes." I force the lie past my lips. "For the past two summers."

The small untruth is necessary to meet my end goal. I'm at a significant disadvantage here, especially considering the high hourly wage being offered and the limited opportunities for career growth in the county.

The interview roster likely boasts applicants who are significantly more qualified for the position than I am. My chances are next to nil without some work history. I'm fortunate to have even made it past the screening stage. I put a random day camp near my old neighborhood on my résumé.

Savannah agreed to be my pretend supervisor. I called her on a whim since she's the least catty among my former clique. Moreover, she's a consummate manipulator and could convince a priest to rethink his vows, which makes her perfect for the task.

I could've asked Meela to participate in my scheme, but I prefer someone with a Texas area code and Southern twang for optimum effect. Savannah didn't agree to help me out of the kindness of her heart. In addition to her other *skill set*, she's an unrepentant gossipmonger and craves recognition. I'm sure she told everyone we know about the *favor* she's doing for me by now and painted herself as a hero.

"Tell me about your time there."

"Being a camp counselor was a very rewarding experience," I respond with confidence. "My responsibilities included activity planning, chaperoning field trips, and ensuring the children's safety. This role taught me patience, how to think on my feet, and how to handle conflict. Also, cleaning the facility, equipment, and grounds throughout the day was an essential part of my duties, as outlined on my résumé."

Now to drive it home. "I'm fully confident in my ability to successfully perform the job functions listed for this position."

Bam! Just how I practiced in the mirror.

Hawk asks a few more standard interview questions and jots down my responses.

"Are you available Tuesday through Friday, six to midnight?"

"Yes," I answer enthusiastically. "That schedule works perfectly for me."

"The weekend schedule is full, but I may need you to cover a shift occasionally. Is that something you can do?"

"Absolutely, I have no problem working overtime," I assure him. "I'll be here whenever you need me."

"Good. Did you bring your driver's license and high school diploma?"

Busted.

I drop my gaze to my clutched hands. "I haven't graduated yet."

"Excuse me?" Hawk snaps, his mouth twisting into a frown. "The qualifications for the job were discussed with you during the screening."

"I just wanted a fair chance at this wonderful opportunity. Please accept my apology for being dishonest. I am eighteen, though."

"Doesn't matter, you're still a high school student." Hawk anchors his elbows on the desk and steeples his fingers, his dark-brown eyes glittering with anger. "I don't appreciate having my time wasted."

"Please give me a chance," I beg, a desperate edge in my voice. "You won't regret it, and I promise to be the best employee you've ever had."

He stands. "My hands are tied."

"Put me to work right now." I lift my chin. "Let me prove myself to you."

He stares a moment longer, unreadable. "Impress me tonight," he says finally, "and maybe I'll forget you lied."

My breath catches. "Thank you. You won't regret this."

I've been on the move nonstop for the last three hours. My body aches from all the bending, scrubbing, lifting, and hauling. Shadows is more or less a brothel. I'm not sure what I was expecting, but it definitely wasn't refilling condom bowls, changing semen-stained sheets, and discarding drug paraphernalia. But here we are.

The second and third floors are for *private* entertainment. I thought that meant birthday celebrations, bachelor parties, and horny men paying extra for butt-naked lap dances. I was way off the mark. Now I understand Hawk's reluctance to hire a high school student. There are twenty rooms total—ten per floor—each with a king-sized bed, nightstand, seating area, dance pole, and bathroom.

Hawk delivered me to Muriel, the cleaning crew lead. I was issued a black polo shirt with the club's logo embroidered on the left side and tan pants. After changing into uniform, I stored my belongings in a locker and was given a two-way radio. Muriel showed me the ropes and gave me the rundown, especially the rule about no dallying with customers.

Fraternizing is strictly prohibited and means immediate termination. Even friendly conversation is frowned upon. Basically, I'm to keep my legs and my mouth shut. Those duties fall to the strippers. Not a problem. I have no intention of engaging in any of it.

The women I've encountered seemed like willing participants, so who am I to judge? In any case, the pros outweigh the cons. Employees get one free meal per shift. I grabbed a fried chicken sandwich from the bar during my thirty-minute break, and it was pretty good. The schedule also means less time spent in the Double Dragon's Lair. That's a win on its own.

The only real problem is getting home. Buses stop running before midnight, and taxis are too expensive. Guess that means I'll be walking home. Roughly five miles—not ideal, but doable. But a teenage girl walking alone that late at night? Disaster waiting to happen. No use dwelling on it. If I get the job, I'll pick up pepper spray and a pocketknife tomorrow.

I refocus, gliding the steam mop over the coal-colored hardwood floors. Once finished, I step into the hall and stow the mop on the cleaning cart. I unclip the radio from my pants and push the talk button. "Room sixteen done."

"You're fast," comes the reply. "Head to room nine."

I smile and press the talk button again. "Fast *and* efficient."

As I'm about to reach down for the door stopper, I spot the air freshener on the nightstand.

"Oh, almost forgot." I secure the radio at my hip and go back into the room.

"Sucks to be you."

I whirl around, instantly recognizing the smug voice. Snake casually leans a shoulder against the doorframe, arms crossed.

"What are you doing here?" I snap, clasping the air freshener to my chest. *Please don't tell me he works here too. Or maybe he's a customer?*

"You honestly don't know." Snake bursts out laughing, shaking his head. "He's going to love this."

I know the "he" Snake is referring to.

"What exactly should I know?"

Snake smirks and walks away. I timidly peek into the hallway, scouting left then right. He's gone. I blow out a relieved breath and move on to the next room. I pull on a pair of latex gloves and clean the bathroom first, then strip the mattress and replace the bedding.

Snake and Sandman can't actually be blood-related brothers. There's not even the slightest resemblance between them, except both are extremely good-looking assholes.

I hear a soft click and pivot on my heel, expecting to see Snake. My gaze clashes with blazing blue instead. I drop the spray bottle and cleaning cloth, fear loosening my grip. Sandman looms in front of the only escape route… imposing… frightening… my worst nightmare.

"Take off your clothes." The growled demand ices my veins.

"P-please," I stammer, hugging my lower belly in a protective embrace. "I'm working."

"My father owns this place," he states, stalking toward me. "And I say it's time for a break."

"Father?" I question, backpedaling around the table. "I thought he died."

"Hell, me too, but on the third day, the motherfucker rose from the dead," Sandman retorts sarcastically. "It's a goddamn miracle."

He flips the table, shattering the chrome glass top. I scream, plastering myself against the wall.

"Do I need to undress you myself?" he asks softly, setting my nerves on edge.

I shake my head and begin slowly peeling away my clothes, unshed tears stinging my corneas. Shoes, pants, shirt—leaving me in my matching pink bra and panty set.

I fix my gaze on the monster's boots… shivering… helpless… entirely at his mercy.

We remain still, no words spoken, his harsh breathing the only sound in the room. I wait on pins and needles, my arms dangling listlessly at my sides.

"The rest," Sandman rasps, charged passion resonating in his gravelly baritone.

I lift my head and the tears flow, distorting his hulking physique into a watery blur.

"Now!" he shouts, startling me into compliance.

“Okay,” I sob, unhooking my bra with trembling fingers.

The lace material slips to the floor. Next, I push my panties down my legs, laying myself bare to him. I cross my forearm over my breasts and place a hand between my legs, instinctively trying to cover my nudity.

“No,” Sandman murmurs, his stone gaze promising dark retribution. “Show me.”

I let my arms fall and seal my eyelids shut, spilling more salty rivulets down my face.

“Look at me!” Sandman bellows, his hand latching onto my throat with unyielding force.

Panicked, I grasp onto his wrist with both hands in a vain effort to ease his crippling hold.

“You will never know peace again.” His grip tightens, completely blocking air circulation.

Within seconds, burning pressure claws through my chest. I feel myself slipping away; my world growing dimmer with each fleeting heartbeat. Strangulation is personal—a slow, agonizing induction to the afterlife.

I can't die. Not like this.

My oxygen-deprived mind races, ruminating on the past, present, and what could have been. Specifically, the catastrophic decision that led to this very moment—the day my cowardice resulted in irreparable damage to my beloved best friend.

I want him back. *My Sam.* My protector, my keeper of secrets, my shoulder to cry on.

But he's gone forever, replaced by this sadistic monster. I study his granite features—the sneer twisting his full, beautiful lips, the throbbing vein on his right temple, the maniacal elation gleaming in his cornflower-blue orbs. He's enjoying choking the life from me. His grip loosens, and air immediately fills my deflated lungs… then he squeezes again.

Over and over.

Taking me to death's door, then pulling me back at the last possible second.

After what seems like an eternity, he releases me. I wilt to the floor, coughing and gasping for breath. He grabs a chair and drags it in front of the dance pole, heavy boots crunching along the broken glass.

“Dance,” he commands, sprawling in the high-back chair.

I clamber to unsteady legs, shuddering sobs ripping through my naked body. I'm in his territory. *The Gods' Territory*. There's no use in calling out for help. Not here, not anywhere. It's pointless and highly dangerous. Sandman is a ticking time bomb. One wrong move and I'm done for.

I stagger toward the dance pole, skirting the shards of broken glass.

"No!" he booms, freezing me to the spot. "Walk through the glass."

I venture forward, body shaking, cautiously placing one foot in front of the other. Mind whirling. Heart thundering. Each step more nerve-racking than the last.

A stabbing pain falters my steps. I cry out, coming to a standstill.

"Keep walking!"

Tears streaming down my face, I limp the short distance to the dance pole, blood painting a trail behind me. My hand wraps around the cool metal—then I hesitate. I don't know what to do.

Sandman opens his cut, revealing the gun stashed in his shoulder holster. The silent threat is loud. *Obey or suffer the consequences.*

"Dance," he growls, freeing his intimidating length. "And make it sexy."

I inhale a quivering breath and circle the pole, awkwardly fondling my nipple. Sandman caresses his erection in slow, deliberate strokes, peering at me with unrestrained lust in his eyes.

Does he plan to just watch, or will he take it further?

He won't be gentle.

My first time is supposed to be special. I want loving kisses and warm embraces.

This afflicted man, whose raw desire is more suffocating than his choke-hold, will only give me pain and scorn. I broke him, and now he plans to break me in turn. Karma is hell on wheels.

Having no clue what to do next, I try to remember moves from my majorette days. I never imagined that knowledge would be the difference between life and death. I execute a scorpion and split combo, hoping it'll be enough.

"Come 'ere," Sandman demands.

I trudge over to him, heart thudding rapidly in my chest, praying I survive the night in one piece. He seizes my waist with strong fingers and pulls me between his spread thighs, his lengthy erection brushing against my leg.

"I want to kill you, but I can't," he states, frustration mirrored in his words. "Why can't I kill you?"

He sweeps his tongue along the cut marring my torso. Then he brandishes his knife and reopens my healing skin. I whimper but force myself to stay still. Attempting to run will only fuel his wrath.

"There, much better," Sandman mumbles, smearing red across my belly. "So much fucking better." He trails his bloody hands up my rib cage and pinches my nipples. "That move you did with your leg, what's it called?"

"Scorpion," I whisper.

"Do it again," he orders, sheathing the knife at his hip.

I shift into position, grabbing my right ankle and stretching my leg taut behind my back, holding my foot directly over my head.

"Don't move." He drops to his knees and buries his face in my folds.

I tense. "Please don't bite me."

He doesn't respond. Instead, he clasps the area just below my ass and pushes his tongue deep inside my body. His tongue moves like waves in an ocean, stroking every nerve ending to awareness. Then he amplifies the pleasure tenfold, licking his way to my hypersensitive clit before sealing his lips around the swollen flesh. He teases me with slow caresses, gliding his tongue back and forth over my sweet spot.

I gnaw on my bottom lip, my eyelids fluttering shut, as heat pools in my lower abdomen. I'm defeated. My mind revolts while my body falls victim to his mouth. I hate it so fucking much—that this monster can play me like a finely tuned instrument.

"I can't stay like this for much longer," I gasp, struggling to remain in position.

His fingernails burrow into my skin, a clear warning not to move. My muscles are going to give out at any moment.

He grips me tighter, lifting me to the tips of my toes.

"Sandman, please…"

The plea dies on my lips as I reach climax, coming so hard my body seizes, raw sensations surging through me like an electric current. I release my leg and topple over his shoulder in a boneless heap, too spent to stand on my own. But he doesn't stop—he laps and nips at my clit, drawing another mind-shattering orgasm from me.

I twist my fingers into his cut, broken sounds spilling from my throat, my core humming with ecstasy.

Before I can come down from my high, he shoves to his feet and carries me into the bathroom. Once inside, he lowers me into the bathtub.

What's next on his torture list? Several possibilities filter through my mind, waterboarding at the forefront. It takes everything in me not to throw myself at his feet and beg him to stop, but I keep my mouth sealed. Any compassion he once had is gone—black hatred replaced it long ago.

Sandman retrieves a small bottle from inside his cut and grudgingly thrusts it into my hand. *Honeysuckle Dreams Bodywash*. It's my favorite, but too pricy for my budget now. I haven't used it in months. After three years, he still remembers.

"Shower."

"W-what?" I stammer.

He turns and sits on the toilet. "You heard me, and leave the shower curtain open."

Another game… another level of Sandman's hell. I twist the valves and let the water run until it's nearly scalding before pulling the lever on the showerhead.

"I need a washcloth," I say monotonously.

"Make it quick," Sandman demands, throwing one at me.

I turn on the shower and step under the spray, trying my best to ignore his presence. Bloody suds cascade down my legs and vanish into the drain. As I glide the soapy washcloth over my breasts, a rumbling growl rends the compact space, kicking my heart into overdrive. His need is tangible, caressing my heated flesh like a physical touch. It stifles the air, mingling with the rising steam.

"Face me."

I follow his command, hesitation clinging to every movement. A sharp breath catches in my throat when I see the cell phone aimed straight at me. He's recording me. My fingers itch to pull the shower curtain closed.

What does he plan to do with the footage? Post it online? Sell it?

"Spread your legs and wash your pussy," he mutters huskily, palming the huge tent at his crotch.

"Please don't record me," I say, my voice small and thin.

"Wash!" Sandman thunders.

I coast the fluffy white cotton between my thighs, tears pouring unchecked down my cheeks. He records, blazing irises cutting a path through the thick steam. He looks almost unearthly, like a fallen angel.

"Enough." Sandman stands, stowing his cell phone in his back pocket. "Go lie on the bed."

This is it. He's going to take my virginity—violate me in the worst way possible.

I hobble from the bathroom, favoring my right leg, dripping puddles of water onto the floor in my wake.

Sandman is a walking tornado at my back.

"On your stomach," he instructs me.

I climb on the bed and lie facing the wall, listening to him undress. Blood swooshes in my ears and more tears come. This isn't real. I'm home, asleep in my bed, having a bad dream.

No, this is real, Zilphia.

"I don't want to lose my virginity like this," I say more to myself than to him.

Words won't sway him. He craves vengeance and not even an extinction-level event is going to stop him from achieving it. The mattress dips as he straddles me, his rock-hard length sliding against my bottom. My spine snaps straight, my hands clutching the sheets in a death grip. A familiar sting just below my nape jolts me into action.

"No, please don't cut me again!" I wail, thrashing beneath him.

The knife's tip being pressed against my temple stills me. "Move again and I will gut you like a fish."

"I'm sorry," I sob, bawling my eyes out. "I'll keep still."

"Your body is my canvas and I'm going to paint it bloody red," Sandman proclaims, then commences his torture, reciting each letter he carves down my spine. "L, Y, I, N, G, S, L, U, T. A fitting moniker for you." I recoil at his derisive laughter. "You're a lying slut, aren't you?" He latches onto my nape, digging nails into my flesh. "Say it."

"I'm a lying slut!" I cry out, wincing against the pain.

His big body covers mine, pressing me into the mattress. "I'm not going to take your virginity tonight," he rasps in my ear. "I'm going to take it when you least expect it. I want you afraid every fucking second, not knowing when I'm going to claim that sweet little cherry." I feel his dick nudging at my puckered opening. "But I am going to take this."

Sandman thrusts forward, savagely ripping into my rimmed entrance. I scream the loudest I've ever screamed in my entire life, the impact sending a bone-jarring jolt through my body. He grunts and snarls, hips bucking wildly against me, but he's too big for my virgin muscles.

"Fuck," Sandman hisses, pushing to his knees. "Too tight."

I look back, watching in horror as he smears my blood all over his dick.

"Please, no more," I croak, barely able to speak. "I'll give you whatever you want."

"Whatever I want, huh?"

"Yes." I let my head fall onto the pillow, fatigue overpowering me.

"Tempting offer," Sandman states, sparking hope in my chest. "There is something I want above all else."

"What?"

"Your pain," Sandman growls before stabbing his erection through my muscular ring.

He violently rocks into me until he's fully seated. I wail in agony, helpless under his pressing weight.

My former confidant is well and truly gone—and the blame falls on my shoulders. I created the perfect storm, and now I'm stuck in the middle of it.

"I know everything about you," he taunts, slamming against my rectum with so much force my vision doubles. "Your father's downfall. Losing your house. The tables have turned, and this time, it's you who's going to get burned."

I black out again and again, my body's only defense against his brutal onslaught. It's never-ending. My screams cease, vocal cords too inflamed and swollen to emit sound. The sick rhythm of blood and flesh, his resounding grunts, and my broken mewls make for a dark symphony.

"Fuck yes!" Sandman bellows, his hips whipping against me at rapid speed.

Then it's finally over. He pulls free from my traumatized body and lies down beside me.

"Meet me in the lobby after your shift," he orders, his tone brooking no argument. "Oh, by the way, you're hired. Congratulations."

He told Hawk to give me the job—easier to keep tabs on me.

"This is just the beginning," he murmurs, planting lingering kisses along my shoulder. "We're going to have so much fun."

CHAPTER 20

Zilphia

"YEAH, ZEUS OWNS SHADOWS AND A LOT OF OTHER BUSINESSES around here," Meela states, spearing a cherry tomato with her fork and popping it into her mouth. "Draco, Sandman, and Snake are heirs to the God dynasty."

"So they're actually brothers, as in blood related?"

"Yep, just different mothers. Why didn't you tell me about your interview? I would've warned you."

"Didn't want to jinx it," I mutter, pouring more marinara sauce onto my pizza fries.

She folds her arms across the table, regarding me contemplatively. "What happened last night? Why does Sandman have it out for you?"

"I'd rather not talk about it," I say, averting my gaze.

"That's cool." Meela raises her empty cup, signaling our waitress for a refill. "I'm all ears when you're ready to talk."

I manage a thin smile. "Appreciate it."

"Here you are." The waitress hands Meela a raspberry lemonade.

"Thanks."

"You're welcome." After ensuring we don't need anything else, she moves on to the next table.

"Look on the bright side," Meela chirps, resuming our conversation. "The pay is good and you're off on weekends."

With Sandman, there is no bright side, only pain and darkness. I don't tell her that, though, electing to change the subject instead.

"What's God's Glory?" I ask.

"Huh?" Confusion knits her eyebrows. "I'm not following."

"Snake mentioned something about *God's Glory* the other day." It can't be good, whatever it is. It had Sully scared shitless. "Remember?"

"Oh yeah." Meela nods in understanding. "I'll tell you what I've heard, but it's all rumors and speculation." She pushes her plate back and gives me her undivided attention. "Supposedly, it's where the Gods punish their enemies and settle disputes among themselves."

"So it's a place?"

She shrugs. "Don't know."

"What happens there?"

"God's Wrath," she answers, her voice low and grave. "Either you come out broken… or you don't come out at all. Beaten, stomped, fucked up beyond repair."

"That's horrible," I whisper, wringing my hands underneath the table. "No one ever goes to the cops?"

"Probably, but they're most likely dead now. Going to the cops is a death sentence as far as the Gods are concerned. God's Eye sees all."

"God's Eye?"

"Yeah, nothing happens in Kent without the Gods finding out."

God's Glory? God's Wrath? God's Eye? This is all too freaking much.

I shouldn't have asked. There's a reason why ignorance is bliss. I have enough to worry about as it is. Damn my curiosity.

Meela refocuses on her buffalo chicken salad, digging in with gusto. I bite into a pepperoni, but I might as well be chewing cardboard. I'm too tense to enjoy my food.

"Quit fidgeting," Meela reprimands, rolling her eyes. "You gotta hernia or something? And your voice sounds a little hoarse too."

"No, my butt cheek itches, and I slept with the fan blowing on me, for your information," I lie and tilt my head sideways. "Wanna scratch it for me?"

"Bitch," Meela mutters, flipping me the bird.

I actually forgot about our plans today, but got my ass up when she texted me. I didn't want to stay in bed all day with my dismal thoughts. I wanted to soak in her sassy energy, and she did not disappoint. My mood instantly improved in her presence.

"And what's with your hair?" she purses her lips, perusing my lopsided ponytail. "No offense, but it's a raggedy mess. I wasn't going to say anything, but you can't be hanging with me looking all bummish. You couldn't gel down those edges and style your hair in a cute little bun?"

My hair got wet last night and shriveled into a puff ball. By the time Sandman took me home, I was too exhausted and riddled with pain to function. Detangling my hair or even putting on a bonnet were the last things on my mind.

"Subtlety obviously isn't your middle name," I say dryly.

"Do you want a friend who keeps it real or a *fake* friend who smiles in your face and talks shit behind your back?" Meela cocks an eyebrow.

I think about my old *fake* friends—Claudette, Phyllis, and Savannah. Yeah, I don't need those types of people in my life. Sandman is enough to contend with.

"I can do your hair next Saturday," she offers. "I'm enrolling in cosmetology school after I graduate, and practice makes perfect."

So there's a silver lining to Sandman's punishment after all. Free hairdo.

"How many tattoos do you have?"

We arrived at Angry Dragon Ink, Draco's tattoo shop, twenty minutes ago. He's not here, but a dozen or so of his brethren are. Some are employees, and others are just hanging out. I try my best to ignore them, which isn't an easy feat. At least I had a heads up this time. The dragon-themed furnishings are breathtaking, particularly the murals on the ceiling and walls. It's giving majestic, medieval-times vibes.

"Five and counting," Meela answers proudly, flipping through the tattoo magazine on her lap.

We're waiting in a roped-off area at the front of the shop.

"Piercings?"

"Sixteen."

I whistle low. "Damn, that's a lot."

"And I'm still not done, girlie."

"Seriously?" I ask incredulously.

"Not even close." Meela grins. "Hey, I have an idea."

"Well, let's hear it."

"You should get a piercing today," she announces, waggling her orange eyebrows—today's featured color scheme. "Maybe a little ink too."

I scoff. "Chile, my momma would flip her lid."

"Aren't you eighteen?"

"Well, yeah, but that doesn't matter to her."

"Listen, you're an adult, babe," Meela says. "Anyway, you can get something small and discreet. She doesn't have to know."

"I'll think about it." I have zero control over my life. Getting a tattoo or piercing would give me some semblance of power. "What are you getting?"

"Garter belt on my right thigh. Wanna see?"

"Sure." Meela passes me her cell phone. "Whoa, that is hot," I gush, zooming in on the picture.

"Damn, girl, you still alive?" Snake chuckles, plopping down in the chair next to me. "I thought you were dead for sure."

Fuck. Where the hell did he come from?

He throws an arm around my shoulders. "Sandman fucked you up something good. You were screaming your goddamn head off."

"Leave me alone," I hiss, moving to the chair furthest from him.

"Watch this one," he says to Meela. "She'll stab you in the back when you least expect it."

Oh no, he's going to tell her what I did.

"Zilphia already told me everything, so go shit on someone else's day," she quips, crossing her arms.

Meela lied for me. She doesn't even know the whole story but still came to my defense.

"You have the worst taste in friends," Snake tsks, shaking his head before looking back at me. "You know Leah's brother is a rapist and murderer, right?"

I want to blurt out, "So is your brother," but I think better of it.

"Stop spreading your lies," Meela snaps at him.

"Leah's brother and my sister were friends," Snake continues, ignoring her. "He wanted more, but she didn't. One day he snapped, raped her, and stabbed her sixty-seven times."

My heart breaks for his sister and breaks for him too. I can't imagine losing a beloved family member or friend under such horrific circumstances. That's got to change a person. Snake's hatred makes perfect sense now, though it's misplaced. Leah shouldn't suffer for her brother's alleged crime, guilty or not.

"That's not true!" Meela shouts.

"Then where the fuck is he, huh?" Snake shouts back at her, bounding to his feet. "Why did he run?"

"He didn't run." Meela is standing now too, and suddenly they're nose-to-nose. "He's dead, you moron. Whoever killed your sister killed him too."

Some avidly watch the heated argument unfold, while others go about their day, but no one steps forward to intervene. I'm afraid they're going to start swinging on each other any moment now.

"Then where's his fucking body? Why would the killer leave my sister's body but take his?" Snake questions. "His father is hiding him, and Leah knows where."

"To throw the cops off their trail, duh. Corey would've never hurt your sister," Meela argues passionately. "He loved her."

"Don't you fucking say that!" he rages, shaking her violently. "That sick fuck didn't love my sister. He was obsessed with her."

"I know what this is really about." Meela smirks, propping her hands on her curvy hips. "You're the one who's *obsessed*."

"What the fuck are you talking about?" Snake growls.

"Leah," she responds, one eyebrow arching with practiced flair. "I see the way you look at her. You want her bad."

Shit, I didn't see that revelation coming.

Snake shoves her hard, and she crashes to the floor. "Shut your fucking mouth!"

"Asshole!" Meela yells, scrambling to her feet.

I rush between them. "Enough."

"Jigsaw is the only reason you haven't been put in your place, but your day is coming," Snake threatens before storming out the door.

CHAPTER 21

Three and a half years ago

SAM

"OKAY, SAM, WHICH COLOR?" ZILPHIA ASKS ME, HOLDING UP TWO small bottles.

We just finished watching the first movie in a slasher trilogy. Not my thing, but it was her turn to choose the movie tonight. I straighten from my slouched position on the sofa to get a better look.

"Definitely the pink nail polish," I answer her. "It suits you."

"It's fuchsia, not pink," she corrects me.

I shrug. "Looks pink to me."

Zilphia rolls her eyes. "You're such a boy."

"Technically, I'm a man," I remark proudly.

"Man? I hate to burst your delusional little bubble, but you're seventeen," she deadpans. "Legally you're still a child."

"Yeah, but I'm closer to being an adult, which makes me more adult than child," I state matter-of-factly.

"Girls mature faster than boys, so technically—" Zilphia makes air quotations, throwing the word I used back at me "—I'll become an adult before you."

I scoff. "That's some made-up bullshit."

"No, it isn't," she counters. "It's scientifically proven."

"Science isn't always right."

"Whatever you say." Zilphia props her foot on the table and begins polishing her big toe.

"I can do that for you," I offer, motioning for her to give me the bottle.

"You? Polish my toenails?" Zilphia shakes her head. "Absolutely not. You'll probably make it all clumpy and ugly."

"I won't," I say. "I'm a nail polish pro."

"Well, if you insist." She places the bottle in my outstretched hand. "Two coats, please."

"Yes, ma'am." I move to the floor and sit cross-legged at her feet.

Zilphia plucks the bowl of candy off the table and starts the next movie. I swallow hard, my blood swooshing in my ears. Finally, I get to touch them—her beautiful, flawless feet. I place a tiny foot on my knee, holding on a little longer than necessary. It's anatomical perfection—suckable toes, accentuated arch, and feather soft.

My dick stirs, extending to full mast. Luckily, the tent in my cargo shorts is hidden from her view in this position. I meticulously stroke the brush over each toenail, taking extra care not to get polish on her skin.

"Go out the front door, stupid!" Zilphia yells at the television. "The killer is going to get you! Don't run upstairs! Okay, you're done, you're done."

She's completely engrossed in the movie, not paying any attention to me. Now is my chance. I lower my head, blowing on her toenails until my nose is only a hairbreadth from her foot. I inhale her scent into my lungs. Sunshine mixed with floral undertones.

"Sam, are you sniffing my foot?" Zilphia asks, amusement clear in her voice.

"N-no," I lie, stammering like an idiot. "I-I w-was blowing your toenails to dry the polish faster."

"You were." She laughs, ruffling my hair. "Do you have a foot fetish?"

"I have to go." I leap to my feet and haul ass out of the tree house.

"Sam, come back," Zilphia calls after me. "I was only joking, and what about the top coat? You're not even done."

CHAPTER 22

Present

SANDMAN

Zilphia. Zilphia. Zilphia. That fucking girl has been stomping around in my subconsciousness nonstop all goddamn day. I'm a junkie for her pain. Nothing has ever gotten my dick harder. Her anguished screams and tearful pleas sent me into a frenzy. I completely spiraled, losing myself in her tantalizing fear.

Terrorizing her was euphoric, better than busting deep inside some gushing pussy. But raping her… that was chef's kiss. Zilphia's delicious virgin ass choked my cock almost painfully, her strained muscles clinging to me with every thrust.

I need another fix. Just a small hit. A grunt rumbles past my lips. *Who the fuck am I kidding?* A small hit won't do it for me. I want to overdose on her.

Seeing her beautiful face for the first time after three long years was a kick to the gut. Gone is her girlhood glow, replaced with womanly allure. Granted, her slender frame hasn't changed much over the years, but there's noticeably more curve to her ass and tits. The most discernible difference is her lean facial features, which were once slightly rounded.

Sam, pathetic bastard that he is, immediately wanted to gather her in his arms and forgive her deceit. Sandman, on the other hand, had no such sentiments. He wanted to fuck and butcher her all at once. I'll be doing the former quite often. The latter...well, I haven't decided yet. I can't hurt her anymore if she's dead.

I veer my motorcycle left, turning onto her street. It's a little past one in the morning. Zilphia spent the day with Meela and arrived home not too long ago. A prospect was on her tail the entire time, periodically updating me on her activities. I park and dismount, dropping my helmet on the seat before heading toward the house. I reach into my cut and pull my phone from the inner pocket, my dick stirring in anticipation.

Me: Open the door.

I gave Zilphia a cell phone last night with strict instructions to answer my texts and calls, no matter the time or place. She can't afford to reactivate her own service with less than nine bucks in her bank account. *The fucking irony.* I made it my business to know everything about her. The easier to control my prey.

The door eases open, revealing my obsession. Her terror-stricken eyes lock on me, tugging a smile on my lips. I clear the porch steps, my possessive gaze taking in her oversized T-shirt and bare legs. I wonder if she's wearing shorts underneath. I'll find out soon enough. She steps back to let me in, then quietly pushes the door shut with a soft click.

I cut my gaze to the living room. "Get on the sofa."

"Not here," she whispers, still facing the door. "Someone could come down."

I'm on her in a flash, plastering her against the wooden surface. "One: You fucking look at me when you're talking to me." I seize her ponytail and yank her head back. "Two: When I tell you to do something, you better goddamn do it. Got it?"

"Y-yes," she whimpers.

"I tell you to get butt naked and take a stroll down the street," I say, running my nose along her jaw, "what you doing?"

"I'm going to do it," she answers, a hitch in her trembling voice.

"What's that?" I tighten my hold in her hair. "Couldn't hear you."

She winces. "I'm getting naked and taking a stroll down the street."

"Glad we're on the same page." I snake my free hand under her T-shirt to put my curiosity to rest.

Panties, no shorts.

I lightly stroke her clit through the cotton material. "You have a fat clit, Zilphia," I murmur, grinding my erection against her ass. "Anyone ever taste it?"

"Yes."

"Who?" I growl, raw jealousy sinking sharp talons into me.

"Redmond," she answers.

"Ended up with that piece of shit after all, huh?" Red-hot rage boils my blood. "And he never fucked you?" I ask skeptically.

I just might have to find that motherfucker and gut him. The thought of another person knowing how she tastes doesn't sit right with me. We were supposed to be each other's first and last everything, but she ruined that possibility for us.

I lost my virginity to a goddamn twinkie instead. The experience was underwhelming, but that didn't stop me from sowing my wild oats. Being the son of the great Zeus got me limitless pussy on demand. If I'm being honest, sex doesn't hold the same appeal for me it once did.

That is, until *she* came crashing back into my life. I want nothing more than to fuck her tight virgin cunt, but first she has to suffer.

"No," Zilphia replies. "My mother wouldn't allow it."

"Of course not," I retort. "I'm going to take a guess and say she told you to seduce him… tempt him with a few touches here and there, but not to give up the goods. No doubt she was pimping you out for self-serving purposes and you let her. Too bad becoming destitute put a wrench in her plans. Am I right?"

"I had no choice," she explains.

"You're fucking pathetic," I snarl, hauling her into the living room, my hand still tangled in her silky curls.

"Sandman, please don't fuck me there again."

"I'm not," I shove her onto the sofa and sink to my knees. "I have something else in mind."

"What?" she asks, her voice catching in her throat.

I latch onto her legs and jerk her forward, making her fall back against the cushions. "This," I say, brushing my fingertips over her concealed pussy.

"No."

"Yes." I tug her panties down her legs and toss the scrap of cotton onto the floor.

"Please," she whispers. "I don't want to lose my virginity like this."

"We don't get everything we want, Zilphia. You of all people should know that." I position my face right at her slick opening and stare at her glistening pink cunt.

So pretty.

My mouth waters. The moon shines in through a gap in the curtains, granting me a clear view of her pussy. I spread her legs further apart and dip my greedy tongue into her sweet nectar, thoroughly exploring every slope and curve. I'm fucking famished for her.

She wrecked me, yet I want her with a hunger more profound than ever before.

I clasp onto her supple thigh with one hand and hurriedly free my throbbing length with the other. Then my mouth closes over her clit, my tongue swirling around the swollen flesh, teasing and sucking, while my hand coasts along my cock.

Zilphia's arms fly above her head, her hands gripping the sofa cushions, soft, husky moans spilling from her lips. Tears leave glittering trails on her cheeks. She doesn't want this, but she can't control her body's natural response. She's completely under my control.

"Oh God," Zilphia gasps, her body writhing beneath my mouth.

I replace my tongue with my fingers and bury my nose at her convulsing entrance, needing to breathe her orgasm into my body. My mind goes completely blank as her sweet, musky scent overloads my senses. I've never smelled anything more decadent in my entire existence.

It's the most powerful high there is.

Every molecule in my body hums, alive with need. I delve my tongue into her sopping hole, fervently lapping her creamy elixir. Once I've had my fill, I pull back and lift her ankles to my shoulders.

"I could eat you for hours," I rasp, skimming my fingers through her downy pubic hairs.

"Please don't do this," she quietly weeps, her sorrowful eyes pleading with me.

"No more begging, Zilphia." I kiss the heel of her left foot. I've always had an obsession with her feet.

I push into her, but just the tip.

My. Fucking. God.

She feels like warm silk. I still, trembling with the effort not to tear through her virgin walls. I'm not ready to fuck her just yet. The goal is to frighten her, even though I have to torture myself in the process.

"I'm not on birth control," she says, desperation dilating her pupils.

The thought of Zilphia's belly swollen with our baby draws my balls taut. *What the fuck is wrong with me?* I dispel the enticing image from my mind.

"Don't care." I shackle my hand around her ankle and bring her foot to my mouth, nipping and kissing right where the arch dips. "You have the sexiest feet I've ever seen."

She inhales a sharp breath, saucer-wide gaze watching my every move.

"Soon, I'm going to fuck these feet," I announce, rubbing my cheek against her heel.

"You can't come inside me."

"Can't?" I rasp. "Who's going to stop me?" I sweep my tongue up her delicate sole and suckle each exquisite toe.

I begin slowly moving my hips in short, jerky thrusts. *Fuck, fuck, fuck.* It's so fucking good. No girl should have this much power between her thighs. Everything about her is addictive. This is only the tip. How would it feel to be fully embedded in her heat? I'll probably lose what little sanity I have left. Goddamn her, and goddamn her good pussy.

Zilphia tenses with every advancing thrust, bracing for the loss of her virginity. I take sick delight in her distress, snapping my hips faster. Nothing compares to this—not killing, not even riding my motorcycle down an empty highway on a bright, sunny day. Sweat cascades down my bunching muscles, molding my clothes to my body like a second skin.

I turn to her other foot, kissing, sucking, and licking to my heart's content. If this is hell, fuck it, give me a first-row seat every day for the rest of my life.

I groan, balls shuddering violently.

"I'm about to come." I throw my head back, pumping my seed into her. "Fucking Christ."

I rest my forehead on her ankle, catching my breath. *She's mine.* I'm never letting her go now. Our fates became intertwined the second she found me hiding in her tree house.

I push to my feet and shove my dick back into my jeans. "Show me where you sleep."

Zilphia plucks her panties off the floor and hurries through a door near the kitchen entrance. I follow her down the stairs, pulling the door shut behind me.

I peruse her sleeping quarters. "Poetic justice at its finest."

Barely any moving space, musty odor, and a dilapidated air mattress to lay her head at night—this is exactly what she deserves.

"I have a surprise for you." I take out my cell phone and go to my photos.

She accepts it with a shaky hand, blanching at the still image on the screen.

"Keep scrolling, there are tons more."

"Did you take these?" she asks, frantically swiping through the pictures.

"No." I snatch my cell phone from her grasp and stash it in my back pocket. "The Gods have a far reach. One phone call and he's dead within sixty minutes."

"Please don't," she begs me.

"Why?" I question, tilting my head to the side. "You hate each other."

"He's still my brother."

"So that slimy motherfucker gets your loyalty, but I got a knife in the fucking back." I clamp my hand around her jaw and shove her onto the air mattress. "Get on your fucking knees." I pull my cock free, slapping her hard across the face with it. "Grab it and dry your tears."

She wraps a slender hand around the thick base, sliding my length over one tear-soaked cheek, then the other.

"Fuck, your tears make me so goddamn hard," I groan, interlocking my fingers behind her neck. "Open wide."

I surge into her mouth, riding her face with ruthless thrusts. Zilphia braces her palms on my thighs, grappling against my vicious assault. The wild hysteria clouding her glossy brown irises stirs my blood, inciting the most primitive part of me. I dig my nails into her nape and jackhammer into her throat until her body goes limp. I release my hold, and she crumples to the mattress, coughing and struggling for breath.

I'm on her instantly, tearing her shirt over her head. My gaze zeros in on her pierced belly.

I run my finger over the shiny jewelry. "Stunning."

This is a pleasant surprise. She must've gotten the piercing done at Draco's tattoo shop earlier. I hook my arms under her knees and hoist her legs over my shoulders, aligning my length at her rimmed opening.

"This is going to hurt," I rasp and drive into her tight muscles.

Zilphia cries out, her delicate features contorted in agony. I lie flat against her soft curves and curl my fingers over her shoulders, thrusting and rolling my hips until she's stretched to capacity, then my control shatters. I plunge into her with punishing brutality, unleashing three years of pent-up anger on her body.

"I've earned this," I groan against her wet cheek. "You're mine to break."

I dip my head and feast on her tits, circling my tongue around the raised bumps on her areolas. The air mattress deflates, but I don't stop. I can't stop. I'm fucking obsessed. Obsessed with her tears. Obsessed with her pain. Obsessed with being inside her.

I fell hard for her back then, and I'm falling hard for her now, but this time I won't play her fool. This time the joke is on her. The familiar warm tingling starts in my balls, then shoots up my cock. I come, filling her tight asshole to the brim.

"Shit," I groan, giving a final thrust.

I roll onto my back, feeling drowsy and sated.

Zilphia curls herself into a tight ball, silent sobs racking her body. I stand and fix my clothing.

"Get dressed and meet me outside," I demand, ambling to my feet.

CHAPTER 23

Zilphia

I cut my blueberry pancakes into square sections before drowning the buttery fluffiness in maple syrup, but it's all for show. I can't bring myself to eat. My stomach's a knot of nerves and nausea.

Sandman sits opposite me, devouring his steak breakfast without a care in the world, like he didn't just brutalize me less than an hour ago. The meat is practically still mooing. Pinkish-red liquid pools on his plate, turning my stomach.

It's jarring sitting at this booth with him, inside this restaurant. *A normal couple enjoying the morning meal together.* That's what people see, but appearances aren't always what they seem. Makes me wonder how many times I've viewed my surroundings through rose-colored lenses.

I'm more than a little surprised he brought me here. I thought for certain he was taking me to some isolated field to murder me. He put me through literal hell, and now he wants to feed me. Why? It doesn't make any sense. Is this his demented way of courting me? I'd rather be at home sleeping my aches away. Maybe I can get some answers.

"How did you find your father?"

Sandman pauses, fork halfway to his mouth, his blue gaze settling on me. I squirm under his piercing stare, wishing I had kept my mouth shut. Curiosity did kill the cat after all. He puts his fork down, the silence stretching between us. I busy myself by shaking pepper onto my cheese grits.

"I didn't," he finally responds, startling me. "My lawyer did. Besides my one *true* friend, she was the only other person who actually gave a fuck about me. I was stupid to ever trust you. I won't make the same mistake twice."

"This is it, then?" My voice wavers. "You're going to hate me forever?"

"Yeah, I am."

"I don't know what you want me to do."

"You can build a time machine, go back to the night you were conceived, and make sure your mother swallows you," he snarls at me. "I want a world where you never existed."

My soul shatters into a million pieces, forming a huge crater in my chest.

"Yo, Sandman," a guy calls out, sliding into the booth beside him. "You sharing?" He reaches over and helps himself to a few potatoes.

"Order your own goddamn food, Cricket," Sandman snaps, elbowing his friend in the ribs.

"Damn, you stingy." He chuckles good-naturedly, turning his attention to me, then back at Sandman. "Interesting night?"

"You could say that."

"Care to elaborate?" Cricket waggles his eyebrows.

"Move," Sandman shoves him out of the booth and stands.

"Where you going?"

"I gotta take a piss," Sandman answers him. "That okay with you, or you wanna come hold my dick for me?"

"I'm sure you can manage your teeny tiny Johnson all on your own," Cricket retorts, sitting back down.

Sandman grunts and saunters into the bathroom.

"I remember you," I say, recognition dawning on me. "You went to Leesburg, right? I saw you and Sandman together all the time."

He's the one true friend Sandman was talking about.

"Shocking," Cricket remarks sarcastically.

"What?"

"That a self-centered bitch like you remembers me."

I also remember the hateful glares he threw my way whenever he saw me. "You never liked me, did you?"

He laughs humorlessly. "Not particularly."

"Why?" I ask. "What did I ever do to you? We haven't even spoken two words to each other until now."

"Can the innocent act," Cricket sneers, his lips twisting in contempt. "I know what you did. I was there that night."

I recall someone coming into the classroom and helping Sandman, but the person's face is a blur. Everything happened so fast.

I swipe at the lone tear rolling down my cheek. "I'm not proud of what I did."

"You aren't good enough for him," he states with iron conviction. "You never were. Now you're back to ruin his life again."

"I don't want to," I argue back.

"This thing between you and him won't end well. I'm willing to stake my life on it." Cricket interlocks his fingers on the table and leans forward, looking me dead in the eyes. "Spare him and kill yourself before you both crash and burn."

I believe him, but there's nothing to be done. Sandman isn't going to leave me alone, and I have nowhere to run. Taking my own life is a hell no. I have too much to live for.

I squeeze my hands into tight fists on my lap. "I'm not going to kill myself."

"Then buckle up," he states, settling back against the booth. "It's gonna be a bumpy ride."

Sandman reappears and nudges Cricket on the shoulder. "Move over."

"I'm heading out." He bounds to his feet instead. "Catch you later."

"You're not eating?" Sandman asks, reclaiming his seat.

"No." Cricket's reproachful gaze lands on me. "I lost my appetite."

"Aight. Keep the rubber side down."

"Always." They fist bump, then he heads out the door.

Cricket hates my guts. I don't blame him, though the kill yourself comment was way over the top.

"Eat your food," Sandman demands, jabbing his fork at my plate.

I squeeze ketchup on my scrambled eggs and force down a few bites, not wanting to make him angry. "Can I ask you a question?"

My last question seemed unwelcome, so I figured I'd seek permission this time. Don't want to poke the bear.

"Yeah," he responds, though his focus remains on his breakfast.

"The video you took of me… What are you going to do with it?"

"Use it to jerk off when I can't get to you."

"Oh." My cheeks heat.

I wasn't expecting that answer. Actually, I wasn't expecting an answer at all. I thought he was going to tell me to shut the fuck up.

"Can I ask you another question?"

I'm pushing my luck, but what the hell.

"Last one," he growls in annoyance.

"*BLOOD GOD*." I nod at the embroidered words on his cut. "What does it mean?"

I'm 99.9 percent certain it means something really, really bad.

"None of your fucking business."

Loud feminine laughter draws my attention to the front. Five scantily dressed women linger near the entrance, waiting to be seated. The hostess directs the group to follow her and leads them to a table diagonally across from us. The last woman halts in her stilettos, catching sight of Sandman.

"Hey, big boy," she greets him, a flirtatious smile teasing her red lips. "Missed you at the bar last night."

A svelte figure, smooth olive skin, and long jet-black hair give her an exotic look. I'm sure she turns heads wherever she goes. She's getting more than a few appreciative glances right now. I wonder who she is to him.

"I was busy."

"Will you be there tonight?" She twirls a finger in his loose blond strands. "I have a surprise for you. It's sheer and red."

"Maybe."

Then her eyes find me. "Who's she?" She fails miserably to conceal the simmering jealousy in her speculative gaze. "Never seen her around here before."

Asking Sandman about me when I'm sitting right here is a blatant snub.

"Call her trash," he replies, his piercing blue orbs boring into me. "That's what she is."

I bit my tongue, squelching the knee-jerk reaction to defend myself.

The woman holds out her purse and drops it onto the floor, a smug smirk on her face. "Pick it up, *Trash*."

"You dropped it," I hiss at her, refusing to budge. "You pick it up."

"Do it," Sandman orders me.

I jerk my gaze back to him, his grumbled command stunning me silent. It's abundantly clear that he loathes my existence, and I even understand why.

On some level, maybe I even deserve it. But to allow other people to treat me lower than dirt is taking it too far.

No. I won't stand for it.

I need to make a move, and I need to make it now. From my window seat, I spot a police cruiser parked several blocks away. *It's now or never, Zilphia.*

I bolt through the restaurant, my heart thrumming in my chest. I head straight for the cruiser, hoping there's a police officer inside or nearby. Meela warned me against going to the cops, but I have to try. There have to be officers in the surrounding police departments who aren't corrupt. A uniformed man exits the pharmacy just ahead. I pull in a relieved breath and slow to a walk.

"Excuse—"

"Sandman," he suddenly calls out, nearly giving me a heart attack. "Ready for your team to lose this afternoon?"

I glance back, finding Sandman only inches behind me.

You've got to be fucking kidding me. Are they friends? I'm in deep shit now.

"The Insurgents won the Super Bowl three years in a row." Sandman casually ambles up beside me and slips an arm over my waist. "When was the last time those sorry ass Mambas won a Super Bowl?"

"They're going to make a comeback this season," the officer claims proudly. "You just wait and see."

"Mm-hmm." Sandman chuckles. "I wouldn't get my hopes up if I were you."

"Yeah, yeah." The officer turns his attention to me. "Who is this lovely young lady? A girlfriend?"

"Come on, Reuben. You know I'm not a one-woman man."

"Still sowing your wild oats." He grins, waggling his eyebrows. "I remember those days. Welp, gotta hit the road before the missus starts calling. See you around."

"Take it easy," Sandman says, steering me back toward the restaurant, his unyielding fingers digging into my shoulder. "Run again and I'm going to fuck you in the ass so hard, you'll be shitting blood for a month."

CHAPTER 24

Zilphia

"Zilphia!" Sheila yells, her tone haughty and annoyed. "Come here please."

What now?

I'm desperate for sleep. Sandman dropped me off hours ago, and even though I was bone-tired, I chose to spend some time with my grandmother. She's my only positive in all this madness. I showered, then crawled into bed with her. Momma was out on a fancy date—still is—so it was just us. We talked and watched her favorite television shows long into the evening.

Since it was getting late and my eyes were growing heavier, I forced myself to leave her comfortable bed and trudge down to the basement. Momma would've blown a gasket had she found me sleeping in her spot when she got back. I used electrical tape to patch up the tear in the air mattress and literally just laid down. An involuntary shudder races down my spine, recalling what caused the damage.

"Zilphia!"

Sighing, I force my feet beneath me and lumber upstairs, finding my aunt standing by the front door. I inwardly roll my eyes at the disgusted look she gives me. I don't have the mental capacity to deal with her right now. I'm exhausted and ache all over. I try my absolute best to avoid her and my cousin whenever possible. What else does this woman want from me?

"You are not allowed to have boys in my home."

Shit. How did she find out?

I made sure to disable the alarm and cameras. My grandmother gave me the codes at the same time she gave me a key to the house. Sheila's going to kick us out for sure now.

"I... um—"

"Quiet." Sheila slices her hand through the air. "He's on the porch. Tell him he isn't welcome here."

What is Sandman doing here now? I expected him to come back later tonight.

"You'll have to do your whoring elsewhere," she adds, her lips twisting in a sneer.

"I'm not a whore." *But I'm pretty sure your daughter is.*

"You better find a job soon," she snarls, narrowing her eyes at me. "The clock is ticking."

"Actually, I already found one." *So there.*

"Then I expect you both gone a lot sooner." Sheila turns on her heel and sashays into the kitchen.

Momma and I can't survive on one salary. She'll need to work too, but solving world hunger is more likely than talking sense into her. My life is so fucked.

I open the front door and blink in surprise. "What are you doing here?"

"We made plans to practice at my place today, remember? For the musical," Jace responds slowly.

"I'm so sorry," I say, pressing my hands to my cheeks. "I totally forgot."

"Hey, don't worry about it." He gives me a reassuring smile. "We can run lines another day."

"Today is still good," I tell him. "Just let me throw on some clothes and we can go."

"Okay, cool. The hideous green truck parked across the street is mine."

I smile. "Be out in a sec."

I won't be able to sleep now; there's too much on my mind. Might as well go out and be a normal teenager for a change. I'm buckled in Jace's four-wheel monstrosity a few minutes later, and then we're off. I attempt to lose myself in the newly released hits playing on the radio, but the shitstorm that has become my life weighs heavily on me. I'm going to need a padded room after all is said and done.

"Zilphia?" Jace's deep baritone intrudes on my dismal musings.

I look over at him. "Mmm."

"Are you okay?" he asks, his eyebrows pinched low on his forehead.

"Yeah, of course," I reply, forcing a small smile. "Why?"

"I called your name, like, five times."

"Oh," I mutter, noticing we're parked in a driveway. "I just have a lot on my mind. That's all."

"Look, we don't have to rehearse today if you're not feeling up to it."

"No, I really want to," I assure him, placing my hand over his on the gear-shift. "It'll take my mind off things."

"Okay. Let's head inside."

I follow Jace into his house and sit on the sofa.

He shrugs out of his hoodie and tosses it on the ottoman. "Want something to drink?"

"Sure. What do you have?"

"Gatorade, tea, or water."

"Water is good."

He bows theatrically. "Your wish is my command."

I survey the one-story home. It has an open-floor design with the living room, dining room, and kitchen all sharing the same space. Small, but cozy and inviting.

"Here you go."

"Thank you," I say, accepting the cold bottle. "Are your parents home?"

"It's just my father and me." Jace settles beside me. "He works on Sundays."

"What does he do?"

"Security over at Bright Horizon."

"That's an indoor amusement park, right? I heard a few kids at school talking about going."

"Yeah," Jace answers. "It's a great place to hang out. Wanna go next weekend?"

"Heck yeah!" I exclaim. I'm already forgetting my troubles, for a little while at least.

"It's a date."

I arch an eyebrow. "A date?"

"Not a date, date," Jace backtracks, his face turning scarlet red. "Just two people hanging out."

I laugh. "Relax, I'm only joking."

"Oh." Jace laughs with me. "You had me going for a second there."

"We should get started. I don't want to be out too late."

Sandman might stop by, and if I'm not there...

"Right, it is a school night," Jace states, his tone becoming businesslike. "Have you ever seen *Beauty and the Beast*?"

"Is that a trick question?" I give him the side-eye. "Hello, I'm a girl. I've seen the animated and the live-action adaptation only, like, a gazillion times. I even saw it on ice once."

"So you're a *Beauty and the Beast* expert?"

"I sure am," I state proudly. "Have you seen it?"

"Only the live-action adaptation," he answers. "You know it's all bullshit, right?"

"What's bullshit?"

"Belle falling madly in love with the Beast. No girl would ever fall in love with a hairy, grotesque beast-man with sharp teeth. Girls are just too superficial."

"Hey." I lightly punch him on the arm. "Don't lump us all into the same category. Some girls look past the physical. And isn't that the pot calling the kettle black? All your testosterone-slinging counterparts care about are looks."

"Not—"

The front door bursts open.

I scream, my heart jumping into my throat, as a barrage of big bodies swarms into the living room. All dressed in black from head to toe, their faces hidden behind ski masks. There's no time to react. My mouth is taped shut, wrists bound behind my back, and a hood secured over my head in less than sixty seconds. Then I'm thrown over a hard shoulder and carted outside.

This is Sandman's doing. I *know* it is. I should scream, kick, *do* something, *anything*. But I can't move. I'm frozen. Oh God, please. I don't want to die. I'm placed in a running vehicle, fear palpable in my trembling limbs. I hear doors slamming shut, then we're moving. Thumping and muffled screams come from my left.

Jace.

I didn't see what happened to him in the commotion. I was unsure if he had been taken like me or killed. A loud whack followed by a pained groan startles me.

"Quiet," comes a gruff demand. "Another sound from you and I'll cut out your fucking tongue."

Though the threat isn't directed at me, I go completely still, afraid to even breathe. These men, whoever they are, mean business. I don't want to do anything to incur their wrath. The zip tie binding my wrists together is painfully tight, slicing through skin and tissue. I bite back my whimpers, keeping as quiet as possible. Blood pools onto the floorboard, coating my fingertips.

Where are they taking us?

I close my eyes and pray. Pray that if I do meet my end tonight, it's quick. That's all I can do. After what seems like an eternity, the rumbling beneath my cheek stops, and the doors creak open. I'm relieved and petrified at the same time, though the latter emotion is more prevalent.

It's extremely loud wherever we are. Roaring engines and revelry greet my ears. A racecar track comes to mind.

"Up and at 'em, sweetheart," someone jeers, jerking me to my feet.

I'm unceremoniously hauled across uneven terrain, losing my footing several times in my failed attempt to match my captor's brisk stride. Bright lights are visible through the threadbare hood covering my face. What is this place?

Oh my God.

I've seen horror movies with this exact premise: a cult kidnaps unsuspecting teenage victims rehearsing for the school musical to sacrifice them to their demonic deity and bring about the apocalypse.

Calm down. You're letting your imagination run away with you.

I'm callously shoved to my knees, the zip tie cut, and the hood snatched off my head. "Welcome to God's Glory, sweetheart."

No, no, no. It takes a few seconds for my eyes to adjust to the glaring lights. Motorcycles surround me, the high beams casting the spectators in shadowy silhouettes. They're silent now, waiting... watching.

This is far worse than any horror movie I could've ever imagined. Several feet away, a hulking bear of a man holds Jace captive in an unyielding headlock. Sandman looms beside them, a fierce scowl contorting his angular features.

I try to speak, to ask him why he's doing this, but the words won't come. I'm going to die at eighteen years old. Die before I've even had a chance to truly live. And my poor, innocent classmate will meet the same fate. *Guilty by association.*

"You really thought you could start some fairytale romance with this asshole right under my fucking nose?" Sandman spits, violent anger vibrating his hard body.

"N-no," I croak, my gaze catching on the knife clutched in his hand.

"Did you let him touch you?" he roars, pressing the tip against Jace's abdomen.

I vehemently shake my head. "I promise it's not what you think!"

Sandman nods at the man holding Jace, and he loosens his grip. "What the fuck were you doing with my property?"

"W-we were r-rehearsing f-for the school m-musical," Jace stammers, his amber eyes filled with stark terror. "I swear on my father's life, I didn't know she belonged to you. I would never disrespect you like that."

"Are there any kissing scenes between you and my property in this musical?"

"Y-yeah, b-but it's… it's just acting."

"Acting or not, that's a death sentence, boy," Sandman growls. "No one touches what's mine and walks away."

"Please believe me," Jace pleads, beginning to cry now. "I would've never agreed to play the male lead had I known Zilphia was yours."

"I believe you, but unfortunately, I have to make an example out of you." Sandman viciously slices into Jace's top lip.

His anguished howls reverberate through the night.

"Oh God!" I scream at the top of my lungs. "Sandman, please stop! He didn't do anything!"

Surprisingly, he does, leaving Jace's lip half dangling. I recoil at the gruesome sight, sick to my stomach. I'm afraid he's going to bleed out; there's just so much blood.

Please don't die.

"Crawl to me," Sandman demands, his wild gaze piercing through me.

I comply without question, for Jace's sake as well as my own.

"Choke on my dick," he orders when I reach him.

"Please, Sandman," I sob, moving to my knees. "Not here."

Not in front of all these people.

"Zilphia, this isn't a negotiation." He coasts the knife's bloody edge down my cheek. "I will fucking gut him and make you wear his entrails around your neck."

I undo his jeans and free his long erection, resigned to my fate. Tears of shame flow as I take him into my mouth. He's warm and silky on my tongue. I cry harder, hearing the whistles and vulgar commentary from our avid audience.

"Deeper, goddamn it," Sandman rasps, tangling a hand in my hair. "I want your throat squeezing my cock."

I slurp his veiny length in deep, long pulls, forcing the broad head past my tonsils. I gag, my eyes watering and nose running, struggling to breathe.

"Fuck yeah… that's it," Sandman murmurs, rocking his hips. "Make it wetter… shit." He bucks wildly into my mouth, releasing his thick, salty load down my throat. "Swallow. Don't waste a single drop," he grunts, thrusting until his balls are empty.

Sandman pulls back and sheathes his knife at his hip, then he's hovering above me, roughly tearing off my shorts and panties, leaving me bare for all to see. "Spread your legs."

He's going to take my virginity and give our audience the ultimate grand finale. I let my thighs fall open, waiting for him to descend on me and complete my humiliation, but he doesn't. To my horror, he stands and aims his length between my thighs. Then he urinates, *marking* me for all to see.

"Let it be known that Zilphia Kensley belongs to me!" Sandman shouts to the crowd, stuffing his length back into his jeans. "Any man who so much as looks in her direction will answer to me." He turns in a wide circle, silently challenging his brethren. No one steps forward. "We're done here."

The crowd disperses, hopping onto their motorcycles and speeding into the pitch-black night. I remain sprawled on the ground, the monster's piss cooling between my legs.

Sandman levels his stony gaze on Jace. "Talk to her again and it's on sight."

With that proclamation, the bear man drags my mangled classmate away and flings his limp body into the back of a black van. I'm assuming the same black van that transported us here. Wherever here is. I spot a large warehouse in the distance, but nothing else.

"Get dressed," Sandman tells me.

Something in me snaps. A sudden, desperate need to get away slams into me. I don't think. I gather my clothes and shoes, then tear across the worn grass. Damn the consequences. It doesn't matter that my chances of escaping are slim to none. I just need to get far away from him, even if it's only for a little while.

One moment my feet are on solid ground, and in the next, I'm careening through the air. I hit earth with a bone-jarring whack, Sandman's crushing weight expelling the oxygen from my lungs. I let out a faint whine, the brutal impact leaving me disoriented.

"Did you really think you could outrun me?" he rasps in my ear.

I hear the hiss of his zipper, then he's penetrating me. No spit to soften his invasion.

"You're my prey… a weak, pathetic nothing with three holes for me to enjoy," Sandman rumbles, working his hardness into my muscular ring. "And I'm king of the goddamn jungle." He fills me to the limit, then past it, stretching me to bursting.

"I'm going to show you how much I fucking hate you," he groans, pinning my wrists on either side of my head.

I scream my agony as he bludgeons my body. There's no other way to describe it. Sandman drives into my rimmed opening with merciless force, each thrust more ferocious than the last.

"I'm never going to let you go." *Thrust.* "This is your life now." *Thrust.* "Running is pointless."

Thrust. Thrust. Thrust.

Sandman bites down on my shoulder, feverishly pounding into me. The attack seems to go on forever. I sob into the dirt as he grunts and growls above me. I feel it coating my face… taste it in my mouth. It's bitter, like the man ruthlessly ravishing me.

"Feels so fucking good," he mumbles huskily, his warm breath fanning across my temple. "Fuck yes… take this nut deep inside that tight ass."

He roars his release, propelling his hips impossibly faster… penetrating me impossibly deeper. Then it's finally over, his body dead weight on my back.

Time melts together, becoming a blurry haze. I don't recall putting on my clothes or shoes—or even straddling Sandman's motorcycle. Every action is done without conscious thought, my mind on autopilot. I rest my cheek against his cut and close my eyes, my arms wrapped tightly around his torso. The vibration beneath my sore bottom and the wind whipping against my face transport me back to reality.

We arrive at a destination unfamiliar to me. Bright flowers, shrubs, and other greenery surround a monument sign rooted on the front lawn. *Burk Cremation Services LLC.* Goose bumps scatter across my skin. Tonight's horror isn't over yet.

"Why are we here?" I ask.

"It's a surprise," Sandman replies vaguely, triggering my internal alarm bells.

He lugs me into the building and down a winding staircase, his calloused hand an implacable shackle on my arm. I hear a click and fluorescent lights flood the cold room. I squint against the brightness, surveying the cavernous space. Three machines hum quietly to the left. Opposite them looms a pair of metal doors. Straight ahead lies a cluttered workstation, surrounded by various pieces of equipment.

"I just want to go home," I say, my voice small and tired.

"Maybe tonight you die." He ambles to the first machine and slams his fist against the green button on the front, lifting the electronic closure. "Get inside."

"What is it?"

"A cremation chamber." A smirk twists his lips. "You know what cremation is, don't you?"

My muddled brain pieces two and two together.

"No," I backpedal, jerking my head side to side.

Sandman glowers at me and opens his cut, displaying the gun stashed in his holster. "I'm not going to tell you again."

Fuck that. I'd rather get shot than be burned alive. I spin on my heel and dive for the stairs. I'm halfway to freedom when Sandman latches onto my ankle.

"Where do you think you're going?" he taunts, giving a hard tug.

I cry out, landing painfully on my side, my ribs taking the brunt of the fall. Sandman drags me back down the stairs and seizes my hair in an ironclad hold, yanking me to my feet. I angle my head and sink my teeth into his bicep and bite down as hard as I can. His blood on my tongue fills me with triumph.

"Bitch!" Sandman thunders, prying my mouth open.

My fist flies at his face, but he catches my wrist midair.

"You wanna play?" His hand shoots out lightning fast, clasping onto my throat. "Let's play."

He flings me into the wall, then he's on me, tearing my shorts and panties down my legs. My head smacking against the plaster leaves me dazed.

"When are you gonna learn?" Sandman sneers, spinning me around.

A few seconds later, he's tunneling his dick into my pussy—just the tip. *For now.* I press my palms against the wall as he moves in and out of me with short, measured thrusts. He sweeps one hand into my thick curls and the other between my thighs, seeking my clit.

"Don't," I whisper.

"You don't want to come?" he murmurs, passion resonating in his husky baritone.

"No."

I don't want anything from him, except to be left alone.

"Too fucking bad. Your body is mine to control and you can't do a damn thing about it."

His fingers stroke, knead, and pluck, forcing me closer to completion. I mentally fight against my body's response to him, but my efforts are in vain. I'm powerless against his touch. My pussy greedily sucks on his swollen head, the wet noises a testament to my surrender.

"I don't want this," I breathe.

"Your mind doesn't, but your body does," he rasps, his lips softly grazing the shell of my ear. "You're about to come. I know because I can feel your clit getting bigger… fuller. Stop fighting it."

My breathy moans sound foreign to my ears. I bite my tongue, shaking with the effort not to roll my hips against his hand.

"Go ahead, make it rain on my cock."

Sandman lightly pinches my magic spot and that does it. I tumble over the precipice, diving headlong into waves of raw ecstasy; my slick walls clamping down on him.

"Fuck yes!" Sandman shouts, his forehead dropping heavily onto my shoulder. "That delicious cunt soaking me, hot and so fucking ripe." His strong grip tightens in my hair as he fills me. "Take my seed… it's all for you."

I melt against his granite frame, my heart racing, my breath intertwining with his. Without warning, he slams my head into the wall, and then I'm being carried. The sudden attack leaves me whirling. Darkness seeps into the corners of my vision, but somehow I manage to stay conscious, though barely.

By the time I become fully lucid, I'm already locked inside the cremation chamber.

"Please let me out!" I scream hysterically, expecting flames to engulf me at any moment. "I'm sorry for going over to Jace's house!"

Death by fire. I wouldn't wish that on my worst enemy. To smell oneself essentially being cooked alive is a horrific way to go.

"Let me out!" I bang my fists against the metal door, oblivious to the pain radiating up my arms.

Seconds stretch into endless minutes, time seemingly distorted, passing by at a snail's pace. Every day he breaks me a little more. Sooner or later, he's going to land me right in the psych ward.

"Let me the fuck out of here!"

The electric hum of the door lifting fills me with instant relief. I launch myself through the opening, toppling awkwardly onto the floor, my shorts and panties still around my knees.

Sandman crouches beside me. "If I find you getting cozy with another motherfucker again..." he says, caressing my cheek. "You burn."

"We weren't getting cozy!" I argue, wanting to scratch his eyeballs out but unwilling to risk being locked inside the cremation chamber again. "We were practicing for the school musical!"

"You were alone with him," Sandman snarls. "I call that getting fucking cozy."

"So I can't be alone with any guys?" I ask incredulously.

"No." Sandman glides his index finger through the semen coating my inner thighs and rubs it on my lips. "You're not allowed to be alone with any male unless I say otherwise. Got it?"

"Yes," I hiss.

"God's Eye is always watching."

CHAPTER 25

Zilphia

"Are you almost done?" I ask, touching the top of my head.

"Stop asking me that." Meela pops my hand with her rattail comb. "I don't rush my work."

"Ouch!" I whine dramatically, snatching my hand away. "That hurt."

So do my ass and back. Meela started on my hair about five hours ago. I'm so ready for her to be done. When she offered to do my hair, I assumed she meant something simple, like a silk press and curl. I've never gotten… *What did she call these?* Oh yeah, passion twists. I've never gotten passion twists before—braids or cornrows either.

She insisted on knee-length, saying it's the rage right now, which is why it's taking so freaking long. I say it's unnecessary torture.

"Are you dying?" Meela retorts, her hazel-green eyes shooting daggers at me.

This is the first time I've seen her without contacts or a wig. Her real hair is a gorgeous deep red. She once mentioned that both her parents are Black, so I'm guessing these features came from a distant ancestor.

"It feels like it." I shift in the chair, trying to alleviate the ache in my ass.

"Girl, you working my last nerve," she gripes, sucking her teeth. "You are the most tender-headed person I've ever met in my entire life. I'm not even doing your hair that tight."

I wonder how many last nerves she has because she's made that claim at least fifteen times already.

"It's not my fault," I snap at her. "I was born this way."

I'm irritable and tired. Between the gentleman's club and Sandman keeping me up most nights, I haven't gotten much sleep. A lot has happened in the last week. I gave up my role in the school musical. Mr. Rousseau did not take my retraction lightly and delegated me to stage crew duties. I used work and helping with my grandmother as an excuse, which softened him a bit. It's not a complete lie. In the end, Deja got the role and couldn't wait to rub it in my face.

Mr. Rousseau may need to find another male lead too. Jace hasn't been in school all week. I haven't called him because I'm terrified of Sandman finding out. Besides, Jace probably doesn't want to hear from me. I just hope he's okay.

"It's not my fault." Meela mimics me in an unflattering tone. "Relax, crybaby. I'm almost done. Twenty minutes."

"Good," I deadpan. "I need to get home and soak my head in some ice water."

"That'll have to wait," she states matter-of-factly. "We're going to a bar tonight."

"I hate to burst your bubble, but we're not old enough to get into a bar."

"Trust me, I'll get us in," she replies smugly.

"Well, I can't wear this." I look down at my T-shirt and sweatpants. "And I sure as heck can't fit any of your clothes."

"Just shower here, then we'll swing past your house so you can change."

"Okay, I'm down with a little teenage delinquency." I could use a little fun and laughter in my life. "Should I call Leah and see if she wants to come?"

I saw her this morning when I went to the hospital for my interview. With her putting in a good word for me, I'm 99.9 percent certain I've got this in the bag. I have a copy of my immunization record on hand, but I would still need to get a TB test done. And that costs sixty bucks. Luckily, Leah said she'd front me the cash.

"Honey, don't waste your time," Meela scoffs, making another part in my hair. "She's not going to come."

"Why not?"

"For one, she was born a grandma. And two, Snake might be there."

"Wait, what?" My entire body tenses. "Will Sandman be there?"

I haven't told anyone about my visit to God's Glory. It's easier to pretend it never happened. My virginity is still intact, but I don't know for how long. Every time Sandman puts the *tip* in, which has been a lot lately, there's always a chance he'll take my virginity. I can't have a baby right now, especially with him.

Thankfully, I was able to get a prescription for birth control pills online for only fifteen bucks a month. I borrowed the money from my grandmother. I hated asking her, but she gave it to me—no questions asked. My first three-month supply should arrive next week.

"Maybe," she answers. "The bar is inside the clubhouse, aka The Sanctuary."

"Then count me out."

I can't show my face there. There's no telling how many of them witnessed my shame the other night.

"I'm gonna tell you the same thing I've told Leah countless times. You can't hide from the Gods in Kent," Meela says. "It's just not plausible. Don't let Sandman or the club kill your vibe. Go out and do you with your head held high."

"I don't know..."

I'm not spunky or badass like her, and Sandman scares the crap out of me. Even her bedroom reflects her personality. She has a carriage bed frame with a sheer pink canopy for goodness' sake. Opposite that is her collection of colorful wigs hanging from hooks on the wall.

But what really made me blink twice is the three mannequins in different stages of undress with tiaras on their heads. Meela is an aspiring fashion designer, among other things. *Go figure.*

"Well, I do," she remarks with conviction. "Waltz in that bar like you're that bitch because you are that bitch. Claim it and fucking own it." She flings a long yellow twist over my shoulder.

Meela isn't wrong. I need to walk through Kent with my head held high, and I can't do that by hiding. Going to the bar will show Sandman and every last God that God's Glory didn't break me.

"And your new do is going to give you some extra bitch pizzazz."

"Okay, I'll go. But I'm still not sure about this color." I finger the curly tip. "It's so... bright and gaudy."

"Ungrateful skank-ass ho!" she scolds me. "This color is fire, and this style would run you at least four-fifty at a braiding shop."

"Dang, really?" I've never paid that much for a hairstyle before. "My mother thinks these types of styles are ghetto."

"Girl, fuck your mother!" Meela squawks. "She on crack or something?"

I burst out laughing. "No, she isn't addicted to any illegal substances to my knowledge."

Meela huffs but doesn't respond.

"Thank you." I turn in the chair and give her a one-arm hug, not wanting to get on her bad side. "I appreciate you taming my mane for free. I absolutely love it."

It's true. I don't share my mother's sentiments.

She smiles, her displeasure quickly forgotten. "No problem, girlie."

"The Sanctuary, huh? A bit cliché if you ask me."

"Cliché as fuck," Meela agrees, and we both laugh.

She resumes her torture on my scalp, but true to her word, she's done twenty minutes later—give or take a few minutes. She showers first, then I hop in next.

I emerge from the bathroom squeaky clean and stroll back into her bedroom, finding her butt-ass naked. I clutch the towel to my chest, taking in her pierced nipples, belly ring, and the stunning chandelier tattoo starting between her breasts and curving over her rib cage. I figured she'd be dressed already and give me some privacy to don my own clothes.

"What?" Meela queries, carefully rubbing Vaseline onto the garter-belt tattoo she got last week. "It's pussy, ass, and titties… the same thing you got. Don't be weird."

She does have a point, and I've seen my fair share of naked girls in the locker room after gym class. I'm not sure why I'm being prudish now.

"Oh my God!" she shouts.

"What?" I shout too, frantically scanning the room.

"Your… your pussy," she squawks, pointing between my thighs.

"Okay." I glance down, seeing that a small gap in the towel has my meow on display. "What about it?"

"What's on it?" Meela asks, scandalized.

"Um… pubic hair." I'm thoroughly confused. Am I missing something here?

"Barbaric," she hisses, her top lip curling in disgust.

"I trim," I grit out, a little offended. "I just haven't in a while."

"Trimming is so middle school." Meela rolls her eyes. "You're a senior for crying out loud. Act like it." She shakes her head in exasperation. "No worries, though. I'll wax you before we go."

"No, the hell you're not." I'm scared to death of getting waxed. "I heard it's painful as fuck."

"Numbing cream, babe. I use it whenever I wax myself or get a new tattoo."

"You wax yourself?" I exclaim.

"Sure do," she replies. "It costs nearly a hundred bucks for a Brazilian wax. I'm not paying that when I could do it myself. Anyway, it won't hurt."

"Okay, I'll let you wax me, but it better not hurt."

"It won't," Meela assures me.

She turns around and pulls on a skimpy thong. I admire the dreamcatcher tattoo spanning the length of her spine and the dimple piercings on her lower back. Meela is a literal walking advertisement for piercings and tattoos. I coast the towel along my body, trying to keep the ugly cut healing on my torso hidden. The last thing I need is to be bombarded with questions, especially if she spots the makeshift tattoo Sandman carved down my back.

"It's your birthday?" I ask, noticing the birthday sash on her bed. "Why didn't you say anything?"

"Oh, it's not my birthday." She smiles. And is that a blush?

I cock an eyebrow. "Then what's up with the birthday sash?"

"I'm on a mission tonight," she responds vaguely.

"Keep your little secret." I feign an attitude. "But whatever you have planned better not get us into trouble."

"I make no promises."

Now it's my turn to roll my eyes.

"Move out of the goddamn way!" Meela demands, her arms folded under her ample breasts.

She's been going at it with the guy manning the bar entrance for the last ten minutes now—neither one backing down. He's stout and a bit nerdy, not at all how I expect an outlaw biker to look. Then again, he's not one yet.

He's a prospect, which means he has to prove himself before he can wear the Gods' colors. Even then, becoming a full-patched member isn't guaranteed. It takes a majority vote.

Meela gave me a crash course in outlaw biker culture on the drive over. Let's just say it's complicated… and dangerous. Honestly, I don't get why anyone would willingly sign up for it. I guess some people like living on the edge. Not me. I prefer life quiet, normal, and far from anything with a body count.

I'm secretly hoping he doesn't let us in. My bravado fled the instant Meela pulled into the parking lot, and I saw the large crowd milling about outside. To say I'm jumpy is an understatement. My gaze scans every face in the vicinity, searching for Sandman. Spotting him first is the only advantage I have.

"Sorry, can't do that," he says, his head shaking in the negative.

"You wanna get kicked in the dick?"

"Look, there's a private party going on tonight," he explains. "But even if there wasn't, I couldn't let you in. Twenty-one and over only, sweet cheeks."

"Call me sweet cheeks again, and I'll rip off your testicles and feed them to you," she growls, taking a threatening step forward.

"My bad." He holds his hands up, palms facing her. "I don't want no problems, but you still ain't getting in."

"Do you have any idea who I am?" Meela's voice rises a few octaves. "My father was one of the founding members!"

"No jailbait allowed inside." His thin shoulders lift in a shrug. "I let you in and it's my ass."

"I'm eighteen, prospect, which means by law I'm a grown-ass woman," Meela gripes in annoyance, pointing at her birthday sash. "Now step aside!"

"Twenty-one and over," he reiterates, widening his stance. "Prez's orders."

Meela throws up her hands in frustration. "For the millionth time, Zeus knows I'm coming. I'm here to see Jigsaw."

"Mm-hmm." He cocks an eyebrow, his steel-gray gaze landing on me. "What about her?"

"She's with me." Meela cocks her own eyebrow. "Jig is waiting on me. You don't want to get on his bad side, trust me."

He sighs but opens the door and waves us inside. "Be good."

"Being good is for pussies." She winks at him and struts into the building.

"I'm gonna regret this," he mumbles under his breath.

I traipse in behind her, literally shaking in my high heels.

What in the actual fuck?

Naked women strutting around in stilettos everywhere, drugs being consumed openly, carnal happenings in dark corners, and everything in between.

I scurry next to her. "Do you think we should be here right now?"

"Yeah," she replies, scrunching her face at me. "Why not?"

"Because," I sweep my arm in a wide arc, "the live-action porn setup is freaking me out."

She rolls her eyes. "Relax, we're going to have an amazing time."

I highly doubt that.

"There he is," Meela whispers close to my ear, her hand clasping onto my arm in a death grip.

I stiffen, prepared to make a swift exit if necessary. "Who?"

"Jigsaw." She sighs, her eyelashes fluttering dramatically. "The man I'm going to marry."

"There are a lot of men here," I deadpan. "Mind being a little more specific?"

She points to a group of men sitting at a table. "The one with the scars on his face."

"What happened?" I ask, jolted by his appearance.

"Don't know, but the scars make him twenty million times sexier." She licks her lips, eyeing him like a popsicle on a hot summer day.

"Um… isn't he old enough to be your father?" *Or grandfather.*

"Haven't you heard?" Meela smiles cheekily, doing the finger-in-the-hole gesture. "The older the dick, the harder the stick."

I laugh despite myself. "You're something else."

"Let's sit over there." She nods at the booth directly across from where her future husband is sitting. "The silver fox with the beard is Zeus."

Sandman's father. He's too busy fingering the woman perched on his lap to notice us, but Jigsaw's glowering gaze is glued to Meela. If looks could kill… she has to feel his eyes on her, but she's doing a good job of not letting it show. It's obvious they have history.

I sit opposite her. "Unless you were held back a grade, I'm guessing you aren't actually eighteen."

"You would be correct."

"What's up with the birthday sash?"

"Tell you when I get back." She sashays to the bar with a little extra razzle dazzle in her steps, but the man she's being extra for doesn't look too happy.

After collecting six shots of tequila, she makes her way back with the same razzle-dazzle.

"I'm bagging my man tonight," she announces, determination in every word.

"Meaning?"

"Jig won't touch me because I'm seventeen." She quickly gulps down a shot. "He doesn't understand that age means nothing."

"Let me get this straight." I rub my forehead. "You're pretending to be a year older just to get some old man's peen?"

"It's more than just sex," Meela snaps at me. "We belong together. He's just fighting it right now."

I regard her thoughtfully for a moment. "You love him."

"Yeah," she says, nodding solemnly. "I do."

"Then I hope it works out."

"I'll drink to that." She downs another shot, and I take my first. "Did Leah tell you about the party next Saturday?"

"No. Whose party?"

"Some douchebag perv who graduated last year, but that's not important," Meela answers me. "It's his birthday and he throws the best parties, hands down. I'm talking free booze, food, and pot. You should definitely come."

"Yeah, sure," I respond, happy for the invite. "What time?"

"Come over at eight," she answers me. "We can get ready together."

"Okay," I say, then gulp down a second shot. "So why do you call him douchebag perv?"

"Because he tries to fuck every girl he comes into contact with," Meela replies, her pretty features contorting with revulsion. "He's not even cute."

"You don't belong here, *Trash*."

I whip my head toward the familiar voice, my spine snapping straight. My gaze clashes with the woman from the restaurant. She's naked, and to be honest, her body looks damn amazing—her makeup and loose, flowing curls are on point too.

"You're the one walking around naked," I retort sweetly. "I think we all know who the trash is here."

Her eyes narrow to tiny slits. "You're going to pay for your disrespect, bitch."

"I suggest you run along and find a dick to suck," Meela quips, flicking her hand in a shooing motion. "Wouldn't want to get that pretty little face messed up."

"You fat pig—"

"Is there a problem, Ivy?" Zeus rumbles, and the woman's mouth snaps shut.

"N-no, e-everything's f-fine," she stammers, her gaze on the floor.

"Then go about your business," he demands.

She marches off, but not before shooting me a disdainful look. This Ivy woman is going to be a major pain in my rear end. I already have enough on my plate as it is.

"What the hell was that about?" Meela asks.

I sigh and relay the restaurant incident to her, though omitting some details.

"I don't personally know her, but I've seen her around," Meela mentions when I'm done. "She's a twinkie and is always chasing behind Sandman. She wants to be his old lady."

"Twinkie? Old lady?" More motorcycle world lingo I don't understand.

Meela quickly absolves my ignorance, supplying the definition for both. "Girls become twinkies for varying reasons. Some just like the mystique of fucking hot criminal bikers, while others hope for an old lady title one day."

"So twinkies fuck countless men a week?" I clench my thighs together. My vagina could never withstand the mileage.

"Don't sound so horrified." She laughs at me. "They know what they're getting into and they obviously enjoy it."

"Is that what you want? To be Jigsaw's old lady?"

"Yep." Meela stands and straightens her tiara. "Now, if you'll excuse me."

I watch on pins and needles as she sashays over to Jigsaw. He watches her too, tracking her exaggerated steps with fire in his eyes. She steps between his sprawled legs and slowly trails a finger down his chiseled arm.

Dang, I wish I knew what they were saying.

Laughter ripples through the people around them. Meela stiffens, her hands clenched at her sides, then storms toward the dance floor like a woman with something to prove. She grabs the first man she sees—tall, lanky, and too eager.

She bends over and starts twerking on him, her white bone-straight wig brushing the concrete flooring. The man enthusiastically gyrates against her, his fingers firmly digging into her fleshy waistline. Her already short white leather dress rides further up her thick thighs, exposing a tiny thong.

I barely register the blur of motion before Jigsaw is in front of them. His fist cracks against the guy's jaw—bone on bone—and the man hits the floor like a dropped puppet.

I gasp, frozen. No one else blinks. Around us, the music thumps, drinks clink, conversations flow. Like a man getting laid out mid-song is normal.

Like violence is just… punctuation. Meela smiles with wide-eyed innocence at the giant towering over her, as if she didn't just light a match. I still can't make out what they're saying, but it's clear Jigsaw isn't happy with her antics.

His face is hard with fury, pulling his scars into harsh definition.

And Meela—insane, glorious Meela—cups his crotch like it's hers to hold.

Has she lost her damn mind?

Jigsaw seizes her wrist and wrenches her arm behind her back, yanking her tight against his chest. She kisses him, and my jaw nearly hits the floor. Meela was serious about getting her man tonight, but now said man looks even more pissed. He throws her over his shoulder like she weighs nothing. She laughs—actually laughs—and smacks his ass as he carts her through a side door.

Then they're gone.

Oh my fuck. What do I do? I knew I should've stayed home.

"What the fuck are you doing here?"

An icy chill settles in the pit of my stomach, scattering goose bumps along my flesh. I turn my head, and there he stands, the person who invokes my worst nightmares and plagues my every waking moment. Golden god comes to mind whenever I look at him. How can someone so astoundingly beautiful have such a black heart?

"I-I c-came w-with a f-friend," I stammer.

He grasps a passion twist between his thumb and forefinger. "What friend?"

Does he like my new look? Does he hate it? Should I have asked his permission before getting the ostentatious hairstyle? Anything is liable to send this unhinged man over the edge.

"Meela," I mumble past the boulder-size knot in my throat. "She did my hair too. Do you like it?"

I could kick myself for asking, but part of me really wants to know.

"Stand up," Sandman orders me and takes a step back.

I slip out of the booth on shaky legs, keeping a hand fastened onto the table's edge for support. Sandman's cornflower-blue eyes drift over my black satin dress, the thin straps barely clinging to my shoulders, then drop to my tiger-print heels. I fixate on a point beyond his shoulder, suddenly feeling very self-conscious.

"It suits you," he rasps sharply, trailing a finger over a delicate strap.

"Thank you," I reply, shyly meeting his gaze.

"You got googly eyes, boy." Zeus's boisterous quip draws our attention.

Sandman goes rigid, his nose flaring in anger. Zeus isn't the only one studying us with avid curiosity. To my utter mortification, our exchange has garnered a small audience.

"You must be Zilphia," he says, guiding his female companion to her knees.

"Y-yes."

"Suck," Zeus orders her. The woman eagerly obliges, freeing his erection and going to town. "You're a pretty little thing," he states, his gaze raking over me from head to toe. "A mite too skinny for my tastes, though. I see why my boy has a hard-on for you."

"You're crossing the line, Zeus," Sandman growls between clenched teeth. "My business is my own."

"You're right, son." Zeus acknowledges, his head dipping slightly. "I can respect that."

Sandman captures my wrist in an iron grip and starts dragging me toward the back of the bar. Ivy appears out of nowhere, looping her arm around his.

"Hey, baby," she purrs seductively. "Lose this bitch and come with me. I'll show you a real good time."

Sandman jerks away from her and shoves her to the floor. "You're here to entertain, so fucking entertain."

Ivy stares up at him, tears swimming in her almond-shaped gaze. I almost feel sorry for her. *Almost* being the operative word. She's a world-class bitch, but I know firsthand how it feels to be on the receiving end of his cruelty. He hauls me forward and veers to the right, entering a separate area for axe throwing. There are six gated sections, all in use. Sandman pulls me to the nearest one.

"Find something else to do," he barks at the group standing there.

A man shrugs and passes him the axe. "I'm not trying to get my ass kicked tonight."

Sandman nods his head at the gate, his eyes pinned on me. "Stand in front of the bullseye."

"What?" I croak, looking at the bullseye, then back at him.

"You heard me," he snarls. "Do it. Now."

It's in my best interest to obey; the alternative could be a whole lot worse. Cremation chamber worse. I walk into the gated section on heavy feet and press my back flat against the bullseye. People are already gathered to watch. At least no one is taking pictures or recording me. More than likely, neither are allowed during these kinds of *private* parties.

"Don't worry, my aim is unmatched," Sandman says and hurls the axe straight at me.

My breath catches. I squeeze my eyes shut, willing myself not to move, not even an inch. The axe whistles through the air, sharp and piercing like a scream. It slams into the target with a heavy thunk, so close it kisses the air beside my right ear.

I flinch anyway. I can't help it. My heart's pounding so hard it drowns out the roar of the crowd erupting in applause. Laughter. Cheers. They love the show.

But through the chaos, I spot Cricket's face. That smug, venomous smile cuts through everything else. He wanted me to flinch. He wanted fear, and he got it.

Sandman raises a fist, silencing them. "Again?"

"Again, again, again…" the crowd chats, filling me with dread.

Sandman saunters inside the gate and retrieves the axe. My corneas burn with unshed tears, but I refuse to let them fall.

"Gotta give the people what they want," he taunts and places a lingering kiss on my cheek. "Remember, don't move."

The next several minutes are a true testament to my endurance. I want to break down and beg him to stop, but I don't. Sandman throws the axe again and again, landing mere centimeters from me each time.

"Show's over!" he finally yells and beckons me forward.

I pad to him on shaky legs, relieved that my only casualty is a nick on the shoulder.

"You did good, but the fun isn't over yet," he murmurs, coasting a finger along my collarbone. "There's more in store for you tonight."

I shudder, imagining the horrors to come.

CHAPTER 26

Zilphia

"IS THIS YOUR HOUSE?" I ASK, FOLLOWING SANDMAN INTO A SPACIOUS foyer.

It smells woodsy inside, like pine with citrus undertones. Sandman closes the front door, then secures the top and bottom locks.

"Zeus's, but I live here," he replies, tossing his keys into a bowl centered on a two-tier glass table. A bronze abstract statue is positioned directly below it, and beside it on the floor is a tall houseplant.

"Wh-where are the dogs?" I ask, remembering how the beautiful beasts chased me down in the woods.

He smirks at me. "Backyard."

Sandman wouldn't say where he was taking me when we left the bar. Just ordered me to get on the back of his motorcycle. I was a nervous wreck on the entire ride, terrified he was going to take me back to the crematorium. I'm not going to count my blessings just yet, though. He brought me here for a reason, and that reason, whatever it is, won't bode well for me.

"Come on." Sandman saunters through an archway, bypassing the winding staircase.

I scurry after him, the sound of my high heels sharp on the black marble floor. "Where are we going?"

For all I know, he could be planning to keep me prisoner in the basement. I'm not being melodramatic. He would definitely do some fucked up shit like that. If he says basement, I'm making a run for it. Fuck the consequences. I'm not sleeping on a dirty mattress and doing my business in a bucket.

Sandman peers at me over his shoulder. "Kitchen."

We enter the opulent space, featuring matte black cabinets, stainless-steel appliances, and concrete countertops. Sandman goes straight to the double glass doors and lets the dogs inside. I plaster my back against the refrigerator, watching as the rambunctious animals jump all over their master, nearly knocking him to the floor. They're almost as tall as he is when standing on their hind legs.

"All right, enough," he grumbles. "I wasn't gone that long. Go on and don't make any messes."

To my complete horror, their inquisitive gazes zero in on me.

"Sandman," I call out in alarm as they pad toward me. "Please help." I'm too scared to move, but to my relief, they don't attack. Wet noses greet me instead, as they investigate the new human in their domain.

I nervously pat both on the head. "What are their names?"

"That's Harley on your left, and the other hound is her brother, Mayhem."

I smile. "They're not so bad." *When they're not chasing people through the woods, that is.*

"I didn't bring you here to make friends with my dogs," Sandman growls at me.

"Why am I here?" I ask him, fearing the answer.

"To bake me a strawberry shortcake," he announces, sitting at the island. "Everything you need is in the fridge and pantry."

My eyebrows stretch to my forehead. I expected shouting, violence, even some bloodshed, but not this.

"Extra strawberries and whipped cream," we say at the same time.

Sandman gives a clipped nod, staring at me with those mesmerizing blue orbs. Anger and lust lurk in their depths. He wants to destroy me just as much as he wants to devour me. It's a losing battle.

I slip out of my heels and set to work, first washing my hands before preheating the oven and gathering the ingredients. *Flour, baking powder, baking soda, sugar, salt…* To the outside world, strawberry shortcake is simply a sweet indulgence, but for us, it's much more. We bonded over the sugary confection on countless nights while ensconced in the tree house. Ultimately, that universe crumbled to dust and scattered in the wind.

Sandman's gaze stalks me through the kitchen like a predator—slow, burning, unrelenting. It coils around me, dragging goose bumps across my skin, lighting every nerve on edge. My hands tremble as I dump the ingredients into the mixer, the roar of the machine barely drowning out the thud of my pulse.

I keep my eyes down and try to block him out, letting the rhythm of baking pull me in. When the batter's smooth, I pour it into three buttered pans with unsteady hands, then slide each one into the oven. Even with my back to him, his presence is suffocating. Like the walls are closing in.

A resounding crash rings out, and I whirl around. Sandman is on his feet, barreling straight toward me, the stool he was sitting on toppled over behind him. He locks onto my shoulders and shakes me so hard my head whips back and forth.

"Was it easy for you to walk over my unconscious body?" Sandman thunders, slamming me against the refrigerator.

"My brother had to drag me out of that classroom. I fought him. I really did. Please believe me," I sob, a hitch in my voice. "I wouldn't have left you like that. I'm sorry for everything. For lying. Your hearing loss. I hate myself for hurting you."

He laughs derisively. "Not as much as I do."

"If I could go back—"

"But you can't go back! What's done is done!" Sandman shouts in my face, ripping my dress down the center.

My breasts spill free, rising and falling with each breath. He seeks out a nipple, suckling my flesh to a taut peak. Then he licks his way to my other nipple, tongue lashing and teeth nipping. I hold myself rigid and brace for the pain that's sure to come. My thong is destroyed with a sharp tug, then his rough fingers explore my velvet folds.

"You shaved?" Sandman murmurs huskily, straightening above me.

"Meela waxed me," I answer him, ensnared in his blue irises.

"Keep your pussy just like this," he orders, raw hunger simmering in his heated gaze.

"Okay," I whisper, tears leaving glistening paths down my cheeks.

Sandman masterfully strokes the heartbeat between my thighs—firm, teasing, relentless. My body becomes a furnace, his unwanted touch stoking a fire within me. A fire that rapidly spreads to my belly and below. It strengthens, wild and unconstrained, evolving from spark to sweltering blaze in minutes. I'm almost there… just a little more. He abruptly pulls his hand away, promptly extinguishing the conflagration.

"You don't get to orgasm tonight," Sandman sneers and brandishes a lighter. "Tonight, we play a game."

"W-what game?"

"I'm going to hold the flame close to your pretty brown nipple for ten seconds," he explains, rubbing the lighter around my areola. "If you can't handle the heat, just say so, but then you lose."

"What happens if I lose?" I question, dreading his response.

"Then tomorrow you get liar tattooed here." Sandman slides his index finger across my throat. "It's fitting, considering what you did. Wouldn't you say?" He rolls his thumb down the spark wheel, expelling the flame. "One, two, three…" he counts, pausing between each number.

Though the flame isn't touching skin, I still feel the burn. I bite down on my bottom lip, attempting to counteract the pain.

Don't give in, don't give in, don't give in.

I can't let him win… not this game. He counts more slowly, one second equivalent to two. More tears come. I'm on the verge of caving in when he reaches the magic number. The air swooshes from my lungs. *I fucking did it.*

"Don't celebrate just yet," Sandman announces, moving the lighter to my other nipple. "The game isn't over."

"What? No," I say, panicked. "You didn't say both."

"That was a test run," he replies, starting the torture all over again. "The real game begins now."

Sandman counts even slower, one second now equivalent to three. There's no question that he wants me to lose his twisted game. His dick is rock hard, my suffering giving him sexual gratification. It's beyond sick. He's *beyond* sick. I wail my agony, the harsh sound reverberating through the kitchen until the game is over.

"See, that wasn't so bad," he croons, palming my drenched cheek. "Round two, or do you prefer a different game?"

"Different game," I choke out.

He smiles and quickly swaps the lighter for the handgun tucked into his waistband at the small of his back.

I inhale a sharp breath. *Out of the frying pan and into the fire.*

"This is a Smith & Wesson. Zeus gave me this beauty for my birthday last year."

"What game is this?"

A sinister gleam shines in his cerulean depths. "Russian roulette."

"No, no, no." I frantically shake my head from side to side. "I don't want to play this game."

"One bullet," he states, pointing the muzzle against my forehead. "Six chambers."

Only one bullet… he already had this planned. Sandman pulls the trigger, and I scream hysterically. He's really going to kill me this time.

"Please stop!"

Click. Again, he pulls the trigger.

"I can't take it anymore!" I heave, debilitating shudders racking my body. "Please. Mercy."

"Mercy?" he mocks, a scowl darkening his features. "Sam had mercy, but Sandman is a fucking animal."

He's exceptionally methodical in his mental terrorism of me. I feel insane, emotionally drained, and mindfucked to the point of no return.

"Here," Sandman says, holding out the gun to me. "Take it."

"W-what?"

This could be a trick. I touch that gun, and who knows what he'll do.

"This is your chance to get rid of me," Sandman explains. "Just aim at my heart and shoot."

"No," I weep, embracing myself in a tight hug. "I can't."

"Take it!" he bellows, shoving the gun into my hand. "Or I'll splatter your brain all over this goddamn kitchen!"

I wrap my fingers around the handle and level the muzzle at his chest. "Don't make me do this."

Despite everything he's done, I can't kill him. He's still Sam deep down inside. Still the abused boy who sought sanctuary in my tree house on that rainy night. My best friend. My protector.

"Pull the fucking trigger, Zilphia!"

I let the gun slip from my fingers. "I can't."

He tilts his head, studying me like an insect under a microscope before picking it up and aiming the barrel at my forehead again. "Now you die."

I clamp my eyes shut and hold my breath, bracing for the end.

The click of the gun pounds through my ears. Empty. I sag against the refrigerator, lightheaded from the adrenaline racing through my bloodstream.

"No bullets." Sandman opens the cylinder for me to see. "Did you really think I'd give you a loaded weapon to fire at me?" He tsks under his breath. "You disobeyed me and now you have to pay."

"I'm not a murderer like you!" I cry out, exhausted from his mind games. "You need psychiatric help!"

"Making you bleed is my therapy." Sandman grasps my chin and lifts my face toward his. "Run." His eyes bore into mine. "I'll give you a five-second head start. You make it out the front door before I catch you, and you're free to go, but if you—"

I bolt out of the kitchen, running as fast as my feet will carry me. Sandman doesn't wait the five seconds he promised. I hear his pounding footsteps right behind me, but I'm too afraid to look back. With no time to spare, I dart up the staircase instead of making a play for the front door.

"Where you going?" Sandman jeers. "There's nowhere for you to run."

I choke down the raw fear clogging my throat, and it settles heavily in my belly. A window is my only chance of escaping. I just need to get to a bedroom. I reach the landing and my heart drops.

Every door in sight is closed. Any one of them could be locked or lead to a linen closet. I'm caught in either case. My head is violently yanked back, then I'm on the floor, gasping for air. Sandman looms above me, several passion twists clenched in his fist. He drags me into a bedroom and flings me onto the bed.

"No!" I yell, frantically kicking out at him.

He seizes my ankles and flips me onto my stomach, then his full weight crashes down on me.

"I'm going to fuck this tight little ass hard and fast all night long," he rasps, pinning my arms above my head with one hand. "There will be no sleep for you."

"Please don't." I weep into the pillow. "I'm so sore."

I need to heal. Day after day he brutalizes my body, never allowing me a moment's respite.

"No rest for the wicked," Sandman whispers in my ear.

I hear the clank of his belt buckle and the hiss of his zipper, then he's driving into me with battering-ram force. He brings his threat to fruition, relentlessly jackhammering in and out of my rear passage.

The bed shakes and shudders under his ruthless thrusts. My tears soak the pillowcase, creating a damp circle beneath my cheek. For Sandman, fucking me isn't just about achieving orgasm. It's about power and control. He needs me to suffer. My betrayal cut him deep, and he's reciprocating tenfold, severing me to the marrow.

"Tell me how bad it hurts," he demands.

"It hurts so much," I croak, my throat raw from crying.

I'll say whatever he wants me to say. Do whatever he wants me to do. I just want him to be done and this night to be over.

"Your pain is like a heroin addiction," he murmurs against my neck. "I wish I could inject it into my veins."

Sandman moves to his knees, pulling me with him. His large hand spans the middle of my back and pushes down, accentuating my arch.

"Stay," he orders, his steel fingers digging into my hips.

He drives deeper into my tight hole, callously pummeling my rectum. Each thrust feels like a bomb exploding inside my body. I scream into the pillow until he finally curls over me, groaning in my ear.

"Take every last drop," he growls, undulating his hips against me.

After a brief pause, he slips out of me and falls onto his back. "Check on the cake."

I can barely move, and he wants me to check on the cake! Fuck the cake! I want to rant at him, damn him to hell, but I clamber to my feet instead and hobble to the door. I'm an utter mess—half naked, bruised and burned, with his semen leaking from my ass.

"Zilphia," he calls out to me.

I squeeze my eyes shut for several seconds before turning around to face him. "Yes?"

I fucking despise how relaxed he looks with his back propped against the headboard and his hands folded behind his golden mane. He spent the last thirty minutes terrorizing me, and he's completely remorseless.

"Don't run."

"Like you said, there's nowhere for me to run."

CHAPTER 27

Zilphia

"IT'S WAY TOO SHORT," LEAH COMPLAINS, PULLING ON THE HEM OF her dress. "You were supposed to make it knee length." She tilts her head sideways, perusing her reflection in the mirror. "It barely covers my ass, and my boobs are practically hanging out. One wrong move and it's hello world."

I stifle a chuckle as I reposition myself against the mountain of pillows on Meela's bed. We're getting ready for douchebag perv's birthday party. I, for one, am looking forward to going. Leah, on the other hand, is not. I'm pretty sure she would rather eat a bowl of rocks.

When she picked me up for my first shift at the hospital this morning, she ranted and raved about how much she detests parties during the entire fifteen-minute drive. I dutifully listened with the occasional nod; after all, she drove ten minutes out of her way to get me. She didn't have to, even though we volunteer at the same time. Afterward, I caught the bus to Meela's while Leah started her shift at the gift shop.

"I was," Meela replies as she zips up the back of Leah's dress. "But I changed my mind. Sorry."

Leah looks back at her, a scowl on her pretty features. "I doubt if you've ever been sorry about anything in your entire life."

"You would be correct," Meela quips unapologetically and walks over to her closet. "Hmm, what am I going to wear?" she mutters, clamping a hand on her hip.

"You're such a witch," Leah gripes and turns back around, studying her reflection in the mirror again.

"Bitch," Meela corrects her. "I'm such a bitch. You must give a queen her due respect."

"Oh God." Leah rolls her eyes heavenward. "You are the most conceited person I've ever met."

"It's called self-confidence, honey," she counters, rummaging through the multitude of colorful clothes in her closet. "Anyway, I've decided your grandma days are over."

Leah sighs. "Isn't it enough that I agreed to go in the first place?"

"I kept my grades up, per our arrangement," Meela shrugs out of her silk robe and flings it onto the back of her vanity chair. "That's the only reason why you're coming. Otherwise, you'd be at home with your nose in a book."

"And?" she gripes defensively. "I like reading. What's wrong with that?"

Meela clucks her tongue disapprovingly. "The fact you even asked that is proof you need an intervention immediately. Teenage years are wasted on you, girl. You should've been born an old woman."

"You look good," I comment. "Honestly, you do. The guys are going to be slobbering all over you."

Sure, it's short as hell and the possibility of a little nip showing is high, but the red bustier-style bodycon dress molds to her lithe figure perfectly.

"See, you're worrying over nothing," Meela states, pulling a peach-colored, patent leather belly shirt from a hanger and slipping it over her head. "Thank God one of you has some fashion sense. Two style-deficient individuals would've been way too much for me to handle."

"Too much skin is showing," Leah says, nervously wringing her hands together. "People will stare."

"Then let them stare. You're sexy as hell," Meela announces with fire in her eyes. "You need to own that shit."

"What she said," I chime in. "I would kill to have a body like yours."

"You're just saying that," she mumbles, her voice small and unsure. "You don't have to lie to spare my feelings."

"Good grief, girl!" Meela yells in exasperation, donning the matching pants to her shirt. "No one is lying to you."

Leah sits on the edge of the bed. "What if Snake's there?"

"I've been going to douchebag perv's parties for two years and haven't seen him at one yet," Meela explains to her. "Anyway, fuck the Gods."

She's been butthurt ever since the bar, literally and figuratively speaking. Jigsaw, aka her scary crush, knew she was lying about her age, and that falsehood earned her a spanking. She couldn't sit comfortably for several days after, but that's not what has her panties in a bunch—it's that her plan didn't work.

I clear my throat. "He might be there."

"What makes you say that?" Meela asks.

"I told Sandman we were going, and he may have mentioned it to Snake." His leash on my life is tighter than ever. Per his demand, I'm now required to report my every move to him.

Leah whirls around and glares at me. "What the hell, Zilphia? Why would you do that?"

"I didn't have a choice." I scoot to the edge of the bed. "I'm sorry."

"Look, I'm not trying to get all up in your business," Leah comments, "but this thing going on between you and the death master affects us too."

"Yeah, it's not fair keeping us in the dark like this," Meela adds, crossing her arms. "Don't you think it's time to let us know what's going on?"

They're right. They deserve to know what type of person they befriended. "I did something really, really horrible," I say, unshed tears brimming in my eyes. "Sandman has every right to hate me."

"Hey, no judgment here." Meela sits beside me and gives my hand a reassuring squeeze. "Whatever is said won't leave this room."

"Neither of you will want to be my friend anymore," I whisper as hot rivulets spill down my cheeks. I wouldn't blame them if they didn't. No one wants a backstabber for a friend.

"We will." Leah sits on the other side of me. "I haven't known you for a long time, but I do know you're a good person."

"I was ten when I met Sandman," I pause and inhale a deep breath. "Back then he was Sam." *My Sam.* An image of him from that rainy night flashes in my mind. He was so afraid—dirty, bruised, and shoeless. I wanted to take him in like a stray animal and keep him forever. It's been eight years, but I remember that night like it was yesterday.

"I found him hiding in my tree house." Tears splash onto my clasped hands. "He was battered and starving." I remember thinking he was going to die. My ten-year-old mind couldn't grasp how someone could be so skinny and be alive. "We became best friends, but we had to keep our friendship a secret, especially from my mother and brother." There wasn't room for him in the world she built for me, so we constructed our own. We were stupid to think it would last. "Everything changed when I started high school."

He loved me, and I broke his heart. I'll never forget the look on his face when I betrayed him. I told a lie, and it ruined his life. If it weren't for me, he'd still be Sam. I wish I could take it all back and rewrite both of our destinies.

"Zilphia?" Leah calls out to me, a note of worry in her voice. "Are you okay?"

I blink, spilling more tears down my cheeks. "What?"

"You completely spaced out on us," Meela says.

"I'm sorry." I cry harder, wiping the wetness from my heated face with shaky hands. "I've never spoken the truth about what happened to anyone." What I told my parents and the detective in the aftermath of the tree house fire was a complete fabrication.

"Let's forget the heavy stuff for now," she chirps, offering me an easy out. "I'm ready to get my party on."

"No." I shake my head. "You both deserve to know what I did." *If they're going to end our friendship, I'd rather get it over and done with now.*

"It was homecoming night," I continue, guilt settling like a boulder in the pit of my stomach. "Sandman punched my date in the face, then dragged me into an empty classroom. We got into an argument, and one thing led to another. The next thing I knew, we were kissing." I close my eyes, recalling the feel of his warm lips on mine.

"My brother and his friends stormed into the classroom. He said he would tell our mother, so I lied." Bone-jarring sobs rack my body. "I lied and said that Sam forced himself on me. They beat him until he was unconscious." I press a hand to my roiling belly. "Later that night, he set the tree house on fire. He didn't even try to run. He stayed and watched it burn."

"That's awful!" Leah exclaims. "And that's why he has it out for you?"

"Yeah." I sigh, suddenly feeling very tired. "I had no idea what happened to him after his arrest until I moved here." *And met Sandman, the monster I created.* "That's when I found out he's completely deaf in his left ear because of the beating. My brother hit him in the head with a desk."

"Sheesh," Meela responds, her eyebrows raised in surprise. "Didn't know that about him."

"Me either," Leah says and releases a long breath. "This is a lot to take in."

I hang my head low, nervously picking at the loose tatters of my frayed jeans. "Still wanna be my friend?"

"I'm not gonna lie, what you did was fucked up," Meela tells me straight up, no sugarcoating. "No wonder he has a bone to pick with you."

"I know," I mumble past numb lips. "I regret it every day."

"He must've really liked you," Leah remarks somberly, peering at me through her prescription lenses. "Did you like him back?"

"I don't know. Maybe." I shake my head. "My mother would've never allowed us to be together. She already had my life planned out, down to my wedding and groom."

"Had?" Leah questions.

"Everything changed when my dad was charged with health insurance fraud," I explain, deciding to lay it all on the line. No point in hiding my past now. "He did it to keep my mother from bankrupting them. All of our friends abandoned us, and my future husband dumped me. It wasn't a total loss because I actually hated him."

"Girl, your life is a complete mess." Meela stands and walks over to her wig wall, selecting a peached-colored afro. "Your mother is a bitch, that's for sure."

"You don't know the half of it." I tell them all about the sordid history between my mother and aunt.

"That's some wild shit," Meela remarks, her nose wrinkling in disgust.

"Is your dad in prison?" Leah asks.

"No, he's a fugitive," I answer her. "He disappeared after he was released on bail. My father isn't a bad man. He just married a bad woman." I pull in a shaky breath. "So what's the verdict? Should I leave? I completely understand if neither of you want to be my friend anymore."

"We're still going to be your friend, Zilphia," Leah says and smiles at me. "We already told you that."

"Yeah, Sandman should practice forgiveness," Meela retorts, plucking a contact out of the pink heart-shaped case on her dresser and popping it into her left eye. And of course, the color matches her outfit. "You made a split-second error in judgment," she adds. "That doesn't make it okay for him to shit on you for the rest of your life. Anyway, who is he to hold grudges? He actually kills people."

Relief washes over me. I won't be ending the day friendless after all.

"You can't accuse someone of outright murder without proof," Leah admonishes her. "If one of the Gods heard you say that..."

"Whatever." Meela rolls her eyes. "Jig wouldn't let any of them touch me," she states confidently. "Come on. I'm ready to go."

"Thanks for not holding my past mistakes over my head," I say, counting my lucky stars that I'm not ending the day friendless.

"You're good," Meela chirps, parking next to a rusted orange Mustang. "Just don't do that shit again or your ass is getting kicked to the curb, girl."

"Trust me, I won't." I slide out of the passenger seat and glance around the large property. "I hear music, but the house looks abandoned."

"It kinda is," Meela replies. "It was douchebag perv's grandparents' farm. They're both dead now and the family let it waste away."

"Where's the party then?" Leah asks as we walk toward the dilapidated dwelling.

"Around back in the barn," she answers, striding ahead of us. "Come on, slowpokes."

"If only she were this enthusiastic about school," Leah retorts sarcastically.

"I heard that, bitch!" Meela shouts over her shoulder.

"Good," she quips. "You were supposed to."

Meela's rebuttal is two middle fingers in the air. I curl my lips together in an effort to hide my laughter, lest our feisty friend liken me to a female dog too. We traipse around the side of the house behind her, and a wooden barn comes into view. The door is open, granting a glimpse into the dimly lit interior. From this vantage point, it looks fairly crowded inside. A group of people stand in a circle nearby, sharing a joint, Solo cups in hand. Their giggles and pungent smoke fill the night air.

"I don't know about this," Leah comments nervously. "Is it even safe?" She gestures toward the rickety red structure. "Look at it. It's a death trap."

"Quit being a worrywart!" Meela snaps, throwing her arms up. "I've been going to parties here for years and I'm still alive."

I loop my arm around Leah's. "It's going to be fine. And look on the bright side, no motorcycles in sight. That means no Sandman or Snake."

"They could always show up later," she cautions, her nervous gaze shifting back and forth as if she expects Snake to jump out of the shadows.

Does he do the same things to her that Sandman does to me? What atrocities has he subjected her to? Now is not the time to ask. Maybe it's better not to ask at all. Maybe, like me, she prefers to suffer in silence.

"Yeah, but we're not going to worry about that right now." After giving me the green light for the party, Sandman texted me a lengthy list of rules to follow, but he didn't say if he was coming. I'm hoping he's too busy doing only God knows what with his biker gang to show.

We enter the barn and follow Meela across the dirt floor to three huge beer kegs situated on top of a table. About two dozen more are stacked against the wall behind it. Reggae music blasts from a tall speaker nestled in the opposite corner. Bales of hay are strategically placed throughout the open space, providing a place to sit for anyone needing to rest their feet.

"One for you," Meela singsongs, handing me a cup filled to the brim.

"Thank you very much," I say and take a small sip. I grimace, my cheeks burning at the tart flavor. I'm not really a beer person, but when in Rome...

"You're very much welcome." Meela fills another cup, then offers it to Leah. "And one for you."

Leah vehemently shakes her head. "I never agreed to participate in underage drinking."

"Fine, whatever," Meela gripes, rolling her eyes. "But what about dancing?" she asks, letting the music guide her movements. "Is that on your 'how not to have a good time at a party' list too?"

"Well, no, but I don't know how to dance."

"No worries, babes." Meela grasps her hand and leads her to the makeshift dance floor. "Just follow my lead."

I trail behind them, my free hand raised high above my head as I belt out the lyrics.

A bead of sweat trickles down my temple. It's at least fifteen degrees warmer in here than it is outside due to the heat emanating from the gyrating bodies. My long passion twists hang like a heavy blanket around my shoulders, raising my core temperature even higher. Thank goodness I decided to exchange my sweater for a crop top.

"You're too stiff," Meela chides, clucking her tongue at Leah. "Stop and watch me." She squats low and resumes her twerking tutorial. I'm one hundred percent heterosexual, but that jiggle is everything. "Up, down, up, down, right, left, then throw that ass in a circle. Now you try."

I laugh behind my cup as Leah awkwardly mimics the sexually charged dance. The girl has zero rhythm.

"It's useless." She sighs resolutely. "I can't dance to save my life."

"We agree on that front. I might have to revoke your Black card."

"At least I know how to cook," Leah huffs, lifting her chin. "All you eat is takeout or ramen noodles."

"No need to get all pissy, babes," Meela quips, playfully pulling on one of Leah's beautiful locs. "It's not my fault you can't dance worth shit. How long have I been begging you to come to parties with me? I could've taught you to dance a long time ago. Anyway, what you cook isn't real food."

"Is too," she grumbles.

Meela rolls her eyes and looks at me. "I need to recharge," she says, then nods at my cup. "You want in?"

"Yep," I reply, passing her my empty cup.

"I can't twerk properly in this thot-length dress without flashing everyone anyway!" Leah yells after her.

A few minutes later, Meela returns with our drinks, and soon we're moving to the beat of the music. Well, Leah does the best she can. I haven't had this much fun in forever.

Before long, I'm on my third drink. I want to get so drunk that I forget the shitstorm my life has become, however temporary.

During the day, I pretend to be okay. I'm just a regular teenage girl with regular teenage girl problems. My father isn't a fugitive from the law, and my mother isn't a selfish bitch. My biggest worries are college applications, senior dues, and deciding what I'm going to wear to prom.

Then the sun sets and darkness falls; that's when the golden-haired devil comes knocking on my door. He brings hellfire and brimstone. *And pain*. Yes, the pain he inflicts on my body is merciless.

The worst part is when his touches turn gentle. My body yields to him, becoming his playground to do with as he pleases, and I hate myself for it. Coming for the devil shouldn't feel so fucking good.

"Oh great, the skank squad is here," Meela spits, her mouth pulling into a grimace. "Look behind you."

I glance back and sure enough, my cousin and her posse are on the other side of the barn, surrounded by boys vying for their attention. I figured I'd see her here tonight. "Remember what I said."

"I know, I know," Meela grouses. "I'll play nice as long as they don't start no shit and stay way over there."

I shake my head. My aunt and Deja are colder toward me than ever. I try to avoid them at all costs, but sometimes it's impossible. I've learned to bite my tongue, but unfortunately, my mother has not. Too many times, Keith and I have had to mediate arguments. My grandmother makes the living arrangement tolerable, though. I spend as much time as I can with her.

"Damn, girl!" I turn toward the rowdy voice and find the owner grinding against Meela's round bottom. I recognize the boy from school. "Your ass gets phatter by the day."

She whirls around and smacks him upside his head. "Keep your scrawny dick away from my booty."

"Don't be like that," he coos, his gaze glued to her breasts. "You know I been crushing on you since fourth grade. Give a brother a chance with your mean self."

"Wasn't interested then, and I'm not interested now. Now move along, little boy," she demands, shooing him away. "You're killing my vibe."

"Wanna get lit?" He pulls a Ziploc bag filled with weed from his jacket pocket. "This that good shit too."

Meela taps her chin in contemplation. "It has been a minute since I've gotten high."

"Then come on," he cajoles, throwing an arm around her shoulders. "You know you want to."

"Okay, let's go." She elbows him in the stomach, then latches onto his shirt, yanking him down to her eye level. "But you better keep your grubby little hands to yourself."

"Damn, girl, you got it." He grins, raising his hands in surrender. "You ain't got to be so violent."

"Y'all coming?" Meela asks us.

"Not me," I answer her. "I want to keep dancing."

"And I need to rest my feet," Leah says.

"I'll be right back." Meela walks out of the barn, with our horny classmate tailing her, and Leah finds a bale of hay to perch on.

I continue dancing, swaying side to side as I sing the lyrics in my mind. The music flows over my sweat-slick body like a warm breeze, and soon the alcohol begins working its magic, numbing me to harsh realities. This is the freest I've felt in months. It's all an illusion, but it'll have to do. Sandman may not come to the party, but he'll be waiting for me at home. He's always around, never giving me a moment's peace.

I push him from my thoughts and glance over at Leah. I smile, seeing a cute boy talking in her ear. She laughs, and on cue, he scoots closer to her, placing a hand on her thigh. I roll my eyes at the blatant move. It's the oldest trick in the horny teenage boy playbook.

Snake appears out of thin air and kicks the boy in the chest, sending him crashing to the dirt floor. I drop my cup, watching in horror as he yanks my screaming friend up by her ponytail. He slams her into the wall and pins her wrists high above her head.

I search the crowd for Sandman. *Where is he?* Maybe the dark prince is solo tonight. Leah's would-be suitor springs to his feet and bounds in their direction, but stops in his tracks. I assume he notices the insignia on the back of Snake's cut. He immediately changes course and hightails it out of here. He knows who the Gods are, and he knows not to fuck with one.

I remain rooted to the spot, unsure what to do. Leah made it clear not to interfere when it comes to Snake. *Meela will know what to do.*

A steel arm bands around my waist before I can take a step. "Mind your fucking business."

The devil has arrived. Fear stalls my breath as I helplessly watch Snake drag Leah from the barn. I send up a silent prayer because only divine intervention can save us now. Sandman sweeps my passion twists over my shoulder and places a soft kiss just below my ear.

"I can't stop thinking about you," he growls, sliding his free hand between my legs. "The same three thoughts cycle in my mind twenty-four-seven. Do you want to know what those thoughts are?"

I nod, though my mind screams no. It doesn't matter what my response is; he's going to tell me regardless. To do otherwise would deprive him of his greatest pleasure—invoking the most fear.

"I imagine the tight sweetness between your thighs soaking every inch of my dick," he murmurs, kneading my clit through my clothing.

"Don't," I whisper, latching one hand onto the arm circling my belly and the other on the wrist pressed against my pubic bone. My mind immediately goes back to the night he took me to God's Glory. Is he planning to do the same thing here? At least half of my classmates are at this party. I won't be able to show my face at school again.

"One day soon, I'm going to pop that beautiful cherry, Zilphia, and pump your body full of cum. Then there's making you hurt." I gasp, feeling his length growing against my ass. "Nothing gets my cock harder. But what I think about more than anything else is cutting this soft, beautiful skin of yours." He rubs his nose along my neck. "The sight of your blood does something to me. *You* do something to me," he rasps accusingly, his voice tortured and thick with emotion.

"I'm so sorry, Sam," I sob, hating that I'm the cause of his anguish. "I was stupid and scared. I wish I could take it all back."

"I warned you never to call me that," he barks, winding his hard fingers into my passion twists.

I lean into his strong body, attempting to relieve the stress on my scalp. "Sandman—"

"Shut the fuck up," he snarls, tightening his grip in my hair.

Pained tears sting my corneas as he forces me through the crowd ahead of him. I slam my eyelids shut against the shocked faces, humiliation heating my cheeks. The mild night air enveloping my slightly damp skin alerts me that we're outside. Still, I keep my vision shrouded in darkness, hearing animated conversations echo around me.

Once the voices and music fade to the background, I crack my eyes open and see that he's steering me toward the farmhouse. I climb the creaking steps and find the front door ajar. A loud cry startles me, and I halt in my tracks. There are people here.

"Move!" Sandman shouts, releasing my hair and shoving me inside.

I crash to my hands and knees on the dusty floor. A musky odor immediately clogs my nostrils and throat, sending me into a coughing fit. I'm no expert, but I doubt it's safe to be in here. It's highly probable this house is infested with mold.

My gaze roams the four corners of the living room, only finding a lone recliner positioned adjacent to the fireplace. The door closes behind me, cutting off the little light the moon provided.

I retrieve my inhaler from my fanny pack and spray two doses into my mouth before pushing to shaky legs. "Why did you bring me in here?"

"Don't talk, Zilphia," he rasps softly, standing so close behind me his warm breath fans my nape. "It's not safe for you to talk."

I snap my mouth shut and stand stock-still, afraid to even breathe. Uncontrolled energy radiates from his body in waves, pouring into me like an electric pulse. I apprehensively wait for his next move, but long moments pass and nothing. I want to shout at him, tell him to get it over with, to stop playing his fucking mind games with me. Instead, I close my eyes and count.

One, two, three, four—

"No!" Leah's terrified scream echoes from upstairs, followed by heavy footsteps and a loud bang. I strain to listen for more sounds of her attack, but silence greets me.

Christ. What is Snake doing to her?

Before I realize what's happening, my face smacks into the wall. I whimper as the metallic taste of blood melts on my tongue. Sandman tears at my jeans, roughly yanking the tight denim down my legs along with my thong. I hold my breath, bracing for the feel of his thick length pushing between my ass cheeks.

"Turn around," he orders.

I should be relieved, but this means he has far worse in store for me. I face him in a daze, head whirling from the violent impact. He's a shadow in the dark living room, mirroring a ghostly apparition.

For all intents and purposes, that's exactly what he is, a restless spirit hellbent on taking over my soul. My tormentor says nothing; he just stands there, several inches separating us. Though his features are an obsidian void, I swear I feel his hot gaze burning a hole into the very core of me.

I plaster myself tight against the crumbling wall when he makes a sudden movement, my breath lodged in my throat. A small flame washes his beautiful face in an orange glow as he lights a joint.

This is all wrong.

The devil shouldn't look this good. The devil *shouldn't* look like a golden god. I stare at his hard angles in wonderment, completely baffled that someone with a heart as black as his could be so handsome. He takes a long hit, then exhales, filling the short distance between us with the distinct smell of cannabis.

"Smoke," he demands, nudging the joint against my lips.

I turn my head. "I-I d-don't d-do d-drugs."

"You're a fucking puppet, Zilphia," Sandman states, his tone hushed and menacing. "And I'm your puppeteer. I control your strings. You don't question. You don't talk back. You obey. Now fucking smoke."

I hesitantly inhale the pungent herb into my lungs and immediately spiral into a coughing frenzy.

"This that A1 shit," he rumbles, clamping a calloused hand around my jaw. "You gotta take your time with it."

Sandman forces me to take hit after hit, initiating level one of tonight's ongoing mindfuck saga. The earthy fumes settle like hot ash in my throat, and soon my body becomes weightless.

"Please, no more," I plead with him.

"*More* is what I crave from you. *More* is what I need from you. And *more* is what I'll have from you, come hell or high water."

The next thing I know, his lips are on mine, his tongue hungrily exploring the depths of my mouth. This kiss is wholly different from the tender kiss we shared in my tree house a little over three years ago. It's wildfire in a field of daisies, the sweetest dream trapped inside a nightmare, and hell in the middle of paradise.

Sandman detests my very existence; even so, he wants me with a desperation that defies reason. His urgency bleeds into me, wrapping phantom hands around my neck and squeezing tight. It must drive him crazy to desire that which he hates most in the world.

He jerks away from me, a frightening roar spilling from his lips. "I swear to God, Zilphia, cross me again and I'll break you like a fucking twig."

"If you want me dead so bad, then do it," I snap, blinking back the hot tears swimming in my gaze. "Torture me, blow my brains out. Just be done with it."

"Eager to die, are we?" Sandman slips a hand between my thighs. "Not until I've had my fill of this," he states huskily, his hands lightly caressing my clit. "After all, I lost my hearing because of it."

I will my body not to respond, but my determination is shit against his skilled fingers. I curl my hands into fists, disgusted that my pussy is wet and aching for him.

Sandman sinks to his knees and places a lingering kiss on my special place, then bestows the same attention to both thighs, his lips firm and reverent on my warm skin.

"Why can't I stop wanting you?" he murmurs.

It's an answer I'd like to know as well. There's nothing extraordinary about me. I just showed kindness to a boy, and that boy fell in love. It's a love I betrayed. Sam wouldn't be Sandman if it wasn't for me. How many people would still be alive if he never became Sandman, the *Blood God*? In retrospect, I'm just as responsible for their deaths as he is.

I ball my fists tighter, digging sharp fingernails into my palms as his tongue explores every inch of my throbbing slit. The pot coursing through my bloodstream heightens my senses, invoking a passion so ravenous it frightens me. I've heard all about the wonders of high sex but never thought I would experience it firsthand.

"No," I breathe, my legs trembling uncontrollably. I need to get away from him before he traps me in his twisted world forever.

Sandman pulls back and indulges in more weed, then angles his mouth over my opening, blowing the pungent smoke into my slick channel.

"Yes," he growls before burying his face in my folds.

My impassioned moans reverberate through the living room as he greedily sucks my pussy. I undulate against his mouth, my hands knotting in his golden strands. He eats me, then smokes. Eats me, then smokes some more—repeating the ritual again and again.

The steady pulse at my center slowly grows into a pounding throb. Then my orgasm comes full throttle, the pleasure so intense my belly clenches violently, trapping the oxygen in my lungs, every cell in my body on fire.

"Oh God," I gasp.

Euphoria quickly turns into anguish as Sandman grinds the smoldering tip of his joint into my clit. I scream and try to run away, but topple to the dusty wooden floor, hindered by the cotton tangled around my ankles. Iron fingers dig into my hips and jerk me to my knees, then I feel his hardness probing my wet entrance.

"Sandman, please don't do this," I beg as tears drip from my eyes. "You loved me at one time."

"And that love came with a heavy price." He seizes my passion twists and slams my head onto the floor. "Arch your fucking back."

Dust mites float all around me as he inches forward the slightest bit, inserting the head of his dick into my pussy. This is it. I'm going to lose my virginity inside this dirty, lifeless house. I hold my breath, bracing for the sting of full penetration—but it never comes. He moves in and out of me with just his swollen tip.

It was never his plan to take my virginity tonight. Psychological torment was his goal all along. Before long, my mind will become a bleak ruin, much like these four walls. I try to pretend I'm not me, that this isn't my life, but his pleasured groans mock me as he takes what was not freely given. I feel him trembling behind me, his control barely hanging on by a thread.

"I'm almost there." His fingers tighten painfully on my hips. "Just a little more. Oh fuck, there it is," he grunts, pumping his release into me. "Fuck, Zilphia."

It's over. Thank God.

I let out a relieved breath, but then he drives his erection into my ass. I scream so loud it feels like my eardrums are about to burst. He thrusts again and again until his erection is fully embedded inside my snug muscles. My hands and knees give out as he pistons into my shuddering body.

All I can do is cry and pray that it's over soon.

CHAPTER 28

Zilphia

"NEXT STOP," I CALL OUT TO THE BUS DRIVER SINCE THE BELL pull isn't working.

After last night and my shift at the hospital this morning, I'm beyond exhausted, not to mention very sore. Neither Leah nor I said a word about what happened inside the farmhouse. I heard her screams, and I'm pretty sure she heard mine. We talked and joked, pretending like the heirs to the God kingdom don't own every breath we take.

One particular patient brightened my day; he regaled me with stories about his deceased sister. Apparently she and I are doppelgängers.

I sigh, dragging my feet along the sidewalk. *Almost home.* Well, the place where I sleep at night. It most certainly isn't my home. I come to a halt, eyeing the unfamiliar car parked in the driveway. Deja is wherever she goes on the weekends, and everyone else is at church. Does my mother have company over? If Sheila finds out, she's going to be pissed, big time.

I go inside the house with every intention of going straight to the basement. I have no idea what my mother is up to, and I don't want to know. My plan backfires the moment my eyes land on the two people sitting on the sofa.

What has she done?

"What?" Redmond chuckles and unfolds to his full height. "You're not happy to see me?" He walks over to me and wraps his long arms around my body. I'm too stunned to speak or move.

"Don't be rude, Zilphia," my mother reprimands, coming to stand beside me. "Doesn't he look handsome? He came all this way to see you."

"But why?" I blurt out. He broke up with me, which was one of the happiest days of my life. What could he possibly want? And why come in person? He could've called or texted. I prefer to have never seen or heard from him again.

My mother looks at Redmond, a fake smile plastered on her face. "Could you give us a moment, please?"

"Absolutely," he responds, sliding his hands into his pockets. "Take all the time you need."

She digs her skinny fingers into my arm and drags me into the kitchen.

"You're hurting me." I jerk away from her and slam my purse onto the counter. "What's going on? Why is he here?"

A conspiratorial gleam shines in her brown gaze. "Our prayers have been answered."

"How?" I ask slowly.

What has she done? More importantly, what does she expect me to *do*? Whatever it is, I already know I'm not going to like it.

"By becoming Redmond's lover," she whispers excitedly. "You know how rich his parents are. Just keep him happy, and the money will keep coming. Imagine spa days, shopping sprees, and vacations. We'll want for nothing."

Redmond is an only child, his parents' pride and joy, their miracle baby. They don't monitor his spending, so it's normal for him to drop a couple grand a week. Whatever he wants, he gets. If you ask me, I think they're afraid of him. Still, I'm not on board with this plan even a little bit. And if Sandman were to find out, he'd kill us both. Very painfully.

"This is insane!" I exclaim, throwing my hands in the air. "I'm not going to whore myself to Redmond. I would sooner live on the streets."

Her features transform into a granite mask. "You're going to do exactly what I tell you to."

I raise my chin. "No." I'm through being her lapdog. Daddy destroyed himself trying to keep her happy. I will not follow in his footsteps. And though I'm not blameless, she's the reason I turned on Sam.

"You ungrateful bitch!" she sneers, her palm cracking across my face.

"You're going to fuck him, and you're going to fuck him good. Do you understand me?"

I hold a hand against my stinging cheek, realization dawning on me. *Money was already exchanged.* "How much did he give you?" She just glares at me, but her silence is answer enough.

"Redmond will be back to pick you up later. You're spending the night with him. End of discussion." She spins me around and shoves me forward. "Go."

"Everything all good?" Redmond queries when we enter the living room.

"Perfect." My mother beams. "Zilphia will be ready in a few hours. Why don't you walk Redmond out, sweetheart?"

I practically run out the door, wanting to get him out of here as quickly as possible. He ambles past me and leans against his car, a self-satisfied smirk curling his lips.

"Are you still a virgin?" he asks, lecherous gaze raking over my body. "I've been wanting to fuck you for a long time, but you were just a tease."

"We can't do this," I tell him. "Sam will kill us."

His eyebrows furrow. "Who?"

"Samuel Hendricks," I clarify, but his facial expression doesn't change. "From high school. Remember?"

Redmond shrugs his shoulders. "Don't know who that is."

Of course, he wouldn't remember Sam. My ex-best friend wasn't popular or rich. "Homecoming night. My house burning down. Any of that ringing a bell for you?"

"Oh, that asshole," he retorts. "What about him?"

I clear my throat. "Well, we're together now." I almost gag on the lie, but the less Redmond knows, the better. Telling him anything about the Gods could get him killed. I can't have his death on my conscience.

He bursts out laughing. "You're shitting me, right?"

"I'm completely serious." I cross my arms. "We reconnected recently. He actually lives in Oregon too."

Redmond closes the distance separating us in three long strides. "I don't give a fuck. Your mother and I have an arrangement."

"My mother's arrangement with you has nothing to do with me."

"Listen, you're going to drop out of school and move into an apartment near my campus." He grips me hard between the thighs. "I'm paying a high price for this and I plan to use it whenever I want."

I push against his chest, but I might as well be trying to move a mountain. "You're insane!"

"You're going to be a good girl, Zilphia, or there will be consequences."

Jesus Christ! How many psychos will I encounter in my lifetime?

"I'm trying to save your life, you fucking asshole!" I shout in exasperation.

"I'm not afraid of your little boyfriend," he sneers and takes a step back. "I'll be back at nine. Be ready."

I look on as he gets in his luxury vehicle and zooms down the street.

What the hell am I going to do?

I glance around, a sudden uneasiness washing over me. Sandman told me he would always have someone watching. I don't see anyone lurking about, but that doesn't mean eyes aren't on me. One thing is for certain—I can't go with Redmond tonight.

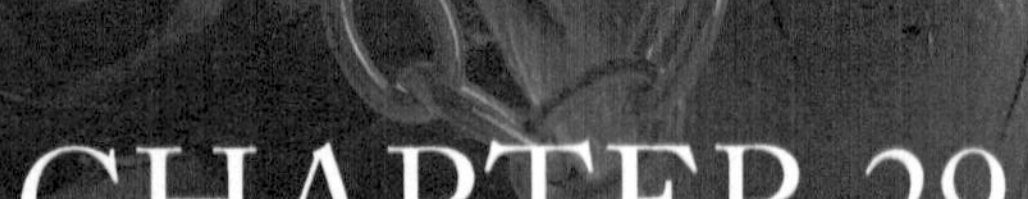

CHAPTER 29

SANDMAN

Tension hangs heavy in the air. The Latin Maniacs occupy one side of the open field while the Gods stand strong on the other, several feet or so separating our groups. Zeus is front and center, staring down their new leader—Silas, Caesar's younger brother. Jigsaw and Draco flank him.

I should be focused on the clear and present danger at hand, but my thoughts are seized on her. My cock twitches, last night's farmhouse exploits filtering through my mind. I hurt her bad, and slept like a fucking baby afterward. And tonight, I'm going to hurt her again.

"Five hundred thousand," Zeus barks, countering Silas's two-million-dollar bid.

"That's not enough." His cold gaze lands on me. "Your son murdered my brother." Silas takes a step forward at my smirk. I slip a hand under my cut and grip the handle of my Glock. *Come on, you pudgy motherfucker, give me a reason to put a bullet in your dome.*

Zeus looks at me and shakes his head. "Again, my deepest condolences for your loss, but the Disciples are at fault here. Spider played us all for fools, but his time is coming. And need I remind you, Caesar tried to fucking kill me."

"But the Gods drew first blood," Lil' Loco spits. "Word on the street is you've got rats in your ranks. None of this would've happened if your fucking house was in order."

"The traitors were taken care of," Zeus growls between clenched teeth. "Our ranks are clean."

"So you say." Lil' Loco shrugs and spreads his arms wide. "There could be a whole lot more, an infestation. The Gods can't be trusted."

Zeus quickly closes the distance between them. "If you like your tongue where it is, don't speak against the brotherhood again."

The shit that went down with Brick and Buffalo put us all at risk—our business dealings too. Word travels quick in the criminal world. What a clusterfuck.

"I'll accept your offer on one condition," Silas states, a smug smile curving his lips. "I want Sandman's head too."

"No," Zeus bites out angrily.

Silas looks at me, the same smirk on his face. "Then give me his bitch."

My hand is back on my Glock in an instant. "Don't have one. I'm a free agent."

How the fuck does he know about Zilphia?

Somebody's running their mouth, and whoever it is, they're fucking dead. Maybe Lil' Loco is right, the brotherhood has an infestation.

"My brother didn't receive a proper burial!" Silas booms, his heavy accent becoming more pronounced. "His remains were discarded like an animal! Five hundred thousand and the girl, then we can call it even."

Every muscle in my body tenses. Zilphia isn't my old lady and doesn't have the privilege of club protection. She'll never be worthy of that title. I cut my gaze to Zeus, quickly scanning his grim features. He's going to accept the offer.

Nah, fuck that. Zilphia is my kill, I've more than earned it.

"Don't do it, bruh," Cricket whispers from my left. "She ain't worth it."

"Zilphia is mine." I yank my gun from my holster and aim at Silas.

Pop. Pop.

Lil' Loco tackles him to the ground, saving the bastard from having his ticket punched. Then all hell breaks loose.

Bullets slice through the air. Bodies scatter. Blood spills.

"I told you not to do it!' Cricket shouts.

"Shut the fuck up and shoot something!" I roll forward and come up on one knee, finding my target once again and letting loose. *Missed!* "Goddamn it!"

Silas and his people retreat toward their vehicles. I line up one more shot. *Just give me one clean view of that bastard's skull.* Pursuing is too dangerous. I can't die, not today.

"Fall back!" Zeus orders.

"Come on, man." Cricket taps me on the shoulder. "We gotta bounce."

I push to my feet and haul ass toward my bike, extending an arm behind me as I return gunfire. Bullets fly all around me, missing me by mere centimeters.

"Fuck, I almost got hit!" Cricket shouts, running along beside me.

The gang piles into their vehicles and zooms out of the field, leaving a few casualties behind. I keep shooting, hoping a bullet finds Silas between the eyes.

"They're gone, Sandman," Snake states, wiping the sweat from his brow. "Fuck, I didn't plan on almost having my ass shot off today."

"You're a God," Cricket replies between labored breaths. "Plan on almost getting your ass shot off every day."

"Jigsaw, how bad?" Zeus calls out in a clipped tone.

He's crouched beside a fallen brother, his large hands firmly pressing against a chest wound. "Bad. We gotta get him to the doc ASAP or he's going to bleed out."

"We got two dead," Draco says, shooting me a death glare. "And it's your fault."

Zeus barrels forward, his gun aimed at the center of my forehead. "You set this club back a fucking decade. No one will trust the Gods."

"What the hell are you doing, Zeus?" Snake shouts, his dark gaze darting between us. "He's your son. Your flesh and blood!"

"And a pain in my fucking ass!"

"They'd be right not to trust the Gods," I sneer, standing my ground. "How did Silas know about Zilphia? Someone's feeding him info."

"Anyone could've given him that intel!" Zeus roars in my face. "Everyone knows you're obsessed with that girl! It's clear as fucking day!"

"Then kill me." I spread my arms wide. "Because anyone who tries to take her from me is gonna eat a bullet."

"Then you better make her your old lady or she's expendable. End of discussion," Zeus warns me before walking away.

"Drop that bitch, man," Cricket says. "She's nothing but trouble."

"You know I can't." *Not now, not ever.*

I feel my cell phone vibrating and dig it out of my back pocket. My heart rate speeds up when I see the name on the screen. "Yeah."

"Zilphia had a visitor today."

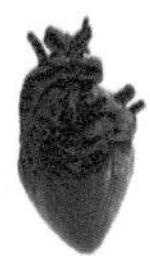

I lounge against my bike, my impatient gaze glued to the front door. I've only been waiting for about five minutes, but when you're addicted to something or *someone*, one second can seem like an eternity. I smile, thinking about the dark surprise waiting for my prey at home.

"Get ready to scream, my sweet Zilphia," I mumble, sliding a hand over my twitching cock. She brought what's to come on herself. She didn't listen, and now she has to face the consequences.

I glance down at my cell phone and type out a text.

Me: You have 60 seconds to get your ass outside.

The front door flies open at the same time I hit send. Zilphia's saucer gaze holds me captive as her trembling legs carry her to me. God, I've always loved those fucking eyes. Those soulful brown orbs almost bring me to my knees, but then I remember what a treacherous bitch she is.

I straighten to my full height and toss her the extra bucket helmet. "Get on."

"I didn't do anything," she rushes out. "I tried to—"

"No excuses." I shake my head, securing my own helmet and straddling my bike in one fluid motion.

Tears gather in her eyes because she knows there will be pain. "It's not my fault—"

"Get on the fucking bike, Zilphia," I growl and rev the engine.

I burn rubber toward home the instant she hops on behind me. She holds onto me tightly, molding her soft curves against my back. I feel something for this girl. I don't know what that something is, but it isn't love. It can't be. I don't believe in it.

On the other hand, love and hate are closely related. Both invoke passionate responses and bring out the worst in people. It's said that people often hurt the ones they love the most. And hurting her is a fucking addiction. Maybe I love-hate her. Is that even possible? Can one love and hate a person simultaneously? Stranger things have happened. My hate for her isn't cookie-cutter. Not by a long shot.

It's beautiful. A beautiful hate.

Before long, I'm dragging Zilphia through the front door and up to my bedroom. She doesn't utter a word, but her sweaty hand clutched in mine lets me know just how scared she really is.

I gesture toward the white box centered on my bed. "A gift for you."

"A gift?" Zilphia repeats, taking a step back. "Why?"

"Because you deserve it," I reply, nudging her forward. "Open it. I made it especially for you."

"What is it?" she whispers.

I push my door closed and lock it. "Go see for yourself."

She shakes her head. "I don't want to."

"Are you sure you want to go down this route, Zilphia?" I ask, coming to a standstill behind her. "There are levels to pain… so many ways to make you hurt." I kiss the side of her neck. "What's it gonna be? Either choice is fine with me."

"I'll open it," she whispers and reaches out with a shaky hand, slowly pulling the red ribbon securing my special surprise loose. "I didn't know Redmond—"

"Shh." I press a finger to her lips. "Keep going."

Zilphia lifts the top, revealing Redmond's severed head. She screams, the earsplitting sound bouncing off the walls. "Oh God! Oh God! What have you done?"

"I warned you, didn't I?" I murmur, gliding my fingertips along her trembling arm. "You're mine, Zilphia. Anyone who tries to take you from me will die a very, very horrible death. Like Redmond here. He was still alive when I started cutting off his head."

Zilphia clamps a hand over her mouth and sprints into the bathroom, collapsing to her knees as she violently vomits into the toilet.

I kneel at her side and hold her hair back from her face. "That's it. Get it all out."

I hum quietly, my hand moving in gentle circles on her back. Once her stomach is empty, I flush the toilet and wet a washcloth. With slow, tender movements, I wipe away the vomit clinging to her beautiful face. I'm a sick fuck, I never denied it, that's why my dick is rock-hard right now. I toss the washcloth onto the floor and position myself behind her, freeing my throbbing cock.

"Please don't," she protests weakly. "I can't."

Unmoved by her plea, I pull her panties and bottoms down just enough to push the tip of my cock into her warmth. Every ounce of my being wants to push deep inside her satin heat, to feel her wetness enveloping my length, but now is not the time.

I move in and out of her sweet gushiness with short, controlled thrusts. *Fuck.* My obsession with her is unnatural, depraved, laced with pain and hate. Despite our tainted history, I can't imagine never knowing her… never touching her. What kind of person would I be had our paths never crossed? It doesn't matter; our fates were predestined, and we're going to crash and burn together.

"When are you going to learn, Zilphia?" I hiss. "You're mine. I'd burn this fucking world to the ground and everyone in it to keep you."

She whimpers as I dig my fingers into her soft ass and spread her cheeks apart. I've never seen a more beautiful pussy in my life. Glistening pink, delectable, and all mine. I push my thumb into her rimmed entrance.

"I'm going to fuck this pretty little rose next." I still, leaving my swollen head inside her slick body. "Squeeze."

"W-what?" she questions, her voice hoarse and tired.

"Your pussy," I rasp, roughly tunneling my thumb through her snug asshole. "Squeeze it." Her suckling walls tighten around my dick, drawing guttural sounds from the back of my throat. "Harder." I begin moving inside her satin heat again. Three strokes in and I'm grunting my release.

Fuck, I've never come so quick before, not even during my first time.

"Take off your clothes," I growl, climbing to unsteady feet. I palm my semi-hard length, tracking her tense movements as she reveals her exquisite curves to my greedy gaze.

"I'm so tired," she says, wrapping her arms around her abdomen. "Please let me sleep."

"You sleep when I say you can fucking sleep." I shove her toward the door. "Walk."

Zilphia stumbles into my bedroom, coming to a stop at the foot of the bed. "W-what d-do you want me to do?"

I stand close behind her, breathing in her addictive scent. "Take the head out of the box and put it on the bed."

She looks back at me, her eyes wide and frantic. "I'm begging you! Please don't make me!"

I latch on to her nape and force her to the bed. "Pick it up. Now."

"I can't!" she wails, struggling to break free of my hold. "You didn't have to kill him, Sandman! He was an only child. Oh God, his parents."

"Oh, but I did." I slide a hand between her luscious thighs. "You see, this belongs to me. He touched it, so he had to die." I dig my fingernails into her nape, and she cries out. "Be a good girl and pick it up."

"God, please help me," she sobs hysterically.

I laugh, a mirthless, coarse sound. "God? Calling out to him is pointless, Zilphia. He can't help you." My fingers seek her satin clit. "I'm your God now. I'm the one who has the power to grant you absolution. The one who can make all your dreams come true or be your hell on Earth. And at this very moment, I'm your worst fucking nightmare."

She reaches into the box, then recoils with a sharp cry. "I can't do it!"

"Disobedience has a price." I bend her over the bed, slamming her face into the mattress. "I'm going to fuck you twice as hard."

"Please don't!"

I brutally work my cock into her ass, her tight muscles giving way to my invasion as she screams her agony.

"Fuck yes," I rasp, fully settling inside her body. I grab Redmond's head and place it next to her face, nose to nose, leaving just a hairbreadth between her and the grisly sight. She whimpers and slams her eyes shut.

"Open your fucking eyes," I demand, withdrawing halfway, then ramming back into her at full force. "And keep them fucking open."

"Okay, okay," Zilphia sobs, hunching forward. "I'll keep my eyes open. Please just stop hurting me."

"That I can never do." I pound into her body mercilessly, each thrust landing harder than the last. "I fucking need to hurt you, Zilphia. It's not a choice. I can't stop. I *don't* want to stop."

I seize her hips, jerking her back to meet my thrusts. Blood flows from her stretched muscles, creating a wet suction around my pulsing length. I groan, the sight an aphrodisiac to my senses. *I'm fucking obsessed.*

Zilphia goes limp beneath me, darkness pulling her under, the increasing brutality too much for her body. It's enough to send me over the edge.

My cock and balls shudder, intense pleasure washing over me. I throw my head back and roar my release, pouring my seed into her bleeding body.

I sink to my knees and lie my cheek against the soft curve of her ass, watching blood and cum trickle down her thighs.

"Disobedience will always have a price, Zilphia," I murmur.

CHAPTER 30

Zilphia

"ARE YOU OKAY?" LEAH ASKS, HER EYEBROWS KNITTED IN CONcern. "You look a little sick." She places a hand across my forehead. "No fever, but you should still go to the nurse's office and lie down for a bit. She might even give you a pass to go home. I can walk you there if you want."

"I don't know what's wrong with me," I say, swinging my locker door shut. "I've been feeling crappy all week."

I'm usually healthy as a horse. It's probably just stress catching up with me. Contending with Sandman, my mother, and the double dragons every day is finally taking a toll on me. Sleep doesn't come easy these days either. I can't close my eyes without seeing Redmond's decapitated head. A certifiable asshole he was, but he didn't deserve to die, not like that. A good ass whooping would've sufficed.

"I spent most of second period in the bathroom puking my brains out."

"Maybe it's something you ate."

"I don't think so." I sigh, rubbing my eyes. "Let's just go to lunch and—"

The words die on my tongue. *No! No! No! That's not possible. I can't be… Please, God, no.*

Leah's worried gaze sweeps over my face. "What's wrong? You look like your puppy just got hit by a car."

"Nothing," I say, fumbling for an excuse. "I just… I forgot… I have to go to the library. Essay deadline for music class."

I could use my cell to Google the question, but I don't know what type of spy crap Sandman has installed.

"Just bring your laptop to the cafeteria and work on it there."

"I won't be able to concentrate with all the noise."

"I'll come with you," Leah offers, fishing her cell phone out of her purse. "I'll text Meela and let her know where to find us."

"No!" I yell. "I mean, there's no need. It won't take me long. I'll meet y'all in the cafeteria when I'm done."

Leah eyes me for a moment, worry etched across her face. "Are you sure?"

"I'm positive." I force out a laugh. "Go eat and tell Meela not to cause any trouble."

She scoffs. "You're kidding me, right? Trouble is that girl's first, middle, and last name."

"True, true," I quip lightheartedly, though my mind is racing. "Well, see ya in a bit."

"Alrighty." We part ways, going in opposite directions.

I glance over my shoulder, watching her until she disappears around the corner before making a mad dash for the library. There are still quite a few kids lingering in the hallway though the late bell is due to ring any minute now. I'm jealous of their smiles, their youthful enthusiasm, their bright futures. I had a bright future once too, but the universe had other plans.

I believe in destiny—it can't be changed, can't be escaped. It simply is.

Tears sting my eyes as I think about what could've been, what is, and what's still coming. I know I'm jumping the gun, but my intuition is telling me that karma isn't done with me—not yet.

Hell isn't a place. *Not for me.*

My hell has blue eyes and blond hair.

I barrel into the library and head straight for the librarian's desk. "Good afternoon," I mumble breathlessly. "Is it okay if I use a computer?"

"Do you have a pass?" Ms. Tandle asks, her slim fingers pausing over her keyboard.

"It's my lunch block."

She nods at a clipboard on her desk. "Sign in first."

I jot down my name and time of arrival, then sit at the computer furthest away from everyone. I don't want my business getting out—gossip travels fast among teenagers. My hands shake as I type my question into the search bar: *Can a virgin get pregnant without full penetration?*

My last period was two weeks before the move. *I think.* I never keep up with the dates. In my defense, I never had a reason to. Redmond and I didn't venture past second base. And Sandman… he didn't take it. Not all the way. I can't be pregnant. *Right?*

A body drops into the chair beside me, nearly scaring me six feet under. "Can a virgin get pregnant without full penetration?" Meela hoots in laughter. "What the hell, girl?"

"Jesus, Meela, shut the hell up before someone hears you," I whisper, my eyes frantically darting around the room.

"Quiet," Ms. Tandle hisses.

"Sorry," Meela mouths, shaping her fingers into a heart, but the no-nonsense librarian's face doesn't soften. She pointedly glares at us for a few more seconds before returning to her task.

"That bitch clearly needs her muff eaten and a good dick down ASAP," Meela mumbles under her breath, then nods at the computer screen. "What stupid-ass assignment are you researching this for?"

"It's not for an assignment," I grit out.

"Researching for yourself, huh?" She bumps her shoulder against mine. "Don't tell me you don't know how babies are made."

I close the page and grab my purse. "Not everyone is a sex expert like you."

"I was joking." Meela grasps my wrist, all traces of humor gone. "What's going on with you?"

"Leave me alone!" I jerk away from her and storm into the hallway. Ms. Tandle sputters in outrage, but I have a whopping zero fucks to give. She's welcome to kiss my whole entire ass.

I slam into the girls' bathroom, startling the two occupants standing at the mirror.

"What the fuck is your problem?" the first girl shrieks, her hand flying to her chest.

"I-I'm s-sorry," I stammer, tears streaming down my cheeks.

The door squeaks open and Meela walks in, coming to a stop beside me. "Out," she orders the pair, jabbing her thumb at the door.

"Make me," the second girl challenges, propping a hand on her hip.

"Bitch, I will dunk your head into the fucking toilet and piss on you," Meela snarls, taking a threatening step forward.

"Let's go," her friend whispers. "I heard she's a mental case."

"You should listen to your homegirl." Meela clucks her tongue. "I'm totally insane."

Meela's challenger pulls her bottom lip between her teeth, her bravado fizzling instantly. "Freaks," she retorts, bulldozing past us. Her sidekick follows suit.

I slump against the wall and slide to my bottom, bringing my knees to my chest.

Meela sits cross-legged opposite me. "We haven't known each other long, but I fuck with you hard," she states sincerely, giving my knee a tight squeeze. "You can talk to me about anything and what's said will stay between us, or you can tell me to mind my fucking business. Either way, I'm here for you."

I open and close my mouth several times, unable to force the words past my tense throat. Saying them out loud gives them credence, but the truth can't be ignored.

"I think…" The words die on my tongue. I draw my thighs tighter against my churning stomach and try again. "I think… I'm… I'm p-pregnant."

I started taking my birth control pills as soon as I got them, but maybe it was too late.

"How late are you?"

Meela asks the question in a calm, neutral tone. If she's shocked by my bombshell, she's a pro at hiding it. I relax a little, grateful for her listening ear and tact in this situation.

"Two weeks, maybe." I hesitate, mentally kicking myself for not knowing the exact date. "I'm not sure."

"Have you ever been late before?" she probes further.

"I honestly don't know." I shake my head, disgusted with myself. "I've never actually paid attention."

"Okay, let's backpedal and not raise the alarm just yet. A late period doesn't necessarily mean pregnancy," Meela explains, covering my trembling hands with her own. "We'll get a pregnancy test after school and—"

"I can't buy a pregnancy test!" I explode, raw panic icing my veins. "Sandman has people watching me everywhere. He can't know. He can't," I reiterate, fresh tears stinging my corneas and spilling over.

There's no telling how he would react. His hatred for me is too potent…

too lethal. I'm afraid he'll hurt me. Yes, it's better to keep him in the dark and pray he doesn't find out.

"Hey, don't worry," she murmurs, wiping my face with her sleeve. "I'll buy the pregnancy test while you wait in the car. He won't find out."

"Thank you." I drop my chin onto my upraised knees, feeling fatigued and lightheaded.

"So let me get this straight," Meela emphasizes, tilting her head in thought. "You've had sex but never full-blown, deep-in-your-guts penetration?"

Humiliation climbs up my neck and seeps into my cheeks. "Yeah. Sandman only puts the tip in."

"Okayyy." She drags out the word, her beautiful features squinching in confusion. "Why?"

"Because he likes toying with me." My harsh laughter echoes through the bathroom. "I want my first time to be special, and he knows it. He can go deeper at any time and take my virginity. It's one of his sick mind games."

"And he comes inside you?"

I nod. "Every single time. I didn't even think pregnancy was a possibility since he didn't go all the way, you know?"

"Whenever semen enters a woman's body, pregnancy is possible," Meela explains.

"But how? How is it possible?" I ask, completely at a loss. "He didn't pop my cherry. I would've known if he had, right? I would've been hurting and bleeding."

I only felt pleasure. Sweet, horrible pleasure.

I shut the door on that treacherous thought immediately. *Not today, Satan.*

"Well, the hymen, aka the cherry, is just a layer of tissue that surrounds the vaginal opening. It doesn't actually cover it, so technically there's no barrier. That's just a myth," she clarifies, and my jaw nearly plummets to the tile floor. "The hymen doesn't break, but it can tear. It stretches and thins over time too. No hymen is exactly the same, and some women don't bleed during their first time."

My fucking God. I'm clueless about my own damn body.

"How the hell do you know all this shit?"

Meela's lip spreads into a wicked grin. "Research, babe. Tons and tons of research."

"I'm so fucking stupid." *Too fucking stupid to be a mother.*

"You're not stupid. That fanciful shit has been drilled into our heads from a young age." She leans in close. "Wanna know a secret? First, you have to promise to keep your lips zipped. I have a reputation to uphold."

"I won't tell a soul." I draw an invisible cross over my chest. "Promise."

"I'm a virgin," Meela tells me.

"Mmm-hmm." I suck my teeth. "And I'm the Queen of England."

"It's true," she responds, a serious note in her tone. "I'm saving my *cherry*."

"For *him*?" I ask, connecting the dots. "That's why you did all the research."

"Yeah." Meela smiles, blushing a bright red. "I want to please him, and to do that, I have to understand how our bodies fit together."

"Yuck. I bet his balls sag to his ankles," I say, making a show of gagging.

"Shut up, whore." She chuckles, lightly punching me on the arm. "No one talks shit about my future man but me."

She's a glutton for punishment. Yeah, she told me she's in love with Jigsaw, but I figured it was just a schoolgirl crush. Her obsession with him is off the Richter scale. That man is going to eat her alive.

Meela stands and offers me a hand. "Come on. Chicken strips are on the menu today, and you don't want to miss that. Nothing does a body good like processed food." She smacks her lips dramatically. "Yum."

"Why didn't you say so? I love processed foods." I say, letting her pull me to my feet.

Meela's right, it's pointless to jump to conclusions. I'm going to stuff my face with chicken strips and put the reason for my late period on the back burner.

I'm fucked.

Completely, utterly fucked.

I can't be a mother.

I can't even take care of myself.

"I can't have this baby," I cry, sobs racking my body. "I just can't. He's a monster."

The four positive tests on the nightstand mock me as my world turns upside down.

"And you don't have to." I feel a dip in the mattress as Meela sits beside me. "There's another option," she adds, rubbing my back in comfort. "You can terminate the pregnancy."

I turn to look at her. "Abortion?" I shake my head. "I couldn't do that."

I couldn't live with myself. My unborn child is innocent in all this. Doesn't he or she deserve a chance to live? Despite how fucked my life has been, I'm happy to be alive, to wake up every day in the land of the living.

"Maybe Sandman will be a good father," Leah remarks, joining us on the bed. "Maybe having a baby will change him for the better."

"And maybe I'll win the lottery next week," Meela retorts. "Maybes don't mean shit, Leah." Meela removes an errant passion twist from my damp cheek and tucks it behind my ear. "Do you really want to be tied to Sandman for the rest of your life? Think long and hard about that. Either way, I'll support whatever decision you make."

"Me too," Leah says. "Your body, your choice."

Sandman swore to keep me prisoner forever, but I was hoping he would tire of me one day and let me go. I know with absolute certainty that if I have this baby—*our baby*—that hope is lost. I'll be his until my dying breath. My stomach twists into knots at the mere thought. He doesn't view me as a human being with feelings. I'm nothing more than an inanimate object to be used and abused for his sick enjoyment.

Just a few short months ago, my plan was to go to college and finally escape my tyrannical mother. Freedom was within arm's reach. Now I have a new warden, and this one is ten times worse. No, I can't let this happen. I've been a puppet since birth. I deserve to follow my dreams and live my life on my terms for once.

I sit up against the headboard. "I'm going to—"

There's a light knock on Meela's bedroom door before it's pushed open just enough for Tulip to poke her head inside. "Hey, girlies. I hope everyone's hungry. I ordered some pepperoni pizzas and a couple of garden salads."

"Boundaries," Meela snaps at her. "I didn't tell you to come in."

"I'm sorry," Tulip says, her smile swiftly dissipating. "I'll give a shout when the food gets here." Just as she's about to close the door, her gaze lands on my face. "Zilphia, are you okay?"

"She's fine," Meela huffs, rolling her eyes. "Can you please go now? You're killing our vibe."

"You don't have to be mean," she admonishes, her voice cracking the slightest bit. "I just want to be your friend."

"Then stop being such a mom and be my sister."

"It's my job to worry about you, Meela," Tulip counters in exasperation. "I know the rift between us is about Jigsaw. This obsession you have with him has to stop. He's not a good man."

"I love him!" she shouts, jumping to her feet. "Why can't you understand that?"

"I'm just having a bad day," I cut in, hoping to derail their argument. "Thanks for ordering dinner."

"Yeah, thanks so much," Leah chimes in. "I'm starving."

Tulip nods, then shoots her sister a disapproving glare before pulling the door shut with a little more force than necessary.

"Ugh, I'm so sick of her self-righteous bullshit!" Meela exclaims, plopping back down on the bed. "Excuse my family drama. What were you saying?"

"I'm going to get an abortion."

"Are you sure?" Leah asks. "You don't want to think about it first?"

"No, I've made up my mind," I say with false confidence. "I need to go somewhere far, at least two hours from Kent." Sandman might be on the same page about ending the pregnancy, but then again, he might not be. I can't chance him finding out.

"Okay. I'll help you find a place," Meela offers. "You want to schedule it for this weekend?"

"Too risky. I'm always being watched." I rub my tired eyes. "I have to get it done during school hours."

Meela pulls off her curly, turquoise-colored wig and tosses it onto the nightstand. "What's the plan?"

CHAPTER 31

Zilphia

MEELA REACHES OVER AND OPENS THE CAR DOOR AS SOON AS she sees me. "Hey," I mumble, sliding into the passenger seat and strapping on my seatbelt.

"Hey," she replies, her gaze roaming over my face. "How are you?"

"Not good," I answer truthfully. "I feel like the worst person in the world."

My emotions are all over the place. Today is the day. I got dressed and went to school like normal, pretending like my heart wasn't breaking. Between Sandman and my nerves, I only got about three hours of sleep last night. If he noticed I wasn't my usual self, he didn't say anything. By the time he left, I was exhausted and sore, but the pain was very much welcomed. It took my mind off what's to come, however briefly.

Meela angles her body toward me. "Listen to me. You're not the first girl to get an abortion, and you won't be the last, but it's not too late to change your mind. We can play hooky at the mall and indulge in a little retail therapy instead."

"I need to do this," I say for my own benefit more than hers. "I need to take control of my life."

"Okay, but the moment you start having second thoughts, just say the word and we're out of there." After my nod of confirmation, Meela puts the car in drive and begins the two-hour journey.

So far, everything is going according to plan. Still, I keep my head on a swivel, terrified Sandman's henchmen are going to pop up out of nowhere. *There's no way they'd recognize me.* Heck, I barely recognize myself in this getup. The oversized hoodie, sweatpants, Crocs, sunglasses, and pixie-cut wig were provided by the girl in the driver's seat. I changed into the disguise after breakfast and made my getaway seconds before the late bell rang for homeroom. Leah stayed behind to explain our absence if necessary.

"Thanks for letting me borrow the rest of the money. I'll pay you back on Friday."

"No problem."

My goal was to save money—that's the only reason I got a job. But that plan went to hell in a handbasket with my first paycheck. I had to pay Leah and my grandmother back. Then my egg donor had her hand out—so did my aunt. After grabbing some essentials, there wasn't much left. The woman who birthed me is my biggest expense, taking nearly half my paycheck. I'll be happy when she finally lands that rich husband. That's for damn sure.

I sigh. Nothing in my life is going the way it was supposed to.

I rummage through my purse in search of my favorite lip gloss. "Shit."

"What?" Meela questions, glancing over at me.

"My wallet," I explain, shaking my head. "I must've left it in my other purse." Maybe this is a sign for me not to go. Should I not go? I feel so torn.

"No biggie." She turns right instead of keeping straight toward the highway. "I'll swing by your house."

"Okay. I don't know how I forgot it."

At least no one will be home except my mother, and she's more than likely still asleep. She won't bother me in any case since it's not payday. Keith left for work hours ago, and my grandmother has a doctor's appointment, so she and my aunt won't be home.

"You have a lot on your mind."

I stare out the window, seeing nothing, blinking back the tears threatening to spill free. A few succeed despite my best efforts. I'm dying inside. I want to curse God, curse the universe, curse fate—curse whoever or whatever allowed this to happen. *The lie you told allowed this to happen.*

"Hey, we're here," Meela announces, concern evident in her voice. "Are you sure you want to do this?"

"I don't have a choice," I whisper brokenly.

"You do—"

"Be right back." I stumble from the car as more tears roll down my cheeks, but I come to a dead stop when I spot Keith's truck in the driveway.

Great. What's he doing here? I hurry inside, making a beeline for the basement door, but banging in the kitchen piques my curiosity. I creep past the basement door, quiet as a mouse, and glance around the corner. *No, no, no, no.*

"What are you doing?" I shout, stepping into full view. "Have you lost your mind?" I place a hand just below my throat, disgusted by the scene in front of me.

Keith leaps away from my mother, who he had bent over the table. His erection stands straight out, glistening with my mother's juices.

I clutch the wall for support. "I'm going to be sick."

"You're supposed to be in school," she admonishes, pulling on her bathrobe. "What are you doing home?"

"That's all you have to say?" I ask incredulously. "What are you doing fucking Sheila's husband?"

"We love each other," she declares with a haughty tone. "We're going to be together."

I laugh mirthlessly. "You're kidding me, right? You're just an easy lay for him."

"That's not true," Keith chimes in. "I'm going to leave Sheila for your mother."

I look at him, thanking the heavens that his male part is back in his pants. "You know their history. How could you do this to your wife? She's pregnant with your baby for God's sake."

My mother struts over to him and curls herself against his side. "The heart wants what the heart wants."

I roll my eyes. "Momma, you can't be serious. We're on the streets as soon as Sheila finds out. And what about Grandma? Don't you care about her at all? Her last wish is for her daughters to get along before she dies."

"Keith will take care of us," she remarks confidently and places a lingering kiss on his cheek. "And we all can't get what we want. Doesn't my happiness count?"

I throw my hands in the air and walk away. Talking to that woman is like talking to a brick wall.

"We're going to get married," she calls after me. "You just wait and see."

"He already has a wife!" I yell over my shoulder. I hurry into the basement and find my wallet on the floor next to the air mattress. I practically run back to Meela's car.

"Everything cool?" she asks once my seatbelt is secured.

I slump against the seat and squeeze my eyes shut, attempting to calm my racing mind. I fucking loathe my mother with every fiber of my being. How can someone be so selfish? Sure, Sheila is a bitch, but she doesn't deserve this and neither does my grandmother. She's too old and fragile to deal with this bucket of bullshit.

I can't tell them. My aunt would throw us out on our asses in a heartbeat. I don't have as much faith in my mother's lover "taking care of us" as she does. Doesn't every married man make the same proclamation to their mistress to keep getting the goods? Rarely does a cheating man leave his wife. What the hell was she thinking? I can't afford to take care of us on my own.

I sigh and pry my eyes open. "Not in the least."

"Wanna talk about it?"

I shake my head. "Not now."

Meela doesn't push for details, which I'm extremely grateful for. I'm just so tired of it all. We barely speak as the miles pass us by, and soon I drift off to sleep.

"Hey girlie." I hear Meela call out to me. "Wake up, we're here."

I blink my eyes open. *Why couldn't this all have been a bad dream?* We make our way into the building, neither of us saying a word. I just want to break down and cry.

"Hi," I whisper to one of the women at the front desk. "I have an appointment. Zilphia Kensley."

"ID and insurance card, please."

"No health insurance. I'm paying with cash," I say, handing her my driver's license.

She makes a copy, then gives it back to me along with paperwork to complete. The waiting room is crowded, but we're able to find seats across from each other. My nerves are shot to shit. I can't stop my hands from shaking.

The next several hours stretch endlessly—urine and blood tests, an ultrasound, and finally a pelvic exam. I mentally check out through it all. I'm five weeks pregnant. That means conception happened the first time Sandman "put the tip in."

"I'm sorry." I pull my gaze from the stained carpet. "Can you repeat the question?"

Maggie, the office counselor, regards me with kind eyes from across her desk. "Are you here of your own free will?"

"Yes," I mumble past numb lips.

She jots down my response, then moves on to the next question. "Have you considered other options?"

"There are no other options," I reply sharply and immediately feel like crap for taking my anger out on her. It's not her fault I'm here. *It's his.*

"There's adoption—"

"There are no other options," I repeat, balling my hands into tight fists. "Are these questions necessary?"

"They are." Maggie leans forward and folds her arms across the desk. "It's my job to ensure you're aware of all possible avenues. What birth control methods have you considered post-procedure?"

"I have the pill, but I was already pregnant before I started taking it." *I would've taken other precautions had I known pregnancy was possible without full penetration.*

Half an hour later, I'm on the exam table with my legs hoisted in the stirrups. A nurse stands beside me, holding my hand for emotional support. Guilt settles heavily in the pit of my stomach.

"You're going to be okay," she tells me, offering a friendly smile. "It'll all be over soon."

"I'm about to inject numbing medication into your cervix," the doctor explains. "You're going to feel a slight pressure."

I close my eyes and pray I'm not making the biggest mistake of my life.

CHAPTER 32

Three years ago

SAM

"Up and at 'em, lazy bones," Zilphia says, a smile in her voice. *"We're going swimming."*

I look toward the door, finding her bikini-clad form standing just beyond the entrance to the tree house with two towels hanging over her arm. My greedy gaze touches on the multi-color fabric hiding her private areas from my view. My mind screams at me to stop staring, but I can't help myself. Every inch of her is perfect, but it's her silky caramel skin that I find most striking. God, I would give anything to be more than friends.

"Why are you staring at me like that?" Zilphia asks, laughter dancing in her beautiful brown eyes.

I instantly jerk my gaze away from her and pretend interest in the comedy playing on the television. "Can't," I comment gruffly, ignoring her question. "Didn't bring any swim shorts."

"Sam, you don't need swim shorts. You're wearing boxer briefs, right? Or maybe you're a tighty-whities type of guy." She waggles her eyebrows.

"I'm a boxer briefs guy, but that doesn't matter. I'm not letting you see me in my underwear." I don't trust myself not to get an erection.

"Don't be a party pooper," Zilphia whines. "Boxer briefs are just like swimming shorts, and hello, I'm wearing a bikini." She clasps her hands together, and it doesn't escape my notice that the action causes her breasts to jiggle just a little. "Pretty please with a cherry on top."

"We could get caught," I say, hoping she drops it and puts some clothes on.

"We won't," she says with an impatient huff. "At dinner, my parents drank enough wine to knock out a horse, and Nolan's at a party."

I reluctantly leave my comfortable position on the sofa. "All right. Lead the way."

My pulse beats a rapid staccato as I follow her down the stairs. A loose thread on her bikini bottoms hangs by the curve of her left ass cheek. It sways back and forth with every step she takes, taunting me. I tempt fate and roll the twisted fibers between my thumb and forefinger.

"Surprise!" Zilphia exclaims and whirls around.

I snatch my hand back and peer over her shoulder, spotting a plate of fried chicken and a couple slices of strawberry shortcake on a small square table. My favorite protein and dessert.

"Nice. What's the occasion?"

"It's our friendiversary." She beams. "Well, I don't remember the exact day we met, but it was five years ago this month."

"Damn, it's only been five years. It seems a lot longer." Zilphia was a godsend that night. Now I can't imagine my life without her.

"Time flies when you're having fun." She drops the towels on a chaise lounge and grabs my hand, impatiently tugging me forward. "Come on, let's get wet."

"Can we eat first?" I attempt to grab a piece of chicken as we pass the table, but Zilphia swats my hand away.

"No eating before swimming. You'll get cramps." She folds her arms and looks at me expectantly. "Well, what are you waiting for? Strip."

"Nuh-uh," I reply, shaking my head and gesturing for her to turn around. Zilphia rolls her eyes, but does as I request. I quickly undress and toss my clothes next to the towels. "I'm ready."

I wade into the frigid water behind her, watching that damn loose thread again. At least the cold will keep me from embarrassing myself.

"Think fast," Zilphia says and splashes water in my face, then tries to swim away.

I latch onto her ankle and haul her back. "Got you."

She squeals and kicks free. I stalk after her, a confident smirk curling my lips. "Prepare to get dunked."

"You better not, Sam," she hisses, excited fear animating her features. "I'm warning—"

I pounce, and we both disappear beneath the surface, but only for a couple of seconds. "Apologize or you're getting dunked again."

"Never."

I shrug. "The hard way it is, then."

The water war escalates, with us battling for the upper hand, though my size and strength give me the advantage. I take hold of her wrists and pin her arms behind her back, bringing her wet body flush against me.

Something shifts, and our playful battle becomes sexually charged, instantly heating the blood in my veins. We stare into each other's eyes, and everything in me wants to kiss her—but Zilphia turns her head, breaking the spell. We had a moment, right? Fleeting, but there nonetheless, or maybe my mind was playing tricks on me.

"Give up?" I rasp.

"Uh-huh," Zilphia responds breathlessly. "I'll apologize, but you have to let me go first."

I raise a skeptical eyebrow but release her. "All right, I'm waiting."

She clears her throat. "I'm… um… What was I saying? Oh, yeah, I'm…"

I grasp her slender shoulders. "Okay, you're going back under."

"Dang, give me a second." Zilphia sucks her teeth. "I'm deeply, deeply sorry for splashing you. Forgive me?" she asks, dramatically batting her eyelashes.

I chuckle at her obvious sarcasm. "I guess."

Before I can think better of it, I remove a silky curl clinging to her bottom lip and tuck it behind her ear, letting my hand linger on her soft skin longer than necessary. The air between us sizzles again. So it wasn't just my imagination. It's real, and she feels it too.

"Race you to the end of the pool." Zilphia propels herself through the water, toward the deep end, but stops short when I don't follow suit. "What are you waiting for? You do know how to swim, right?" she jokes.

"Never learned." I climb out of the pool and begin drying off.

I'll never be good enough for her. I don't even know how to swim. She's going to go off to college and make something of herself. My greatest achievement will probably be becoming assistant manager at the local grocery store.

I hear the swoosh of water as she pulls herself onto the deck. "I'm sorry, Sam. I was only joking."

"No big deal," I mumble, keeping my back to her. "I gotta get home." I grab my well-worn polo and yank it over my head.

She walks around me and places a hand on either side of my face. "I'll teach you."

"You don't have to."

"I know." Zilphia smiles and grabs the hem of my shirt, lifting it over my head. "But I want to." She leads me back into the water and begins my first swimming lesson.

CHAPTER 33

SANDMAN

I GLIDE ACROSS THE SMOOTH SURFACE OF THE WATER, THINKING ABOUT her. When the fuck am I *not* thinking about her? My feelings for Zilphia confuse me. Could I be falling in love? *Nah.* Hate is my love language.

And by fucking God, I hate that fucking girl with an intensity that burns brighter than the sun. Besides, I decided a long time ago that love doesn't exist.

Do I want to fuck her? More than my next breath. Do I want to make her suffer? Absolutely. Do I want to make her bleed? That's a hell fucking yes.

But love? Love is a fucking fairytale, the elusive unicorn for the dumb and desperate, only existing in unrealistic romance novels and television, filling impressionable young minds with bullshit aspirations and a false idealism that one day they'll find their happily ever after… their soul mate… their better half. *Idiots.* All of them, but then again, everyone plays the fool once, twice, or several times in their life.

I once coveted the illusion until reality gave me a swift kick in the balls. Seeking the four-letter word came at a great cost to me, but the tables have turned, and my personal brand of revenge is a dish best served piping hot. So fucking hot, it singes the roof of the mouth.

Making her suffer won't be enough to sate my bloodlust. I need something more, but I don't know what that something is. If only I could reanimate the dead, I would fuck her, kill her, then bring her back over and over again—each homicide more gruesome than the last.

Blood rushes to my cock at the thought. I would gladly surrender my soul to the devil himself in exchange for the ability to kill Zilphia a thousand different ways.

I reach the end of the indoor pool and push into a flip turn. Once upon a time, I couldn't swim, but Zilphia taught me how. Lesson after lesson, I became stronger, more confident in the water. Zilphia never lost patience with me. She was always kind, always nurturing, and that only made me love her more.

My cell phone rings, snapping me back to the present. I swim to the edge of the pool and tap the speaker icon.

"Yeah."

"We have a problem," Snake growls, raising the hairs on the back of my neck.

"What is it?"

"Zilphia's not at school," he informs me.

"What the fuck do you mean she's not at school?" I snarl, already out of the pool and bounding toward the house, a million and one thoughts racing through my mind. Did she run or was she kidnapped? Probably the former, but the brotherhood has many enemies, so a kidnapping isn't far-fetched. "Where the fuck is she?"

"I don't know. Me and a few brothers searched the entire building," he explains. "We couldn't find her anywhere. Meela isn't here either. Could be a coincidence, but more than likely they're together."

"What about her other friend?" I ask, taking the stairs two at a time to my bedroom.

"She's here but says she doesn't know where they are."

"You believe her?" I toss my phone on the bed and step out of my swim shorts.

"She's lying through her fucking teeth, but I can get her to talk," Snake states with grim promise.

"Take her to The Sanctuary," I instruct him. "I'll be there in twenty."

"Will do."

I'm dried, dressed, and out the door in less than ten minutes. I called Zilphia, but as expected, my call went straight to voicemail. I installed a tracker on her phone, but little good that'll do me with the damn thing shut off. If she left on her own, she's going to regret the day she entered this world.

I put wheels to asphalt, burning rubber toward The Sanctuary. Once there, I storm to the basement and into the hidden room where many of our enemies met their demise. Snake sits at a table alongside the two fuckers who were supposed to keep an eye on Zilphia, the trio entertaining themselves with a card game. Leah cowers in the opposite corner, her face stained with tears.

"I swear I don't know where she is," she sobs, pushing to her feet. "Please let me go."

I ignore her and stomp over to the motherfuckers responsible for letting my property slip away. A fist to the jaw unseats prospect one, sending him crashing to the concrete floor. "You pieces of shit were supposed to keep an eye on her!" I roar and prospect two finds himself next to his counterpart with a bloody nose.

Leah makes a break for it, but Snake's right behind her in an instant, seizing her long ponytail and flinging her into the wall. She plummets to the floor in a sobbing heap.

"My glasses!" she cries, reaching out toward the broken plastic and glass.

"Run again and broken glasses will be the least of your worries," Snake warns her.

"I'm sorry, Sandman," prospect one says, his eyes bulging with fear. "I don't know how we missed her. We were watching the building, but didn't see her come out."

I drop to my haunches and coast a finger through the blood trickling down his chin. "I wonder how long it takes a person to die from being skinned alive. Minutes? Days? Weeks perhaps?" I ask softly, but the threat is loud and clear. "You two better hope she's found sooner rather than later." I rise to my full height. "Get out, but do not leave The Sanctuary."

A few of the brothers are already waiting upstairs to keep them company. It's all hands on deck until Zilphia is found.

I stalk toward Leah, but Snake steps in my path. "I got this."

"Go grab a drink at the bar," I say, stepping around him. "You don't want to be here for this."

He places a firm hand on my shoulder. "I said I got this."

I scowl at the offending appendage. "Do you want to keep that hand, little brother? One way or another, she's going to talk."

"I'll get her to talk," he rumbles, his turbulent coal-black gaze daring me to challenge him. *Challenge accepted.* I ball my hands into fists, ready to beat the fuck out of him, but his next words deflate my anger. "She's mine."

I understand now, this isn't him trying to compare the size of our dicks. Leah is his, in the same way Zilphia is mine. No one else is allowed to hurt her; that privilege belongs to him and him alone. I nod. "I'll give you ten minutes, little brother."

Snake fastens a hand into her micro locs and hauls her to her feet. "Where the fuck is she?"

"I don't—" he flings her into the wall, and again she crashes to the floor.

"The clock is ticking, Leah." He saunters over to her and lifts a booted foot to her throat. "Are you prepared to die today?"

She clamps both hands around his ankle, trying to relieve the crushing pressure on her trachea. "Please," she croaks, wheezing for breath. "I'm telling the truth."

The girl is loyal, I'll give her that, but my patience is wearing thin. A bullet to the kneecap will have her spilling her guts real quick, but I'll let Snake do his thing first. For the next several minutes, he tosses her around the room like a rag doll, but she doesn't break. She maintains that she doesn't know where Zilphia is.

"I know what'll get her talking," Snake says to me, then leaves the room.

Leah grabs the leg of the table and pulls herself into a sitting position. "I don't know where she is!" she wails. "Let me go before he kills me!"

"This is child's play," I remark, gesturing toward her. "When it's my turn, the real torture begins."

"You're an animal," she accuses, her tear-filled gaze flashing fire at me.

I laugh and dig my cell phone out of my back pocket, making a show of checking the time. "Yeah, I am, and in about three minutes, you'll see firsthand just how much of an animal I can be."

"No wonder Zilphia's…" Leah starts, but then snaps her lips together.

"No wonder Zilphia what?" I question, straightening from my slouch on the wall.

My inquiry is met with silence. Just as I'm about to snatch her ass up and introduce her to the *animal,* Snake strolls back into the room with his pet python coiled around his neck.

"No! No! No!" Leah screams and crawls beneath the table. "Take it away! Take it away!"

Snake looks at me and smirks. "She has a *snake* phobia."

"Clearly," I deadpan.

He flips the table, and she scurries across the floor on all fours. "Keep it away from me!" she shouts, plastering herself into a corner.

"Tell us what we want to know," Snake barks, kneeling in front of her. "Or you can spend the night with Marla." He removes the six-and-a-half-foot reptile from his neck and places it around hers.

Leah's terrified screams rend the small space, and I'm of a mind to knock her the fuck out. Zilphia's screams are music to my ears, hers, not so much.

Snake rubs the top of Marla's head. "Do you want me to take her?"

"Yes! Please get it off me!"

"Then you know what you need to do, sweetheart," he whispers and places a kiss on the corner of her mouth.

"She went to have an abortion!" Leah cries hysterically. "Get it away from me!"

I stumble backward, my heart nearly stopping in my chest at her revelation. Snake jerks his wide gaze to mine, displaying the same shock I'm sure is mirrored in my own. Of all the scenarios that ran through my mind, this wasn't even a bleep. I expected her to be on a plane heading halfway around the world. My turbulent emotions morph into raging anger. If Zilphia killed our unborn child, her fate is sealed.

"Where?" I growl between clenched teeth.

"I swear on my father's life, I don't know!" she shouts, her eyes wild with fear. "They didn't tell me. Please get it off me."

Long strides carry me from the room and up the stairs. I need to round up as many brothers as I can to search for Zilphia. Time is critical. I have to save my unborn child.

CHAPTER 34

Zilphia

"SURE YOU DON'T WANT ME TO COME IN WITH YOU?" MEELA ASKS.

"I'm sure." We're parked a block down from the clubhouse.

It's dark out now. After leaving the clinic, we turned our cell phones back on—only to be hit with a barrage of missed calls, voicemails, and texts from Sandman. He knows everything. I don't blame Leah for telling my secret; anyone would have under the circumstances. Her tear-filled voicemails begging for my forgiveness broke my heart.

I spoke to her briefly and assured her there was nothing to forgive before powering off my cell phone again; Meela did the same. I wasn't ready to go back, so we had lunch and browsed a few stores. Later, we saw a movie, wandered around the mall a bit more, and then had dinner.

As we neared Kent, I switched my cell phone back on and saw more missed calls, voicemails, and texts from Sandman. His threats have my stomach in knots, especially the threats concerning my grandmother. The last voicemail was from ten minutes ago, and from the loud music and chatter in the background, I knew he was at the bar.

"You don't have to face him alone."

"Yeah, I do." I sigh and undo my seatbelt. "I already put Leah in danger. I'm not going to put you in danger too."

"I can take care of myself," Meela quips in her usual sassy tone.

"I know you can, but this isn't your fight," I say, turning in my seat to face her. "Thank you so much for being there for me. We haven't known each other long, but you've been an amazing friend, but no one can protect me from him. And anyone who tries will probably end up dead." I push the car door open. "I'll see you tomorrow." *I hope.*

"Okay." Meela leans over and gives me a tight hug. "Call me if you need me."

"I will." I inhale a fortifying breath and exit the vehicle.

I could very well be walking to my death, but there's no point in running or hiding. Sandman said he would always find me, and I believe him. He hates me too much to ever let me go. I square my shoulders and walk through the gates of the clubhouse.

The men guarding the entrance let me pass, no doubt recognizing who I am. Quite a few people linger outside, and dozens of eyes track me as I make my way to the bar entrance. I'm sure they've all heard about my disappearing act.

"You should've stayed gone. Sandman's gonna fuck you up six ways from Sunday, girl."

I glance over, finding my antagonizer slouched against his Harley. I raise my chin, refusing to show fear. "Where is he?"

"Inside, getting wasted." Cricket ambles toward me, a beer in one hand and a cigarette in the other. "I've seen him in a rage plenty, but never like this. He just might put a bullet in your skull tonight. Something he should've done a while back if you ask me."

"But he didn't ask you, now did he?" I retort sarcastically.

"He didn't," Cricket admits. "But trust me, your days are numbered, baby killer." He tilts his head sideways, his intent gaze appraising my physical attributes. "I don't understand his obsession with you. Never did, honestly. There's absolutely nothing special about you. You're average at best. Sandman has a string of beautiful women itching to get at him."

"Then tell him to take his pick and leave me the fuck alone." I push past him and storm into the building.

Cricket is a fucking asshole, but I can't fault him for hating me. He's protective of his best friend, always has been.

I scan the smoky interior and spot Sandman sitting at the bar. His messy golden mane is unbound, falling in loose silken waves around his broad shoulders. I gasp in surprise, noticing his slumped posture and the way his forehead rests heavily in his upturned palm. He looks so defeated.

It's a foreign concept to associate with this deadly man. Did he feel the same defeat the night I betrayed him? "*I have no idea who this guy is. He forced me in here and started kissing me...*" Those words were bile on my tongue, but still I said them and ignited an all-consuming hate that led me to this very moment.

No one in history has ever hated someone the way he hates me. His hate for me is a living, breathing thing. It's the monster under my bed, the boogeyman in my closet, and the dark phantom in my nightmares.

"Good choice," Zeus rumbles. "Coming back that is. My boy was prepared to mount a full-scale search for you in the morning."

Of course, the great tattooed leader of the Gods has two scantily dressed women perched on his beefy thighs. At least there's no funny business going on this time.

I narrow my eyes at him. "You turned him into a monster."

Zeus flashes his teeth at me. "Sweetheart, he was already a monster. He just needed a little nudge to reach his full potential."

Before I can unleash my sarcastic tirade on him, I'm sailing through the air at breakneck speed. I hit the wooden floor with a bone-jarring thud, knocking the literal wind out of me. My teeth stab into my tongue, filling my mouth with blood. Though my head is spinning and my vision is blurry, there's no question about the identity of the shadowy figure looming over me.

"Sandman," I croak.

He hauls me up by my throat and slams me on top of a nearby table, sending the occupants scurrying. Beer bottles crash to the floor, sending shards of broken glass flying in every direction.

"You don't know what real pain is, Zilphia," he sneers in my face, so close his lips brush against mine. "Real pain is felt here." He jabs a finger against his temple. "It's wanting a person that you can never have more than your next breath. It's when that person lives in your fucking head twenty-four-seven. It's when that person stabs you in the fucking back and twists the blade so goddamn deep it pierces your heart." He runs his nose along my cheek. "Physical pain can leave scars, but mental scars run deeper. That's why I take immense pleasure in mindfucking you. I *need* you to feel the same mental anguish I felt."

The anguish I still feel.

The last part wasn't spoken out loud, but I swear I heard him say it in my mind. It's a universal truth that hurt people hurt people—and his hurt simmered for three long years, slowly reaching a boiling point. This time, I'm the one who's going to get burned.

Sandman's steel hand squeezes tighter around my neck, slowly draining the life from my body. I release my hold on his forearm and accept what is. No one bats an eyelash at the crime taking place, the music doesn't stop, games are still being played, and conversations continue. Murder is a trivial thing in the outlaw biker world, as mundane as brushing one's teeth.

Sandman jerks me forward, lifting me to the tips of my toes. His grip loosens just enough for me to pull oxygen into my starving lungs. "Did you kill my baby?"

I say nothing. I'm just so fucking tired. Tired of him. Tired of my mother. Tired of everything. He launches me over the table, and once again, I find myself on the dirty floor. I stay where I land and close my eyes. I have no more energy left in me.

"He's going to kill her," I hear Jigsaw comment.

Zeus chuckles in response. "Nah, he won't."

"Uh-huh. If you say so," he replies, skepticism clear in his voice.

"Zilphia is his favorite toy. He may bang her up a little bit, leave a few cuts and bruises, but he won't kill her," Zeus states matter-of-factly. "That would mean no more playdates, and where's the fun in that?"

"Get the fuck up," Sandman snarls, seizing my hair and bringing me chest to chest with him. "Did you kill my baby?" he asks again and again, but my lips remain sealed. His wild blue eyes bore into me, promising retribution and blood. "Many horrors await you, Zilphia. Many, many horrors."

He drags me to a metal door at the back of the bar and presses a button on the intercom attached in the center. A camera is built into the small electrical device, ensuring only authorized persons are granted entry.

"Open the fucking door," he growls impatiently. "It's Sandman."

Click.

We step into a security room, evident from a control panel and the row of monitors lining the wall above it. Sandman drags me past two prospects, and we're buzzed into a lounge-style recreation room. Laughter and conversations abound—club members, their old ladies, and even children enjoy the first-class amenities.

Overstuffed sofas, chairs, and bean bags provide ample sitting for anyone looking to kick back and relax. Bowls of popular brand-name snacks sit atop a stainless-steel island with plush bar stools on either side. A matching refrigerator is positioned in the corner behind it. Beyond that, an arcade can be seen behind a glass enclosure. A fireplace is situated beneath one of eight huge flat-screen televisions mounted to the taupe-colored walls. The Gods must pull in a ton of money to be able to afford such luxuries.

Sandman rounds a corner and bounds up a curved staircase to the second floor. I struggle to match his long strides, my scalp throbbing from his rough fingers. He shoves me into a room, his hand still tangled firmly in my passion twists, and flings me onto the bed. I flip onto my back and quickly scramble against the headboard.

"Come 'ere," he growls, capturing an ankle and yanking me across the mattress. I instinctively kick out at him with my free foot, connecting with his mouth.

"I'm sorry," I breathe, my stomach roiling with fear.

Sandman swipes his tongue over the bead of blood on his bottom lip. "You'll be far sorrier by the time I'm finished with you." He roughly strips the lower half of my body bare and spreads my legs wide. A long laceration covers my left hip from where my panties dug into my skin.

His searching gaze studies the feminine folds between my thighs.

"No blood?" he bellows and shakes me so hard my vision goes black for several seconds. "Did you get an abortion? Were you ever pregnant?" He plucks my ruined panties off the bed beside him and examines those too. "Is there a baby?" He shakes me again. "Speak!"

"Yes, there's a baby!" I shout back at him, my body vibrating with raw emotions. "No matter how much I hate its father, I couldn't do it!" Tears spring to my eyes and fall unchecked down the sides of my face. "I couldn't kill my baby."

His icy blue gaze cut me to the marrow. "You hate me?" he questions gruffly, his breathing fast and erratic.

"Yes, I fucking hate you!" I yell at the top of my lungs. "I've never hated anyone as much as I hate you!"

"Good," Sandman rasps, frantically tearing his jeans open and freeing his thick erection. "I hate you too." He falls between my thighs and positions his length at my entrance. "I hate that you exist." My earsplitting scream reverberates through the room as he ruthlessly drives his steel length into my body.

"I hate that we ever met." He rears back, then swings his hips forward again, gaining another inch inside my slick walls. "I hate that I can't get you out of my goddamn head." Another thrust brings him past the point of no return. "Most of all, I hate that I fell in love with you," he groans, fully settling inside my pussy.

My ruin is complete.

Sandman lies flush against me and goes full throttle. The sounds of my virginity loss echo through the room. There's no mercy, no gentleness, no sweet nothings whispered in my ear. This is what hate looks like—it's ugly, brutal, and without an ounce of remorse. It's said that love hurts, but I say hate hurts a whole lot worse.

He stares into my eyes as he pounds into my pussy. *No, it's more than that.* He's staring into my very soul.

"Treacherous bitch," he hisses, hooking his arms under my knees and spreading my legs wider for his assault. "I would've given you anything."

The bed creaks as his dick tunnels in and out of my pussy. I dig my fingers into the smooth leather covering his shoulders and hold on for dear life. Soon the pain turns into a dull ache, then the dull ache turns into a tingling throb, blurring the lines between lust and hate.

"No," I moan, vehemently shaking my head. I don't want his toxic pleasure. I don't want anything from him.

"There's no stopping now," he replies huskily, then his lips are moving against mine.

He kisses me like I'm his salvation, like without me, there's no him. The throb in the pit of my stomach grows to a pounding tempo as his tongue sweeps into my mouth. Sandman was the first boy I ever kissed. It was beautiful, innocent, wholly different from the wild intensity of this kiss.

Our tongues duel in a sensual dance, his lips firm and demanding against my own. Foreign sensations take over my body, and I find myself yielding beneath him. I try to resist, but the pleasure is too much.

Sandman laces our fingers together and pins my hands on either side of my head, his dick making my pulsating pussy weep in the best way. Touch, sound, taste, sight, smell—every sensation is magnified tenfold. I feel his desperation with every frenzied thrust between my sweat-soaked thighs. His need. His anger. It all bleeds into me. This is a claiming, nothing more, nothing less.

He jerks my bra and hoodie over my breasts, then pulls a pebbled nipple into his strong mouth. I thread my fingers into his sleek golden strands, tightly holding him to me. His warm tongue explores my areola while deft fingers expertly knead my other breast.

Suddenly, his thick hardness leaves my body, and he trails soft lips down my quivering torso, stopping to tongue-kiss my belly button.

I clench the sheets in my fists, frantically gyrating under his greedy mouth. I'm on fire for this man, though I shouldn't be. He's guided by vengeance and filled with rage—no conscience to speak of and zero empathy. Even so, his touch calls to the most primitive part of me. The part that knows I belong to him and always will.

Probing fingers seek the heated flesh at my center, lightly grazing my swollen pussy lips before pushing into me knuckles deep. There's no resistance, my slick walls already sopping wet for him. His fingers are rough and hard inside me, but *fuck, it feels so good*. The cotton sheets cling to my hot skin as he brings me closer to completion. His soul is hell, but his hands, mouth, and dick are heaven.

He moves lower, kissing his way to the sensitive place between my legs.

"Oh God!" I scream, trying to twist away from him, but he wraps his arms around my thighs, holding me in place. "It's too much!"

"No," he rasps, breath fanning my engorged clit. "It'll never be enough."

I thrash against the mattress as he feasts on my feminine folds like a starving man, tongue flicking back and forth over my clit. Passion clenches my belly, consuming my entire being. My eyes roll to the back of my head. I come hard, so hard my breath stalls in my throat. Sandman continues licking and slurping long after my orgasm subsides.

"Please, no more," I whisper, weakly pushing at the top of his head.

He finally pulls back, a look of confusion marring his handsome features. "How can it be this fucking good?"

"We have to stop," I plead with him. "I can't take any more."

"You can and you will." He rips his cut down his arms and tosses it on the floor. "I'm going to fuck you so hard and so fucking deep you won't be able to walk straight for a week."

His shirt goes next, revealing the six-pack I've become all too familiar with. Any normal warm-blooded woman would admire the proud organ between his thighs and his gladiator body—but it's my worst nightmare. *At least that's what I tell myself.*

He flips me over and yanks me to my knees, filling me to the hilt in one savage thrust. I cry out, searing pain slicing through me.

"Fuck, it's dripping," he groans, wildly hammering into my pussy.

"Sandman, please," I sob, inching forward. "It hurts."

"Where you think you're going?" he snarls, tightening his grip on my hips and slamming me back on his dick. "Get the fuck back here."

He's relentless in his destruction of me. I bury my face into the pillow and pray it'll be over soon. Rough hands slide to my ass, spreading my cheeks so far apart it hurts. Sandman pummels my body with hard, deep thrusts. I plummet to the bed in a weak heap, his heavy weight pressing down on me. He tangles one hand in my long twists and delves the other into my folds, teasing my throbbing clit with nimble caresses. My greedy pussy clamps down on his length as the fever in my core comes roaring back to life.

"No," I whimper.

"Your nos mean absolutely nothing to me, Zilphia," he whispers in my ear. "Your pussy is mine. If I want to eat it, I'm going to fucking eat it. And if I want to fuck it, I'm going to fuck it. Your pussy has my name written all over it, and I'm going to take it whenever the fuck I want it."

Sandman trails his tongue along the rounded curves and dips of my ear before pulling my earlobe into his mouth. My whole world shakes from the force of his body driving into mine, creating a whirlwind of ecstasy within me.

"I know you feel it," he tells me. "The fire consuming every inch of your beautiful body. I know because it's burning in me too."

"I don't want to," I whisper back.

"And you think I do?" he growls. "You're a fucking disease, Zilphia. A disease I have no cure for."

"No, Sam, I can't," I moan, my pussy clenching and unclenching on his dick.

"Fuck, fuck, fuck," he groans. "I'm coming. Fuck."

Sandman finally stills, settling his full weight on top of me. I said his name. The name he ordered me never to speak. I wait with bated breath for my punishment. After a minute or two, he slips from my body and rolls me onto my back, then retrieves a pair of handcuffs from his nightstand drawer.

"What are you doing?" I question, apprehensively eyeing the metal restraints.

"Making sure you never run again," he mumbles.

It takes a few seconds for his words to register, my gaze transfixed on the semi-erection resting between my breasts as he fastens my wrist to the headboard. The softening flesh is covered in my feminine juices and virgin blood.

"I wasn't running. Please don't handcuff me." He ignores me and promptly secures my other wrist before lying on his side, facing away from me. "Sandman, please. I have to go to the bathroom."

He says nothing, and soon his soft snores fill the room.

CHAPTER 35

Zilphia

I LIE AWAKE, WAITING FOR SANDMAN TO SLIP BETWEEN MY THIGHS and push into my weeping body. Like clockwork, my internal alarm had coaxed me to consciousness, my throbbing core hungrily anticipating its dick breakfast.

Every morning, he fucks me like it's the last time he'll ever fuck me—like a man on death row and my pussy is his last meal. His touch should make me sick to my stomach, but it doesn't. *God help me.* Toxic is bad. Toxic is dangerous. But with him, toxic feels so damn good.

He's a killer, the worst kind of human imaginable. There's no doubt in my mind that the fiery place awaits him in the afterlife. Until then, he owns me—body and soul. Being with him is equivalent to being on a tugboat stranded in the middle of a raging hurricane. I'm liable to get swept overboard at any moment, but my pussy doesn't give a damn.

I kick the duvet down my legs, sighing contentedly when the cool air hits my lower region, still tender from yesterday's sexcapades. At times, he fucks me slow, gentle even, as if he's making love to me. Other times he fucks me like a rabid animal, pounding into me so hard and so deep I bleed a little. It's confusing.

I peek over at his slack features, causing pain to shoot down my stiff arms. I'm handcuffed to the headboard, the same as every night, despite Mayhem and Harley keeping guard outside the bedroom door. My wrists are chafed and sore, the metal digging into my soft skin. This has been my life for the last week.

We fuck before the sun rises, fuck in the shower, fuck during his lunch break, fuck when he gets home in the evenings, fuck before we go to bed, and fuck in the middle of the night.

I'm not allowed to leave, not even to go to school, though I'm granted a daily phone call with my beloved grandmother. I've only spoken to my mother once, letting her know I'd be staying with a friend for a while. *"I don't care what you do. Just keep your mouth shut about Keith and me."* With that order—and a few choice words about Redmond disappearing on her—she ended the call. Redmond disappeared all right, but not in the way she thinks.

Whenever he's gone or asleep, I'm left handcuffed to the bed. I'm truly a prisoner now, both mentally and physically. He wouldn't even let me go home to pack any clothes. Instead, he went out and bought me all new things.

I peer at my captor again, my gaze roaming over his naked form. *He. Is. Glorious.* Even in sleep, he emits a powerful aura. His mussed strands lie in golden waves on the pillow behind him. I dig my teeth into my bottom lip, vividly recalling the feel of his silken mane between my fingers as his skillful tongue caressed my clit.

My gaze travels lower, lingering on his tattoos and mouthwatering six-pack. Flashes of the smooth, taut skin bunching and shuddering as he pounded into me just a few hours ago surge through my mind. But the crème de la crème is the male organ resting on his abdomen. It's huge, even in its dormant state. His dick should be categorized as a weapon of mass destruction because damn if it doesn't make my insides explode.

My breath hitches when my captor begins to stir, and a heartbeat later, the reason for the soreness between my thighs grows to full length. Sandman rolls to his side, hand instinctively seeking the heat at my center, though his eyes remain closed. His fingers softly stroke my clit, and my body instantly answers, becoming hot and soaking wet.

I throw my head back and slam my eyes shut, swirling my hips in tandem with his stroking fingers. It's amazing how this man can take me to the brink in seconds. I widen my legs as his fingers move faster. *It's coming. I feel it.*

"Please," I beg.

He pushes a thick finger into my pulsing pussy in answer, and then it happens. An explosion of raw ecstasy rushes through my core. My eyes fly open to his blazing blue orbs intently watching me as my slick walls clamp down on his finger.

I jerk against my restraints, my injured wrists completely forgotten. When he makes my body sing, I can pretend he's not a monster and I'm not the person he hates most in the world. He moves between my thighs, his gaze still boring into me, and enters my body in one fluid thrust. I whimper, my pussy struggling to adjust to his girth. *It hurts.* It hurts so fucking good.

"Your pussy is always so fucking wet and so fucking tight," he whispers in my ear, his muscular form lying flush against my pliant curves. "It almost makes me forget how much I loathe your fucking existence."

"Uncuff me," I moan, pulling against my bonds. His warm flesh feels amazing pressed against my own, golden silk over steel. I want to touch him. *No, I need to touch him.* "Please, Sandman."

A tortured sound rumbles from his chest, then his full lips are on mine. In true fashion, he begins fucking me like there's no tomorrow. I cross my ankles at the small of his back and roll my hips upward to meet his thrusts, my pussy becoming wetter for him.

Sandman groans, his tongue sweeping into my eager mouth as we feed off each other's desperate energy. The pressure builds, each hard thrust bringing me closer to orgasmic fulfillment. He's not just fucking my body, he's fucking my soul, and it's the sweetest agony. I cry out, breathless and trembling, overwhelmed by the white-hot sensations throbbing in my pussy.

"Damn you," he rasps, gripping the back of my knees and pinning my legs to the bed. "Damn you to hell."

"You are my hell," I moan, my lips brushing against his.

"And you're mine," Sandman whispers back, then he's devouring my lips again.

I completely lose myself to him, to this man who hates every fiber of my being. And he loses himself to me too. I turn my head, my lungs burning as I gasp for air. He keeps his lips on me, placing open-mouthed kisses along my jawline and down my neck, sucking the space where my neck and shoulder meet into his strong mouth. Seconds later, he groans his release, spilling his thick cum into my wet body. I come too, milking every last drop he has to give. After one last jolting thrust, he stills on top of me.

Once we float down from our climactic high, Sandman uncuffs me and leads me to the bathroom. I shuffle behind him, my steps uneven due to the ache between my legs. He flips on the bathroom light, and my breath catches at the reflection staring back at me in the mirror.

My mass of black curls is all over the place, the elastic hair tie lost sometime during the night; I've been sporting my natural look for two days now. Hickeys mar the left side of my neck, matching the dark fingerprints on my hips. My wrists look a mess and could do with some medical attention. The evidence of his desire glistens on my thighs. I'm a girl who has been thoroughly fucked.

I blink, my inspection halted by the sharp sound of the shower coming to life. Sandman takes hold of my hand and tugs me under the nearly scorching-hot water.

"Wash me," he orders, his blue gaze glued on my face.

"Okay." I grab his washcloth and bodywash off the shower rack.

The familiar spicy pine scent fills my nostrils as I wash his perfectly sculpted torso. I thoroughly clean one arm and then the other, his intense gaze never wavering from my face. Steam quickly fills the spacious bathroom, cloaking us in a dreamlike state. Folding my bottom lip between my teeth, I sink to my knees. His thighs, like the rest of him, are beautiful and toned.

I'm busy with my task, gliding the washcloth over a solidly built leg when something pokes me on the cheek. My eyes widen seeing his erection a hairbreadth from my parted lips. One week of fucking practically nonstop, and I'm still amazed by his stamina. I'm not sure how much more my pussy can take.

"What the fuck you waiting for?" he questions me. "Suck it."

I place the washcloth on the porcelain tub and wrap my fingers around the base of his erection, squeezing tightly. Sandman hisses, curling his hands into fists at his sides. I glance up at him from beneath my eyelashes and meet blue fire. It's said that the eyes are the windows to the soul and nothing could be truer. I can see the longing for the girl he vowed to hate forever shining in his hooded gaze.

Keeping my eyes glued to his, I begin lightly kneading his heavy testicles, eliciting another hiss from him.

"Suck," he orders, sounding more animal than man. "Now."

I slowly shake my head before blowing on his slit. His face contorts into a mask of pure rapture as his eyes drift shut. Emboldened by his responses, I swirl my tongue around the bulbous tip.

In the blink of an eye, his large hands are knotted in my curls. "Didn't your mother teach you not to play with your food?" he growls, forcing my head back to look at him. "Open your mouth and eat your breakfast like a good girl."

The moment my lips part, he goes feral. I latch onto his thighs, anchoring myself as he relentlessly fucks my mouth. I can barely breathe, my jaw stretching painfully to accommodate him, but I'm not afraid. He may hurt me, maim me even, but he'd never kill me. *Since I'm his favorite toy.*

Tears slide down my cheeks, mixing with the saliva dripping from my chin. Though my gag reflex has gotten better over the last week, I'm still no match for his above-average-sized dick. Sandman moves closer, placing a foot between my splayed knees. I instinctively tilt my hips forward, rubbing my pussy against his leg. I moan, sending vibrations along his length.

"Again!" Sandman demands, surging between my lips faster.

I emit another throaty moan while clasping his full balls in a firm hold. That does the trick; his salty load overflows in my mouth, spilling down my chin.

Sandman takes a step back, slipping his dick from my mouth. Before I can inhale my next breath, the left side of my face is plastered against the tile wall with his semi-hard length pressing into my ass.

"You missed some," he whispers, dragging a finger through the cum trickling down my chin and pushing it between my lips.

I coil my tongue around the long digit, sucking it clean as his now fully erect length enters my yielding pussy. My eyes flutter closed.

He snakes a hand around my throat, squeezing ever so lightly. I place my palms flat against the shower wall as his other hand seeks the heartbeat between my folds. Hot water cascades down our joined bodies, heightening the passion consuming me.

"Please," I breathe when he doesn't move.

"Please what?" he replies gruffly, softly stroking my clit.

"Please fuck me," I answer unashamed.

Sandman withdraws until only the tip of his dick remains in my body before sinking back into my warm depths. We groan, caught in the whirlwind ecstasy consuming us both.

"You're dangerous," he murmurs, tightening his hold around my neck.

"How am I dangerous?" I whisper.

He drops his forehead against my temple. "You make me weak."

"Then let me go," I say, my voice cracking the slightest bit.

"Not even if Hell froze over." He rocks into me over and over again, stroking my insides with long, languid thrusts, pausing briefly when he reaches the hilt of me.

A firestorm of pleasure tilts me on my axis, spreading from my core to the tips of my polished toes. It grows to a fervent crescendo until unadulterated rapture buckles my knees. My lips part, a soundless scream surging from the core of me.

"Zilphia," Sandman rasps, finding his own release.

CHAPTER 36

SANDMAN

I SET TWO FULL PLATES OF WAFFLES, SAUSAGE LINKS, AND SCRAMBLED eggs on the island, sliding one over to Zilphia.

"Thanks," she says, offering me a small smile.

I shrug and look away from her. "It's food, not a fucking marriage proposal."

She looks down at her plate, her smile disappearing. What the hell am I doing? I cooked her breakfast like some lovesick idiot. That chore usually falls to her, but I took over this morning. I still can't explain why. I've never cooked a meal for the opposite sex before; it's not my style. A good dick down is the best I can offer.

Woof! Woof! Harley barks, basically telling me to hurry the fuck up with her breakfast in dog language. I scoff at her audacity. She's always been a spitfire. Mayhem, on the other hand, is calm, cool, and collected for the most part, despite his moniker.

"Yeah, yeah," I grumble, topping their hearty breakfast with several multivitamins. "It's coming." They've been on a raw diet since they were eight weeks. I prepared their favorite today—beef liver, chicken hearts, raspberries, and broccoli.

I feel Zilphia's eyes on me as I place the ceramic bowls on the floor. Mayhem and Harley stay on their bellies near the kitchen entrance, watching me expectantly. They know to wait for my command. I'm alpha here.

"Could you pass me the ketchup, please?"

I nod and grab the tomato-based condiment from the fridge, then hop onto the stool beside her.

"Thanks," she says, plucking the bottle from my grasp.

Harley and Mayhem are on all fours now, whining for their breakfast.

"Eat," I instruct them and they bolt across the kitchen, almost knocking each other over. I shake my head, my lips tilting upward in a half smile. You'd think they were starving.

"They eat better than most people," Zilphia comments before shoving a forkful of ketchup-covered eggs into her mouth.

I grimace, gesturing toward her plate with my fork. "That can't taste good."

"It does, actually. You should try it."

"Nah, I'm good," I mutter, liberally dousing my waffles in maple syrup. "Ketchup doesn't go on eggs."

She shrugs. "So how long have you had Harley and Mayhem?"

"Two and a half years," I answer, my gaze lingering on her.

She's so goddamn beautiful, it hurts to look at her. I ache for her morning, noon, and night. Even now, after a night buried inside her, my body still burns for her, aching to feel her soft, all-consuming heat again.

Her eyebrows knit together in thought as she cuts into a waffle. "I never figured you for a dog person."

"I wasn't." I slam my glass onto the island, spilling orange juice over the rim as dark memories cloud my mind. "Zeus thought they'd be good for me. I was fucked up for a long time after I got here, getting high and drunk every day, starting fights, ditching school. I should be dead."

"Because of me," she whispers, her eyes lowered in shame. "Sandman, I—"

I seize her ponytail and yank her head back, drawing a whimper from those perfectly formed lips "Another apology, Zilphia?" My bitter laugh echoes in the kitchen. "Keep that pretty little mouth of yours shut and finish your breakfast before something bad happens." I tighten my hold on her hair. "We on the same page?"

"Y-yes," she stammers.

I let her go, but our silverware lies forgotten on our plates as tense silence fills the space between us. I shake my head, attempting to dispel the dark memories from my mind, but they refuse to go away. My head swims with the need to hurt her. But I can't—not the way I want to, now that she's carrying our child. I zero in on her trembling hand. She's afraid, and she has good reason to be. The monster in me lurks just beneath the surface, demanding to be let out.

I ball my hands into fists as my breathing accelerates, matching the tempo of my racing heart. A clear drop of liquid splashes onto the marble countertop, landing beside her still trembling hand. I lift my gaze to her face, seeing the trail of a single tear on her smooth cheek. It's not enough. I need more of her tears. Before I can stop myself, I close my hand around her slender neck and jerk her to me.

I lick the wet path on her caramel-kissed skin, savoring the salty flavor on my tongue. "Tastes so fucking good." I run my nose down the side of her face. "Cry some more."

"The-the ba-baby," she croaks, latching her hands onto my forearm. "P-please."

"Be a good girl and cry for me." I suck her plump bottom lip into my mouth and bite down hard.

My chest rumbles as her distinct metallic flavor assails my taste buds. Zilphia cups my cock through my jeans, and it twitches in response, my need to fuck her instantly overpowering my need to hurt her. Smart girl; she knew awakening my libido would save her from my wrath.

I band an arm around her petite waist and pull her between my legs, claiming her lips in a possessive kiss. Our lips clash again and again, tongues tangling, every movement perfectly matched—like we're reading each other's thoughts. She moans and melts against me, her fingers clenched in my shirt. I cradle the back of her head and deepen the kiss. Fuck, I want her more than my next breath.

"Off," I growl, tearing her pajama bottoms and panties down her legs.

"Yes," Zilphia pants, hurriedly stepping out of the soft fabric pooled at her feet.

I swipe my arm across the countertop, sending my plate and orange juice crashing to the floor. I lift her onto the island and spread her legs open for my greedy gaze. My jaw tightens, saliva thick on my tongue, as I drink in the delectable sight before me. *Glistening pink*. My favorite color. I never had a favorite color until I laid eyes on her pussy.

I pull her legs over my arms and bury my nose into her slit, inhaling her scent into my body. My throbbing dick grows harder, straining against the denim containing it.

"You make me feel insane," I rasp, meeting her gaze. "But I welcome the madness, because it means I get to have you." I dip my head between her folds again and rub my face in her sweet juices. "You're my curse and my salvation."

"Is this all it'll ever be between us?" she asks, her voice thick with emotion. "You hating me. Fucking me. Hurting me. I'm so tired, Sandman. I'm so goddamn tired."

"That's all I have to give." I grab the maple syrup and pour the amber liquid all over her pussy.

"Oh God," she breathes, clutching the edge of the island.

"God has nothing to do with what's about to happen." I lower my mouth to her sweet paradise and slowly tease my tongue along her velvet-soft pussy lips.

She undulates against my face as her sexy as fuck moans serenade my ears, making my painfully hard cock jump. I burrow my hands under her top and grasp her waist. My fingers meet at the small of her back, grazing the letters I carved into her flesh. That was the first night I was inside her. The first night I knew I would die a thousand deaths before I'd ever let her go.

"Best dessert I've ever had," I rasp and close my lips around her clit, suckling it like it's my favorite candy.

"Yes! Yes! Yes!" she shouts, clutching the back of my head. "I'm going to… Oh God… I'm going to co—"

Zilphia's passion-filled cries reverberate through the kitchen as I flick my tongue back and forth over her clit. I feel the squeeze of her soft thighs against my head as her orgasm ripples through her.

"Sandman," she gasps, frantically thrusting against my mouth. "Please don't stop."

I lick and suck her swollen sweet spot until her tremors subside. With jerky movements, I free my throbbing length and pull her astride my lap. My cock melts into her slick heat. *Sen-fucking-sational.* It's so goddamn good, my entire body trembles.

In my twenty-one years on this Earth, I never had pussy so good it made me tremble like a little bitch. Zilphia got that top-tier pussy. That toxic pussy. The type of pussy that can make a motherfucker commit murder just to feel her dripping treasure.

I place my hands on either side of her neck, sliding my thumbs under her chin and tilting her head back until her gaze finds mine, burning with a fire that mirrors my own. "Ride my cock like your life depends on it."

Zilphia rolls her hips, gliding the wet suction between her thighs up and down my erection. I pull her close, wrapping my arms around her waist, and she leans into me, her arms locked around my neck, holding me just as tight as we stare into each other's eyes. I give up complete control, allowing her to set the rhythm and pace. And my God, she rides me slow and steady, and fuck if my toes don't curl. *Shit.* Our lips touch, but we don't kiss.

"You can't hate me and hold me like this," Zilphia whispers, cupping my face in her small hands. "You can't hate me and fuck me like this." She places lingering kisses on my lips, and I kiss her back, until we're both breathless, clinging to each other tighter. She pulls back and peers at me with those alluring mocha eyes. "You *can't* hate me and kiss me like this."

"That's where you're wrong, Zilphia," I murmur against her lips. "My hate for you is what gets my dick hard." I thrust upward and she moans. "It's what makes me come so hard I can barely stand afterward. I can fuck you and still hate you. I can fuck you and still want to put a bullet in your head. Don't ever confuse what we have for a fucking fairytale."

She shakes her head. "I don't believe you."

"You should." I dig my fingers into her soft, round ass and slowly guide her gushing pussy up and down my length.

I groan, pressing my forehead to hers as my balls draw taut against the base of my cock. I'm completely fucked. I'll never get tired of being inside her. Fucking her isn't a want, it's a profound need. I need to feel her hot sheath wrapped around my dick, and I *need* to find completion within her delectable body. Killing was my addiction before she crash-landed back into my life. Now my every waking thought is filled with her. We come together, bodies straining, hands rasping, lips clinging.

We wash away the evidence of our fucking in the downstairs bathroom and return to the kitchen afterward. I sweep up the mess on the floor while Zilphia washes the dishes. We look like a normal couple, doing normal couple shit. I scoff at the thought. What we have is far from normal.

"Hey, cut it out or time out for you both!" she exclaims good-naturedly.

My unruly pets nearly knocked her over with their roughhousing. She's taken a liking to them, and they've taken a liking to her too. That wasn't supposed to happen. They were supposed to help me keep her in check. After I finish sweeping up the broken glass, I return the broom and dustpan to the hall closet just beyond the kitchen entrance.

"Done," Zilphia announces, folding the dish rag over the faucet.

"Let's go," I say, motioning her forward. "I gotta get going."

"No," she responds, jutting out her chin defiantly, but it's all for show. There's no mistaking the fear in her eyes.

"What the fuck you just say?" I growl, taking a menacing step in her direction.

Zilphia bolts to the other side of the island. "Take me to work with you. You can't possibly keep me handcuffed to the bed forever."

"That's exactly what I plan to do." I stalk after her with long strides, but she runs again. "The more you run, the greater the punishment will be."

Sensing the tension between us, Mayhem and Harley position themselves in front of her, whining plaintively.

What the actual fucking hell? "Goddamn traitors," I grumble before narrowing my eyes at her. "You turned my dogs against me."

"Can you please be reasonable for once in your life?" she asks, throwing her hands up in exaggeration. "Staying in bed all day isn't healthy for me or the baby. I need to move around and get some exercise."

I halt my pursuit and contemplate her words for several long moments before coming to a decision. "You stay within my sight at all times. Do you understand me?"

She breathes a sigh of relief. "Yes."

"You don't even take a piss without my permission." I walk into her personal space and grasp her chin between my thumb and forefinger. "Don't test me, Zilphia."

"I said I understand," she deadpans, rolling her eyes in annoyance. "I won't even wipe my butt without your permission," she adds sarcastically.

I inspect the 1977 Chevrolet Camaro with a discerning eye as I coast a hand over the gleaming orange surface. This profession kinda fell into my lap. Zeus brought me to the shop one day, and the rest is history. Once I got my shit together, I practically came here every day after school.

When I graduated, Zeus signed Empire Auto Repair Services & Custom Paint over to me. The repair shop is on the other side of the building, but I leave the repairing to the mechanics, though. Fixing shit ain't my jam, but I'm a fucking Picasso when it comes to painting.

"Soooo," Zilphia starts, drawing out the one-syllable word behind the respirator mask covering the bottom half of her face. I gave it to her to protect both her and our unborn baby from the fumes back here. The ventilation system is top-notch, but it's better to be safe than sorry. "This is what you do for a living?"

"Yep." I glance back at her. "What about it?"

"Nothing." Zilphia shakes her head, lifting her shoulders in a shrug. "I just thought you um…"

She trails off as she fidgets in the overstuffed chair I carted from my office for her explicit comfort. I only did it to shut her up. Her incessant whining about the folding chair being too hard, her ass hurting, and future back problems started grating on my nerves.

"You thought I killed people for a living?" I finish for her.

"Well, you said it, not me."

I chuckle and refocus on my task. "I don't kill people every day, Zilphia." As an afterthought, I add, "I would if necessity called for it, though."

"But why kill people at all?" she asks me. "Why not just do this? You're obviously really good at it."

It's my turn to shrug. "I'm really good at killing too, and some people need killing." I spread my arms in a wide arc. "Call me Mr. Jack-of-all-Trades. I paint during the day and blow motherfucker's brains out at night."

She scoffs. "And who decides who lives and who dies?"

"Zeus, of course," I answer her.

"And who made him judge, jury, and executioner?" I hear the loathing in her voice. She thinks my old man is dirt. Zeus is no angel, that's true enough, but he isn't all bad either. He does a lot of good too.

"Get off your high horse, Joan of Arc," I retort, moving my gaze to the black flames painted on the hood of the car. "Every asshole I kill deserves it ten times over."

"Why does it have to be you?" she questions, refusing to drop the subject. "Can't someone else do it?"

"Nah, I like killing." I saunter across the garage and come to a stop several inches in front of her. "If you thought I spent my days killing people, why'd you beg to come to work with me? Looking to learn the trade?"

"Of course not!" she exclaims. "It didn't cross my mind at the time. I just didn't want to be handcuffed to the bed."

I reach a hand out and coast a thumb over her delectable lips, recalling how they stretched so beautifully around my cock this morning. "Why do you care that I kill people?" I raise an eyebrow at her. "Concerned for my soul, Zilphia?"

She gasps, her gaze widening on the bulge growing in my denim jeans. "Don't you ever get tired of having sex?"

I laugh out loud. "What twenty-one-year-old male gets tired of sex?" I ask, stepping closer to her. "Do you hate my fucking that much?"

I shouldn't care whether she hates it or not. Her pussy is my property to do with as I damn well please—but I do care. I want her to crave the feel of my dick moving inside her wet, warm depths. I *need* her to crave my touch. I *need* her to be addicted to me.

"It's amazing most times," she whispers, averting her gaze. "Sometimes you're too rough and I bleed."

"Good." I grab her hand and press it into my erection. "I like your blood on my dick."

"Hey, hot stuff!" A familiar voice intrudes on our intimate moment, instantly raising my hackles. "Are you free tonight? I've been missing…" Ivy's smile falters when she spots Zilphia. I took her to pound town once, and she's been on my nuts ever since. I thought about slinging some more dick her way, but she became too damn clingy for my liking. "Oh, she still around?"

"Yeah, *she* is," Zilphia snaps, glaring daggers at her. Do I detect a hint of jealousy? Only one way to find out.

"For now, but the clock is ticking," I lie. My dick doesn't get hard for other women anymore. "Where's my hug?"

Ivy sprints across the concrete floor and launches herself into my arms. I slide my hands to her ass and squeeze, never taking my eyes off Zilphia. The dark scowl on her face confirms what I already suspected—she's jealous.

She leaps to her feet. "What the hell, Sandman?"

I place Ivy on her platform heels and press a lingering kiss on her neck. "I'll meet you at the clubhouse at eight. Wear something sexy."

"Anything for you, baby," she purrs, shooting Zilphia a triumphant smirk before sashaying out of the garage.

"Tell me you're not going to fuck that skank," Zilphia demands, balling her fists at her sides.

I brush past her and enter the lobby area. "Camaro's done," I inform the purple-haired girl sitting behind the reception desk.

"Okay," she chirps, picking up the receiver. "I'll give Mr. Simmons a call and let him know."

I continue to my office with a fuming Zilphia on my heels. "Answer me!" she yells, slamming the door shut behind her.

I take my sweet time settling behind my desk, just to piss her off a little more. "What I do doesn't concern you."

She rips off the respirator mask and launches it at me. I duck, and it smashes into the window behind me, shattering the glass. "So you can fuck any skank you want, but I can't even look at another guy?"

"That is correct." I lean forward, steepling my fingers together. "Unless you want him to lose his head."

"Do you…" she draws in a deep breath, blinking back tears. "Do you feel anything for me at all?"

I cock my head to the side. "Are you asking me if I love you, Zilphia?"

Tears escape her eyes despite her efforts to hold them back. "Do you?"

I stand and walk around my desk, coming face-to-face with her. "Your name and the word love will never leave my mouth in the same sentence." Because I can't help my fucking self, I cradle her smooth, damp cheek in my large palm. "You were my first kiss. You were supposed to be my first everything."

Zilphia leans into my touch. "What if that night never happened? Our lives would be so different."

"What if?" I laugh mirthlessly. "What-ifs are shit. What-ifs don't matter. What *is* does."

She places a trembling hand over my heart. "What *is* can change."

"No, it can't." I cover her hand with my own. "It's not blood that pumps through my veins. *It's hate.* I'll always hate you, Zilphia. That'll never change."

"What about the baby?" she whispers, her pleading eyes boring into mine. "We both grew up in a household without love. We've both been abused. We can't do that to our child."

"I would never hurt our child!" I tear away from her, anger thrumming through me. "Our child will be loved and cared for."

"Hating me will hurt our child." Her voice hitches as more tears flow down her cheeks. "Hurting me will *hurt* our child. You know it will."

"I have to hurt you, Zilphia," I murmur, coming to stand in front of her again. "I've told you this. If I was on my deathbed and was granted one last wish before leaving this Earth, it would be to make you bleed one last time."

"And I'm just supposed to be docile while you abuse and cheat on me for the rest of my life? No, I can't." Zilphia shakes her head, taking a step back. "I won't." She whirls around and bolts for the door.

I chase after her, slamming her against the wall, my chest pressing against her back. "There's nowhere you can run where I won't find you, Zilphia."

"I can't live like this," she wails, sobs racking her slender body. "Please let me go. I swear, you'll never see me again. Do it for our child. You know in your heart our child doesn't belong in your world."

"Never," I murmur against the side of her neck.

"You're a selfish bastard," she hisses.

I smirk. "That I am. I enjoy fucking you too much to ever let you go."

She scoffs. "You don't need me to bust a nut. There are plenty of club skanks for you to choose from. Have your pick. I'm pretty sure they're all eager to please the great Sandman."

"That's true, but I say the more the merrier." I grind my erection into her ass. "How do you feel about a threesome?"

"You're a disgusting manwhore and I hope your dick falls off!" she screams at the top of her lungs. "Just fucking let me go!"

I spin her around and pin her wrists to the wall. "I've been obsessed with you since I was twelve years old, Zilphia. There's no way in hell I'm ever letting you go."

"What do you want from me?" she whispers, her doleful gaze searching mine. "Do you want me to love you?"

"No, my sweet, sweet Zilphia." I press my lips against her ear. "I want you to fear me." I tear at her jeans, yanking them down her thighs along with her panties.

"No!" Zilphia shouts, shoving past me, but she stumbles and face-plants onto the carpet. She scrambles to her hands and knees, then frantically crawls toward the door.

"Come 'ere." I grab her ankles and flip her onto her back. "What did I tell you about that word?"

"You can't keep raping me, Sandman!"

"Who's going to stop me? You?" I sit back on my haunches and motion her forward. "Okay, give it your best shot."

Zilphia rears up and punches me square in the face, but I barely feel it. Maybe it's the adrenaline coursing through my dick. I've never wanted to fuck her more than I do at this very moment. "Is that all you got?" I taunt her. "I'm disappointed."

"Fuck you!" she screams, swinging at me again, but I catch her wrist midair.

"My turn." I seize her throat and slam her onto the floor. "You shouldn't have poked the monster. Now he's hungry." I strip her bare as she kicks, scratches, and damns me to hell. Then I free my cock. "Ready or not, here I come." I drive into her as hard as I can, pounding into her pussy over and over again.

She sobs beneath me, feeding the darkness in my soul. That darkness thrives off her pain, so I fuck her harder because the harder I fuck her, the more she cries. I dig my fingers into her calves and push her legs back as far as they'll go, driving deeper into her magic pussy. It grips me so goddamn tight, I can barely move inside her.

Fuck.

I'm not ready to come. It's not about me getting my rocks off. It's about domination—and fear. I need the mere thought of me to instill her with terror. I need her complete surrender… for her to understand that she'll never escape me in this lifetime or the next. She's mine forever.

I still, balls deep inside her warmth, and press my forehead to hers. "Does it hurt?"

"Yes," she whispers, her lips a soft caress against my own.

"Yes, what?" I growl, pushing deeper into her.

She whimpers. "Yes, it hurts."

I tighten my hold on the back of her legs, piercing her soft skin. Blood trickles from the deep grooves, pooling around my fingertips. Zilphia's pained gasp twitches my cock, and it takes everything in me to keep my monster at bay.

"Are you afraid?" I ask, my voice grating and unfamiliar to my own ears.

"Yes, I'm afraid!" she shouts, crying hysterically now. "I'm afraid every fucking day!"

"That's what I wanna hear." I fist my hands in her hair and lie flush against her soft body. "Now I can come."

I piston into the silken flesh between her thighs, my hips thrashing and rolling. Before long, I plunge headfirst into the black abyss where insanity meets ecstasy. I open my arms in welcome, embracing the madness, because in that madness awaits the greatest pleasure I've ever known.

Sweat pours from my body onto her flawless brown skin. She has an unbreakable hold on me, but I don't give a damn. I'm too far gone—too pussy wasted to care about anything other than the snug warmth cocooning my manhood. The only thing that can bring me back is finding release inside her sweet, wet walls.

I swear to every deity known to man, hers is the best pussy I've ever had. It's my crack, the best kind of poison. One minute it has me floating on cloud nine, only to send me crashing back to Earth in the next. But it isn't the impact I remember most, it's the rush I feel as I'm falling.

I bury my face against the slender column of her throat and breathe in her addictive honeysuckle scent. It's innately her, ingrained in her essence after all these years. Zilphia cries out as a surge of wetness soaks my dick. There it is, the fall. And what an amazing fall it is.

"Fuck, fuck, fuck," I groan, releasing hot spurts of cum into her wet core. "Fuck, it's so goddamn good." I settle my full weight on top of her, sated and weak.

"I can't breathe," she whimpers, squirming beneath me.

I push to my forearms and stare into her tear-filled gaze. "Your pussy soaked my dick all up. So it begs the question: Is it really considered rape if you come?"

Her mouth trembles. "You're the devil."

I smirk. "No, you got it all wrong, sweetheart. I'm far worse than the devil." I slip free of her body and slump back against my desk.

I couldn't stand right now to save my life. Zilphia stays on her back, legs slightly agape, staring up at the ceiling. I wonder what she's thinking but decide not to appease my curiosity for the moment. Instead, I retrieve a doobie and my favorite lighter from the inner pocket of my cut. I light up and admire the view through the earthy smoke permeating the air. My gaze follows the rapid rise and fall of her dark-brown nipples. Everything, and I mean every-damn-thing, about her is perfection. And she's all *mine*.

"I want to go back to school and spend some time with my friends," she announces.

I scoff, releasing a thick stream of smoke from my nostrils. "Not happening."

She sits up and stares at me with pleading eyes. "Can you at least think about it?"

"Isn't bringing you to work with me enough?" I growl in annoyance. "I swear, you goddamn women are never satisfied. You're staying home tomorrow."

"Snake can keep an eye on me at school," she presses, pulling her shirt over her head.

I shake my head. "Not all the time and I can't trust you not to kill our baby."

"I won't." Zilphia lowers her gaze and rests a hand on her still-flat belly. "I hate myself for even thinking about doing it."

"But you *did* think it. That's the fucking point," I sneer at her. "And you could think about doing it again. But remember this, if our baby dies, you die." I lean forward, staring straight into her rich, chestnut irises. "You remember the cremation chamber, don't you?" Tears immediately fill her eyes and spill down her soft cheeks. *Yeah, she remembers.*

"I'll burn you alive, and I won't stop there. Your entire family will feel my wrath. On second thought, I'd kill them first and make you watch. Make you choose who I slice up first. Yeah, that's what I'll do. That'd be an awful way for dear ole grandma to go. Oh, and your extended family will feel my blade too." I grasp her chin with a thumb and forefinger. "Your entire bloodline will be wiped from this Earth."

"I was afraid, okay?" she whispers through trembling lips. "I still am, but my baby—"

"*Our* baby," I snap. "Never exclude me. It's my baby too."

"Our baby is my life now." Zilphia places a hand over her heart. "Nothing else mattered after I heard our baby's heartbeat. Our child deserves all the kisses, hugs, and cuddling we never got as kids."

She seems sincere enough, but her words ring hollow. I can never trust her again—not after that night.

CHAPTER 37

Zilphia

"GOD, I CAN'T BELIEVE HE KEPT YOU HANDCUFFED TO HIS BED for an entire week," Meela says, pulling her purse strap over her shoulder. "Someone should cut off his balls and stick them up his ass."

Leah sighs and nudges her glasses higher on her nose. "Why must you say the most vulgar things?"

My eyes land on the tape holding the plastic frames together. Leah says everything's cool, but I still feel guilty about her glasses—and about what Snake did to her. She ordered a new pair, but delivery takes two to three weeks.

"Someone should cut off his testicles and lodge them up his rectum." Meela crosses her arms under her ample breasts and cocks a sardonic eyebrow. "Better?"

Leah's eyes roll heavenward. "I'm sick of you," she grumbles.

"Aw, darling, don't be like that," Meela croons, pinching Leah on the cheek. "You know you love me."

Leah slaps her hand away. "With much difficulty."

I laugh. "I've missed you two."

"Duh, what's not to miss?" Meela hooks her arm around mine and pulls me toward the exit. "Come on. Let's get the hell out of here."

A smile curves my lips as we shuffle down the hallway. Honestly, I'm surprised Sandman didn't change his mind about letting me come back to school. Of course, Snake watched me like a hawk all day. I even caught him standing outside some of my classes.

"I never thought I'd be so happy to be back at school."

"Oh God, she's delusional," Meela gasps in mock horror and speeds up her steps. "Hurry, we have to get her to the mall ASAP."

"Don't forget, Leah is taking me to see my grandmother first," I remind her. "Wanna come with? We'll just be a half hour, tops."

I miss my grandmother so much. I can't wait to feel her wiry arms around me.

Meela scoffs. "Absolutely the fuck not. I can't be in the same house as your bitchy cousin."

"You and me both." Deja hasn't seen me in a week. For all she knew, I could've been dead in a ditch. And all I got was the stink face and a snarky *"The whore is back"* when we passed in the hall this morning.

"I'll hang out with the ice queen for a bit." She draws in an annoyed breath. "Just pick me up after. Ugh, I can't believe she revoked my car privileges again."

"Is it necessary to call your sister that?" Leah asks, always the voice of reason. "Anyway, what did you expect? You kept staying out past curfew."

"Okay, Little Miss Ice Queen Number Two. I have a man to win, so fuck Tulip's curfew."

Leah clucks her tongue disapprovingly. "He's so inappropriate for you."

"What can I say? I'm a naughty girl."

Leah shakes her head but says nothing.

"What happened to Levi and Theo?" I was afraid to ask Sandman.

He tasked the prospects with watching over me the day I slipped away to have the abortion. Sure, they aren't pillars of society, but I don't want anyone else's blood on my hands.

"Heard they were taken to God's Glory and got the shit beat out of them," Meela answers me. "I haven't seen them since, though."

"Do you think... do you think they're dead?" *Please don't be dead.*

"Nah, they were probably told to leave Kent and never show their faces again," she assures me. "Now, had you gotten the abortion, they'd definitely be..." Meela drags a long stiletto-shaped fingernail across her throat.

Redmond's decapitated head flashes in my mind's eye, sending a chill down my back. *I know what that chill is.* It's death.

The stench of it surrounds me; it flows through my veins and fills my lungs, leaving its decadent flavor on my tongue. It's death that fucks me senseless every single day, ruthlessly, with a potent fervency so violent it vibrates through my soul.

Then, when I'm drained of all energy—sweat-slicked, muscles limp, and body weak—it fucks me again, more ruthless and harder than before.

Even now, I feel death's phantom fingers between my thighs, stroking my most sensitive area. I never imagined death would be a man with the bluest eyes I've ever seen and hair the color of the sun. Death is a siren's song, and I'm firmly trapped in its grasp.

"Zilphia, are you okay?" Leah asks, dispelling my carnal thoughts.

"Yeah." I blink several times, attempting to dispel my troubled thoughts. "Why?"

"You zoned out on us, girl," Meela says as her probing eyes roam over my face. "You do that a lot. What were you thinking about?"

"Nothing," I mumble, looking down at my shoes. "It's just that I have a lot of schoolwork to catch up on."

I don't want to talk about Sandman. I just want to have a good time with my friends.

"Ugh!" Meela exclaims. "What the hell does he want?"

I jerk my head up and follow her gaze, spotting Snake propped beside the double glass doors, his arms folded across his chest. Leah's breaths quicken as his dark gaze slowly sweeps over her lithe figure. It promises ecstasy, pain, and the filthiest sex acts that can be performed on the human body. I know because it's the same way Sandman looks at me.

Leah lowers her gaze and protectively wraps her arms around her torso. Snake smirks and steps into her path, whispering something in her ear. Whatever he said had the desired effect, which no doubt was fear. Tears roll down her cheek as he pushes a hand under her shirt and draws slow circles on her belly.

"Leave her alone, *Lucien*," Meela snarls.

She knows full well that using his given name in public is a sign of disrespect—something I learned from her. The girl loves playing with fire, and if she's not careful, one day that fire is going to burn out of control.

"Watch yourself," Snake snarls. "Jig won't be your protector forever. And man, am I looking forward to knocking you down a peg or two."

Meela bats her eyelashes. "Little ole me? But I'm sweet as a five-pound bag of sugar, *sugar*."

"On second thought, I hope Jig gives you exactly what you want." Snake moves closer to her, bending his head until his hard gaze is eye level with hers. "There's a side of him you've never seen. He's going to fuck up your entire world."

"Good, because I want him to fuck up my world in all types of ways."

Snake's signature smirk curves his lips again. "Not like this, baby girl. Not like this," he warns before pivoting on his heel and pushing through the doors.

"What a butthole," Meela says, glowering at his back. "What did he say to you?"

"Nothing important." Leah angrily swipes at the wet trails on her cheek. "I can't wait to graduate and move far away from here."

We walk out into the cool autumn day, and I stop in my tracks, my breath catching in my throat.

There he is.

The bane of my existence.

The blond devil.

He casually lounges against the side of his motorcycle. I drink him in, my gaze sweeping over his jean-clad legs. I know just how powerful those legs are. An unwelcome image of him on his knees as he pounds into my body filters through my mind, making my pussy clench.

I shake my head and continue my perusal, admiring the thick veins covering his muscular arms, identical to the thick veins on his dick. Our gazes clash, and the intensity reflected in his blue orbs nearly bowls me over. It's the same look he gives me right before he fucks me senseless.

A slight breeze ruffles his loose golden mane, and several strands flit across his blindingly beautiful face. Fuck him to hell and back. No man should look that good, especially him.

"Jesus Christ," Meela grumbles. "Zeus's offspring are annoying as fuck."

I hurry down the stairs and march straight up to him. "What are you doing here?" I whisper-yell at him. "You said I could see my grandmother and go to the mall after school."

He tosses me a helmet. "I'm taking you."

"But why?"

"Because I don't trust you." He straddles his motorcycle and motions for me to get on behind him. "Get on."

"I said I wouldn't—"

"Get on the fucking bike, Zilphia, or the only place you'll be going is up and down on my dick," he bellows. My cheeks heat in embarrassment. God, I fucking hate him!

I look back at Meela and Leah, blinking back the tears threatening to spill free. "I'll meet y'all at the mall." I hold out my backpack to Leah. "Can you take this for me?"

She gives me a sympathetic smile. "Yeah, sure."

"She's sorry for what she did, okay?" Meela fumes, her hands forming tight fists at her side. "Are you going to shit on her for the rest of your miserable life?"

"Not just shit, I'm going to piss on her too," he counters, gracing her with the same sardonic smirk perfected by his brother, and obviously inherited from their father. "Wait, I already did that."

Meela frowns, blinking in confusion. I haven't told them about my visit to God's Glory and most likely never will.

"Get on the bike, Zilphia," he orders again. "Or should I give your classmates something to really talk about?"

I avoid the faces around me, slipping the helmet on before climbing onto the bike behind him. Once we're away from prying eyes, I allow my tears to fall. I can't be at his beck and call for the rest of my life. I just can't, and bringing a baby into this toxic shit is crazy. I don't know what to do. Killing him isn't an option. The Gods would never stop searching for me. Anyway, I can't stomach the thought of killing him, though I'd be doing myself and the world a favor.

He makes a sharp turn down an alley, and I instinctively tighten my arms around his waist. One of these days, he's going to send us both to an early grave. I frown, noticing there's no outlet at the other end. He kills the engine, but before I can ask any questions, he's off the bike and yanking me in front of him.

"Why—" I gasp, the words dying on my tongue as he snatches my helmet off, dropping it beside his on the ground.

In the next instant, my back is pressed against the crumbling brick wall, my arms pinned high above my head. Then his mouth is on mine, hard and demanding. He tastes like desperation, lust, and something… dangerous. It's suffocating. His hungry tongue sweeps past my lips as his dick grows long and thick against my belly.

"I need you," he growls, yanking my jeans down to my thighs.

"Stop," I pant, latching onto his wrists. "I'm not going to let you fuck me in a dirty alley."

"You don't get a say in where or when I fuck you, Zilphia," he snarls, ripping my thong from my body.

"No, Sandman, no!" I plead with him. "You can't keep treating me like this. I'm going to be the mother of your child."

"You think I want to be obsessed with you?" He slips a hand between my thighs. "Obsessed with this? To crave you more than I crave my next breath?" he rasps, burying his nose against the side of my neck and inhaling my scent. "To crave your smell, the warmth of your skin, the wet suction of your hot pussy? You consume my every waking moment. I fucking hate you, Zilphia. But I hate myself even more for wanting you so badly."

"I never wanted to be your obsession," I sob in frustration. "Please stop this. I can't take it anymore. Please, for our child's sake."

"You should've stayed in your bedroom that night, Zilphia," he says, sinking to his knees.

"No good deed goes unpunished," I whisper.

He looks up at me from under those long golden eyelashes and blows on my clit. I cry out in ecstasy, my knees nearly buckling. It shouldn't feel like this—hot, consuming, perfect. Not with him. He's a monster.

"No good deed goes unpunished," he echoes, then slowly licks me from my throbbing entrance to my clit, keeping his gaze locked with mine.

I cry out again, my head thrashing from side to side. I'm on fire for him.

"Want me to stop?" he asks, his eyes daring me to lie.

I shake my head, my eyes burning with tears. There's no sense in denying it. My body's reaction reveals the truth.

"Say it," he demands.

"I don't want you to stop."

"Good girl." He slides his thumbs along my folds and spreads my pussy lips apart. "Beautiful and all *mine.*"

His strong mouth closes over my clit, and my entire body jerks with pleasure. I grab fistfuls of his flaxen mane and scream out his name, wanting to pull him closer and push him away at the same time. Thick fingers plunge deep inside my aching pussy, deliciously stretching my slick walls as his tongue flicks back and forth over my swollen clit.

"Oh God," I slur, undulating against his face, completely out of my mind with need. "Oh God, Sandman."

I fall over the edge into blissful euphoria, my body dripping and writhing uncontrollably.

He brings me to climax again and again—urgency in every caress of his tongue and thrust of his fingers. Maybe this is what happens when unrequited love turns to hate, then to lust, and finally to obsession. It's the perfect storm, and the worst part is, I'm starting to enjoy the thunder.

I collapse against him, my legs folding beneath me. "I can't… I can't. Sandman, please."

"More," he rasps, yanking my shoe off and peeling one leg free from my jeans. "I need more."

He guides my thighs over his shoulders, then his mouth is back on my clit. He sucks my swollen flesh while his fingers seek my warm depths again. He slides his other hand under the curve of my ass and works a finger into my rimmed opening. My moans reverberate through the alley as the throbbing pressure in my feminine core builds again, but it's different this time. I feel something more… but what that more is, I don't know.

"What's… what's happening?" I moan.

Sandman moves his fingers and tongue with purpose—wild, wet, and greedy. *Oh God, it's coming.* A raw sound escapes my throat as a stream of milky liquid gushes from between my thighs, soaking his face and the front of his shirt. Wave after wave of paralyzing ecstasy consumes my entire being as he ravenously drinks from my body. He drinks every drop I have to give, leaving me depleted and limp from exhaustion.

Before I can fully regain my senses, Sandman pins me against the wall with his big body and pushes into me from behind, filling my pussy to the hilt. I brace my hands on the crumbling red brick, waiting with both anticipation and dread.

He stills and presses his mouth to my ear. "I've waited for this all day."

"Show me," I whisper before I can stop myself.

He digs hard fingers into my jaw and angles my face toward his. I meet his gaze and shiver at the feral desire shining in the blue depths. "Tell me you're mine, Zilphia," he demands.

My body clenches around his erection, desperately needing him to fuck us both to completion.

He groans. "Tell me."

"I'm yours."

"I've wanted you for so long," he murmurs, then begins moving inside me, fucking me so achingly slow my toes curl. "I'd lie awake for hours, fucking you a thousand different ways in my mind, wishing it was your pussy instead of my hand giving me pleasure. Now my child is growing in your belly."

I give him my complete submission because I don't have a choice, and even if I did, I don't know if I'd want him to stop. My mind knows he's the embodiment of toxic as fuck, but my body doesn't give a damn. Fate won't be denied, and neither will he. It's a never-ending cycle of fucked up with him.

He places a lingering kiss on the spot just behind my earlobe, while his expert fingers softly stroke my engorged clit. "You hear how wet she is for me?"

"Yes," I breathe.

"That's the sound of your surrender," he murmurs and pulls back until only the tip of his length is left inside my throbbing center. "I'm the villain in your story, but I'm the one your pussy purrs for. The one who makes you come so goddamn hard you forget your own name." He slowly sinks back into my heat and stills again. "Prince Charming could never make you this wet."

He begins pounding into my pussy with bone-jarring force.

"Too rough," I whimper, but he only fucks me harder.

It hurts, but damn, he's hitting all the right spots. Each frenzied thrust into my body lifts my feet off the ground. I position a hand beneath my cheek to protect my soft skin from being scraped raw. Our ragged breathing and flesh slapping against flesh echoes in my ears.

The dread I felt is forgotten, replaced with a need beyond my comprehension. *I'm becoming just as twisted as he is.* He takes without asking and hurts without empathy, but I stay wet and ready for his dick. Our type of fucked up can't be replicated.

"You're the air in my lungs, the blood in my veins, and every beat of my goddamn heart," he rasps, placing a large hand beside mine on the brick wall while keeping the other between my thighs. "Fuck you, Zilphia. Fuck you."

He's wrong—I'm none of those things. Hate is the air in his lungs, the blood in his veins, and the driving force in his every heartbeat. Hate is intoxicating. Hate is powerful. Hate is pain. Hate is *beautiful.* Hate can be many things, but for him, hate is life.

He seeks my lips, and I readily give him what he wants. Our lips and tongues clash together in a kiss that steals my breath as he ferociously surges in and out of my pussy.

"Fuck yes," he groans against my kiss-swollen lips, the urgency of his thrusts increasing.

"I want you to soak my insides with your cum," I moan, drunk on pleasure. "I want it dripping from my pussy."

"Zilphia, Zilphia, Zilphia," he chants my name over and over, pounding into me so deep, I swear I feel him in my womb.

Finally, I fall headfirst into unadulterated rapture. My eyes roll to the back of my head as my slick walls contract around his rock-hard dick. I want this feeling forever, but there's a steep price to pay. I can't have the man without the monster.

"That's right, squeeze that dick," he rasps as his hot cum floods my pussy.

He comes and comes and comes, his seed overflowing onto my thighs.

I'm an emotional wreck by the time he slips from my body. Sex is powerful; my mother drilled that into my head when I was a little girl. She said sex makes men weak, and that's what makes women superior. She's obviously never gotten fucked by someone like Sandman.

I turn around, using the wall for support. He watches me with a blank expression on his stone features as he secures his belt buckle. How can he not be affected? He felt it too, didn't he? It couldn't have been just my imagination.

"Get dressed," he bites out.

"I need help," I say softly, pointing at my jeans. I'll topple over if I try to move now. His nostrils flare in annoyance, but he crouches down in front of me and roughly shoves my foot into my pant leg.

"Wait!" I exclaim and shyly gesture toward the sticky cum on my thighs. "Do you have a napkin or something?"

"No," he barks, yanking my jeans up. "Hurry the fuck up."

I blink back tears. How can he fuck me like that, then treat me like shit afterward? He's so confusing. After several failed attempts, I finally managed to fasten my jeans. Sandman is already sitting astride his motorcycle, glaring at me.

"Hurry up!" he yells. "I don't have all fucking day."

I walk over to him on wobbly legs, but I don't climb on behind him just yet. "Have you ever been with anyone the way you are with me?"

He chuckles sarcastically. "Does it matter?"

"Yeah, it does."

"Every bitch I fuck is treated to the Sandman special. Did you think it was only reserved for you?"

I shake my head. "I don't believe you."

"I don't give two fucks about what you believe, Zilphia. Don't take what I say when I'm horny to heart. That's just my dick talking." He cocks his head sideways, his lips tilting upward in a subtle smirk. "You don't think you're the only girl I'm fucking, do you?"

I raise my chin defiantly. "If you were fucking other girls, you wouldn't be fucking me multiple times a day."

He shrugs a shoulder. "What can I say? I have a high sex drive."

"Stop fucking lying!" I shout.

Sandman launches himself at me, seizing my throat in a vise grip. "Have you forgotten who's in charge?" He sneers in my face. "You're nothing more than a piece of meat to me, Zilphia, so don't get any fanciful ideas about what's happening between us."

He releases me, and I fall to my knees, gasping for breath. I look down at my belly, and a sense of calm envelops me. There are dark days ahead, but my baby will make those days a lot easier.

CHAPTER 38

SANDMAN

SHE CAN CRY ME A FUCKING RIVER. I CAN'T FORGIVE HER FOR WHAT she did, not now, not ever. The lie she told royally fucked me up mentally and changed me for the worse, starting a chain reaction that put a Glock in my hand.

For all intents and purposes, she inadvertently created Sandman. The events of that night forever changed me physically too. Because of my hearing loss, it's difficult for me to pinpoint voices and sounds, especially in loud places. That can be dangerous in my line of work.

Yeah, I can walk, and I have all my limbs, my sight, and my dick gets hard without issue. For the most part, my hearing loss doesn't affect my quality of life, but when you're hurt by the one person you love most in the world, the degree of the offense doesn't matter. Betrayal is betrayal.

Despite her treachery, she lives rent-free in my head twenty-four hours a day. Obsession is more detrimental and addictive than any drug. Somewhere deep inside me is the teenage boy still vying for her affection. I despise that fucker. He's weak. I thought I killed him the night of the fire.

The excuse I gave Zilphia for picking her up from school is bullshit. I needed to see her, to touch her, to smell her, but most of all, I needed to *fuck* her. Hell, I still need to *fuck* her. It takes everything in me not to detour down another alley and bury my cock inside her wet, warm goodness again.

And fuck, when she squirted all over me, I nearly lost my goddamn mind. I want her sweet juices all over me again. Fuck it. I don't care what I told her. I'll take her to see her grandmother, but after that, we're going home.

I park across the street from the house and kill the engine. Angry shouts reach my ears from the open door.

"Oh no," Zilphia mumbles, then bolts across the street, narrowly avoiding getting hit by a car.

If the driver hadn't swerved around her at the last second, she'd be dead. The motorist hurls several obscenities at her before giving her the bird and speeding away.

"Zilphia!" I shout, chasing after her. What the hell is wrong with her? I enter the living room a second behind her into chaos.

Her aunt and cousin are beating the fuck out of her mother. The aunt's husband is in the middle of the brawl, trying to separate them. I have to hand it to her, though—she's giving as good as she gets.

Zilphia's grandmother struggles to make her way downstairs, crying hysterically and yelling at her daughters to stop.

I spot her little cousin peeking from behind the sofa, a cell phone plastered to his ear, most likely talking to a 911 dispatcher.

"I should've never let you anywhere near my husband!"

"It's not my fault you weren't taking care of your man!"

"Let go of her hair, Sheila!" The man responsible for the fight bellows. "You're both pregnant for Christ's sake!"

His wife turns on him and starts swinging. "You got the bitch pregnant!"

I blow out a breath. "Fuck, I didn't see that coming."

Now there are two fights instead of one, and I ain't breaking up shit. I lean back against the wall and cross my arms. Five-O better get here quick.

"Let her go!" Zilphia wails and latches onto her cousin's arm before she can rain more punches down on her mother's head.

She whirls around and shoves her hard, sending her crashing into the glass coffee table. Zilphia screams in agony, cradling her bloody forearm to her chest. I pounce on the bitch, slamming the back of my hand across her face and knocking her into darkness.

"Deja!" Her mother races to her side and glares at me with hate-filled eyes. "Who are you and what the hell are you doing in my house?"

The matriarch of the family's limp body lands at the foot of the stairs. Anguished screams reverberate through the living room.

I leap into action, kneeling beside her and placing two fingers on the right side of her neck. "No pulse."

"Don't let her die, Sandman," Zilphia begs. "Please don't let her die."

I start CPR just as several policemen rush into the house, their weapons drawn. They quickly assess the situation and take over. I pull Zilphia into my arms and hold her tight as she bawls her eyes out.

CHAPTER 39

One month later

Zilphia

I BURROW CLOSER TO MY GRANDMOTHER'S FRAIL BODY AND REST MY HEAD on her chest. The soft mattress seems to swallow her tiny frame whole. "I'm so happy you're okay."

"I'm fine," she assures me. "You don't have to worry about me anymore."

I lift my head and stare into her soft, rheumy gaze. "I have to tell you something." I inhale a deep breath as tears spill from my eyes. "I'm pregnant."

She smiles and wipes the wetness from my cheeks. "I know, sweetheart. You're going to be a great mother."

"How-how do you know?" I ask her. "I haven't even told Momma yet."

"I know these things."

"You're not disappointed in me?" I love my grandmother so much. She's always been my biggest cheerleader. I would hate to upset her in any way.

"I could never be disappointed in you. You're my sunshine."

"What am I going to do, Grandma?" I sob and bury my face against her thin shoulder. "I'm not ready to be a mother."

"Listen to me very carefully," she orders in a stern voice. "God won't give you *anything you can't handle." She places a gentle kiss on my temple. "I have to go home now. But I'll always watch over you and your children."*

I frown and lift my head again. "What are you talking about, Grandma? You are home."

"Goodbye, my darling. I love you."

One second she's there, and in the next, she's gone. I scramble off the bed and spin in a circle, but she's not here. Where did she go?

"Grandma, come back!" I shout frantically. "Please don't leave me! I need you!"

"Grandma!" I scream, waking with a start, my heart pounding in my chest.

"Fucking hell, Zilphia," Sandman grumbles and pulls me into his strong embrace. "It was just a dream."

I stare up into his beautiful blue eyes. "I miss her so much."

It's my first Thanksgiving without her. We didn't always spend the holiday together, but we never missed a phone call. She died of a massive heart attack. It's been a little over a month, but it still feels like yesterday. The paramedics tried to revive her, but it was too late.

I haven't heard from my mother since. My texts and calls go unanswered. I thought she'd at least come to the funeral. Instead, she ran off with her married lover, leaving nothing but wreckage behind. I hate her so fucking much. Who skips their own mother's funeral? Even Nolan showed up, though he barely spoke two sentences to me.

I live with Sandman now. Sheila wasted no time kicking me out. I don't blame her, but I shouldn't be punished for my mother's sins. I carry enough of my own. But the lowest blow was not including any of our names in the obituary.

My grandmother had a few good years left—maybe more. But the hatred between her daughters wore her down. In the end, it killed her.

He sighs. "People die. It won't get easier, but some days will be better than others."

"I want her back!" I wail, crying my heart out. "I can't make it in this world without her." I'm so lost without her.

God, why did you take her from me? I just want to hug her one last time. *Grandma!*

"I can't console you, Zilphia," he tells me. "I'm not that man, but I can give you this." He brushes his lips ever so gently against my own.

Sandman is still Sandman. My grandmother's death didn't soften him toward me. He's less monstrous in a way, but I don't know how much longer that'll last. Every day, his control slips a little more.

Because I need to dull the pain in my heart, I thread my fingers into his golden strands and return his kiss. He yanks the comforter off our naked bodies and rolls me onto my back, settling between my thighs. I spread my legs wide for him, and he fills me in one fluid motion. He doesn't give my body time to adjust to his invasion. In true Sandman fashion, he recklessly plunges in and out of my pussy.

It burns, but I need this.

I need *him*.

There are a million different paths my life could've taken, but I ended up here, in his bed and completely under his control.

I cross my ankles at the small of his back and roll my hips upward, meeting his hard thrusts. I'm still hurting, but he gives me a different kind of hurt. A hurt that feels good. A hurt that overpowers my senses and makes me forget my grief, even if only for a little while.

Soon my body accepts him with little resistance, melting over his erection like liquid silk. Our sweaty bodies meet again and again, in tandem with our hungry lips and dueling tongues.

I score my nails down his back as the throb between my thighs intensifies with every passing minute. Sandman anchors my legs over his shoulders and intertwines our fingers, pinning my hands to the bed, then he pounds into me with a fierceness that thrills and frightens me. He trails open-mouthed kisses down my throat and along my collarbone. I turn my head and suck his earlobe into my mouth, twirling my tongue around his small hoop earring.

"Fuck, Zilphia," he rasps, fucking me harder and faster than ever before.

I implode, succumbing to the white-hot sensations at the center of my pleasure. Sandman shouts his own release, pouring his seed deep into my convulsing walls. He settles onto his back, his semi-hard length resting on his belly, slick with my juices. The pain of my grandmother's loss hits me like a wrecking ball, and all I want to do is cry.

"Please hold me," I whisper.

Sandman pins me with his steel-blue gaze, and I know for certain he doesn't want to provide the comfort I so desperately need.

"Please."

He growls in annoyance but pulls me into his arms. For the next thirty minutes, I cry my sorrows against his chest.

I scan the lounge, a knot of discomfort tightening in my chest. These men almost seem normal—eating, laughing, and joking. Not the hardened criminals I know them to be. Sandman sits to my left at the island, scarfing down the food on his plate. Cricket occupies the stool on his other side, making quick work of his own meal.

All kinds of grilled meats, seafood, sides, and desserts stretch across the long tables against the back wall. My stomach churns at the mix of smells assaulting my senses. Between the football game blaring on all eight flatscreens, the cacophony of sounds from the arcade, boisterous conversations, and little God offspring running around, I can barely hear myself think. I really just want to go back to bed.

I don't want to celebrate. I want my grandma.

It all seems so surreal, like I'm watching someone else's life through a television screen. I'm not two and a half months pregnant. My grandmother is still alive and healthy. My brother and I get along. My father isn't a fugitive. My mother is the perfect housewife with a heart of gold. And my aunt and cousin don't hate my guts.

I blink back tears and check my cell phone for the millionth time, even though my notifications have been silent. My mother and brother still haven't responded to the Happy Thanksgiving texts I sent this morning. I shouldn't have texted them. But it's Thanksgiving, and I felt… alone. Stupid, I know.

I throw my phone back into my purse. I'm done. I'm not extending the olive branch again.

"Eat," Sandman commands, jabbing his fork toward my untouched plate.

I stiffen but hold my ground. "Not hungry."

"I didn't ask if you were hungry," he growls. "I said eat."

I push the plate away, a quiet rebellion.

He leans in and presses a forkful of pasta against my lips. "Open."

I turn my head. "I said I'm not hungry."

"You've been losing weight. If you're not healthy, neither is our baby."

"Just because I lost a few pounds doesn't mean I'm not healthy," I retort.

Sandman grabs a fistful of my long, knotless braids and yanks my head back. "Don't make me hurt you, Zilphia."

"You're such a fucking hypocrite," I snap at him. "In one breath you claim to be worried about my health, then in the next you're threatening to hurt me."

He drops my hair, his jaw clenched. "I'm going to take a piss. When I get back, a quarter of that food better be gone." With that edict, he stomps away.

I turn back around in my seat, locking gazes with a smirking Cricket. "What the fuck are you looking at?"

Cricket's smirk melts into a scowl, and he shifts in his seat to face me. "That baby in your belly is the only thing keeping Sandman from putting his foot up your ass," he states matter-of-factly around a mouthful of cheeseburger. "Do yourself a favor and do what you're told. You won't be pregnant forever, and you and I both know he has a very long memory."

I reach for my cup of peach tea, intending to throw it in his face, but familiar arms wrap around me from behind. "Hey girlie, how's your day going?"

"It could be better," I answer, relaxing into Meela's embrace. My baby daddy's asshole best friend is consigned to the back burner for now. I admire his loyalty, but that doesn't make him any less of an ass.

Meela hops onto the stool Sandman just vacated. "How about you stay with me tonight? I'll do your toes and nails, and give you the best full-body massage you've ever had. The works, honey. What do you say? I'll tell Leah and make it a girl's night."

I sigh. "I have to ask Sandman."

As the days pass, his leash around me gets tighter and tighter. It's been school and then home most days, unless we're together. I don't know if it's concern for me, for our unborn child, or for both of us. On the rare occasion I'm allowed to go out solo, he's always lurking in the background somewhere.

Meela rolls her eyes. "God, tell him to loosen his grip a little. He's stricter than a preacher whose daughter likes doing the Lord's work on her knees."

If only it were that easy.

"Where's Tulip?" Our heads snap in the direction of the growled question.

"Oh my God," Meela mumbles under her breath. "Here we go."

Draco hovers beside her, his arms crossed over his expansive chest. "Where is she?"

We both know who the "she" is.

I have to admit he's freaking hot. Although we live in the same house, I've never seen him this close up before. We're rarely in the same room together, probably because he doesn't get along with the middle child of the family, aka my baby daddy. I've heard them arguing from the safety of the bedroom at least a dozen times.

Though he and Sandman are the same height, he's more muscular in build and has the most vivid green eyes I've ever seen. They almost seem to glow. Even his beard is sexy, and I don't care too much for beards. He has beautiful hair too. The curly ginger strands are pulled into a top knot on his head. Like his psycho siblings, he has a lot of tattoos.

Most notable is the intricate red dragon tattoo spanning the length of his right arm. How can all three brothers be sexy *and* crazy as hell? The red demon, the dark prince, and the stone-cold killer. Actually, where is the dark prince? I haven't seen him all day. He's probably off somewhere terrorizing Leah.

"She's at home, Draco," she replies, her tone flat and uninterested. "Did you really think she'd come here of all places?"

"Alone?" he presses, stepping closer to her. Depending on the answer, all hell might break loose.

"Yep. Plans to watch movies all day."

"I'll take her a plate," he mumbles, more to himself than anyone else, and turns on his heel.

"I'm taking her one later," Meela calls after him, but he keeps walking.

"No need."

See, crazy as hell.

Meela rolls her faux-blue eyes. "How does one become pussy whipped without actually getting the pussy?"

"I suppose the same way someone becomes dick whipped without actually getting the dick," I counter, fluttering my eyelashes.

She grins, bumping my shoulder with hers. "Touché, bitch."

"Aren't you going to warn her?" I ask, watching Draco as he piles food on two paper plates.

"Hell no."

"That's not very sisterly."

She shrugs. "I don't give a damn. I hope he fucks her until her back gives out. Anyway, he would never hurt her. He worships the ground she walks on."

"That doesn't matter if she doesn't want him." I'm tired of these fucking men thinking they can have any woman they want.

"Listen, she needs to get fucked and fucked bad. And not just regular fucking either," she adds, plucking a string bean off my plate and tossing it between her blue-painted lips. "Tulip, the prude, needs the type of fucking that will have her walking bowlegged for a month. I swear, sometimes it's hard to believe we came from the same penis and vagina."

"Still, it's her choice whether—"

Meela holds up an index finger. "Hold that thought, because I know this bitch is not all up on my man."

I follow her gaze to where Jigsaw sits with a pretty brunette snuggled on his lap. "Meela, don't do anything crazy. There are children here."

"Please, these little snots have seen way worse on television." Meela drops onto her shiny blue platform heels and smooths her hands down her skin-tight multicolored jumpsuit. "How do I look?"

I look her up and down, from her blue knee-length lemonade braids to the tips of patent leather boots. "Like the next twerk star."

"You give the best compliments." She blows me an air kiss, then squares her shoulders. "Watch my purse."

I sigh, watching her sashay toward the unsuspecting duo.

Cricket grins, his gaze tracking Meela too. "This should be entertaining."

Meela taps Jigsaw on the shoulder and starts giving him the business. I can't hear what's being said over the din in the room, but her stance says it all. One hand is propped on a curvy hip while a long acrylic nail is pointed dangerously close to his face.

He pushes the woman off his lap and stands to his full height, towering over Meela's small frame. Even in her heels, the height difference is astounding. The two begin to argue, and as scary as he is, she still doesn't back down.

I squirm in my seat as they shout at each other. I'm able to hear bits and pieces now. Meela says something about him being a dog in heat and needing to keep it in his pants. He counters with something about her being a brat and needing to stay in a child's place.

From the corner of my eye, I see several women herding the children into the hallway with promises of candy and a Disney movie marathon in the movie theater. *Good idea.* They don't need to witness this craziness. Meela angrily shoves at his chest. Jigsaw's companion shoves her in return, and Meela sucker punches her in the face. Well, that escalated rather quickly.

"Oh snap," Cricket chortles, throwing his head back in laughter.

The woman screeches in outrage and charges at Meela, her fingernails poised to do some serious damage. She swipes at her, but Meela ducks and rears back her fist for another punch. Jigsaw holds Meela back with an arm and grabs the brunette by the throat, snarling something in her face before shoving her away.

Their shouting match resumes, and he says something that makes Meela stagger back a few steps. She slaps him hard across the face, then attempts to slap him again, but he latches onto her wrist. Not one to be bested, she tries to knee him in the balls, but he twists away and shakes her like a rag doll.

I look at Cricket. "We have to do something."

"Nah." He shakes his head. "That's their business."

Afraid for my friend, I hop off the stool, determined to defuse the situation. "Well, I'm going to put a stop to it."

"Sit the fuck back down," Cricket growls at me.

Who the hell does this bastard think he is? "Fuck—"

A loud boom tears through the room, trapping my words in my throat. The once-secured metal door that led to the bar now lies damaged on the floor.

Everything seems to happen all at once. A group of men pours into the room, releasing a hail of gunfire. Bullets riddle the brunette's torso, killing her before her body hits the carpet.

Jigsaw bounds across the room with a screaming Meela in tow. He shoves her inside the arcade with a dozen or so cowering kids and jumps into the fray.

"Get down," Cricket shouts, yanking me to my knees behind the island, a gun already in his hand.

"What's going on?" I ask, shaking so hard my teeth chatter. "Who are those men?"

"Fucking Lawless Disciples," he hisses. "Get to the kitchen and hide. I'll cover you."

"Have you lost your mind? If I go out there, I'll get shot to bits."

"Do what I say, goddamn it!" he yells at me. "I'm not going to let you die."

"I'm scared," I say, my voice trembling as tears burn my eyes.

"Just stay behind me." He pulls a second gun from a holster. "On the count of three, okay?"

I nod. *Where's Sandman?* As much as he hates me, I know he'll protect me.

"One. Two. Three!"

We make a break for it. I stay hidden behind him, praying I don't get shot.

"Oh, you want some, motherfucker?" Cricket bellows. *Pop, pop, pop...* "Oh, you too, bitch? Fuck you!" *Pop, pop, pop...*

It only takes seconds to reach the doorway, but they were the longest seconds of my life.

"Go, Zilphia! And don't come out until it's over."

I race to the kitchen as fast as my legs will carry me, grab the biggest knife I can find, then shut myself inside the pantry. Little good it'll do against a gun, but my choices are limited.

I didn't think to grab my phone; everything happened so fast. Has anyone called the police? The better question is: *Will anyone call?* People usually turn a blind eye where the Gods are concerned. Besides, the gunfire is probably too muffled for anyone outside to notice.

I recall Sandman mentioning that while the clubhouse isn't fully soundproof, the construction crew went to great lengths to get it as close as possible. If that wasn't bad enough, the few stores around here are all closed for the holiday.

I sink into a corner and pull my knees to my chest. Blood pounds in my ears as my breathing turns ragged. *Shit.* My asthma medication is in my purse right along with my cell phone.

Okay, stay calm and focus on your breathing. Long, deep breaths, like the doctor taught you. In and out. In and out. In and out.

"Where are you, little mouse?" a man croons. "I saw you come in here."

Fuck, fuck, fuck. I wipe the sweat from my eyes and push to my feet, holding the knife out in front of me. I press deeper into the corner, my heart thundering against my rib cage.

"Come on out like a good little gash and I'll make it quick. Well, I might have a bit of fun with you first." He chuckles.

I remain stone silent, hoping against hope that he goes away. *Sandman, I need you.*

The door opens, revealing a tall, thin man. "Hello, love." He smiles, showcasing teeth too tiny for his mouth, and aims the gun at my heart.

"Please, I'm pregnant," I say, praying my pending motherhood will sway him from killing me.

"I know, darling." He motions me forward with his gun. "Drop the knife and come on out."

I place my only means of defending myself on the shelf. "Sandman will give you anything you want," I sob, slowly walking toward him. "Just don't hurt me."

"You gotta die, darling," he states matter-of-factly. "Prez's orders. He wants Zeus and his entire bloodline dead."

A shot rings out, and my would-be executioner is hit in the arm. Before

I can react, he latches onto my wrist and spins me around, snapping his forearm across my throat. I whimper, feeling his gun pressed against my temple.

Sandman stands before us, his weapon raised and pointed at the man at my back. I draw in a sharp breath, seeing something in his eyes I've never seen before… *fear.* "Let her go."

"Drop it or I'll blow this bitch's brains all over this goddamn kitchen!"

"Not a fucking chance," he growls, taking a step forward.

His forearm tightens on my neck. "Don't fuck with me! I'll end this bitch and your bastard right here and now!"

Neither man moves for what seems like forever, but finally, Sandman places his weapon on the floor. "You'll never make it out of here alive."

"Don't care," the man jeers, aiming his gun at Sandman. "As long as I take you with me."

"No!" I shout, elbowing him in the gut with all my strength.

He grunts in pain, loosening his hold on my throat. I dive for cover, scrambling out of his reach.

Sandman charges forward with a roar and tackles him to the floor. I crawl underneath the kitchen nook and hide behind a chair.

Both men are on their feet now, throwing punches at each other. Sandman dodges the next punch thrown his way and comes back with a jab to the man's ribs.

He doubles over and gets a knee to the face. Cartilage breaks and blood spills, making my stomach roil.

"Motherfucker!" the man roars, grabbing a cast-iron pan off the stove and slamming it across Sandman's face.

I watch in horror as his body hits the floor with a hard thud. He doesn't move. *Oh God, please don't be dead.*

The man turns his wild gaze on me. "Now, where were we?"

I scramble from my hiding place and swing a chair at him. "Stay away from me!"

He laughs and easily plucks it from my grasp.

"Sandman, get up!"

"Darling, he can't help you," he taunts, stalking toward me. "He's knocked out cold."

I try to run, but he captures me and slams me into the wall, his large hands locking around my neck. I lash out, scratching at his face and arms, but he holds firm. My arms fall limply at my sides, my vision darkening. I feel myself fading away.

Something splashes onto my face, then his hands are gone.

I crash to my hands and knees, sucking big gulps of air into my burning lungs. A gurgling sound reaches my ears, and I scurry backward, afraid of what it is. I can't see clearly. Panicked, I rub my fists against my eyelids, trying to clear my vision. I blink my eyes open, and a small cry slips past my lips at the sight that greets me.

It's like a horror movie. Blood is everywhere—on the counters, oven, refrigerator, walls, and even the ceiling.

Sandman is on top of the man, plunging his knife into his lifeless body over and over again. He's soaked in blood; his once blond hair is completely red and covered in chunks of human flesh.

The man's face is unrecognizable, reminding me of hamburger meat.

Bile rises in my throat, and I spill the meager contents of my stomach all over the floor.

"Please… stop," I croak. "For God's sake… please stop."

I don't think he can even hear me. It's as if he's possessed.

Zeus rushes into the kitchen—Cricket, Smokey, and Jigsaw follow close on his heels. They all take in the bloody scene, their faces frozen in shock.

"He's dead, goddamn it!" Zeus bellows, attempting to pull his son off the lifeless man.

In the end, it takes all four of them to drag Sandman away from his latest victim.

A sudden rush of dizziness sweeps over me, then everything goes black.

CHAPTER 40

SANDMAN

"HOW THE FUCK DID THIS HAPPEN?" ZEUS GROWLS, PACING BACK and forth among the blood and carnage.

We're on high alert after the shit that just went down. Brothers are already scouring the streets and surrounding counties for any signs of Disciples.

Jigsaw leans against the wall, his lip split and knuckles bloodied. "They caught us sleeping," he says, his voice hard. "That can't happen again."

After taking a piss, I went out back for a smoke break and to get away from the noise. I needed to get away from Zilphia too, before I snatched her little ass up for being disobedient. I was heading back inside when I heard the explosion. Those fuckers hit us when they knew our guard would be down.

The blame is on us, though. We got too cocky… thought we were untouchable. This is the price. We suffered heavy losses—brothers and civilians. Naomi and Hawk, who's an ex-military medic, are in the basement, patching up the wounded.

The Disciples took heavy losses too, but that means nothing. They still got in. They breached our sanctuary. That shouldn't have happened.

Once word gets out, it's highly probable every criminal syndicate in the surrounding area will try their hand. We have to save face and quick. The only way to do that is to kill every last Disciple.

I coil one of Zilphia's long braids around my index finger. She's still unconscious, head resting on my lap. I've showered and dressed in clean clothes, though five minutes under the water didn't remove all the blood from my hair and body.

I almost lost her and our baby today. My heart is still racing. When that fucker had the gun on her... The image materializes in my mind, twisting my stomach into knots. I had never been so scared in my life. If anything ever happens to them, I'll make this world bleed.

"No, it can't." Zeus stops in his tracks and aims his gaze at Butch. "Contact all the chapters. Tell them what happened here and to send any available brothers our way."

He nods, cell phone already at his ear.

"Where the fuck are Draco and Snake?" Zeus barks. "I want them here now."

He's trying not to show it, but he's worried. I am too. They could be dead or being held hostage. Draco and me, we have our differences, but he's still blood.

"Neither answered when I called," Smokey says, digging his phone out of his back pocket. "I'll try them again."

"We can't sit on this." I push to my feet and gently place Zilphia's head on the sofa. "We need to go after them now before they run."

Zeus shakes his head. "They're not going to run. Spider won this battle, so now he'll figure he can win the war."

"Those bastard Disciples might not run, but they'll go underground," Tank adds, a scowl on his dark-brown face. "They won't be easy to find."

Tank walks up beside me and drops a heavy hand on my shoulder. "I know what they tried to take from you today, but don't get reckless. We can't lose any more brothers."

"I can't just sit here and do nothing," I snarl. My hands are itching to spill Disciple blood.

"Keep a cool head," Zeus tells me. "They're going to pay, son. You have my word."

I dip my head, though every fiber of my being demands that I prowl the streets and get every Disciple I can find.

"Snake is en route," Smokey announces, stuffing his cell phone back into his pocket. "Still no word from Draco."

"Shit, I forgot," Cricket says, pausing with his beer a hairbreadth from his lips. "He's at Tulip's."

"Fucking boy is always thinking with his cock when it comes to that girl." Zeus sighs and drops into an armchair.

"I'll get her number from Meela," Jigsaw offers, then disappears into the hallway.

After the bullets stopped flying, Meela wound herself around him and wouldn't let go. He tried to force her to leave with the women and children, but she only held on tighter. He could've shaken her off easy, but I think her tears did him in. Instead, he took her to his room.

Tank strides across the room and whispers something to Zeus.

He gives a clipped nod and stands. "We have a lead on a Disciple safehouse."

Looks like a club informant came through for us.

"Let's go," I say, lifting Zilphia in my arms.

I'll leave her in my room and post a couple brothers on the door. Naomi checked her out, said she's fine, just in shock.

"Burn these pieces of shit and put our fallen on ice," Zeus tells the prospects.

I'm driving one of three SUVs to the safehouse. We just crossed into Wicomico County, a little over an hour from Kent.

Snake pounds a fist on the dashboard. "I still can't believe this shit, man." He and Draco arrived at The Sanctuary within minutes of each other. Zeus tore into them for not answering their phones.

"We'll get them back," Cricket comments from behind me.

"Where the hell were you, Snake?" Smokey asks.

"Nowhere," Snake answers, shrugging a shoulder. "Just hanging around. You my mother or something?"

Smokey scoffs. "By hanging around, do you mean stalking Leah?"

"Stay the fuck out my business," he growls, throwing a punch back at him.

"Chill, man." Smokey laughs, dodging the fist that was meant for his face. "I won't bring up your girlfriend again."

"Stop fucking around," I order them, parking behind the SUV in front of me. "We're here."

We exit the vehicles and gather on the sidewalk. We're twenty deep and roaring to fuck some shit up.

Jigsaw points out a dilapidated house about three blocks up the street. "That's it."

The house is big but unassuming, nothing out of the ordinary to indicate a Disciple safehouse. It's a good place to hide in plain sight. The lights are on, so somebody's home.

"Basement?" Tank asks him.

"Yeah, an attic too," Jigsaw confirms, gaze scouting the rundown neighborhood. "Lots of places to hide. I'll do some recon, make sure the coast is clear. Be back in five."

"Watch your six, brother," Butch states gravely.

"Always," he replies and saunters across the street before disappearing behind a house.

You can take the man out of the military, but you can't take the military out of the man.

"We go in hot and heavy." Zeus drops an open duffel bag full of MAC-10s at his feet. "The bullets keep flying until every last Disciple in that house is dead."

"Fuck yeah." Snake grins, arming himself with one of the machine guns. "That's what I'm talking about."

The other brothers follow suit, echoing his excitement.

I grab a weapon too, relishing the feel of it in my hands. "What about the rest of them? We need to kill them all."

I won't rest until every last Disciple is ash.

"We will," Zeus states with grim determination. "No matter how long it takes."

"Clear," Jigsaw announces, rejoining the group. "Thirteen bikes are parked in the alley out back. We can assume there's at least that many of those fuckers inside."

"Let's show these bastards you don't fuck with the Gods," Draco growls.

"At my whistle, we go in and light 'em up," Zeus says.

We split up to cover both entry points into the house. I lick my lips in anticipation, the prospect of killing Disciples lighting a fire in my blood.

Zeus lets out a sharp whistle, then kicks the front door open with one booted foot. We bound into the house behind him, our weapons drawn and ready. It's a fucking pigsty in here.

"Motherfucker!" a man roars, reaching for a gun on the coffee table.

Zeus pumps him and the man beside him on the sofa full of lead. The rat fucks sitting at a table in the back corner scatter. Two run for an alcove to the left and the other three bolt for a doorway to the right.

Shouts and rapid gunfire rip through the house. The brothers fan out, taking cover wherever they can. I dive in front of the sofa with Cricket and Smokey, bullets flying all around us.

I shoot at the men sheltered in the alcove, ducking every few seconds to avoid their return fire.

"Fuck!" Cricket yells. "The stairs! Shoot those motherfuckers!"

He's hit. Blood pours from a gaping hole in his shoulder. I flip the coffee table, using it as a shield between us and the deadly projectiles. We unleash a hail of ammunition toward our targets, dropping two. The rest haul ass back upstairs.

"Shit," Cricket hisses through gritted teeth. "Hurts like a son of a bitch."

"Want me to kiss it and make it better?" I quip, digging a clip out of my cut pocket and reloading my MAC-10.

"Gee, would you, Mom?" he deadpans.

"Later. I got some Disciples to kill first." I make a run for the stairs, squeezing off rounds along the way.

I reach the landing intact and scan my surroundings for immediate danger. Five doors—two open, three closed. *Fuck.* My thirst for vengeance clouded my common sense. I can't cover this floor alone. I'd take my chances if I didn't have Zilphia and a baby on the way.

"You got a death wish, asshole?" Cricket grumbles from behind me.

I smirk and glance over my shoulder. My day one, Snake, and Smokey creep up the stairs, locked and loaded.

"Glad you could join me."

He flips me the bird, and I chuckle. They mimic my position, crouching beside me on the landing, gazes sweeping over the cluttered hallway.

"And where the fuck you been, little brother? Out back smelling the daisies while we were in here doing all the killing?"

Snake scoffs and, following my best friend's lead, extends his middle finger at me. "Whatever. The back of the house was thick with Disciples. Definitely way more than thirteen of those fucks in the house," he adds. "How many up here?"

"Not sure. Three, maybe four," I answer him. "We check every room and dead any Disciples we see."

We clear the first room, then the second, searching closets and looking under beds. The third door leads to a bathroom, so we continue down the hallway with measured steps.

The organ in my chest beats a mile a minute, but it's not because I'm afraid. I live for this shit. It's the thrill of hunting my enemies. I tighten my grip on the sleek metal in my hands as we reach the fourth door.

The crunch of aluminum echoes through the hall. I look back, my gaze zeroing in on the soda can under Cricket's boot. I narrow my eyes at him.

"My bad," he remarks sheepishly.

Before I can break my foot off in his ass, bullets tear through the door and walls. We dive onto the floor, narrowly escaping death. A higher power is looking out for us, and it ain't God, so it must be the devil. Chunks of debris rain down on us, creating a cloud of dust over our heads.

"Nice going, dickwad," Smokey growls, elbowing Cricket in the ribs. "You almost got us killed."

"Lick my hairy balls, man. It was an accident."

"What's the move?" Snake asks, looking to me for answers. "We can't stay here with our tails between our legs."

"Give me a fucking second to think," I bark. Maybe my chances would've been better alone. As I'm contemplating what to do next, the bullets stop. I stiffen, hearing muffled voices from inside the room.

"Go check. They gotta be dead or booked it back downstairs."

"And get my head blown off? Nah, I'm good."

"You're the lowest-ranking member here, which means you do what the fuck you're told."

Spider. I recognize his voice from the few run-ins we've had over the years. I can't let him leave this house alive.

"Let's light 'em up." I leap to my feet and kick the door open with a resounding bang.

I aim my bullets at Spider, but the big bastard is too damn fast. He jumps out the window, leaving his men to fend for themselves. *Spineless fuck.*

Snake guns down the man making a break for the bathroom. Two others, posted behind a dresser, return fire. We dart back into the hallway, pressing against the wall for cover. One of the men attempts the same escape route as his leader, but he isn't as fast. We turn that fucker into swiss cheese.

"You're dying tonight," I state matter-of-factly. "Might as well come out and face God's Wrath."

"Enough blood has been spilled," the man calls out. "How about we call it a night?"

A slow, venomous laugh slips past my lips. "Too late for that, wouldn't you say?"

"Come on, fellas. I got a new baby at home."

"Should've thought about that before you fucked with the Gods," Snake snarls.

"I'm out of bullets," he says, and two pistols clatter across the floor. "Don't shoot. I'm coming out." He cautiously emerges from his hiding place, his hands raised. "Listen, I can be an informant for the Gods. Fuck Spider. He left me for dead, so anything you want, I'm your man."

"Not interested." I step into the room, my weapon trained on him.

"You wouldn't shoot an unarmed man, right?"

"Wrong." I smile and light his ass up. "Night, night motherfucker." He crumples to the stained carpet, dead as a fucking doornail.

The familiar roar of a motorcycle echoes into the bedroom. We rush to the window, seeing Spider speeding down the street.

"We have to go after him," I growl.

"How?" Cricket asks. "He'll be long gone by the time we get outside."

"Fuck that." I launch myself out the window without a second thought. I land on my side, cracking several ribs on impact. "Fuckkkkk!" I bellow, rolling onto my back.

"What the hell, Sandman!" Snake yells down at me.

"Crazy asshole. Just because you got a tattoo of a bird on your neck doesn't mean you can fucking fly."

"Shut the fuck up, Cricket!" I stand, ignoring the sharp pain just under my left pectoral and sprint to the SUV, determined to catch up with Spider.

I hop into the driver's seat, fingers tightening on the wheel. Just as I'm about to floor it, the back door swings open. Snake and Smokey climb inside. Cricket dashes around the front and slides into the passenger seat.

I smirk. "Decided to jump?"

"Can't let you go off and be stupid by yourself," Cricket says dryly.

"Psycho motherfucker," Snake mutters under his breath.

"You're a God baby, bro. Psycho is in your DNA too," I quip, then slam my foot down on the gas.

All four tires squeal on the asphalt as I peel around corners and blow through red lights. The streets are mostly empty, so it doesn't take long to find Spider. He has a good head start, but his luck is about to run out.

"Blast that fuck," I tell Cricket.

"With pleasure." He rolls down the window and serenades the night with gunfire.

Up ahead, warning lights begin flashing at the railroad crossing. Within seconds, the blaring horn of an approaching train cuts through the air. Spider makes it across the tracks moments before the gates drop. I press forward, refusing to let victory slip through my grasp. The leader of the Lawless Disciples dies tonight.

"What the hell you doing?" Snake snaps, leaning forward between the driver and passenger seats. "You got eyes, so I know you see that fucking train coming."

"We can make it," I growl.

"No, the fuck we can't," he argues back, his eyes locked on the locomotive barreling full steam ahead. "We'll get Spider another day."

"Snake's right," Smokey says, panic rising in his voice. "It's coming too fast."

"You know I'm usually down for whatever, but this is some insane shit," Cricket adds, shaking his head at me.

I click my seatbelt into place. "Buckle up. It might get a little bumpy."

They all strap in under protest. *Tough shit.* I'm too close to ending this piece of dog shit to turn back now.

"If we die, I'm gonna spend the rest of eternity whooping your ass in Hell," Cricket grumbles.

"We ain't dying tonight." I have Zilphia and our unborn child to live for now, and neither will be safe until Spider stops breathing.

We're nearly clear of the tracks when the train clips the rear panel, sending the SUV into a violent tailspin. My head slams against the window, and everything blurs as I fight to stay conscious. Blood pours down my face, filling my vision with crimson red.

We crash sideways into a tree. My head hits the window again—then everything goes black.

PART FOUR

New Year, Same Shit

CHAPTER 41

Five and a half months later

Zilphia

I BITE INTO MY PEANUT BUTTER–COVERED, SWEET-AND-SOUR-FLAVORED pickle and hum in gluttonous ecstasy.

"Calm down, girl," Meela quips, dropping into the chair beside me. "Are you going to ask the pickle to marry you?"

Leah, who sits across from me, unsuccessfully tries to hide her laughter behind her hand. I give her my best death glare, but that only increases her laughter. I roll my eyes and turn my ire on the instigator instead.

"Shut the hell up, Meela," I say around a mouthful of the savory sweetness. "I'm seven and a half months pregnant with twins. I'm allowed to be greedy."

"That you are," she replies in her usual cheeky manner. "You're as big as a goddamn house." She cocks an eyebrow. "Sure there's only two in there?"

"Fuck you very much," I deadpan and dunk my half-eaten pickle into the jar of peanut butter in front of me.

She leans close to my pickle. "Let me have a bite."

I snatch my hand back. "Mine!"

"Dang, I was only joking," she says, amusement in her artificial pink-colored eyes. "Pickles and peanut butter? Nooo, thank you."

"Hey, don't knock it till you try it," I tell her. "But not this one. This one is mine."

"Pregnant people are weird." Leah chuckles and pops a salt and vinegar chip into her mouth.

We've both been snacking, waiting impatiently for the food to get done.

"All jokes aside, you look absolutely stunning," Meela comments, giving me a once-over.

I smile from ear to ear. "Thank you. You look stunning yourself."

Meela skims a hand over her butterfly locks. "I always do, don't I?"

I roll my eyes at her smug remark, but she's not wrong. She even wears sexy little pieces to bed. Practice for when she finally gets her man. Her words, not mine.

Today, she's sporting a yellow, long-sleeved crop top with a smiley face on the front, paired with ripped, skin-tight jeans. A pair of sky-high platform sneakers in the same sunny yellow completes the look.

I'm looking pretty fashionable today too—thanks to my stylish friend. She picked out a long, flowy blush-pink dress and silver flats with rhinestone buckles. The dress drapes off my shoulders, showing a hint of cleavage. A matching tiara sits atop my bohemian knotless braids. Meela had it custom-made by a girl she found on Instagram, along with the sash that proudly declares me "Mother-to-Be."

She and Leah were up at the crack of dawn, decorating the clubhouse for my baby shower. I'm genuinely impressed. Blush pink, silver, and ivory decor fill the room—from the table centerpieces to the balloon bouquets. Zeus covered the cost, but my friends handled all the planning.

Soon, I'll be the proud mom of twin daughters. I still can't believe it. Sandman didn't speak for a full ten minutes after the ultrasound tech told us there were two babies growing inside me.

"You were supposed to be back two hours ago," Leah comments, arching an eyebrow at Meela.

"What can I say? I needed my beauty rest."

"Oh God," Leah scoffs, rolling her eyes.

I smile, grateful for them both. Without Meela and Leah, I'd be a wreck. My grandmother is gone. And the woman who gave birth to me? Vanished.

Loretta Kensley never had a maternal bone in her body, but it still hurts that she hasn't reached out. That silence cuts deeper than I expected.

I'm especially grateful Leah is here. She hates anything to do with the Gods, but she still came to support me. Thankfully, Snake is keeping his distance, though I've caught his eyes on her more than once.

I glance around the crowded room—the same room where the Thanksgiving massacre happened. I don't recognize half the faces. Most of them showed up after the attack and never left.

The war between the Gods and the Disciples is still raging, with both sides suffering losses. Spider has managed to stay under the radar so far. Even today, security is tight to prevent another bloodbath. It's not every day you see men with machine guns at a baby shower.

I sigh. The past five months have been rough. I'm mostly on lockdown, though I'm still allowed to attend school. I know it's for my own protection, but the cabin fever is real.

To make things worse, two detectives showed up about a week after the attack, asking about Redmond. Sandman saw it coming and coached me on what to say. I played it cool and answered all their questions. Yes, he visited me. No, I didn't agree to the arrangement between him and my mother. Yes, to my knowledge, he left after I refused to be his whore. I was terrified, but I didn't let it show.

Sandman was questioned too, since he and Redmond knew each other once upon a time. With no evidence of a crime, the detectives hit a dead end.

"Food's ready," Leah squeals excitedly and bounds to her feet. "Want me to make you a plate?"

I drop my pickle into the jar of peanut butter. "Absolutely, and give me some of everything."

"Roger that, food for three coming right up." Leah speed-walks toward the buffet-style setup as the designated cooks place a serving utensil on top of each covered dish. I requested vegan options just for my plant-eating friend.

"Greedy as fuck," Meela mumbles under her breath.

I point my index finger in her face. "Didn't I tell you to shut it?"

She plucks said finger, and I whine dramatically. "Ouch, that hurt."

"Aww, let me kiss it better." Meela grabs my wrist and attempts to kiss the ache away.

"Quit being a menace!" I giggle, pushing at her forehead. "You're going to make me pee myself."

My gaze catches on Sandman's piercing blue irises, and my breath stalls in my throat. The way he watches me sends an icy prickle through my veins. I know what he's thinking, or rather, what he's fantasizing. I've seen that look a thousand times before.

He wants to fuck me in the most savage way possible. I don't have to touch between his thighs to know he's rock-hard right now. My growing midsection hasn't tempered his lust or hatred for me. In fact, the larger my belly gets, the more possessive he becomes.

I should look away, but his stormy gaze holds me captive. The hate, anger, and lust radiating in those alluring blue orbs suffocates me just as effectively as a hand around my throat. Sandman is a train wreck waiting to happen.

He barrels forward, though there's a sharp curve in the tracks ahead. Self-preservation would have a sane person braking, but not him. Not this brutal, savage man. He stays the course, and when the train derails, crashing in a fiery blaze, he'll emerge from the ashes—broken and bloody.

Still, he would board the next one, continuing the dangerous cycle because all he knows is chaos and destruction. It's his Achilles' heel—a deadly obsession that's bound to destroy him one day, but until then, his reign of terror will consume anyone caught in the crossfire.

Unfortunately for me, I'm in the middle of it all. Unlike him, I'm not strong enough to walk away from the wreckage.

"How are things between you two?" Meela asks, interrupting my dismal thoughts.

I blink and finally tear my gaze away from him. "Same ole, same ole."

"I've been thinking," she whispers for my ears only. "I can help you get away. I've got some coins saved and I'm getting more when I turn eighteen. Just say the word."

"Do you really think I can escape him? He'll find me, Meela."

And when he does, there'll be hell to pay. Right now, I have a little freedom—not much, but enough to breathe. If I run, he'll lock me up for good.

In any case, whatever money Meela gives me won't last, and she's not turning eighteen for a while. I don't have a cent to my name. Sandman made me quit Shadows after the abortion debacle.

And let's be real—I wouldn't get very far with two babies hanging off my coattails. It's a pipe dream.

"Here you go, baby mama," Leah says, depositing two overflowing plates in front of me.

I force a smile on my face. "Thanks."

"Welcome." Leah turns on her heel and heads back to the buffet.

I begin eating, and the subject is dropped, though my appetite is completely gone now. After several minutes, I give up the pretense and just sit there, contemplating Meela's offer.

Even if I were to escape Sandman somehow and disappear, witness-protection style, I don't know the first thing about taking care of a baby—let alone two—on my own. Heck, I can count on one hand how many times I even held a baby.

"Chop, chop," Meela orders, clapping her hands at me. "It's almost time for games."

I nod and force down a couple more bites before dropping my fork onto my plate again. "I'm ready."

Two hours and way too many games later, I'm exhausted and desperately need a nap. Knowing how my newfound family turns any occasion into a party, my baby shower won't end until late evening. Even then, the revelry will continue well into the early morning hours.

"Heading upstairs to rest for a bit," I tell Meela and Leah. "Let me know when it's time to open gifts."

I leave the noise behind and make my way upstairs to Sandman's room. Once inside, I slip off my shoes and climb onto the bed, humming under my breath as my body sinks into the soft mattress. In an hour or two, I'll be recharged and ready to go back down.

I toss my tiara onto the nightstand and pull the blanket around me. Just as my eyes start to close, the door creaks open—and my karma in human form walks in.

I jackknife into a sitting position, clutching the blanket to my chest as if the cotton barrier will protect me from him. "W-what do you want?"

"Let's not play games," Sandman replies gruffly and shrugs out of his cut. "You know exactly what I want."

"I'm tired," I whisper.

"Don't care." He begins undressing slowly, deliberately, taunting me with the knowledge that I'm powerless. My gaze tracks his every movement until he stands naked before me. "Are you going to open your legs willingly, or do I have to pry them apart? Either way, you're getting fucked."

All these months later, and I'm still in awe of his beauty. His body is sculpted perfection, hard yet silky smooth. I can't help but stare at the virile organ between his muscular thighs. It's long and so very thick. Even from my position on the bed, I can clearly see the throbbing veins in his proud flesh. Sandman has the power to give me immeasurable pleasure or the worst kind of pain. It depends on how he chooses to wield what he was blessed with.

I shake my head. "No, you can't force me. Not while I'm pregnant."

"Sweet Zilphia, you're about to see just how wrong you are," he hisses and begins tearing at my dress.

"No!" I scream, trying my hardest to fight him.

I kick, scratch, and punch with everything I have, but he's too damn strong. Even with my big belly, he still outweighs me by at least fifty pounds. He effortlessly rips my dress, bra, and panties from my body, leaving me bleeding where the fabric dug into my skin. He locks his big hands around my ankles and spreads my legs apart, exposing me to his wild gaze. He swallows hard, his Adam's apple bobbing.

"Mine," he proclaims, yanking my legs over his shoulders. "All mine."

"Let me go!" I yell, tears of frustration burning my eyes.

In a last-ditch attempt to escape, I throw myself onto my side and reach for the lamp on the nightstand. Victory is at my fingertips, but he flips me onto my back and slams into my pussy, rocking his hips until he's fully seated inside me.

"Fuck yes," he rasps, his handsome features twisting with unadulterated rapture.

He won. He always does. I turn my head, tears slipping from my eyes.

"Fighting is pointless, Zilphia." He bands his forearms across the area just below my knees, holding me tight against his chest. "And so are your tears."

He pounds into me without an ounce of humanity. I place a hand on his abdomen and clasp his thigh with the other, anchoring myself against his assault. Each thrust reverberates through my entire being, hitting every erogenous zone inside my warm depths and shaking me to my very marrow.

Throbbing pressure explodes between my thighs and spirals outward, making me dizzy with pleasure. A throaty moan sweeps past my lips as my wet passage clenches around Sandman's length, sending him into a primal frenzy. He looks like his club's namesake towering above me, plunging in and out of my pussy, whisps of his blond mane clinging to his sweaty face.

"So goddamn good," he praises, then licks along the bottom of my left foot before sucking each toe into his hungry mouth.

My back arches off the bed. *I'm so close.* "Oh God, I feel it. I feel it, Sandman."

"That's right, sweet Zilphia," he groans between open-mouthed kisses on my foot. "Come for me. Fuck, so good. I'm going to fill that pretty little pussy up."

"Oh God!" I cry out, squirting all over his dick, soaking the sheets beneath my undulating body. "Yes, yes, yes!" I claw my fingernails into his golden skin, my legs shaking violently.

"Zilphia!" he shouts, driving into me so hard my body lifts off the bed. His cum floods my pussy, spilling from my spasming walls and trickling down to my ass. "Good girl. Grip my cock just like that. Fuck." He gives one final bone-jarring thrust before slipping from my sore pussy and resting his head on my round belly.

One of the little humans in my womb does a somersault, or at least what feels like a somersault, and Sandman pops his head up, a genuine smile stretching his lips. I've never seen him smile like this before. He already loves them unconditionally. Will he ever love me? To be loved by him must be a powerful thing, ten times more powerful than his hate.

"Having fun in there?" he says, peppering kisses along my swollen midsection.

A knock sounds at the door. "Sandman, you in there?"

"What the fuck do you want, Cricket?" he growls, looking back at the door. "I'm busy."

"Zilphia has a visitor."

Sandman turns his narrowed gaze on me. "Expecting someone?"

"No," I frown, clueless about who it could be. Besides my two best friends, I didn't invite anyone else.

Sandman saunters to the door without bothering to cover up his nakedness and jerks it open. "Who is it?"

"Zilphia's mother."

Sandman nods and closes the door, then turns to face me.

"I haven't spoken to her since she left." I can't believe she has the audacity to show up here after all the chaos she caused.

He grabs my duffel bag off the dresser and tosses it on the bed. "Get dressed."

I packed a sweater and leggings just in case I wanted to get comfortable later. It's a good thing too, since Sandman ruined my beautiful dress. Meela isn't going to be happy about that one bit.

We dress quickly, and I follow Sandman into a small sitting room near the front of the clubhouse. Cricket and the woman who birthed me sit on opposite ends of the sofa, staring daggers at each other. He vacates the room with a mumbled, "Bitch thinks she's royalty."

Anger clogs my throat at the sight of her. I want to scream, rant, call her every obscenity in the human language, but no words come out. I'm too angry to speak.

Then I take in her appearance. No makeup, bags under her eyes, hair pulled back into a loose ponytail, clothes rumpled and stained. She's had it rough. It's no less than what she deserves.

"I guess congratulations are in order," she states, gesturing toward my round belly. "I hear you're having twin girls. I'm having a daughter too." She shifts her gaze to Sandman. "The father, I presume?"

"Why are you here?" I snap, not in the mood for fake pleasantries.

She leaps to her feet. "How dare you speak to me like that? I'm your mother—"

"You are not my mother!" I yell so loud she jumps. "You brought me into this world, but you were *never* a mother to me. Answer the fucking question."

Sandman stands to my right, watching the argument unfold in silence.

"I'm not perfect, Zilphia," she says, fat tears rolling down her cheeks. "I never claimed to be, but I raised you the best way I knew how."

"Spare me the fucking crocodile tears, *Loretta*." She sucks in a sharp breath at the use of her given name. "How could you miss her funeral? Your own mother?" I lose it then, several errant tears tumbling down my cheeks.

"We didn't want to cause trouble."

I laugh. "Then you shouldn't have fucked your sister's husband. Leave, you're not welcome here."

"Zilphia, please. I have nowhere else to go." Loretta Kensley begging. Never thought I'd see the day.

I cock an eyebrow at her. "Where's Keith?"

"He abandoned me." She places a hand on her plump stomach. "What kind of man abandons his pregnant fiancée?"

"Oh, I don't know," I comment sarcastically. "Maybe the same kind of man who abandons his pregnant wife." What is this woman smoking?

"She's your sister, Zilphia. No matter how you feel about me, remember that. I have no money, nowhere to go, and I haven't eaten since yesterday. I need prenatal vitamins and medical care. Are you really going to send me away to sleep on the streets?"

I want to tell her to kiss my ass, to leave and never show her face again, but I can't. I need to know that my sister is going to be okay.

I look at Sandman. "Please, for my sister."

His contemplative gaze studies me for long seconds, and I'm afraid he's going to toss her on the streets. He isn't exactly known for his empathic nature, but he surprises me.

"You better get yourself together pronto after that baby's born, because you ain't living off my dime," he tells her.

CHAPTER 42

Seven years ago

Zilphia

I PACE THE LENGTH OF THE TREE HOUSE, TOO EXCITED TO STAY STILL EVEN *for a moment. Sam should've been here by now. I huff out an impatient breath and force myself to sit on the sofa, bouncing a leg in anticipation of his arrival. What's taking him so long?*

"Come on, Sam." I lean back against the soft cushions and tuck my legs beneath my bottom.

Just as I'm about to stretch out and rest my eyes, I hear the faint sound of approaching footsteps and leap to my feet, a huge grin tugging at my lips.

"Surprise!" I call out the moment Sam walks into the tree house, though I keep my voice low.

I don't want to wake my brother, or worse, my parents—particularly my mother. If she finds us out here, she's going to whip my butt something good.

"What's going on?" Sam asks, looking very confused.

"It's your birthday, silly." I grab his hand and lead him to the table. "This is all for you," I announce, gesturing toward the ham and cheese sandwiches, chips, candy, cupcakes, soda, and a small black case.

"For me?"

I giggle. "Yes, for you. Don't you remember your own birthday?"

"Yeah, but no one else ever does." He turns away and begins to cry, his thin shoulders trembling with each sob.

I throw my arms around him and squeeze him as tight as I can. "I'll always remember your birthday because you're my best friend and I love you."

"You." He pauses, sniffling softly. "You love me?"

"With all my heart," I tell him, squeezing him tighter.

He faces me again and encircles me with his rail-thin arms, squeezing me as hard as I squeezed him. "I love you too," he whispers with a shuddering breath. "With all my heart."

The moonlight shines down on us through the window. That and the glow from the television is the only light in the tree house, though I always make sure to turn the brightness down so we aren't caught.

I pull back and grab the black case off the table. "Open your gift first."

"Did you buy all this stuff with your own money?" he asks, hesitantly taking the case from my grasp.

"Yep." I grin at him. "I saved my allowance for two whole months."

He starts crying again. "You didn't have to do that for me. I don't have any money to buy you anything for your birthday."

"It's okay, Sam. I wanted to do this for you." I look down at the case clutched in his hand. "Open it."

I bite down on my bottom lip as he reveals the digital watch. It's blue, almost the same color as his eyes. That's why I chose it out of all the other options.

"You like it?"

He smiles at me, and I smile back, happy to see the sadness leave his eyes.

"Yeah, very much. Thank you."

I give him a quick peck on the cheek. "You're welcome."

CHAPTER 43

Zilphia

I can't believe we're under the same roof again. We're due for a long talk, but I can't even bring myself to be in the same room with her. Earlier today, the woman formerly known as my mother strolled into the kitchen with a beaming smile and cheerful "Good morning." I wanted to vomit; instead, I escaped to the nursery to unpack and organize.

That was two hours ago, but I'm still hiding out, surrounded by pink decor and baby items. I'm enjoying the peace and quiet while my baby daddy's out. Though it's Sunday, he left for the shop before sunrise to put the final touches on a rush order.

I inspect the small bookshelf I just finished putting together and nod in approval. A handyman I am not, but I did a damn good job. Now for the books. I clamber to my feet, which isn't an easy task with my big belly, and pad across the hall to my bedroom. I stored the books in my closet for safekeeping.

Leah, the intellectual that she is, bought the books for my girls months ago, affirming, *"It's never too early to foster young minds."* I shake my head, recalling her serious tone. I swear that girl is an old soul.

As I pull the bag of books from the closet shelf, a shoebox tumbles out and lands at my feet. I go still, seeing a familiar blue watch lying among the scattered mementos. *I can't believe it.* He still has it after all this time.

I put the books down and pick it up, reading the words written in permanent black marker on the back.

Best Friends Forever, Love Zilphia.

I remember writing those words like it was yesterday.

Rough fingers snatch the watch out of my hand. I spin around, coming face-to-face with a scowling Sandman. "What the fuck you doing?"

"N-nothing, I-I—"

His fingers lock around my wrist so tight that pain lances up my arm. "Stay out of my fucking business!"

"I didn't touch it," I whimper, afraid my bones might snap at any second. "It fell when I grabbed the books. I swear."

"Get out," he barks and shoves me away. "Now, before I hurt you."

I should leave and thank my lucky stars I got off with just a bruised wrist. Instead, I stay rooted to the spot, watching as he gathers the scattered items and places them back in the shoebox.

My eyes widen, realization washing over me. "Oh my God."

The hair scrunchie, socks, bracelet, lip gloss—things I thought I lost. He had them all.

"Why do you have my things?" I whisper.

Sandman throws the shoebox right past my head, and then he's on me, crowding me against the wall with his big body. His ragged breaths fan across my temple with each rise and fall of his chest. Anger pours from him in waves, raising the fine hairs on the back of my neck.

He's close to breaking. And when he breaks, no one is safe—especially me.

"Because I was obsessed with you from the moment I saw you." He leans in, his hard body brushing against me. "Have you ever been obsessed with someone, Zilphia?"

I shake my head. "No."

"Your mind becomes fixated on that person." He pulls the strap of my camisole down my shoulder, exposing my right breast. "You can't think about anything else, and when you're not with that person, it feels like your heart is going to explode," he continues, circling the pad of his thumb over my nipple with featherlight caresses. "You would move heaven and earth… sacrifice everything for that person, even your own life."

"I never asked to be your obsession," I respond breathlessly.

"Liar," he hisses. "You called to me that night and begged to become my obsession."

I frown up at him. "What are you talking about? I saw you go into the tree house, but I didn't call out to you."

"You did." He presses a palm to his forehead. "Here, you called to me here. You told me to come to you and everything would be okay. And for a while it was. I loved you so fucking much, Zilphia. I loved you more than I loved myself. Before you, I wanted to die."

He was beaten so badly that night, whatever he thought he heard was nothing more than a hallucination. That's the only logical explanation—or maybe he's straitjacket crazy, like Meela said. Regarding the latter, I knew his feelings for me grew beyond friendship, but nothing could've ever come of it. We lived on the same planet, but we were from two different worlds.

"We created something magical inside that tree house," I say, choosing my words wisely. "The pressure to be perfect in everything made my childhood a living hell. Without you, I wouldn't have survived it. I loved you, but we couldn't be together. You know we couldn't."

"Thought you were too good for the trailer-trash white boy?" Sandman snarls, glaring down at me. "But look at you now, belly round with my babies and pussy on call for my dick." He slips a hand into my panties, pushing long fingers deep inside my wet heat.

"I never thought that," I moan, latching onto the front of his shirt with both hands. "I swear I didn't."

"You were always going to be mine, Zilphia," he rasps, nudging my legs further apart with a booted foot. "I was biding my time, but fate brought you to my doorstep. Did you think I had forgotten you?"

No, and I hadn't forgotten him either. I thought about him every day.

His fingers stroke my slick walls, his calloused palm sliding back and forth over my clit, shooting white-hot sensations straight to my core.

"I want to come," I beg, rolling my hips, my movements frantic with need. "Please, Sandman. I want to come."

"Your orgasms belong to me," he whispers in my ear. "You come when I say. Understand?"

"Yes," I breathe.

"You're dripping down my fingers," he murmurs. "Pregnancy made your pussy wetter."

I grasp his shoulder and bear down on his hand, matching him thrust for thrust. He hooks his fingers inside me, teasing the sensitive spot behind my pubic bone. I gasp as a ball of heat rushes through me like a freight train.

"I'm about to… I'm about to—"

Sandman snatches his fingers from my body and puts several inches between us. "What I tell you?"

"No, no, no." I reach for him, but stay pressed to the wall, my legs weak and unsteady. "Please come back."

"No orgasms for you, but I still gotta get mine." His gaze rakes over my body, lingering between my thighs. "Strip, then lie on the bed."

"Go to hell!" I shout, my voice cracking with fury.

He smirks. "I've already been. It was a luxury experience. Be a good girl and I'll take you sometime."

"Fuck you," I spit, lifting my chin. "I'm not getting on that bed and you can't make me."

His gaze alights on my trembling hand, and his smirk morphs into a full-blown smile.

"Sweet, sweet Zilphia," he croons, excitement shining in his blue orbs. "You just made my day a whole lot better."

I suck in a sharp breath as he swoops down on me like an avenging angel, grabbing me under the arms and tossing me onto the bed.

"Are you insane?" I shriek, pushing up on my elbows to glare at him. "Do you see how big my stomach is? You can't just be throwing me around like a sack of potatoes!"

"Am I insane?" he laughs, latching onto my ankles and pulling me to the edge of the bed. "We both know the answer to that question, don't we?" He stares into my eyes as he rips my pajama bottoms down my legs and drops them onto the floor. "Tell me, who's to blame for my lack of sanity?"

"Me…" I breathe, though a response isn't needed.

He nods, turning me onto my side. "I was chasing heaven but ended up in hell."

Having that much power over a person can be a blessing and a curse. In my case, it unleashed an all-consuming hate. I never want that much power again.

"You wrecked me, Zilphia," he continues, positioning his knee just above my ass on the bed while keeping his other foot firmly planted on the floor.

"You were supposed to be my salvation, but you turned out to be a Trojan Horse."

I bite down on my wrist, holding my breath, as his fingers coast over the soaked cotton clinging to my labia. Moments later, I hear the hiss of his zipper, and my panties are pulled to the side. Cool air caresses my heated sex, and a sound I didn't know I could make escapes my lips.

"Hurry," I beg, needing him inside me.

"Say my name," he growls through clenched teeth.

"Sandman. Sandman. Sandman," I chant, his name an entreaty on my lips.

"No, say my other name."

"Sam," I whisper so softly, for a second, I question if I said it. He warned me never to call him by his given name—he was adamant that Samuel Hendricks died long ago. But maybe he was just buried under Sandman's hate.

He seizes my hip with strong fingers and slams into my pussy in one spine-rattling thrust. Raw pleasure explodes through my body, dispelling all logical thought and reason from my mind.

"Again!" he orders, pounding into my weeping walls.

"Sammmm!" I scream so loud that my ears ring.

"Again!"

"Sam! Sam! Sam! Sam! Sam!"

I scream his name over and over again, our flesh colliding in a violent symphony, amplified by the slick desire between my thighs. The bed shakes beneath us with each frenzied thrust. I reach back, placing a hand against his hard abs.

"Nah," he rasps, pushing me further onto the bed while remaining thick and full inside my pussy. He lies down behind me, his chest pressed firmly against my back, and then he's moving inside me again. "Take all of me."

"Yes," I moan as his hungry lips settle over the spot where my shoulder and neck meet. He sucks the sensitive area, every pull of his strong mouth a thunderbolt to my throbbing core. His mouth and dick move in sync, and soon the velvet heat growing between my thighs ignites into a firestorm of smoldering sensations.

"How can it be this good?" he rumbles against my neck, delving his hand into my panties and expertly kneading my clit. "You make me fucking crazy."

"You don't think you make me crazy too?" He's taken over my body, my mind, and my soul. There's nothing left of me. He consumes every inch of my being but constantly wants more.

He flips me onto my back and kneels between my thighs, yanking my legs over his shoulders. A sharp gasp bursts from my lungs as he fills me up again, hammering into my pussy like a wild animal. Sweat runs in rivulets down his handsome face and drips onto my belly.

"I'm coming," I pant, my slick walls tightening around his erection.

"Fuck," he groans, his features going slack with pleasure. "Milk every last drop."

A split second later, he drops down boneless beside me. I take a measured breath and ask the question weighing heavily on my mind.

"Do you still hate me?" He allowed me to call him Sam. Maybe he doesn't hate me as much anymore. Maybe we can be a semi-normal family.

Without so much as a glance, he storms into the bathroom and slams the door behind him.

Where is he?

He's been gone for hours. After showering, he left without saying a single word to me. I knew there was a possibility my question would set him off, but I needed to know. Guess I have my answer.

I don't know why I needed to know when I'm unsure of my own feelings. I still fear him. Always will. But I'm starting to crave his touch more and more. When he's inside me, I forget he's a monster, at least for a little while.

God, my life is a soap opera. I have a psycho baby daddy, and my mother is pregnant by her sister's husband. No point dwelling on either situation now. What's done is done.

I already love my daughters and sister unconditionally. They are my life now, and I would gladly die for them. My sister will not have the same fucked up childhood I had. I will protect her from our mother at all costs. Speaking of the woman who birthed me, it's about time we had that talk.

Sighing, I push away from the island and slide off the stool onto swollen feet. With my empty bowl and glass in hand, I pad over to the dishwasher and deposit both inside. Dinner wasn't exactly a gourmet meal, but the ramen noodles and boiled eggs feel good in my stomach.

"Thanks for keeping me company," I coo at my adopted fur babies, giving both a pat on the head. We had a rough start, but now they're my shadows.

Due to my extended belly, it takes longer than usual to reach the second floor. I linger at the landing for a few minutes to catch my breath.

"Stairs can go kick rocks," I mumble before trudging on.

As I approach my mother's bedroom, her condescending voice slices through the quiet. "No, I am not going to write a character letter for him. Let him rot," she says with a bitter laugh. "And tell him I want a divorce!"

I clasp a hand over my mouth in shock. *Daddy?*

"Oh, and let him know that he is not the father of my children," she boasts proudly.

My heart leaps into my throat. *No. No. No. She's lying.* I slam the door open, the impact rattling the frame. My mother jumps, dropping the cell phone onto the bed.

"Tell me it isn't true." My voice shakes. "Tell me my father is my father."

She clambers to her feet, holding her head high. "It doesn't matter."

"It matters to me!" I scream, tears streaming down my face. "You lied to me my whole life! Who is he? Who is my real father?" The truth hits like a punch to the gut. "Nolan and I… we have different dads, don't we?"

We look nothing alike, but I never thought much of it—siblings don't always resemble each other.

"It doesn't matter," she reiterates, shooting me a look that instilled fear in me as a child.

I'm going to be sick.

"You're evil," I hiss, every word laced with venom. "I want to speak to my father now." I nod toward the bed. "Was that his lawyer?" I spring across the room, intent on getting my hands on that cell phone, but my mother beats me to it.

"Don't you dare," she snarls, holding the device behind her back.

"Give it to me!"

I try to reach around her, but she shoves me back.

"I hate you!" I shout at the top of my lungs. "Keith figured out what a heartless person you are and couldn't get away from you fast enough!"

"Ungrateful bitch!" she screeches, grabbing a fistful of my hair and yanking hard. "Your father was and still is a spineless, weak little man who couldn't give me children! If I hadn't found myself a real man, you wouldn't exist!"

I pry her fingers from my braids and fling her away from me. "You're pathetic. No education. No job. No future. Who's going to want you now?"

"You little whore!" she rages, her hand slicing through the air toward my face, but Snake appears, stepping between us.

"Whoa, what the fuck is going on in here?"

"I want her gone. Now," I say between labored breaths. "She can't stay here anymore."

Snake pinches the bridge of his nose before addressing me. "Where the hell am I supposed to take her?"

"I don't care. Just get her the hell out of here."

His gaze cuts to Draco, who I hadn't noticed looming in the doorway, a bored expression marring his features. "Can you take her to The Sanctuary?"

He scoffs. "Do I look like a fucking chauffeur?"

"Okay, then you can babysit Zilphia until Sandman gets back," he counters, cocking an eyebrow at him.

"Fucking nursery school," Draco grumbles, glaring at my mother. "Pack your shit. We leave in five."

My mother props a hand on her hip. "I'm not going anywhere."

"Yes, the fuck you are," Snake tells her, folding his arms across his chest. "The Sanctuary or the streets. Your choice."

"How can you do this to me?" she sniffles, crocodile tears filling her eyes. "I'm your mother."

Amazing. Loretta Kensley should've been an actress. Draco snorts and spins on his heel, looking none too happy.

"I don't have a mother."

She shoots me a look that could cut glass, her mask immediately going from crestfallen to angry. "You'll regret this."

I flee to my bedroom, unable to look at her a second longer.

Snake strolls in a beat later, his gaze sweeping over my face. "You good?"

"No," I answer and start bawling my eyes out. I don't need to look in the mirror to know I'm ugly crying the ugliest cry ever.

"Fuck." Snake tunnels a hand through his inky-black strands. "I'm not good at this type of shit. You want me to call Sandman? Hell, he's no good at this comforting shit either, but maybe he can lay some pipe and make you feel better."

I shake my head. "I just need to be alone."

"Aight," Snake says, already heading out the door. "Shout if you need me." He might get off on Leah's tears, but mine don't seem to matter.

I close the door behind him and perch on the edge of the bed, attempting to organize my thoughts. I have to find out who my father's lawyer is and help in any way I can. We may not share the same blood, but he'll always be my dad. Eventually, I do want to find my real father. I have another whole family out there, and I want to know them. Once they learn of my existence, hopefully they'll want to know me too.

My chest knots with emotion, and a fresh wave of tears spills from my eyes. *I need to get out of this house.* I'm starting to feel a bit stir-crazy, like my skin is too tight for my body.

I push my swollen feet into my slides and wobble downstairs. Before I can make it out the front door, Snake saunters from the living room with Harley and Mayhem traipsing behind him.

"You know I can't let you leave. Sandman would chop off my balls if anything happened to you."

"I'm going for a walk." I grab my jacket from the foyer closet and slip my arms into the sleeves. "I won't be gone long."

"I'll go with you."

"No, I'll be right—"

"Then you stay here." He shrugs. "You going out alone ain't happening."

I sigh. "Fine."

"Cool." Snake plucks the dog leashes off the table next to the staircase. "We'll take the mutts too."

We secure the excited Dobermans and leave the house, walking in companionable silence as the blocks slip by, which I'm grateful for. I zip up my jacket against the chill. It's spring, but the nights haven't quite warmed up yet.

"You're good for him," Snake remarks unexpectedly, pulling me from my turbulent thoughts.

I glance at him. "Really? Doesn't seem like it."

"He's… less psychotic."

"Yeah, if you say so."

Out of nowhere, a rusted pickup truck drives up on the curb and comes to a screeching stop in front of us.

"Run!" Snake shouts, reaching for the gun concealed inside his cut.

Before I can process what's happening, two men jump out of the pickup truck and fire their weapons at Snake. I'm not sure how many times he's been hit, but he goes down fast.

"Snake!" I watch in horror as crimson spreads across his shirt. Harley attacks one assailant, latching her strong jaws around the man's forearm.

"Get this fucking dog off me!" he yells at his accomplice, who takes aim and discharges a single shot. Harley whimpers and flops to the ground at Snake's feet.

I don't know who these men are, but I sure as hell know those cuts. *Disciples.*

"Run, Zilphia," Snake wheezes between gurgling breaths.

I tighten my grip on Mayhem's leash and take off, but there's no way I can outrun these men. Still, I pump my legs as hard as I can.

I have to get away. For my girls.

Hard hands grab me from behind. Mayhem lowers his head and lets out a deep growl, his eyes locked on my captor. Fearing for him, I drop the leash and yell for him to run. Despite the bullets flying all around him, Mayhem makes it to the next block in one piece.

"Come on, man," the guy holding me hisses, his gaze darting around nervously. "Let's get the fuck outta here."

They begin dragging me toward their getaway vehicle. I can't let them take me. Chances are, if I get in that pickup truck, I'll never be heard from or seen again.

"Help! I'm being kidnapped!" I scream, struggling against the strong hands holding me captive. "Somebody, help me!"

A fist connects with the side of my face, making the world spin around me. I'm tossed into the backseat, and moments later, we're speeding down the street.

Oh God, what have I done? I'm being taken to God knows where. Snake and Harley are at death's door. And it's all because I wanted to go for a stupid walk. If I survive this and they don't, Sandman's going to hate me more than ever.

CHAPTER 44

Zilphia

"WHERE ARE YOU TAKING ME?" I YELL AT THE DRIVER AS HE veers into the woods. It's pitch black—no signs of life. No one to hear my screams. I cradle my belly with trembling arms. *Please, God. Not now. Not like this.*

The man beside me digs his gun into my ribs. "I told you to shut the fuck up."

I glare at him. "You better pray Sandman never finds you."

"Darling, the Gods are finished," he says, a grin cutting across his face. "We've been recruiting. Soon there won't be a single God left. Long live the Disciples."

The truck jerks to a stop. "We're here."

I look out the window, my frantic gaze searching, but there's nothing—just endless trees and darkness.

"Time to meet your maker, darling," the man taunts, yanking me out of the backseat.

The truck's headlights cut through the night, revealing two figures in the distance. As my captor hauls me closer, their faces come into focus. I do a

"I've seen you before. You were a patient at Sibley back in October. I brought your meals."

We shared a few casual conversations, and he seemed nice enough.

"Well, I'll be damned." He chuckles. "It's a small world."

I freeze, one particular patch on his cut catching my eye. "You're the president of the Disciples."

He grins. "The one and only."

My heart drops into my stomach. "Are you going to kill me?"

"I am, but it's nothing personal, sweetheart."

"Do you know who I am?" the blonde standing beside him asks. She runs a teasing hand over his bulging bicep, smug satisfaction curling her lips.

I study her features, but I don't recall our paths ever crossing. "No."

"I'm Sam's mother."

"What?" I whisper. How is she mixed up in all this?

She was a sore spot for Sandman, so we rarely spoke about her. I've never even seen a picture of her.

"Why are you doing this?"

"I came to visit Sam a couple months ago." She releases the arm she'd been admiring and approaches me with a confident sway in her hips. "I wanted to make things right between us, be part of his life, but he slammed the door in my face like I was nothing," she spits, bitterness contorting her features into a hard mask. "I've made mistakes, but nobody's perfect."

Sandman didn't say anything about his mother's visit, but he's not exactly forthcoming with me.

"Please don't do this." I grasp her hand and place it on my swollen belly. "I'm pregnant with your granddaughters. Whatever issues you and Sandman have, we can work them out together."

She jerks back and laughs, a sinister sound that crawls down my spine like ice. "I no longer have a son. I want Zeus and everyone who shares his blood gone, starting with the little whores in your womb."

"Is it money you want? Sandman will pay whatever you ask. Just don't do this!"

"We know." Spider ambles up behind Sandman's mother and wraps his arms around her waist. "We're killing two birds with one stone." He nods at his henchman, who then drags me over to a shallow grave.

Oh God, they're going to bury me alive.

"No, no, no!" I scream hysterically, pulling against the hard hands holding me. "Please don't!"

They shove me into the makeshift wooden coffin. That's when I feel it—a small pop, then a warm gush between my thighs.

One of the men laughs. "Little bitch pissed herself."

"Her water broke, idiot."

"Hurry the fuck up," Spider growls. "We got people to kill and moves to make."

They nail me inside the crudely made casket. Dirt falls through the cracks, filling the confined space with dust and debris. I hear their elated laughter and taunts, muffled by my pounding fists and frantic screams.

Soon their voices fade away, and I'm left in complete darkness. I slam my fists against the wood until my knuckles are raw and slick with blood.

The familiar tightening in my chest unleashes a new level of terror. I don't have an inhaler. My chances of survival have just dropped to zero. *Be strong for your girls. If you don't survive, neither do they.*

I take deep, even breaths, inhaling through my nostrils and blowing out through my mouth. Wait—I *do* have one.

I dig the canister from my jacket pocket and inhale the life-saving medication into my lungs. Thank God I slipped it in there the last time I went out.

I press down again.

Nothing.

It's empty.

Oh no.

I pray the little medicine I got is enough to keep me alive until help arrives.

If help arrives.

I whimper as a wave of pain slices through my abdomen and lower back. My contractions have started.

SANDMAN

"You goin' act like somebody pissed in your cornflakes all night?" Cricket asks with a chuckle.

"Fuck off," I growl and down another shot, savoring the clear, bitter liquid as it slides down my throat.

He chuckles. "You're in love, bro. That girl has had you wrapped around her pinky finger since you were twelve."

"I can't love." I grab the bottle of tequila and pour myself another shot. "Don't know how. Even if I did, I could never love her. Not after what she did."

Zilphia broke me in every way a person can be broken. If Zeus hadn't found me and put a gun in my hand, I would've been six feet under long ago. Killing became my therapy. Killing gave me power. Killing made me forget… *her.*

Wishful thinking on my part. Zilphia was always in the back of my mind, like a fucking fly that wouldn't go away.

"Yeah, you do." He reaches into the bowl of mixed nuts between us on the bar and pops a few into his mouth. "Your brand of love is just all kinds of fucked up."

"Keep yapping, and I'm going to beat your ass up and down this bar."

"Damn," he tsks, shaking his head. "You need anger management, dude."

I grunt. "Smart ass."

Cricket shoots me a thoughtful look, all traces of humor gone. "I never liked Zilphia, but you chose her. Just don't lose yourself again."

Before I can respond, the music dies mid-beat, and the lights snap on. I bound to my feet, Glock gripped tight in my hand, scanning the room for danger. Cricket is at my side, his weapon drawn.

"If you're not a God, get the fuck out!" Jigsaw shouts at the crowd.

"What the fuck is going on?" Cricket mumbles.

Zeus watches me from across the bar, fear and anger etched on his rugged features. The fine hairs on the back of my neck rise. In almost four years, I've never seen him show fear.

Draco, Jigsaw, Tank, and Butch stand huddled with him, whispering among themselves. We push through the throng of bodies toward them. A good number of brothers are here tonight.

The room hums with low voices and restless energy as they await orders.

"What's up?"

Zeus and Jigsaw share a look, but no one answers.

"Somebody gonna talk?" I snap.

"Snake's been shot," Zeus replies, his voice raw with anger. "He's in surgery now."

"What are his chances?" My blood is boiling, but I force myself to stay calm for now. But make no mistake, I'm going to paint the streets red with the fuckers who went after my brother.

"Don't know, they wouldn't say over the phone." He lets out a thunderous roar and flips the nearest table.

Jigsaw places a firm hand on his shoulder. "That kid's been tough since he was in diapers. A few bullets won't take him out."

Zeus gives a sharp nod before continuing. "Snake was conscious for a bit. Said it was the Disciples that shot him."

I squeeze the weapon in my hand until my knuckles burn. It's time to end those bastards once and for all. "What's the move?"

Again, my question is met with silence. I level a pointed look at Zeus. "What aren't you telling me?"

He hesitates, his jaw clenched tight, then his words land like a sledgehammer. "Zilphia's been kidnapped."

Without a word, I holster my gun and pull my cell phone from my back pocket as I race toward the exit. The voices and footsteps behind me fall on deaf ears.

Zilphia is my only priority.

By now, the streets will be buzzing about what happened. One or more of our informants might have some intel. A text notification from an unsaved number stops me in my tracks.

I turn around, my heart pounding so hard it hurts. "Spider wants fifteen million tonight. Wants me to come alone or Zilphia's dead."

"Spider?" Loretta questions from her seat at a booth. Despite news of her daughter's abduction, she devours the food in front of her with gusto.

Draco showed up with her about an hour ago. Zilphia kicked her out. I didn't give a fuck. Didn't want her there to begin with.

"What part of get the fuck out didn't you understand?" Draco snaps at her.

"I live here now, remember?" she retorts haughtily. "I'm only asking because I knew a Spider a long time ago."

"I doubt it's the same Spider," Cricket deadpans.

"Well, I heard someone mention Disciples. The Spider I knew was the president of an MC with the same name. He's tall, right? Six three, dark-brown skin, with a crescent-moon-shaped scar on his left cheek?"

I'm standing in front of her before she can blink. "How do you know him?"

The bitch smirks, and I have to remind myself not to knock her ass under the booth. A sudden thought hits me, and I narrow my eyes at her. If she had anything to do with Zilphia's kidnapping, Jesus Christ himself won't be able to save her from my retribution.

"Talk," I hiss.

"Spider is Zilphia's father."

It takes a few seconds for her words to sink in. "What the fuck did you say?"

"We had a fling in Vegas," she explains around a mouthful of food. "I never told him about Zilphia because I was married and he was just for fun."

"You've got to be fucking kidding me," I hear Cricket grumble behind me.

Didn't see this coming, but it works out in my favor. From what I've heard, Spider's big on family. Chances are, he won't kill his own daughter. "Get up, you're coming with me."

"What? Why should I put myself in danger? I'm sure it's Zilphia's own fault she was kidnapped. She's always been stupid."

I snatch her out of the booth. "You're coming with me. End of fucking discussion."

"How dare you?" she squawks in outrage. "Are you all just going to stand there and watch him manhandle a pregnant woman?"

I look at Zeus. "Do you have the money on hand?" Loretta is my trump card, but the money is still needed as a backup.

"Of course, but you're not going alone."

I shake my head. "I won't risk my family."

"They're my family too," he counters. "We go in this together and send those fuckers to Hell."

I nod, and we embrace in a quick hug. I don't let it show, but I'm scared out of my mind. If they die, I die.

"Draco, go to the hospital and keep me updated on Snake's condition," Zeus orders, then singles out Tank and Smokey. "You two go with him and watch his back."

All three make a swift exit while the rest of us gather and plan our next move.

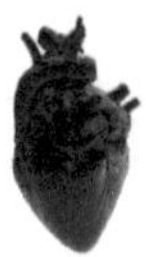

"I never should've been dragged into this," Loretta gripes from the passenger seat. "It's not my fault Zilphia got mixed up with a criminal. Men like you are for fun, not for building a life with. Frankly, I knew you were trouble the day you nearly burned my house down."

I'm already on edge and this bitch won't shut the fuck up. "I happen to enjoy trouble." I brandish my weapon, lying it across my thigh, making sure the barrel is pointed directly at her. Loretta shifts in her seat, my actions having the desired effect. "Especially killing. I use my Glock most times, but for a more personal touch, my Bowie knife is my go-to choice. Wanna see it?"

"No," she responds, a slight tremor in her voice.

"Sure you do." I pull the Bowie from the sheath at my hip and hold it out to her. "Take it."

She shakes her head. "I don't want to."

"I said fucking take it," I demand, the threat underlying my words unmistakable. With an unsteady hand, she takes the twelve-inch blade from my grasp. "Feel how heavy that is?"

"Y-yes."

"I remember gutting some poor bastard for saying some disrespectful shit to me." I chuckle, but no one would call the sound humorous. "My knife slid into his belly like a perfectly cooked steak. Guess what happened next."

She lets out a soft whimper before answering. "I-I don't know."

"The fucker shit and pissed himself," I continue, flashing a smile at her. "Guess what happened after that? What the hell, I'll just tell you. I disemboweled him and stuffed his intestines down his throat. The interesting part is he was still alive while I did it." I bore into her eyes. "I don't think you should talk anymore. What do you think?"

"I-I'll be quiet."

"Good."

The rumble of engines echoes through the night, and every muscle in my body tightens. If the plan goes south, I could lose them.

Butch up and get your shit together. Now is not the time to second-guess myself.

I'm a God. I will not falter. I will bring my family home.

"How certain are you that Spider's her father?"

"One hundred percent certain."

"You better be," I warn, stashing my weapons. "Stay here."

I exit the vehicle, leaving the money on the backseat for now. We're deep in the desert, away from prying eyes, with only the moonlight keeping the darkness from swallowing us whole.

In the distance, riders emerge from the pitch black and slow to a stop about six feet from where we stand. Their arrival kicks up a thick cloud of dust, obscuring visibility and making a dangerous situation even more dangerous.

I lock my gaze on Spider and the woman sitting behind him. It takes every ounce of my self-control not to shoot her dead as she climbs down from the bike.

"What the fuck are you doing here, Katherine?"

"Is that any way to speak to your mother?" she mocks, striding forward until we're barely a breath apart. "Oh, that's right. You told me you didn't have a mother and never to show my face again."

"Where is she?" I growl, fighting to keep my cool.

"We buried her alive," she taunts, fluttering her eyes up at me. "She begged for her life and the lives of your bastards."

I close my hands around her throat and squeeze as hard as I can. Abject terror replaces the triumphant glint in her eyes as she struggles to pull oxygen into her lungs.

Spider comes to her rescue, leveling his gun between my eyes. "I can't let you manhandle my bitch. That's my job. Be a good stepson and let her go."

I shove her away from me, though I would like nothing more than to break her fucking neck. "You're pathetic."

"How dare you treat me this way after all the sacrifices I made for you!" she rages between gasping breaths.

"It's okay, baby," Spider croons and nestles her against his side. "He just needs a little discipline." His gaze narrows past my shoulder, trying to see through the tinted glass. "I told you to come alone."

"Oh, that's a surprise for you," I say, then wave for Loretta to come out. The door slams, and seconds later, she's standing beside me.

Spider looks at her, then back at me. "What's this pregnant bitch doing here?"

"I thought it was time for a reunion," I state sarcastically.

"What the fuck you talking about? I don't know this bitch."

Loretta bristles. "We had a fling nineteen years ago."

Spider throws his head back in laughter. "So? Is there a fucking point to all this?"

"Well, this fling produced a child," she deadpans.

"I'm going to take a wild guess about what's going on here," Spider drawls, his voice dripping with amusement. "You want to do an exchange, right? Your gash for a kid I supposedly fathered nineteen years back?"

"Zilphia is your daughter," I bark, my hands clenched at my sides. "Where is she?"

He scoffs. "Bullshit."

"I know who my child's father is," Loretta snaps at him. "We met at a bar in Vegas called District Lights and hooked up for a week. Your friend's name was Bear. I stayed at The Gold Orchid, and you were at Motel Sin. Ring any bells?"

Spider regards her contemplatively, which is a good sign. Maybe he's starting to remember.

"Oh, and your sister's face is tattooed on your left shoulder blade. She died in a store robbery, right?"

"Name?" he grits out.

"Loretta Kensley."

"Don't listen to them, baby," Katherine purrs, running a finger down his chest. "They're lying. Let's do what we came here to do."

That's Katherine for you, always the manipulative bitch. "You're going to kill your own daughter? Your own grandchildren?" I ask, playing on his soft spot for family.

"For heaven's sake," Loretta huffs, rolling her eyes. "Just get a DNA test from the drug store and be done with it."

Spider nods. "I'm on board, but the girl stays with me until the results come in. If she's my daughter, I'm willing to let bygones be bygones and negotiate a partnership beneficial to both clubs. After all, we'll be family."

"What?" Katherine screeches. "If doesn't matter if that little bitch—"

Spider ends her tirade with the back of his hand, hitting her so hard she lands a good three inches away from him. "Speak when spoken to."

"I'm-I'm sorry," she stutters, staggering to her feet. This woman gave birth to me, and I give zero fucks that Spider just laid her out.

"No deal. We get the DNA test done tonight, but Zilphia comes home with me."

There's no way in fucking hell I'm leaving her with the Disciples. I need to get to her ASAP. By now, she's running out of air. *If she had an asthma attack, she could already be…*

No.

I refuse to finish that thought.

A man pushes through the crowd, moving toward Spider with grim determination. "This piece of shit killed my father," he snarls, his eyes locking on me. "You promised me his murder would be avenged tonight."

His brothers echo his rage, hungry for violence. I inch toward my car, sensing the imminent mutiny.

"What about the money, Spider? It's as much ours as it's yours."

The shouting grows louder and more volatile as tempers ignite.

"Disciples, fall in line!" Spider bellows and the complaints die down. "I am the founder and president of this MC. My word is law!"

"Fuck that!" The guy, whose father apparently met his demise at my hands, centers his weapon on me. "Burn in Hell."

Before he can pull the trigger, his brains are splattered all over the ground.

"Sniper!" someone shouts.

About fucking time.

I yank Loretta behind the car just as gunfire lights up the night. My brothers swarm in with lethal precision.

Spider picked the wrong place for this meeting. The ridges and outcrops provided the perfect cover for an ambush.

Bullets and death rattles serenade the night as blood spills and bodies drop. The Disciples don't stand a chance—we've got more manpower, the element of surprise, and bulletproof vests.

"Stay here and keep down." Ignoring Loretta's screams not to leave her, I join my brothers, pouring lead into any Disciples that find themselves in my sights.

A few get away on their bikes. If they've got half a brain, they'll leave Kent for good. We're taking hits too. I never want to see a brother fall, but unfortunately it comes with the territory. One day you're fucking your favorite twinkie, and then the next day, you're dead.

I spot Spider making a run for his bike. *Not today, motherfucker.* I sprint after him but don't shoot, even though my trigger finger is itching to do him in. I need him alive… *For now.*

I catch up to him with ease and tackle him to the desert floor. He scrambles for his weapon, inches from his fingertips, but a hand snaps in and plucks it away.

"Not so fast, dipshit."

Cricket. He's saved my ass too many times to count. I climb to my feet, pulling Spider with me.

"It's over. We kicked their asses."

I was so fixated on my target; I hadn't noticed the shooting had stopped. Cleanup's already in full swing. The brotherhood works as a unit—rounding up the wounded, collecting our fallen, and hunting down every last Disciple who bolted on foot.

"It's not over until I get Zilphia back," I growl and stand toe-to-toe with the man who fathered her. "You're going to take me to her, and you better pray she's still alive."

I pat Spider down, taking a gun and several mags off him. I slide the former in the back of my jeans and store the latter in my cut.

"Holy sweaty balls," Cricket blurts out. "Is that your mother?" I follow his gaze to the blonde woman kneeling at Zeus's feet.

"She's not my mother." I push Spider ahead of me. "Walk." I would take care of her myself, but right now, every second counts.

Cricket falls into step beside me. "Ain't leaving you to handle this alone."

"You going for Zilphia?" Zeus calls out to me.

"Yeah."

"Take some brothers with you."

I shake my head. "No time. Cricket got my back."

He nods, then motions toward Katherine. "What do you want to do with her?" Betraying the Gods is an automatic death sentence, but because she pushed me out of her body, Zeus is giving me the privilege to decide her fate.

"Please don't let him kill me, Sam," she pleads. "I'm still your moth—"

I discharge two slugs into her abdomen without missing a step. She slumps to the ground, still breathing, but she'll bleed out soon enough.

"Told you never to show your face again."

Cricket whistles. "Remind me never to get on your bad side."

As I approach my bullet-riddled vehicle, my gaze narrows on the scene ahead. Jigsaw kneels beside Loretta, slicing his knife across her lower abdomen.

"You done this before?" I ask, reaching him. As suspected, Loretta is no longer among the living, a gaping hole in her neck the cause of her departure.

"No, but I have to try or the baby will die," he replies.

I nod and leave him to his task, then pin my gaze on Spider. "Driver's seat. Now."

My Glock stays trained on him the whole time. Cricket hops into the back.

"How far?" I ask, sliding into the passenger seat.

"About an hour."

"Nah. You get us there in thirty."

As the minutes tick by, thoughts of Zilphia suffocating run rampant in my mind. No matter how hard I try, I can't shake the haunting image. Is she alive, or is she dead? The uncertainty is driving me crazy.

"Fuck!" I roar, slamming my fist into the dashboard again and again, oblivious to the pain.

"Easy," Cricket says, catching my wrist mid-swing. "She's going to be okay."

"You don't know that, Cricket." I don't want to hope. Hope is for the weak. I once believed in it as a kid, and it bit me in the ass. "I can't fucking take it." If God exists and is merciful as people say, he won't let them die.

"I know, bro. We're almost there."

I shove my gun against Spider's temple. "If they're dead, I'm going to make you bleed until all you know is pain."

And after I'm done with him, I'll put a bullet in my mouth.

In the ensuing silence, my morbid thoughts return with a vengeance. Time seems to stretch, and just when I'm about to lose my shit again, Spider turns onto an overgrown trail and throws the car in park.

"This is it."

I rip the car door open and leap out, feeling like a death row inmate about to take the last walk.

I wave Spider ahead with my gun. Cricket and I follow in his wake, scanning the perimeter for moving shadows, the headlights guiding our steps.

I stumble over my feet, my stomach knotting tighter with every step I take.

Cricket catches my arm. "I got you, bro."

I nod my gratitude and force one foot in front of the other. I never wanted to be a father. Didn't think I was cut out for it—but the second I learned

Zilphia was pregnant, I knew I'd move mountains to ensure my kid's every happiness. Even more so when I found out we were having twins.

Now… I might never get the chance.

"Just up ahead," Spider says, pointing at a patch of soil lighter than the flat, darker earth surrounding it.

I fire a single shot into his leg.

"Son of a bitch!" he bellows, dropping to the ground.

"Move and it'll be your balls next," I threaten.

"Fuck, no shovels," Cricket mumbles.

Of course not. Spider never had any intention of following through with the exchange. I holster my Glock and drop to my knees, clawing at the soft soil with my bare hands. On the other side, Cricket starts digging at the opposite end, matching my urgency.

My nails peel back in my desperation to reach her, but the pain's nothing compared to the hell waiting for me if I'm too late.

Finally, my hands hit wood.

"I've got you," I breathe, frantically working my fingers along the edge of the boards. My heart's pounding so hard I can't hear anything else.

I wrench the top off with all my strength, a broken sound ripping from my throat when I see Zilphia's tear-streaked face.

She's alive and in active labor, gasping through a full-blown asthma attack, her panties and leggings bunched around her thighs, the top of a tiny head already visible.

"Grab her legs," I bark at Cricket, hooking my arms under her shoulders. She's covered in dirt from head to toe.

I lie back against the nearest tree, positioning her between my thighs. Cricket tears her shoes off, then yanks her panties and bottoms down her legs.

"I have your inhaler." I pull the canister from my cut pocket and give it a firm shake. I never leave home without it, even when she's not with me.

I spray two doses into her mouth, and within minutes, her breathing starts to steady.

I toss the inhaler aside and grip her spread knees. "I need you to push, Zilphia."

She shakes her head, sobbing. "It hurts… I need a hospital."

"There's no time," I murmur, pressing a soft kiss on her temple. "Our girls need you to push."

"Okay." She draws in a deep breath and bears down, straining with everything she has to bring our daughters into the world.

"She's coming," Cricket yells. "Keep pushing."

Moments later, a sharp cry pierces the chilly night.

"I officially declare myself the God Daddy," Cricket grins, gently placing the squirming bundle on Zilphia's chest.

"Oh my God," she weeps, her voice thick with emotion. "Oh my God… she's here."

She's beautiful and so damn tiny with a wild mop of golden curls. I trail a finger down her soft cheek. "Don't cry, sweet angel. Daddy will always take care of you."

I unsheathe my Bowie knife and cut the umbilical cord.

Zilphia gasps. "Her sister is coming."

Cricket rubs his hands together. "Okay, baby number two, let's go."

Zilphia pushes and pushes until our second daughter makes her debut with a shrill cry.

"Congrats, it's a boy," Cricket announces, lifting the little human for us to see.

I'm speechless for a second or two, then a smile spreads across my face. "Hear that, Zilphia? We have a son."

"The tech was wrong," she says, smiling back at me.

Cricket lowers him beside his sister. I slice through his umbilical cord—feeling like a million bucks. Like his twin, he has a head full of golden curls.

"I have to push again," Zilphia pants, bearing down.

Cricket recoils, his eyes fixed between her thighs. "What the fuck, man? She just delivered two aliens."

"Those are the placentas, you moron," I retort, securing the Bowie back at my hip. "Every baby has one. Keeps them alive."

"How was I supposed to know?" he grumbles. "It's my first time delivering babies."

"Apologies, Zilphia," Spider says, his voice low. "I didn't know you were my daughter. I spent a week with Loretta and never saw her again after that."

"What's he talking about?" she asks, peering back at me, confusion in her beautiful brown orbs.

"He speaks the truth, but it doesn't matter." I ease her against the tree and stalk toward him. "Any last words for your daughter?" I draw the gun from the waistband of my jeans and aim the barrel at his forehead. "Speak now or forever hold your peace."

"Sandman, don't!" Zilphia shouts. "If he's truly my father, I'm begging you not to kill him. Please do this one thing for me."

"I can't do that." I glance at her over my shoulder. "Too much blood has been spilled."

"Thought we were going to let bygones be bygones," Spider growls, narrowing his gaze at me. "I want to know my daughter and grandchildren."

"Bye." I empty two bullets into his skull. "Now you're gone."

Zilphia looks at me with dead eyes, tears slipping past the grime on her face. It had to be done, and I don't give two fucks about it.

CHAPTER 45

Six weeks later

SANDMAN

I GRIND MY TEETH, WHAT'S LEFT OF MY PATIENCE HANGING BY A thread. I have better things to do than wait on this red-headed motherfucker, but Zeus decided it was time for us to squash our beef once and for all.

So here I am, waiting to go toe-to-toe with Draco. No weapons. No dirty tricks. Just good old-fashioned fists.

Personally, I don't have a problem with the fucker, except for the stick lodged so far up his ass it'd take the Jaws of Life to remove it.

The last month and a half have been a rollercoaster. Zahara and Zeppelin are healthy and whole, though they spent two weeks in the NICU just to be safe.

We buried Loretta, and with a little bribery, Zilphia was able to adopt her sister, Liliana.

With Spider gone, the Disciples slinked back to the shadows. Maybe they'll attempt a comeback one day, maybe they won't. Either way, we'll be ready for the fuckers.

Harley pulled through and will be fully recovered in another week or two. I can't say the same for Snake. He's his own worst enemy right now and has a long road ahead of him.

"Think he chickened out?" Cricket asks to my left. We both sit astride our bikes, shoulder to shoulder with our brothers.

I grunt in response, too fucking pissed to speak. I just want to get back home to my family. That's where I spend most of my time these days, much to Zilphia's annoyance. She'd love nothing more than for me to go back to my sixty-hour weeks at the garage. *Tough shit.*

I'm not missing a moment. I've been peed on, puked on, and everything in between. I've given bottles, given baths, and made it to every doctor's appointment. I've even pulled my share of night duty—those 3:00 a.m. feedings can be brutal. Who knew something so tiny could cry so loud?

Still, despite the sleep deprivation, I love every second of being a father.

Caring for three newborns isn't for the weak, so we hired a nanny. Meela and Leah help when they can. Naomi too, whenever she's not at the hospital.

"It's Saturday night, man," he complains. "I'm supposed to be at the bar balls deep in some pussy."

I echo his sentiments. Yesterday I was so fucking hard I could've drilled through brick.

"Here he comes now," Cricket says, nodding toward the approaching motorcycle. "Looks like he decided to grace us with his presence after all."

I swing off my bike and shrug out of my cut, wanting this over and done with. The leather hits the seat with a dull thud. My shirt follows, landing beside it.

"Good luck," Cricket says, winking at me.

"Luck is for pussies," I quip, rolling my shoulders before striding into God's Glory with steadfast confidence.

Soon after, Draco joins me, bare-chested and wearing a scowl that says he's just as ready to throw down as I am. This fight's been a long time coming.

"I'm owed an apology," I drawl, closing the small distance separating us. "You kept me waiting."

He smirks. "You were an entitled little shit from the moment I met you."

Zeus ambles over to us. "The fight only stops when the beef between you two is settled."

The moment Zeus turns to walk away, Draco blindsides me with a jab to the temple, then slams me with a savage right hook. My head snaps sideways, stars bursting behind my eyelids. *Motherfucker caught me lacking.*

Our bloodthirsty brothers roar with excitement, always eager to watch a fight.

"You need some discipline beaten into you, boy," he growls.

I dip low, dodging his next swing by a hairsbreadth, then bury my fist into his gut with everything I've got. He doubles over with a ragged whoosh, all the air ripping from his lungs.

"And you think you're man enough for the job?" I snarl, driving my knee into his nose with bone-crushing force. He hits the ground hard, blood pouring from his nostrils like a busted faucet. "Okay, give it your best shot."

I raise a booted foot, aiming to shatter every bone in his face, but he rolls away at the last second, and my foot slams into the dirt. Before I can make my next move, Draco seizes my ankle and yanks my leg out from under me, sending me crashing to the earth beside him.

His elbow smashes into my mouth, splitting skin on impact. Blood spills onto my tongue, harsh and bitter.

We lurch to our feet and circle each other, waiting for the smallest opening to strike. He got hands, I give him that, but I wouldn't expect anything less from the son of Zeus.

"You're a hothead and one day it's going to get you fucking killed," he spits, his voice sharp with unrestrained anger.

"Didn't know you gave a damn," I retort sarcastically.

"You're my brother," Draco snaps, frustration cutting through every word. "Of course I give a damn. I don't want my nieces and nephew growing up without their father." He stills and pierces me with his intense gaze. "I don't know what happened to you as a kid, but you need to get the hell over it."

"Easy for you to say!" I thunder. "You didn't get the shit beat out of you nearly every fucking day!" I hammer him with three punishing body shots, smirking in satisfaction at hearing the pained grunts spilling from his lips.

We trade blow after blow until we're both left sprawled in the dirt—bloody, breathless, and drenched in sweat.

"I'm sorry your childhood was fucked," Draco says between heaving breaths. "But that's not going to stop me from riding your ass every time I catch you doing some reckless shit."

"Like you said, I'm a father now," I shoot back, just as winded as he is. "I've got no intention of being reckless, you fucking carrot."

Zeus appears above us. "Is this done?"

"Yeah," we grunt at the same time, ending our feud for good.

Mayhem barrels into me the moment I walk through the front door, a whirlwind of fur and uncontained energy.

"Hey, buddy." I crouch down to his level and gently scratch behind his ears. "How's our girl doing? You taking good care of her?" He lets out a happy bark. "That's my good boy."

I glance into the living room to check on Harley and find her passed out on her bed before making my way upstairs.

Zilphia will be in the nursery. She's been sleeping there for the past six weeks, but that changes tonight whether she likes it or not. I've tolerated her silent treatment and cold stares long enough.

I head into the bathroom, snag the first aid kit from under the sink, and face the wreckage in the mirror. Draco really did a number on me. One eye's almost swollen shut. Blood's crusted under my nose. My top lip is split open. My cheek is a mess of red and purple. And that's just above the neck.

No doubt I'm covered in bruises from head to toe.

I patch up my battered face as best I can, then step beneath the steaming spray of the shower. The near scalding water cascades over me, a searing balm to my bruised and aching body.

Once I'm dry and wearing nothing but a pair of boxer briefs, I step into the nursery and freeze at the doorway, drawn in by the quiet intimacy before me. Zilphia is fast asleep in the rocking chair, her robe hanging open, revealing one plump breast. A pearly thread of milk glistens as it escapes her soft brown nipple.

Zahara is nestled in her arms, sleeping peacefully, her tiny body rising and falling with each subtle breath.

I step deeper into the room and sink to a crouch in front of them. My eyes hungrily drink in the woman who brought our twins into the world.

Thick, wild curls barely tamed by a hair tie. Long lashes rest like shadows against her smooth, caramel-brown skin. Her full, heart-shaped lips parted ever so slightly, soft and irresistible. Shapely, pliable legs give way to dainty feet, each toe perfectly proportioned, her copper-colored nails meticulously trimmed. I trail a finger over one, barely grazing the surface.

This woman possesses every inch of me. Always has and always will.

I carefully lift Zahara from her arms, and Zilphia's eyes snap open.

"What are you doing?" she murmurs, groggy but alert.

"She's asleep," I whisper, easing Zahara into her crib with a tenderness I never believed a man like me was capable of.

I steal a glance at Liliana and Zeppelin, both slumbering in their own cribs. Liliana may not share my blood, but she's my daughter all the same.

I turn to face Zilphia, who regards me with the same icy disdain I've grown used to over the past few weeks.

"I'm sure that beating was well deserved."

I ignore the jab. There are more pressing matters at hand. "It's been six weeks."

Her eyebrows knit in confusion, but the moment comprehension dawns, fury swiftly takes its place. "Go fuck one of your club groupies."

I stalk toward her, and she scrambles out of the rocking chair, backpedaling until her back hits the wall. "I don't want them. I want you."

She yanks the robe closed, catching my gaze lingering on her cleavage. "I don't give a damn what you want because you've made it crystal clear you don't give a shit about what I want."

"Spider had to die," I growl, stepping into the last inch of space separating us. "There was no other option."

"I wanted a chance to get to know him and any other family I might have," she snaps, shoving at my chest. "You took that away from me."

"We're your family." I glance toward the cribs, then settle my gaze back on her. "The Gods are your family."

"I may be forced to stay here, but you will never touch me again."

"Don't fight me, Zilphia," I snarl, fisting the velvet belt of her robe. "I'm going to have you, willingly or by force."

Her fingers wrap around my wrist, her voice soft but resolute. "No."

"You belong to me." My hand encircles her throat, firm and possessive, but without pressure. "Forever and always. You don't get to tell me no."

"And when we die?" she asks defiantly. "You can't follow me in death. We both know you're going to Hell."

"On the contrary, sweet Zilphia," I rasp, my voice low and dark. "Not even the Almighty himself can protect you from me. I'd storm the pearly gates and drag your ass back to Hell with me." My palm presses against her throat just enough to make her breath catch. "Nothing will ever keep us apart. No man, no deity, or any other divine force. We'll fuck and burn together for eternity."

"I'm going to fight you with everything in me," she hisses, her eyes flashing angrily at me.

I brush a thumb over her plush bottom lip. "Okay."

I seize her arm and drag her across the hall, flinging her into our bedroom. As promised, she scratches and throws punches along the way. I shut the door behind us and lock it with a definitive click. But I don't pounce on her just yet. My gaze wanders over the woman who's held me captivated since I was twelve years old.

Her perfectly round breasts rise and fall with each wild breath. *So fucking beautiful.* My cock doubles in size, needing to be inside her warmth.

"Stay back," she commands, her frantic gaze darting to the bathroom.

I smirk. "You won't make it two steps before I'm on you."

Zilphia snatches my favorite cologne off the dresser and launches it at me before dashing toward the bathroom. The glass bottle slams into the bridge of my nose. I stumble backward from the impact, my eyes watering, feeling like a bomb exploded in my face. It hurts like a son of a bitch, but I recover quickly, capturing her around the waist when she tries to run past me.

Her teeth tear into my left pectoral, biting hard and deep.

"Fucking dammit," I hiss, winding my fingers into her hair and yanking her head back until she releases me with a pained whimper. "Had enough?"

"No," she snaps, the vivid red evidence of her attack smeared across her lips.

"Figured you'd say that." I wrestle her against the wall, pinning her wrists high above her head with one hand. The other, I slip into her silken folds. "No panties? You made it way too easy for me."

Tears gather in her eyes, turning them into simmering pools of rich brown. "You can't keep doing this."

"That's where you're wrong, Zilphia," I murmur, trailing my fingers through her downy-soft pubic hair. "You're mine." I work two fingers inside her snug pussy to the hilt. "This is *mine*."

"I'm not yours," she bites out, her voice cracking with fury.

"No?" I move in and out of her body with excruciating slowness, relishing the wet softness grasping at my fingers. "My cock is going to be buried inside your pussy in the next five minutes. Tell me again how you're not mine."

"Taking me by force doesn't make me yours," she fires back. "It makes you a rapist."

"I can live with that."

I drive into her slick center faster, and her body responds, melting over my fingers like warm, sticky honey.

"No," she breathes, then sinks her teeth into my top lip, tearing my wound open again. Blood spills onto my tongue, but I'm too high on adrenaline and violence to feel the pain.

I curve my fingers, fucking her as deep and hard as I can. Zilphia cries out as liquid heat spurts from between her legs in thick waves, soaking the carpet beneath our feet. Completely enraptured, I fall to my knees and lap up the essence glistening on her thighs.

My cock twitches as her sweet, earthy taste explodes on my tongue, awakening the most primal part of me. I lick my way to her folds and eat her pussy with a ravenousness only she can sate. With her, there is no control or reason. Just a relentless need so profound it defies all logic.

I grip her round, supple bottom and draw her closer, deftly dragging my tongue back and forth over the heartbeat of her pussy.

"I hate you," she sobs, nails biting into my shoulders as her hips writhe against my mouth. "I hate you so fucking much."

"But your pussy doesn't," I rasp. "Let me demonstrate." I push two fingers inside her satin walls and lock my lips around her clit, sucking the engorged flesh into my mouth with strong, rhythmic pulls.

My mouth and fingers move in sync, creating the perfect storm inside her warm, delectable body. Within minutes, she's squirting all over me, sounds of ecstasy tearing from her throat. I seal my lips over her swollen mound, drinking her until she's depleted and lying boneless against me.

My cock strains against the cotton containing it, needing inside her now. I yank her to the floor, ripping the velvet robe from her body and shoving her onto her back.

She grabs one of my leather boots, tossed carelessly on the floor, and smacks me in the face with it. "I said no!"

My skull vibrates from the blow, and for a moment, my vision splits in two. I wrestle the boot from her grasp and chuck it out of her reach. She's giving me a run for my money, but the outcome will remain the same. I'm going to fuck her and fuck her hard.

"Get off me!" she yells, clawing her fingernails down the side of my face.

I clamp my hand over her face and slam the back of her head onto the floor. She whimpers, her eyes glazing over.

"This ends only one way," I hiss, jerking her onto her stomach.

"I'm the mother of your children," she gasps between gut-wrenching sobs. "If that means anything, you'll stop right now."

"Sweet Zilphia, that's like asking me to stop breathing." I push my boxer briefs down my legs and surge into her snug pussy balls deep.

I groan, lying flush against her back, the air rushing from my lungs. It's so fucking good. The moist ridges of her slick walls contour to my dick like a second skin. One stroke in, and I'm already about to come. I hold steady, shaking with the effort to contain my orgasm as Zilphia quietly weeps beneath me.

"Don't cry," I murmur, kissing her wet cheek. "I'm going to make you feel good."

I roll my hips, fucking her slow and deep. She is so fucking wet, so wet even my balls are drenched in her juices, and with every stroke, she gets wetter. I dip my tongue into her ear, kissing, sucking, nipping. Her soft cries turn into throaty gasps, increasing in volume as we both spiral toward the edge of carnal oblivion.

"So warm. So wet. So tight," I praise, fucking her like she's my oxygen and I'm a dying man.

I'm high on her, entrapped in the raw pleasure only she can give me. I delve my hands into her slippery folds, positioning a thumb on either side of her clit, lightly kneading the throbbing flesh.

"No," she moans, her breath hitching.

"Surrender to it, sweet, Zilphia," I whisper huskily. "You know you want to."

"Sandman, please," she pleads, undulating beneath me. "I don't want… Oh God."

A guttural sound rumbles from my chest as her dripping pussy spasms around my hard flesh, sending a violent jolt to my aching balls.

"Zilphia," I rasp, spilling my seed inside her sweet wetness.

I give one last thrust and drop onto my back, my chest heaving. Within seconds, my cock is fully erect again—throbbing, hot, and ready.

"Come sit on it," I murmur, squeezing just below the sensitive head.

"Leave me alone," she fumes, lurching to her feet. "You got what you wanted."

"That was just an appetizer." I move into a crouched position, my muscles coiled tight with excitement. "I'm going to fuck you until I'm too weak to stand."

She grabs a plastic jar off the dresser and hurls it at me, a furious scream bursting from her lips. I dodge whatever the hell it is and lunge at her before she's able to get her hands on something else.

"Let me go!" she shouts, struggling to wrench free from my grasp.

I swipe the remaining products onto the floor and wrestle her onto the wooden surface. She swings her fists at me, fighting like a wild animal.

"Stay still, Zilphia," I snarl, slamming her back against the mirror so hard the glass shatters where her head hits. "Move again and I will hurt you."

"I hope you die," she spits, tears swimming in her brown orbs.

"I will one day, but not today."

I pull her legs over my arms, staring at the glistening pink treasure between her thighs. *Fuck, her pussy is overflowing with my jizz.* My mouth waters, my gaze following the sticky white trail to her pretty rimmed hole.

"Beautiful," I mumble, grasping my cock and gliding the tip from her cum-filled opening to her clit, then back again.

My eyes catch on my reflection in the mirror, and I barely recognize the person staring back at me. Not because of the tangled state of my hair or the bruises marring my face—it's the raw need burning in my blue gaze. How is it possible that she can make me feel grounded but out of control at the same time?

I align my length at her dripping entrance and drive into her depths. The hot grip of her walls shoots a soul-searing shockwave down my spine, almost sweeping my feet from under me. *Fuck yes.*

My fingers dig into her waist, holding her tight, as my body plunges into hers over and over again. Her tits, full and round from pregnancy, bounce with every frenzied thrust into her pussy.

"Six weeks without this and I nearly lost my fucking mind," I slur, dazed with my need for her.

I lift one of her legs over my shoulder and grip the back of her other thigh at the crease, spreading her wider and fucking her deeper.

Zilphia's face is a mask of passion, her gaze half-lidded, teeth sinking into her bottom lip. A thin sheen of sweat clings to her body, casting a shimmering glow across her velvet skin. Her hair tie is long gone, lost in her frantic struggle to escape me, leaving her silky mane flowing free and wild. *She's a goddess.*

I anchor a hand at the top of the mirror and piston into her sopping cunt so hard the dresser collapses to one side with a crack. Sweat runs down my body in rivulets as I push us both to the brink of release. *Fuck. Fuck. Fuck. She makes me fucking insane.* I feel as if I'm about to burst out of my skin, every cell in my body on fire for her.

I stare at where our bodies meet, and it's a sight to behold. My cock, covered in her creamy nectar, stretches her pretty pink cunt to the brim.

"Your body comes alive for me, Zilphia," I whisper, my voice strained and foreign to my own ears. "No matter how much you try to deny it. It craves my cock, my lips, and my tongue. It drips for *me*."

Pearly-white milk leaks from her pebbled nipples and rolls down the curve of her bouncing breasts, dripping onto her belly.

I want some of that.

I guide her legs around my waist and lift her in my arms. Our gazes collide, and an all-encompassing desperation arcs between us, nearly knocking me on my ass. In that desperation lies pain and hate, lust and passion, need and obsession. We're bound by all these things.

If there's a more tragic story in history, I never heard of it. She turned my world upside down and set me on the path that led to Sandman. Still, I wouldn't change meeting her for anything. Despite the shit I've said and done, I can't imagine my life without her.

I'd rather have never drawn a breath than live a single moment without knowing her. When it comes to this girl, I'm all kinds of fucked up.

I carry her across the room and climb onto the bed, settling on top of her lush curves. She locks her ankles around my lower back, staring up at me with wet eyes, as my hips grind between her supple thighs in circular motions. Not too fast or too slow, just the right pace to prolong the intoxicating delirium pulsing through my veins.

"Don't bite me," I mumble before sealing my mouth over hers.

I swallow her broken sob just as she turns away. "No."

"What'd I tell you about that word?" I growl, seizing her jaw and crushing my lips to hers again.

An anguished cry rips from her throat as she returns my kiss with the same violence. Our lips slam together again and again, tongues clashing with burning urgency. The split in my lip tears further, smearing blood across both our faces, but that pain is trivial compared to the crippling hunger she stokes within me.

I cup her left breast and kiss a red path to her taut nipple, sucking the extended flesh into my mouth. The taste of her honey-sweet milk explodes on my tongue, tantalizing my already wrought senses. Pussy and breastmilk… decadent… delicious, a combination I never knew I needed.

"What are you doing?" Zilphia breathes, her back arching off the bed. "You-you can't—"

She threads her fingers into my hair, squeezing me tight against her breast, her protest ending on a low, ragged gasp. We undulate against each other like waves in an ocean, her hips rising to meet my powerful thrusts, our bodies on fire and slick with sweat. Once again, I'm losing my sanity to her, but what a sweet descent into madness it is.

I drink my fill, drawing the rigid peak into my mouth with deep, long pulls. Zilphia goes wild beneath me, legs shaking, back arching, head thrashing, as she screams her pleasure. The smells of sex and her honeysuckle scent seep into every corner of the room, enveloping me like sun-kissed silk.

I nip and lick my way to her other breast, coiling my tongue around her erect tip before resuming my feeding frenzy. Her body is fucking amazing, soft and thick in all the right places, even more so since she became a mother. My steel frame fits seamlessly against her hourglass figure, every womanly curve and dip cradling my hard angles like a caress.

And she thought she was going to deny me this. Not a chance in hell. I'm a junkie for her, irrevocably addicted and under her spell indefinitely.

"Yes," she moans, her contracting pussy an iron brand on my dick. "Oh God, yes."

"Ah fuck," I grunt huskily as warm, tingly sensations rise from my throbbing balls to my cock. I bury my face against her neck, her scent teasing my nostrils as my hips pump between her thighs harder, faster.

Zilphia cries out, raking her fingernails down my back as she orgasms again.

"Sweet Zilphia," I groan, coming so hard my back bows.

I collapse onto the bed, my energy and balls drained for the moment. Zilphia rolls onto her side, pulling the blanket over her shoulders. She thinks she can go back to barely speaking to me. Not going to fucking happen. We have children to raise and six weeks of fucking to make up for.

I coast my hand along my semi-hard length. There's one more thing I want, then she can rest, for a little while at least. Soon my dick is at full mast again, and I yank the blanket down her body.

She lets out an angry cry and jerks around, her palm flying toward my face.

I capture her wrist and flip her back onto her side, securing her in place with a forearm across her collarbone and a leg over her thighs. “Still got some fight left in you, I see.”

“Fuck you,” she spits venomously.

“Stop resisting, sweet Zilphia.” I position my cock at one of my favorite places on her body. “It’s going to be a long while before I’m sated.”

She inhales a sharp breath, her spine snapping straight as I thrust into her tight ring until I’m fully embedded inside the snug muscles.

“Fuck, I’ve missed this,” I groan, feeding my dick into her ass while stroking the engorged flesh nestled at the top of her slit.

Before long, she succumbs to my cock and skilled touches, the line separating pleasure and pain dissolving, becoming one. I hold her tight against me, peppering lingering kisses along her nape, the salty taste of her skin igniting a fire in my blood.

She grasps the hand wedged in her folds, gyrating her hips in tandem with the fingers on her clit. Then she reaches back, her slender fingers fisting in my hair. I close my lips over the pulse on her neck, teasing the rapid beat beneath her skin with the tip of my tongue.

“Sandman,” she gasps, coming apart in my arms for the fourth time.

I move to my knees, pulling her with me, my front pressed to her back. “Hold on to the headboard.”

She shakes her head. “You can go straight to hell.”

“I gave you plenty of chances to obey. Now you’ll have to be punished.” I lock my hands around her wrists and squeeze enough to hurt, forcing her to grab onto the headboard.

“What are you going to do? Kill me?” she taunts, her voice dripping with contempt.

“We both know I’m too obsessed to ever kill you, but there are worse things than death.” I trap her hands beneath mine and savagely pound into her ass.

“Stop!” she begs, frantically twisting against my hold. “You’re hurting me!”

“Just let it happen,” I murmur against her neck.

Her teeth slice into my forearm, each one sharp as a razor blade and drawing blood. I exhale through gritted teeth, biting back a curse, but I don’t stop. I plunge into her clenched entrance with the force of my entire body, pouring all my strength into every thrust.

“Get off me!” she screams, thrashing with desperate fury.

My balls contract, drawing taut against my body. "Sweet, sweet Zilphia," I rasp, releasing thick spurts of semen inside her ass.

I fall limp to the bed. Zilphia lands on top of me, crying hysterically.

"Shh," I croon, wrapping my arms around her. "It wasn't so bad."

She bursts from my embrace, shrieking in outrage as she throws punches at me. "You're an animal!"

I tackle her onto her back, imprisoning her under my weight and pressing her wrists to the bed. "You created this animal, so don't act surprised when it goes on a rampage."

After a few minutes, her muscles soften beneath me, her resistance crumbling. Only then do I release her and saunter to the bathroom. I wet a washcloth at the sink and wipe away the remnants of sex and blood from my body. Once I'm clean, I dampen another washcloth and return to the bedroom.

Zilphia lies motionless as I part her legs, her gaze on my face, accusation and defeat shimmering in the chocolate depths. A sense of power and sick pride swells in my chest, watching my cum leak from both holes.

Entranced, I drag my index finger through her inflamed slit to her ass and write MINE across her inner thigh. Then I kneel beside the bed and trace each letter with my tongue, savoring the sweet, salty taste of our combined essence. The flavor lingers in my mouth as I gently clean her swollen pussy.

"Do you love me?" Zilphia asks, her voice thick with emotion.

"This again," I snap in annoyance. "You're mine. That's all you need to know."

"But do you love me?" she presses.

"I'd kill for you," I growl, glaring at her. "If you ever left me, I'd set the world on fire searching for you, and Lord have mercy on anyone stupid enough to get in my way." I run the back of my fingers down her cheek. "Love is just a fucking word, Zilphia. It's easily said and quickly forgotten. That's not us. What we have is forever."

A small cry erupts from the baby monitor on the nightstand. I glance back at the screen and see that Lily's awake, her tiny mouth trembling and face scrunched in distress. I'm on my feet in an instant, tossing the washcloth into the hamper on my way out the door.

I need to get to her before she wakes the twins. After a quick stop at the changing table for hand sanitizer, I scoop her swaddled body into my arms. She instinctively turns toward my warmth, seeking nourishment.

"Hey, sweet girl," I coo, pressing a kiss to the silky ringlets at the crown of her head, right on her soft spot. "Ready for some milk?"

I amble across the hall, gently rocking her back and forth in my arms. Zilphia is lying on her side, her head cradled on a pillow.

"She's hungry," I say, placing Lily next to her.

Zilphia pulls her closer, and she hungrily latches onto her nipple. "Oh, stop acting like you're starving to death," she chides, laughter in her voice. "You ate three hours ago."

I walk over to the closet and retrieve the small box I hid there earlier.

"For you," I say, placing it on the bed.

Zilphia eyes it warily. "What is it?"

"You'll see. I promise it's not a human head."

She bites her bottom lip as she opens the box, then looks up at me. "You got me a cut."

I nod, my possessive gaze locking on the patch that declares her mine—*SANDMAN'S GIRL*. "You're my old lady now."

I set the box on the nightstand and stretch out beside them, quietly watching her as she nourishes our daughter. Until our paths crossed, I didn't believe there was any good in the world. I was in the darkest part of hell, but she reached inside that hell and brought me into her light. Zilphia healed me—the broken, dirty boy from the wrong side of the tracks. Then she stabbed me in the back and twisted the blade, turning my heart into a black hole.

Now she's the mother of my children, and my heart is whole again. I grasp her chin between my forefinger and thumb, lifting her face until her eyes meet mine.

"I'm *never* letting you go," I murmur, conviction resonating in my tone. "You're my forever."

THE END

Want more of Jigsaw and Meela? Joinmy newsletter for a bonus chapter!

THANK YOU FOR READING

I hope you savored every twisted, intoxicating moment of *Sandman* and *Zilphia*! It was a decadent, messy descent—full of pearlclutching shocks and delightfully dark turns. Four more *Gods of Ruin* books are stirring in the shadows, each a standalone journey into chaos, obsession, and desire.

If you dare, leave a review and sink your teeth into my other wicked tales. For more whispers from the dark, connect with me on social media:

Facebook – Author Lorrain Allen

Instagram – author_lorrain_allen

TikTok – authorlorrainallen

Maverick's Madness is a raw, dark highschool bully romance that dives headfirst into trauma and obsession. Maverick grew up under the weight of his father's bigotry, shaping him into the hardened, volatile guy everyone fears. Then Cocoa, a biracial new girl, arrives—bold, defiant, and immediately in Maverick's crosshairs.

PROLOGUE

MAVERICK

I'm drunk out of my fucking mind. Usually, I can deal, but my past came nipping at my heels relentlessly. Painful memories bombarded me until I couldn't take it anymore.

My mother, Grace Carolyn Carter, hanged herself eleven years ago today, taking the coward's way out. *Fucking bitch.* She should've killed me too, instead of leaving me in the clutches of my sperm donor.

I crave numbness, so I find myself at Duke's, the bar on the outskirts of town. I have no clue how many beers I've chugged down—enough to let some cougar reeking of cigarette smoke and strong, musky perfume drag me into a bathroom stall, sit me down, and ride my cock.

Fortunately, I did have enough functioning brain cells to snag the condom stashed in my wallet and sheath my length.

The woman looks rough—leathery skin, deep wrinkles, brittle box-colored bright red hair… let's just say she won't be winning any beauty pageants. What the hell did she say her name is?

Shit, I forgot. I do recall her mentioning her age.

Thirty-six, but damn if she doesn't look fifty. It's clear life hasn't been kind to her. The universe is a fickle motherfucker. In the end, the bastard fucks us all over. My vision doubles. Goddamn, my head is spinning. I blink rapidly in an attempt to regain focus. Fuck me… still seeing two of everything. I'm going to have a bitch of a hangover in the morning.

"Your cock is amazing," the woman purrs.

Too bad I can't say the same about her pussy. She has the loosest cunt I have ever had the displeasure of fucking. It's no easy task to stay hard, but I'm desperate for a nut.

"Yes, baby!" she shouts, bouncing up and down on my dick. "You like this wet pussy? Argh, I'm coming!"

She orgasms, screaming at the top of her lungs.

My erection deflates. Guess I'll be relieving myself later.

"Baby, that was fantastic," she moans.

I grunt in response.

"Wanna come by my place tomorrow night?" She stands, tugging down her skirt. "My husband goes to work at seven."

"Nope, your pussy is horrible," I slur.

"You little piece of shit!" she shrieks in outrage and storms out of the stall.

I pull the condom off and drop it into the toilet. That was the easy part. Standing and getting my jeans up is a completely different story. Fifteen minutes later, I stumble to the bar and plop my ass onto a stool. Ralph, the bartender, regards me warily.

"Give me another beer."

"You're shitfaced, Maverick." He shakes his head. "I'm cutting you off."

I slam my fist on the scarred wooden surface. "Give me another goddamn beer."

"No can do, and I'm gonna need your car keys."

I reach across the bar and latch on to his collar. "You going to take them from me?"

"Come on, Mav." The bar's namesake slides onto the stool beside me. He's a big, burly motherfucker—pushing six seven, bald head, beard, and covered in tattoos—not the type of dude a girl brings home to meet her folks, but would give up the pussy to. "Can't have you roughing up my employee."

"Small disagreement," I say, relinquishing my hold on said employee.

Duke's an outcast because he doesn't conform to the townspeople's standards. He's always played by his own set of rules. For that, he has my respect—something I don't give lightly. Being a former juvenile delinquent himself, he allows underage drinking in his bar, but has no problem banging heads together at the first sign of trouble. Fighting isn't allowed under any circumstances. He calls the apartment upstairs home, so he'll protect this place at all costs, even with his life.

"Demons riding you hard today?"

"The fuckers won't leave me alone." I sigh, rubbing the nape of my neck.

"Ralph, tequila, please."

"Coming right up."

Ralph hands him a shot filled to the brim. Duke swallows the liquid fire in one gulp, then slams the glass on the bar.

"Wanna talk about it?"

"Nah."

"I'm around if you ever need a listening ear, but you gotta go home."

"Fine," I grumble.

"Make some java for our inebriated friend here."

"You got it, boss," Ralph replies.

"Be back in twenty, then I'll give you a lift home." Duke squeezes my shoulder before sauntering out the door.

A couple minutes later, a cup of steaming coffee is placed in front of me.

"Drink up," Ralph says, then hustles to the other end of the bar to flirt with a woman sitting there.

"Look who's here," Jake sneers.

Even in my drunken state, I recognize the asshole's voice. I swivel in my seat, holding the mug in my hand. My archnemesis and two of his cronies surround me. The bad blood between our schools runs deep. This year, the stakes are higher because our futures hang in the balance. I've been named quarterback of Montgomery Academy's football team. Jake received the same title at Louisville, over in the neighboring county.

He surveys the dimly lit bar. "Where are Dee and Nix?"

"I ditched them."

"It's not smart to drink alone."

I give a half shrug. "I can take care of myself."

"Getting drunk isn't going to curb your psychotic tendencies," he jeers, face twisting in contempt. "Your nickname is Mad Maverick for a reason. Everyone knows you belong in the loony bin."

"How's the finger?" I smirk.

His jaw clenches.

We got into a brawl several weeks back that resulted in his pinky being broken.

"Just say the word, Jake." Crony one cracks his knuckles.

He holds up his hand and wiggles his fingers. "All good now, but you know what… I *do* owe you an ass whooping."

I stand, prepared to throttle the first motherfucker who steps in my direction. "Is that so?"

Crony two swings and I duck, barely missing the blow. I throw the hot brew in his face and he howls in agony.

Jake punches me in the nose, and I crash into a nearby table, blood pouring from my nostrils. The patrons scramble for cover. Three against one and I'm wasted… hell, this won't end well for me. I could take them all on if I weren't plastered.

"Duke's gonna be pissed." I hear Ralph groan.

I smash the mug across Jake's temple, and he drops to his knees, clutching his bleeding head. Crony one takes ahold of my right arm and crony two seizes the left. They drag me to the pool table and slam me on top of it, pinning my wrists to the slate. Jake clambers over.

"I'm going to enjoy this," he snarls and starts hammering on my midsection.

Damn, this fucker hits hard. A gunshot rings out, effectively putting an end to the scuffle. I push up on my elbows and see Duke pointing a gun at the ceiling.

"No fighting in my fucking bar!" he bellows.

It's so quiet you could hear a pin drop.

"Took you long enough," I joke, breaking the silence. "My insides were getting rearranged."

"You three"—he jabs his thumb behind him—"out."

The trio bolt towards the exit. They know better than to challenge Duke.

"You good?"

"Right as rain," I reply, wiping the back of my hand across my bloody nose.

"You're more trouble than you're worth, kid."

Story of my fucking life.

Craving more? Head over to Amazon and dive back into Maverick and Cocoa's story.

ACKNOWLEDGMENTS

To Fabiola Cadet, what can I say? A whole damn lot. You've been my cheerleader since the early days of my author journey. Whenever I vent my frustrations on Facebook, you're always there—commenting and offering words of encouragement. No matter what, you make it your mission to uplift me.

When I launched my bookish merch website, you were my very first customer. When I started my Patreon page, you were among the first subscribers. When I formed my ARC team, you were one of the first to join. You even volunteered to become the admin for two of my Facebook groups. Even though you receive a free copy of every new release, you still choose to purchase a copy. You continuously go above and beyond to support me. I see it, and I appreciate it more than words can express.

To Morgan Brittany, thank you from the bottom of my heart for being such a trusted member of my ARC team and an incredible admin for one of my Facebook groups. I truly appreciate you volunteering to be the final set of eyes on my books before publication. Your thoughtful feedback and sharp eye for catching things that were missed by me, my editors, and proofreaders have played a significant role in improving the quality and readability of my work. You're seriously awesome.

To my amazing Patreon subscribers—you are all absolute rockstars. I know I'm not always as consistent with posting as I'd like to be, but your support never wavers, and that means the world to me. Every dollar earned through Patreon is reinvested into my author business, helping me create, grow, and keep doing what I love. I want to thank you all for your patience, generosity, and continued support. Hugs and kisses to each of you!

To my amazing ARC team, thank you all for reading and reviewing my books. Your support plays a crucial role in helping my new releases gain visibility on Amazon—something that's never easy. I truly appreciate your time, dedication, and the part you play in the success of each book. Sending much love to each one of you!

ABOUT THE AUTHOR

Lorrain Allen currently resides on the East Coast and has one amazing son. She finds escape and inspiration in the pages of a good book. Her long-term goal is to craft dark, erotic, paranormal, contemporary, new adult, and young adult romance novels. The themes she explores may be controversial, but then again, what's life without a little controversy?

OTHER BOOKS

Standalones

Consumed: A Dark Stalker Age Gap Romance

Maverick's Madness: A Dark High School Bully Romance

Living in Cin Duet

When Art Rises: Living in Cin (A Dark High School Romance)

When Art Falls: Living in Cin (A Dark Romance)

A Little Taste of Sin Series

Sweet Peach

Midas Touch

Gods of Ruin MC Series

Beautiful Hate: A Dark MC Romance

www.authorlorrainallen.com

www.ingramcontent.com/pod-product-compliance
Lightning Source LLC
Chambersburg PA
CBHW030351310726
48979CB00001B/264

9781734230987